Infernal

THE MARKED

BIANCA SCARDONI

INFERNAL, THE MARKED #4

First Edition: July 2018

All characters and events depicted in this book are fictitious. Any similarity to
real persons, living or dead, is purely coincidental.

ISBN: 978-1-9993874-2-6

For my readers,
who patiently (and not so patiently)
waited for this book to be here.

And for my dad, Victor,
who is not allowed to read this book.

CONTENTS

Hell is empty.
The Devil is here.

PREFACE

There is no road so long and winding as the one that leads you to the finish line. Every bend is meant to test you, every junction meant to bring you closer to that place where love and sacrifice meet. To that place in the valley where the sun doesn't quite reach.

I know now that my life will only ever be a battle against that darkness—a darkness that is infinite and eternal in its very nature—and it will remain that way until the inevitable day when the darkness takes my last breath.

That is my purpose.

That is my *destiny*.

My name is Jemma Blackburn, and this is my Hell.

1. RUN TO THE HILLS

Dark, looming evergreens lined both sides of the road, as if to usher me head-first into my final chapter. The rain was still falling hard, battering down against the windshield and making it hard for us to see two feet in front of the black SUV. I could hear Dominic and Gabriel screaming at each other in the front seats, their voices loud and disjointed, but none of their words were registering. Nothing was registering except the memory of Trace's vacant eyes.

The haunting scene from Angel's Peak replayed in my mind like a death wish I never wanted, an omen I couldn't stop from happening. Dizzying flashbacks of the black smoke entering Trace's body bombarded my mind. Each time, I scoured the memory looking for something that wasn't there before...a clue...a kill switch...some way to undo it all. Each time praying that the memory wouldn't unfold like the last time, that my horrifying new reality would instead disintegrate into nothingness and yield the happily-ever-after I had always dreamed of.

But my happily-ever-after never came.

I shook my head and pressed my palms down over my ears,

blocking out the noise around me.

The Roderick Sisters had opened the Gates of Hell and unleashed Lucifer onto our world—onto my world and into the boy I loved, and I wasn't sure there was anything I could do to get him back. Frankly, I wasn't sure about anything anymore. The only thing I knew for certain was that I was in Hell.

Only I hadn't gone to it...*it* had come to me.

"That's the stupidest thing you've said yet," snapped Dominic.

"It's the only way," retorted Gabriel, his tone markedly calmer. "The Order will know what to do."

"Is that so? And when have they ever helped us before?"

"Had we been transparent with them from the start—"

"Had *we* been transparent?" scoffed Dominic. "All they've ever done is falsify facts and hide the truth from Jemma. The only help they provide is the kind that serves themselves." Dominic turned in his seat to face me, beads of water dripping off his alabaster skin like falling gemstones. "Are you hearing this?"

His muffled words faintly broke through my covered ears. I pressed my palms down harder.

"Angel? Are you listening to me?"

"Shut up. Just shut up." I wasn't sure the words actually sounded from my mouth or if I'd just thought them inside the slowly crumbling barricades of my mind.

I didn't want to listen to them argue about the Council or hear all the what ifs and could've beens. I just wanted them to shut the hell up so I could think. I needed to get my thoughts together and figure out a way to put all these broken pieces back together again—to put Trace back together again—and I couldn't do that with them planting grenades inside my brain every two minutes.

"She's in shock," said Gabriel, eyeing me from the rearview

mirror. His dark brows pulled down over his olive eyes, as if to offer me sympathy. But it felt like pity. "Let her be."

"We need to get out of town, brother. Tonight. The Council can clean up their own mess."

"And the others?"

I glanced over at my mother's lifeless body slumped in the seat beside me. Gabriel had gone back to get her as soon as Trace and the Roderick sisters left the area. My wooden stake was still protruding from her heart—a painful reminder of what I'd done, of the grave mistake I made believing a single word out of the sisters' filthy mouths.

But I wouldn't make that mistake again.

The death of my childhood naivety had come to pass. I trusted no one and I feared nothing, not even death itself, for everything I loved in this world had already been taken away from me. Ripped from my heart like a bandage. There was nothing left inside but darkness...darkness breeding darkness, and I was at one with it now.

"And what of her Keeper?" continued Gabriel. "We can't just—"

"He's as good as dead, if he isn't already."

More bombs exploded in my head as his words sounded back to me.

He's as good as dead.

Trace was as good as dead...

A guttural scream ripped out of my lungs, the force of it so sharp and anguished that it blew out every window in the car, sending shattered glass raining through the air like shrapnel. Dominic and Gabriel threw their hands over their heads as the car hit the medium and then swerved off the road towards the embankment.

My eyes locked onto the tree ahead of us as we barreled straight for it.

It was the last thing I saw.

A thick, familiar fog passed over my legs as I sat up and glanced around at my surroundings. Crumbling headstones peeked out from the hallowed ground, letting me know in no uncertain terms that I was in a cemetery, but I had no idea how I had gotten there or what had happened to the car.

And where the heck were Dominic and Gabriel?

I parted my lips to call for them as a strange aftertaste of rain settled on my tongue. It felt sticky and wrong—unnatural in the way that it weighed down my voice. I pushed up from the dewy grass and straightened myself. Had I been thrown from the car? My eyes scanned the area looking for signs of a wreckage, but there was none to be found.

Something wasn't right.

This scene wasn't right.

A dark silhouette appeared in the distance, too far for me to make out any of its features but close enough to know I wasn't alone.

"Dominic?" His name fermented on my lips as I waited for the shadowy figure to call back at me.

No response. Instead, it moved closer to me, its husky form becoming clearer as inky black hair and a pair of eyes as blue as the Caribbean Sea made an appearance through the mist. My breath hitched because I knew it was him.

My happily ever after.

"Trace!" My skin buzzed with electricity as he closed the gap between us.

"We need to talk, Jemma, and we don't have much time."

Dumbfounded, I stared at him like an apparition from a past life. He wasn't supposed to be here, *couldn't* be, and yet he was. The wind howled around me, ruffling my hair as it hissed its warnings to tread ever so carefully.

"Jemma—"

"No." I shook my head. This wasn't Trace. It wasn't possible. I watched Lucifer enter his body with my own eyes. This was a trick. A con. I stumbled backwards, putting as much distance between us as I could.

He let me back away as though he could hear the faint whisperings of my suspicion.

"Don't be afraid, Jemma. You're fast asleep right now. It's only a dream." With a wave of his hand, the cemetery faded away, and suddenly, we were standing on my old street back in the Cape; the one we came to all those months ago when he took me to the past to visit my father. "See?"

"How did you do that?" I hissed my question as I took another step back.

"We're *dreamwalking*," he said as though that explained anything." It's the only way I can see you now." He lowered his head and his broad shoulders quickly followed. "He's taken over, Jemma. I can't fight him off."

"I'm...you're...this..." Okay, so I couldn't create an actual sentence anymore. I shook my head as I tried to dislodge all the cobwebs swirling around my brain. "This is a dream?" I asked, trying to make sense of the senseless.

"Yes. Well, sort of." He took a cautious step towards me, intensifying the electricity zipping over my skin. "I don't know how much longer I can hold on, Jemma. It's so cold now," he said as his teeth clattered together. "S-so dark."

The defeated look on his face sent a bolt of panic through my abdomen.

"I needed to s-see you...one m-more time, in case—"

"Stop!" I couldn't stomach hearing him finish that sentence. I'd sooner die than put that out into the world where the Angels of death could hear it and make it true. "You have to hold on, Trace. I'm going to find a way to get you back.

7

Everything's going to be fine," I promised blindly and then moved in to touch him, but he took a step back from me—forever and always just out of my reach.

"I've never f-felt evil like this before, Jemma." He shook his head as though conceding the war. "He's too s-strong."

"You're stronger!"

"Jemma, I'm so sor—"

"No. No! Don't you dare say it!" I quickly cut in. "It isn't over yet. Do you hear me? I'm not giving up on you, Trace."

His lashes lowered, covering the full blue of his eyes as his body slowly began to fade away.

"Trace! Wait!" I lunged forward to trap him inside my arms, to barricade him against my body, but there was nothing but air left in his place. I was too late. I'd lost him again.

I crumbled to my knees as tears brimmed in my eyes.

"*Jemma, can you hear me?*"

My head snapped up at the sound of a warm, familiar voice.

"*Open your eyes.*"

Gabriel?!

I looked around, frantically searching for him as the scene from the Cape began to tremble and then bleed away like water running down an oil painting. I dug my hands into the earth, bracing myself as it all disappeared into nothingness.

2. INTO THE VOID

My lids sprang open, and I blinked the sleep and confusion from my eyes. Gabriel was standing by my side, his eyebrows knitted as he looked down at me, staring as though I were some newly discovered alien life form. Apparently, I wasn't in the Cape anymore, or at the cemetery, or in the car. I was indoors now. That is, unless this was a dream too...

Freaked out and thoroughly confused, I immediately tried to lift myself up, but the room twirled around me like some out of control carnival ride that no longer had a working off switch. Or maybe I was the broken one who just couldn't stop spinning myself into Hell.

That definitely seemed more likely.

"I was starting to worry about you," he said with a tight smile as he wrapped his hand around my elbow and helped me sit myself up.

I could see the fire burning at the far end of the room, and I knew we were back at Huntington Manor, though I had no recollection of how we'd gotten here. My body shook as I tried to fit the hazy pieces back together, but nothing seemed to fit. Everything was disjointed and out of sorts, like puzzle pieces thrown into the air with nobody there to catch them.

"You hit your head pretty hard," he said, his voice calming and soft. "But you're okay."

I wasn't, though. Not by a long shot.

"How long have I been asleep for?" I asked him as I rubbed the hazy clouds from my eyes. Every part of my body ached something terrible, and despite the fact that I had obviously just been asleep, I felt utterly drained.

"You've been out for a few hours."

A few hours? My eyes snapped back to his. "Where's Trace?"

"Trace?" His brows furrowed as though he didn't understand my question. Or maybe he just didn't want to answer it. Either way, I knew I was headed for Shit's Creek.

"Yes, Gabriel. Trace. Where is he?" My eyes scanned the room and immediately stumbled onto my mother's incapacitated body sitting lifelessly on a chair in the corner of the room.

"You remember what happened at Angel's Peak, don't you?"

The look on his face coupled with the daunting presence of my mother's body let me know that it hadn't all just been a horrible dream.

This was real.

Hell on earth had come, and Trace was really gone.

I squeezed my eyes shut as my teeth clattered together painfully.

"I'm sorry, Jemma," he said as everything came back to me all at once.

The pain of it slashed through my body in nauseating waves before settling heavily in the pit of my belly. I tried to hold it together, to hold it down, but I couldn't. Overcome, I bent over my knees just as my stomach emptied itself all over the wooden floor. Gabriel quickly moved out of the way to avoid the backsplash and then grabbed a throw blanket from behind me, wrapping it around my shoulders.

My body continued to shake uncontrollably as I tried to stop myself from heaving.

"Drink this," he said as he handed me a water bottle from the coffee table. "You need to get something in your stomach. It'll help you feel better."

I highly doubted that. I wasn't sure there was anything that could help me now.

"Please."

Lifting my head, I took the bottle from his hand and twisted off the cap, but the bottle never made it to my lips. My eyes magnetized back to my mother and remained there, as though unable to look away. For the first time in my life, I found myself longing for her—for that safe place from the storm that only a mother could provide.

"Why haven't you reanimated her?" I asked him, my voice teetering along the edge of breaking into a million pieces.

She was slumped back in the chair as wisps of her dark hair cascaded across her face. She looked as though she were fast asleep in a peaceful slumber. Well, minus the ash color of her skin and the stake protruding from her chest, that is.

The stake I planted…

I slapped the horrifying memory away from my consciousness. It was just another painful reminder of how I'd played right into the Roderick sister's bloody hands.

"I thought it was best to wait for Tessa to get here," he answered, his tone soft but cautious.

"Why?" I asked as he ran a hand through his short dark hair and leveled his eyes at me.

"She should be here for this."

"She should be here for a lot of things," I retorted without bothering to hide the bitterness from my words.

"Jemma—"

"Forget it," I said, cutting him off. "I don't want to hear it." I wasn't in the mood to hear the Tessa-is-so-great speech. The one about how everything she does is for me. And that she's just trying to keep me safe. Honestly, if that was really the case, she was doing a piss poor job of it so far.

"I just thought it was best for the two of you to decide this together. As a *family*."

I huffed out a humorless laugh as the world's worst family reunion flashed through my mind.

And still, as hard as it was for me to digest the very concept of a *family*, the notion of it still tugged on something inside of me, because deep down in the gallows of my truth, I still longed for exactly that. Family. Love. Normalcy. All the things that were destined to never be mine.

I looked up at Gabriel as a hollow, hopeless feeling pressed down inside of me. The Hellgate had been opened, and I still had no idea what that meant for all of us. "How do we find him?" I asked, hoping he had plan, because I sure as shit didn't.

"I'm not sure we can. Not unless he wants to be found."

"You're kidding me, right?" That was so not the answer I wanted to hear. "So, what the hell do we do in the meantime?"

"We wait."

I gawked at him like he'd sprung a second head. "You can't seriously expect me to sit around here and do nothing. We should be out there looking for him. For all we know, he's hurt, and he needs our help."

"Jemma, he's Lucifer's vessel," he stated somberly, as though that should end all future discussions on the matter.

Like hell it would.

"How do we know for sure? It's not like we stuck around to interview him." Okay, so I was grasping at straws again, but who could blame me? I had nothing else to hold onto but the hope that Trace was okay—that the transference of Lucifer's energy didn't take. And I would hold onto it until the Devil himself told me otherwise.

"I have to find him, Gabriel. I have to at least try."

"We don't know where he is or what they have planned," he pointed out. "Going after them without any information would be suicide. Besides," he added gravelly, "You need to rest. You may have accelerated healing, but those stitches aren't going to stay put unless you do."

"Stitches?" The memory of being stabbed in the stomach wafted back in. I pulled up the hem of my shirt to reveal a neat row of stitches about an inch long across my abdomen. Great, just what I needed. Something else to slow me down.

"It's healing nicely," he added as I padded my finger along the suture.

"Very nice indeed," said a honeyed voice from the doorway.

My gaze somersaulted to Dominic. He was leaning against the threshold with his arms crossed over his chest and the semblance of a tickled grin on his face. Leave it to him to find something amusing about this.

"I see you started the party without me," he said, gesturing with his chin to my exposed flesh.

I glared at him and then yanked my shirt back down. "I'm glad you find this funny."

"I didn't say it was funny, love. I was simply admiring the view."

"Well, don't, okay?!" I didn't have the energy to wordplay with him. Not today. "I don't need this right now."

"Then tell me what you need." The intensity of his unrelenting gaze made my head feel as though it were swimming through muddy waters, and that was exactly the kind of thing I *didn't* need.

What I needed was a way to undo this mess and get Trace

back. Better yet, I needed someone to tell me none of this was happening. That it was all just some twisted nightmare I'd dreamed up from years of watching too many horror movies. And most of all, I needed Dominic to stop staring at me that way or I'd never be able to put one foot in front of the other one—ever again.

Gabriel straightened to his full height upon noticing my distress. "Knock it off, Dominic."

"I'm not doing anything, brother." He pushed off the doorway and calmly strolled towards me, a calculating smile teasing the corner of his lip. The closer he got to me, the more my tension eased.

And he knew it too.

He stopped at the coffee table and sat down directly in front of me, his knees brushing up against mine as he leaned in towards me. "Tell me what you need, angel, and I will provide it."

My eyes dropped to his mouth as the savory memory of his charmed bite drifted in and out of my consciousness with promises of a cure, and I loathed myself for it. How could I even think about that at a time like this? There was obviously something very wrong with me.

"Dammit, Dominic. She just woke up," gritted Gabriel. "Give her some space."

"She doesn't need space from *me*. In fact, I'd venture to say she needs the exact opposite of space." Dominic's eyes were pinned on me, focused only on sending me good vibrations through his proximity. "Isn't that right, angel?"

My mouth opened to deny him, but I couldn't find the words to tell the lie.

The truth was, I craved our exchanges, and I calmed in his mere presence, and there wasn't anything I could do to change that. Dominic and I were bloodbonded—looming apocalypse or

14

not.

His full lips pulled into a knowing grin as Gabriel ran his hand down over his face. Obviously, Gabriel was thinking the same thing I was: that we were so royally screwed right now.

"Besides, brother," continued Dominic. "You're the one who insisted we stay in town and fight this doomed war, remember?"

"What is your point?" answered Gabriel.

"My point is that you're going to need your golden Slayer if you have any hope of stopping the apocalypse, and we both know I'm the only one who can restore her to her former glory."

"Excuse me?" I scoffed.

Where did he even get off? Arrogant ass!

"I think you've done enough to her," answered Gabriel.

"*For* her," corrected Dominic.

Gabriel crossed his arms over his chest and grimaced.

"Can we stop talking about me like I'm not in the room?" I tried to stand up with the intention of getting away from the both of them, but apparently my shaky legs had other plans. I pitched forward towards Dominic, my hands fumbling onto his shoulders, though he quickly grabbed my hips and steadied me.

"Thanks," I mumbled under my breath.

Without removing his hands from my body, he straightened to his full height and peered down at me through those dark, enigmatic eyes. "Let me heal you, angel," he said as he brushed his thumb over the tennis ball sized lump on my forehead, instantly soothing the ache like his hand were made of the same medicine his mouth was.

My traitorous body leaned into him as though it belonged there, as though it were the natural thing to do. The reaction was immediately followed by a thunderous burst of guilt that turned my stomach around until it burned from the inside out. "I'm fine." I pushed his hand down and tried to step around

15

him, but he blocked my path.

"You're not fine, love. Your nerves are shot, and you're *hurt*."

Unfortunately, there wasn't a remedy for the kind of hurt I was feeling. It wasn't the kind of hurt you could fix with a first aid kit or even a Revenant bite. It was the kind of hurt that chipped away at your heart, disfiguring it until nothing remained but scar tissue. "You can't help me, Dominic. Not with this."

"I can make the pain go away," he insisted, his voice barely above a whisper, and I knew he was right.

He *could* make me feel better, and for a second, I seriously contemplated it. But I knew that taking the easy way out—escaping into Dominic and leaving this unbearable pain and darkness behind me—was only a temporary fix. It would not heal the hurt inside of me, and when it was over, it would only bring me closer to Dominic and farther away from Trace. And that was something I couldn't allow to happen.

No matter how tempting the escape was.

No matter how much the bloodbond begged me for it.

"Just get out of my way," I said, my voice shaky as I forced my way around him.

His raised his palms to me, expressing his innocent indifference, but the dark glint in his eyes said otherwise. There was nothing innocent about that man, and everyone in the room knew it. "I'm only trying to help you, love."

"I don't need that kind of help."

His eyes narrowed. "You should know by now that pushing me away is only going to make it worse for you," he warned, but I chose to ignore him entirely.

I had no other choice.

Instead, I turned to Gabriel. Sobering, constant Gabriel. I could always rely on him to put me back in the game. "How do

I get him back? Tell me everything you know about Lucifer's vessel." If I had any hope of finding Trace and stopping this so-called apocalypse, I was going to need a major crash course in all things Lucifer.

"I wish there was a simple answer," he said as he ran a hand through his ebony hair and took a small step towards me. "I've read the Scripture front to back more times than I care to remember, and while there's always been plenty of information about the apocalypse, there's never been anything about the vessel or the soul that previously occupied it."

Previously? I swallowed a mouthful of blades. I couldn't stomach hearing him speak about Trace in the past-tense—as though he were merely just some vehicle for the Devil.

As though he didn't even exist anymore...

"You have to understand, there is no precedence for this," he continued.

"I don't need to be reminded." I was well aware of the fact that I was the one and only village idiot to release Lucifer from his tomb. "I just need to know how to get him back."

His expression pinched. "I'm not entirely sure that's possible, Jemma. There might not be anything there to bring back."

"Come again?" I said, nearly choking on my own breath. "Are you saying he might not be alive?"

"It's hard to say one way or the other. As far as I can understand, Lucifer should have full control over Trace's body—much like a typical demon possession. But make no mistake, this is not a typical demon possession. *If* Trace is somehow still in there, it won't be long before Lucifer takes over completely and eliminates the link entirely."

If Trace was still in there?

His words replayed in my mind like the music score to a Shakespearean tragedy. I decided I wasn't going to focus on the big, fat *if.* I was going to dig through the smothering darkness and hold onto that tiny fragment of light. "But there is a chance he's still in there, right?"

I mean, it wasn't as if he was just some run of the mill mortal. He was a Descendant of Angels—a Reaper for crying out loud. That had to mean something. It had to.

"Theoretically, yes. But not a very good chance, and that's assuming they've translated the texts correctly."

That was good enough for me. There was only one thing I needed to know now: "How do I kill him?"

Gabriel's shoulder's slumped at my question.

"There *is* a way to kill him, right?"

"Yes," he said, but the hopeless look never left his face.

"Then what is it?" I pushed.

His eyes skirted away for a moment before meeting mine again. "I don't know that we can kill one without killing the other."

The air thinned in the room as I shook my head at his words.

No. Nope. Just no! That couldn't be the end of it. There had to be another way…

"What if we figured out a way to get Lucifer out of Trace's body first? Trace would regain control and come back, right?" Gabriel started to shake his head, so I quickly added, "I mean, theoretically, of course."

He thought about it for a moment. "I suppose, but it isn't very likely, Jemma."

"Which part?"

"All of it," chimed Dominic, sans bedside manner. "The chances of Lucifer allowing Trace to occupy the same vessel as him are next to non-existent. And you certainly cannot simply exorcise the Devil out of him like he was some common demon."

"Why not?"

"Because, he's not a demon, buttercup."

"Dominic." Gabriel tightened his jaw and shook his head at him.

"Would you rather I lied to her, brother? Giving her false hope will only make her run off and do something foolish."

"Excuse me?" I snapped, glaring at him.

"You're excused, angel," he said offhandedly before turning his attention back to Gabriel. "You know as well as I do that Romeo is done for. The only thing we should be concerning ourselves with is the end of days. Or am I the only one who hasn't forgotten?"

I narrowed my eyes at him. "You just can't help yourself, can you?"

"Not usually, no, although I do need you to be more specific."

"To throw Trace to the hellhounds and be done with him!"

"That's hardly what I'm doing."

"Bullshit." I didn't trust his intentions for a minute. Not when it came to Trace. "I know what you're trying to do, but it doesn't matter to me one bit, because I'm not giving up on him until there isn't an ounce of hope left."

"I'd say we crossed that bridge when that temptress blood of yours hit the ground."

My back stiffened as fresh tears scorched the corners of my eyes. "You don't know that! You don't know anything!"

Gabriel himself said there was no precedence for this. They were just as much in the dark as I was, and the way I saw it, if Lucifer found a way inside of Trace, then there had to be a way to get him out.

I only hoped Trace's soul would still be in his body when I found it.

"You're letting your emotions cloud your judgment, and

it's going to get you killed," Dominic said, taking a slow and calculated step towards me. His voice was softer now, more urgent. "Is that what you want, angel? Because there are more pleasant ways to die if that is what you desire."

"I don't care about what happens to me," I said stubbornly, matching his advance. "This isn't about me!"

He lowered his head so that we were at eye level now. "It's always about you, angel. At least it is where I am concerned." There was something strangely sincere about his words and the tone in which he spoke them.

"If you're so concerned about me, why don't you help me?"

"That's precisely what I'm trying to do."

"Well, it doesn't feel that way," I said lowly, trying not to lose my breath from his closeness.

His eyes dropped from my gaze, surveying everything from my lips to my neck to the bump on my head and then back again. "We both know you don't allow yourself to feel anything where it concerns me."

I flinched at his words—at their implication. "What the hell is that supposed to mean?"

His lips parted to say something before pressing together again.

A blanket of static passed between us, charging the air with muted words and tethered emotions. My chest heaved as I tried to fill my lungs with the air that was never enough. Afraid of what I might say or do with him standing so close to me, I tried to push him away again, but he caught my wrists and pulled me into him.

"Perhaps if you stopped pushing me away," he said as he lowered his head again, his breath caressing my lips as he spoke, "you'd see that I only want to keep you from peril."

The intensity of his eyes made a flutter of heat ripple through my insides.

Obviously, this wasn't going anywhere. Well, nowhere good, anyway. This was exactly the reason I needed space from him. I couldn't think straight when he was this close, nor did I have the energy to keep pushing him away, especially when his proximity was the only thing that quelled the growing volcano inside of me.

I pulled my hands free. "If you want to keep me from peril, you can start by staying the hell away from me." There was destruction in my tone, but I wasn't sure if it was meant for Dominic or myself.

"That isn't what you want, and we both know it."

"Wanna bet?" I said, my jaw clenching so hard I could hear my teeth gnashing together.

"Alright, angel," he said as he looked at me for a harrowing moment and then nodded, "It's your funeral."

"That's right! It is my funeral, so stay the hell out of it!"

Wait, what? Did I really just say that?

He shook his head at me and then picked up his drink from the coffee table. My heart sank a little as I watched him leave the room, but that wasn't nearly as disturbing as the immediate ache that followed his departure. It was the kind of separation anxiety that made my skin crawl and my head pound from the inside out. I immediately tried to shake it away, forcing myself to stay focused on what was most important. You know, the latest nightmare unfolding within my life. And it took every bit of strength I had to accomplish the feat.

"Does the Council know?" I asked Gabriel as I rubbed my temples in an effort to ease the gnawing discomfort.

"Yes." He nodded. "They're aware that Lucifer is earthbound."

"Do they know that Trace is the vessel?"

He shook his head. "He has yet to show himself since Angel's Peak."

21

"Why not?" Hope immediately ignited inside me. Maybe something went wrong. Maybe the ritual didn't take. Maybe Trace was fine and just waiting for me to get out there and find him. "That has to mean something, right?"

"Yes. If he's laying low, it's certainly for a reason." He paused, his forehead creasing as he continued. "Most likely it means he's biding his time, or worse, he's making plans."

And there went my bloom of hope.

"So, no news is bad news," I surmised. "And my sister?"

"I haven't been able to reach her yet. I'm guessing the Order's already mobilized her."

We both knew what that meant. The clock was ticking.

His eyebrows furrowed when he added, "You should know, they've requested a meeting."

"The Council?"

He nodded. "I think you should hear them out. If there's a way to save Trace, the Order will know."

"I don't doubt that," I answered dryly. "I just don't trust them to tell me about it."

Not even Gabriel could argue that one.

"I'll leave the final decision up to you," he said, his moss eyes glimmering with sincerity. "But I don't see what other choice we have right now. We're completely in the dark, Jemma."

I needed another option more than I needed air right now. Unfortunately, I was too tired and spent to come up with any useful alternatives. I folded my arms across my chest as the unease continued to slash its way through my body.

"You know it's only going to get worse," he cautioned, his ominous tone further aggravating my anxiety.

"What's that? My life?" I snorted tartly. "Tell me something I don't know."

"I meant the bloodbond."

22

Moisture left my mouth as I met Gabriel's eyes. We had yet to have a conversation about the bloodbond, and frankly, I wanted to keep it that way. I wasn't exactly comfortable with Gabriel knowing that I had sealed that deal with his brother and willingly offered myself up to him on more than one occasion.

"I can handle it," I said, knowing full well what my consequences were.

"The longer you reject it, the more painful it's going to be for you."

I lowered my head into my hands. "I know that."

"I don't think that you do, Jemma."

I met his eyes again, startled by the force of his words. It wasn't as if I hadn't been warned before, but somehow, hearing it from Gabriel made the reality that much scarier to face.

"Well, what would you have me do instead, Gabriel? The more I give in to him, the more I want him." My confession appeared to surprise him, but not as much as it surprised me.

"I'm not sure," he said, his gaze veering away from me and then returning with determination. "But you can't just avoid it. My brother was right about one thing. No good will come of it, and with everything that's going on, we can't afford to have you at half strength."

"Are you telling me you want me to go full blood-whore on him?" I leered at him skeptically.

His cheeks darkened when he answered, "Of course not." He pushed his hands through his hair as he considered it. "But you will need to be on some kind of regimen," he decided. "Small doses at regular intervals should keep your body optimal and the withdrawals at bay."

My face twisted as his words. "You're making it sound like I'm an addict."

"Give it a few more days."

His words knocked the air out of my lungs.

Regret immediately skewed his features. "I shouldn't have said that. I apologize."

"Don't. It's fine." I forced my chin back up and digested his words, no matter how sour they tasted. "I never let the truth break me before, and I'm not about to start now." As awful as it was, as difficult to swallow as it might be, knowing was always better than not knowing.

At least it was to me.

"I hate him for doing this to you." His voice was low, but it still packed a meaningful punch.

"I wish I could hate him too," I muttered, mostly to myself. But the truth was, I didn't hate Dominic.
Not even at all.

3. PULL ME UNDER

The rain fell in sheets outside my window as I climbed into the guest bed and pulled the comforter up to my chin. Gabriel had forced—*insisted* that I get some rest and give my body a chance to heal, and while it was becoming a chore to keep my eyes open, it still felt wrong being in a warm bed while Trace was still out there.

Granted, there wasn't anything I could do for him until we knew exactly what we were up against, but it still didn't make it any easier for me to accept the waiting game we were now stuck in.

Turning onto my stomach, I tried to calm my mind enough to sleep, but every time I closed my eyes, all I could see was tormenting images of Trace's hollow eyes staring out at the lake. I'd never seen his eyes look so lifeless, so void of all the light he carried like a second skin. It shook me to my very core.

I kicked the sheets off my legs and turned again, and then again. My body was restless, and my skin felt as though something were crawling just below the surface of it. I couldn't stop my mind from running rampant over the future, over what remained of it. There were so many unanswered questions, so many horrible ways this thing could play out, and once again, I was completely in the dark. Was Trace still alive? Would I be able to find a way to get him back? And worse, what if I couldn't...

What then?

The thought sent a whole new level of anxiety through my body. One I couldn't stomach to save my life. I tried to think of other things, easier things, but nothing seemed to stick. No matter how hard I tried, my mind raced back to the catastrophe unfolding within my life. And his eyes—those haunting eyes.

Flopping onto my back again, I stared out at the wall across from my bed. I could hear movement in the next room— Dominic's room—and while he was close enough that I could hear him, he wasn't close enough to make me feel any better.

The longer I allowed myself to think about him, the more the bond summoned me, begging me for reprieve from the one person that could quiet the ache. Of course, I refused to give into it, but it only made falling asleep that much harder.

I turned over in the dark and searched the night table for my phone.

4:32 A.M.

Realizing I wasn't going to be getting a lick of shut-eye anytime soon, I climbed out of bed and decided I needed to put something in my empty stomach. Maybe that was the reason I couldn't fall asleep.

I quietly made my way downstairs and fixed myself a bowl of cereal. In the quiet of the empty kitchen, I leaned against the counter and took a spoonful of cereal, mulling over what Gabriel had said about the bloodbond. The more I thought about it, the more I realized he was right: I *was* going to need something to help me survive this connection without losing myself in it completely, and if dosing myself regularly was the way to do it, then I was all in.

Anything was better than the agonizing pain of these incessant withdrawals.

After forcing a few more bites down, I rinsed out my bowl and tiptoed back up the stairs. My heart and mind had every intention of going right back to my room, but I found myself standing outside Dominic's bedroom door, utterly conflicted. There was a war going on inside of me, one that threatened to rip me in two. On one hand, my heart was screaming at me to go back to bed—to suffer through the pain no matter the cost to me. And then there was the other side. The part of me that made my feet refuse to move no matter how much I inwardly cursed at them.

Apparently, my body had a mind of its own, and it wasn't willing to suffer the way my heart was.

Conceding the battle, I knocked on his door.

No answer.

I knocked again and waited an entire two seconds before opening the door myself.

Apparently, patience wasn't one of my virtues.

"You do realize the point of knocking is to wait for someone to answer," chided Dominic, his tone as flat as an out of tune piano. He was lying on his bed, bare-chested, with his feet crossed at his ankles and a book in his hands.

"Thanks for the etiquette lesson." I shifted uncomfortably, still hovering by the door. "Can I come in?"

"Well, that depends," he said as he placed the book down beside him and lifted off the bed. The taut muscles on his abdomen pulled and flexed as he sauntered across the dim-lit room to me.

"On what?" I asked, forcing my eyes to stay topside.

"On what you're here for."

I wasn't entirely sure of that myself.

"I can't sleep," I admitted, my eyes accidently dipping

down to his bare abdomen as he met me where I stood. I immediately regretted it as my cheeks flushed with heat. When I looked back up at him, he was smiling triumphantly.

"You like what you see?" he asked as he leaned his forearm against the doorframe as if to give me a better view.

I immediately bristled. "Cocky much?"

"You have no idea." He smiled wolfishly, and the heat in my cheeks damn near scorched me.

This was a bad idea…

So very bad.

"I shouldn't have come here."

"Probably not," he agreed.

Jackass.

I turned and tried to walk away, but he quickly caught my arm and hauled me back inside, shutting the door behind me and then locking it.

I'm in trouble. "Dom—"

He pressed his finger against my lips, silencing me.

For a moment, I was confused, thinking maybe he had heard someone coming down the hall, but when his hand slid away from my lips and caught my waist, I knew this had nothing to do with company and everything to do with us.

"Why don't you tell me why you're really here," he said, looking at me like he already knew the answer. Like I was here to satisfy the bloodbond.

"I'm not here for that," I said, though it tasted like a lie.

His gaze travelled down to my mouth and then my neck, eyeing both hungrily. "Then why are you here?"

"I…don't know."

His eyes flicked back up to mine. "Stop playing games with me, angel. I don't like it."

"That's not what I'm doing."

"Isn't it?"

"No."

"Then what are you doing?"

The truth was, I had no freaking idea what I was doing. "I just...I couldn't sleep, and I didn't want to be alone."

"I see." He appeared to be considering it. "So, you're just using me then," he stated simply.

"What? No!" My face immediately reddened with embarrassment. "That's not what I'm doing."

I mean, at least I didn't think it was.

The corner of his lip pulled up into a lopsided grin. "I didn't say I minded."

I couldn't help but crack a smile at that, but it quickly fell away as my shame rushed in to bury it. How could I be smiling at a time like this?

"Don't do that," he said, brushing his thumb against my lips.

"What?"

"Hide your smile." He picked up my chin so that I was looking directly into his eyes. "You deserve to smile, angel. Don't ever let yourself believe differently."

I wasn't sure why, but his words loosened something inside me, and suddenly, my throat felt thick with sorrow.

"I really should go back to my room now," I said, avoiding his eyes, even though he was standing close enough to me that I could almost taste him.

"Why is that?"

"Because I'm about to start crying, Dominic, and I'd rather not do that in front of you."

"I think it's a little late for that," he said as he reached out and brushed away a tear with his thumb. His dark eyes remained transfixed on me when he said, "You know I hate to see you cry, angel."

That may have been true, but he sure as hell was watching

me.

"Feel free to look away then," I offered plainly as more tears fell, streaking my cheeks with their salty residue.

"I can't for the life of me figure out how to do that."

My breath stalled in my throat, momentarily pausing my waterfalls as I met his eyes. I couldn't take it when he spoke to me that way. Words too soft and stripped down to be from someone like Dominic, and yet they were. It was confusing and frustrating, and it did strange things to me...like urging me to get closer to him, to touch him, to let him in...things that threatened me with absolute annihilation.

"Stop saying stuff like that to me," I said as I white-knuckled myself in place.

"Why?"

"Because it confuses me," I answered honestly, not bothering to dilute the truth.

"You'd rather I insult you then?"

"Yes." *Wait.* "No. That's not what I meant."

"I see what you mean about being confused."

I jabbed him in his stomach, and he quickly caught my hand, a smile tugging at his lips as he covered it with his own. Something inside of me came to life again as the invisible cord between us shortened. And then suddenly, my fingers were splayed against his skin, riding the ridges even though I'd meant to pull my hand away.

He ducked his head down, eying my hand with a mixture of amusement and curiosity. "This is new."

"What is?" I asked, feeling myself slip deeper into the mesmerizing feel of his skin.

"You...touching me."

And then I was touching him with both my hands, my fingernails dragging against his skin as though I were no longer in control of my own extremities. He exhaled a growl that

30

vibrated at the back of his throat, letting me know it felt just as nice to be touched by me as it did for me to touch him.

"Angel." His voice was a quiet warning to tread carefully, but his eyes were already hooded with desire. "You ought to stop while you still have the chance."

But stopping was beyond my paygrade.

I knew no good would come of this. I knew being this close to Dominic was dangerous, but somehow, under the blanket of nightfall when my demons came to stir me, he was the only one that could silence the screaming.

"I don't want to stop." The connection throbbed harder, calling for me to move closer to him. My body was flush against his, my fingers digging into his back, and somehow, it wasn't enough. I could still feel the pain from the outside world, still see Trace's eyes in the back of my mind. I didn't want to feel pain anymore.

I didn't want to see those eyes…

My hands came back around the front, this time moving upwards and then wrapping themselves around the back of his neck. Another growl escaped him as he pressed his forehead against mine, his eyes brimming with fire and flames.

"I have to feed, angel." His voice was low and gruff with need.

My heartrate picked up at the mere mention of the act. It was no surprise to me. After all, this was exactly the place I'd been pushing him to. It was exactly where I wanted to go, and though I'd never admit it to myself in the light of day, it was exactly the place I wanted to be.

"Then feed." I picked up my hair and pushed it over my shoulder, clearing a path for him.

He pulled his head back, scrutinizing me as though he hadn't trusted his ears.

I was going to defend myself by telling him how Gabriel

said it was better if we found a way to control the bond—the urges—to dose ourselves in small increments to ward off the need, but I knew that he'd see right through it. While I had agreed with Gabriel, that wasn't even almost the reason I'd wandered into Dominic's room tonight, and we both knew it. So, I pressed my lips together and swallowed the excuse down.

"What are you waiting for?" I asked when he failed to make a move.

He didn't waste another second.

His fangs immediately clicked out as his pupils dilated, making the dark pools of his eyes appear boundless. The sight of it caused my heart to stall mid-beat and then race off into overdrive. Fear, anticipation…excitement, they were riding my body like a caged stallion with a small taste of freedom.

There was no stopping this now, and I didn't want to.

A veil of darkness riddled with lust and yearning flickered across his face as he cupped the nape of my neck and lowered his head to my jaw, his lips brushing against my skin as he made his way down to his favorite spot below my ear.

Anticipation rocked my body, but only for a second, and then he broke through the skin, drawing from me as though he had every right to—as though he owned me.

Perhaps in some small way he did.

I tightened my grip around his neck, my knees wobbling below me as ecstasy seeped into my bloodstream. Pleasure and pain. With Dominic, it was one and the same. The longer he drank, the further I slipped from reality, and it was every bit as wonderful as I had needed it to be. Every second that ticked by brought me closer to my twisted heaven on earth, deeper into my own self-made prison where no one could touch me.

Not even the devil himself.

4. EXODUS

I woke up the next day alone in the guestroom with no memory of how I'd gotten back there. Vivid flashes of last night's escapade trickled into my mind—Dominic's fingers in my hair, his mouth on my neck—but I quickly buried it in that secret place I put all the uncomfortable things I didn't want to deal with.

So, I fell apart yesterday. I let the bloodbond win the battle. Sue me. It wasn't the first time, and I doubted it would be the last time. Either way, I wasn't going to let that stop me from what I had to do.

With my mind on auto-pilot, I took a quick shower and got dressed and then made my way downstairs. Gabriel and Dominic were already in the den, their voices wafting through the house like the whisperings of a distant ghost.

"Good morning, angel," said Dominic as I peered my head into the room. "You look particularly rested this morning."

Gabriel's eyes cut away from me and I immediately reddened at the obvious scarlet letter I was wearing. We were really going to need to get that whole blood regimen thing underway, or this uncomfortable scene was going to repeat itself over and over again every morning. And trust me, once was enough.

"Any news on Trace?" I asked, crossing my arms over my chest as I moved the conversation along.

"No." Gabriel shook his head. "Well, not exactly."

"Not exactly?" I repeated, fairly certain that was a yes or no question. There was a thickness in the room that made the tension almost palpable. I hadn't noticed it when I first walked in, but I did now.

"Gabriel's been on the horn with the Council all morning," offered Dominic as he waggled his eyebrows.

"About what?"

Gabriel motioned for me to sit down, and I did, worried my legs would fail me if he decided to hit me with even more bad news than we already had.

"Okay, I'm sitting. What is it? What's going on?" I finally managed to croak out when he didn't immediately begin talking.

His forehead lined as he looked down at me with a hard edge to his eyes. "There's been a heavy influx of demon sightings all night. Far too many to be considered a coincidence," he added, making sure I knew where he was going with this. "As far as we can tell, they're slowly moving inland and closing in on Hollow Hills."

A thick, strangling knot formed at the back of my throat. If the demon population was suddenly heading this way, it was for a reason. Something was luring them here.

"But we're still *warded*, right?" I asked nervously as I tried to remember what I'd learned about demons during my training sessions with Gabriel.

From what I could remember, the fight against demons consisted of two things: vanquishing demons using well-trained, cut throat Slayers who weren't afraid of getting their hands dirty on the front lines. And apotropaic magic to ward off demons and other lowly creatures from specific areas, and sometimes even entire cities. They believed in proactive prevention as much as they did eradication.

"Not exactly," he said, his voice gruff with tension. "They're overriding the sigils."

"How is that possible? I thought the seals could only be broken by the Caster who inscribed them?"

"Yes and no."

"Seriously, Gabriel? Pick one."

"Well, that's the way it always worked in the past. That is, until now."

"Dammit." If the demons were somehow breaking the seals the Order had in place, we'd just lost the first line of defense against them. None of us were safe anymore. Not that we ever really were, but that was beside the point.

"Okay, so how do we stop them?"

"The Council's already mobilized some of their top Rigs, but it's a temporary solution at best. There's too many of them and not enough of us. Whatever's happening, it's connected to Lucifer, and the Council knows it." He paused briefly, searching for the right words before he continued. "They want to speak with you, Jemma. They're not asking anymore."

"Uh-uh." I swallowed the knot as I tried to think of a way out of this. "Not yet—not until I find Trace." There was no way I was going into a meeting with the Council completely clueless about what we were up against, or what *their* intentions were. The last thing I needed was to be at their mercy, especially when Trace's life was on the line.

For all I knew, they were looking for me to lock me up and throw away the key for good.

"And how exactly do you plan on finding him?" asked Dominic, irritation heavy in his tone. "Being that the Council has yet to pinpoint his whereabouts."

"Honestly? I don't know." The only thing I knew for sure was that I needed information and I needed reinforcements. I needed to find someone who would be willing to help me get answers—someone who would put Trace's life above their own. The Order wouldn't...but maybe his father would.

I had to start somewhere.

"But I have an idea," I said as I stood up from the sofa, my legs shaky with anticipation. "I need a ride to All Saints."

"For what?" asked Dominic, following me as I stalked across the room to grab my jacket.

"What do you think?"

He snagged my elbow and turned me around. "This is hardly the time to visit the local watering hole, love."

"You think?" I pulled my arm free. "I'm going to talk to Peter." Because if there was any hope of reaching Trace, Peter Macarthur would help me find a way.

At least, I hoped he would.

5. A TOUCH OF EVIL

The lunch crowd at All Saints was thick with all the usual suspects, all of them happily stuffing their faces as though the end of days weren't upon us. It had been a while since I'd been back here, and in a weird way, it almost felt like coming home. After everything that had gone down with Engel, I hadn't exactly been in the right frame of mind to nonchalantly serve chicken wings as though I wasn't the one destined to bring on the Apocalypse.

Dominic followed closely behind as I weaved my way through the happy patrons to the employees-only area at the back of the building. Gabriel decided to stay behind and continue his research, which was perfectly fine by me. I only needed one licensed Huntington brother anyway.

So, what's the plan, love? asked Dominic to my mind. His voice slid through my brain like silk.

"I don't have one," I said evenly. Even though the place was vibrating with music and chatter, I knew he could hear me through the noise. Revenants could hear a mouse squeak from five blocks away, but Dominic and I were bloodbonded, and that made our connection even tighter. He was tuned into me on a frequency that no one else could hear.

He hooked his arm around my waist and drew me back into his chest. I tried to ignore the way my body easily leaned into his, as though it wanted to take refuge there.

"Don't you think you ought to come up with one before going in there?" he whispered close to my ear, his hand splayed against my stomach.

"I don't need a plan," I said, ignoring the swelling heat in my belly. "I'm just going to tell him the truth."

I mean, what the hell else could I do?

"Is that right? And when has that ever worked out for you in the past?" he asked.

Heck, it was a perfectly valid question.

"Never," I answered honestly. "But what choice do I have?" I turned slowly, my lips nearly grazing his own as I faced him. "If I have to lie to him to get him to help me save his son, then I don't need his kind of help anyway." Ignoring the goosebumps prickling over my skin, I pushed his arm down and continued walking.

He didn't bother to object again.

With my hand on the doorknob, I pulled in a deep breath and barged in through the office door.

Peter Macarthur was sitting at his desk, talking to someone on the phone. His mouth drifted open as he caught sight of me. "I'm going to have to call you back," he muttered into the receiver before hanging it up.

"Jemma, darling. Didn't expect to see you here." His lips spread out into a toothy grin. "What a nice surprise."

"I'm sorry to burst in like this, Mr. Macarthur, but we need to talk."

"Hm, sounds serious." He eyed Dominic, who stood silent-but-deadly at the back of the room, and then returned his focus to me. "Forgive my manners. Please have a seat," he offered, extending his hand to the chair in front of his desk.

I sat down and tucked my hair behind my ears, buying myself an extra second or two before I had to explain to him what had happened to his only son. Unfortunately, I could buy myself an entire century worth of time, and I'd still never be ready enough to have this conversation. "It's about Trace," I finally managed to say.

"Trace?" His forehead lined with curiosity before his gaze shifted over my shoulder. "Well, speak of the devil."

Speak of the—what now?

"What about me?" said a deep baritone voice from somewhere behind me.

My back straightened into a rod as chills zipped down my arms. I knew that voice—I'd know that voice anywhere. I gripped the armrest on my chair and *slowly* turned around, almost too afraid to look.

But I did look. And then my jaw dropped.

"Tr-Trace?" I could barely get his name off the roof of my mouth.

He smiled down at me, setting off both of his dimples in tandem as the light in the room lit up his gleaming blue eyes. He looked healthy and beautiful and completely alive.

And I couldn't do anything but stare at him like a deer caught in headlights.

His brows furrowed. "What's wrong, Jemma? You look like you've seen a ghost."

A ghost? Try the devil. Or was it? I honestly couldn't tell just by looking at him. Not that it mattered. I knew better than anyone that looks could be deceiving.

And then my brain clicked back on.

"Holy shit!" I said and jumped up from my chair. The abrupt movement sent it screeching back into a filing cabinet.

"Jemma, darling, what's gotten into you?" asked Peter,

eyeing me as though I was batshit crazy.

And I hoped to God I was, because the alternative…the alternative didn't make a lick of sense.

"What's gotten into *me*?" I huffed out a maniacal laugh, and then another one. "I think you should be asking what's gotten into him!" I cried, pointing an accusatory finger at Trace.

His eyebrows pulled together as a mixture of hurt and confusion coated his expression. "What's that supposed to mean? Why are you acting like this?"

This had to be a dream. It had to. That or some sick joke that everyone was in on but me. My eyes snapped to Dominic for answers—if anyone would know what was going on, it was Dominic.

Don't look at me, love, he said to my mind with a minute shake of his head. *Try to keep him talking.*

Easy for him to say. He wasn't the one who had to talk to his maybe dead/maybe fine/maybe possessed boyfriend.

Ignoring the painful pressure building in my chest, I turned back to Trace. I needed to get a hold of my damn self and get some answers. You know, assert my dominance and whatnot.

"What the h-hell is going on? What are you d-doing here?" I stuttered as I slowly backed away from him.

That went well.

Pressing my back against the wall, I followed the edges of the room and inched my way back to Dominic's side. I figured I could be just as dominant from the other side of the room.

"What do you mean, what am I doing here?" Trace's eyes bounced between me and Dominic, and I swore I saw hurt flicker through them at the sight of us together. "I work here."

"Goodness, Jemma. Are you feeling alright?" asked Peter as he rose from his chair. "You seem out of sorts."

Oh, my God, I was in the freaking twilight zone. Obviously, I'd hit my head a lot harder than I thought.

Paula knocked on the door and then poked her head all the way, her eyes landing on each of us before settling on Peter. "Mr. Macarthur, April needs you at the front."

"Thank you, Paula. I'll be right there."

I shot Paula a get-me-the-hell-out-of-here look, but she seemed to miss the message as her pained eyes landed on me and Dominic. She abruptly left the room, and as soon as she did, I shoved Dominic in the same direction. The only thing I wanted to do was get my butt out of that room and away from Trace...or Lucifer...or whoever the hell he was until I figured out exactly WHO THE HELL HE WAS.

Something was severely wrong here, and honestly, I couldn't stomach another minute of everyone staring at me like I was crazy. Like last night hadn't happened. I came here with the intention of talking to Peter—of asking him for his help. I hadn't braced myself for *this*. For Trace being here and acting as if nothing happened.

This was utter insanity.

"Where are you going?" asked Trace, following us as I tripped over Dominic's foot in my frenzy to run us out the door. "What's going on, Jemma? Please talk to me."

Dominic caught me mid-stumble and straightened me out. His eyes remained fixed on the Reaper before us, but he didn't say anything. He just watched him, his dark eyes narrowing with unspoken suspicion.

"What's going on?" I repeated his question while trying not to nervous-laugh. "I think I should be asking you that, Trace. Or should I call you Lucifer?"

"Lucifer?" His head ticked back a notch. "You're not making any sense, Jemma. You're starting to scare me."

My hands shot up to my temples. My head was pounding like someone planted a drum right between my ears.

Maybe I *was* losing it?

His gaze snapped to Dominic. "What did you do to her?" he accused, his jaw flexing aggressively.

"I beg your pardon?"

Trace stomped towards Dominic, his eyes glowing and fueled by fire as he grabbed him by the lapels of his trench coat and shook him. "Did you compel her again?"

"Kindly remove your hands from my person." Dominic shoved him back a step. "Compel her to do what, exactly?"

Trace's jaw tightened. "I don't know what you're up to, but you're not going to get away with this, dead boy!"

My eyes bounced between the two of them, along with doing other crazy things that looked a lot like twitching. "Get away with what? What are you talking about?"

"Listen to me, Jemma," pleaded Trace. His eyes were fixed on me as he approached me with caution. "Whatever he's telling you, it's not real, okay? He's compelling you again."

"The hell I am."

"No." I shook my head. "I watched you take in Lucifer with my own eyes."

"Take in Lucifer? Jemma, come on. Are you hearing yourself? This is crazy." He picked up my hand and gently guided me towards him, and I let him because I wanted so badly to believe him—to touch him. "It's me, Jemma. Look at me. He's making you see things that aren't there."

Dominic scoffed. "He's lying, angel. It's what the old snake does best."

"You have to fight him, Jemma. It isn't real."

Panic descended on me as the fragile walls around my sanity began to quake. "I was there. I saw it happen."

"Where, Jemma? I was at work every night this week. Ask my father!" he said and motioned over his shoulder to Peter, who was still watching us like a train wreck just happened outside his office.

"It's true," confirmed Peter, looking at me as though I'd just escaped the loony bin.

No. Nope. My knees knocked against each other as I fought the urge to crumble to the floor. "You were there."

"I swear I was here all night. Come on, Jemma. Think! He's compelling you. I told you you couldn't trust him."

But I saw him.

I saw it happen with my own eyes…

Didn't I?

Shit! What if Trace was telling the truth? What if the whole thing was nothing more than a hallucination brought on by Dominic? It wouldn't be the first time he'd played mind games with me.

I thought we were passed all that, but what if I was wrong?

"Angel, please tell me you're not actually buying this cheap load of crap, are you?"

"I…I…" I had no idea what was going on or who to believe. My mind was spiraling out of control, and I was afraid I was going to lose it all over again. Oh, my God, this isn't happening.

This isn't happening.

THIS ISN'T HAPPENING.

"That's it. We're leaving," said Dominic as he tried to reach for my hand, but Trace quickly spun me around, putting his back to Dominic and keeping him just out of my reach.

"Not today, Revenant," said Trace with a smile I didn't recognize. A smile that made my insides tremble. My body temperature dropped abruptly as the room began to melt away from us.

This just went from bad to worse.

And just like that, we were gone.

6. THE MARK OF THE BEAST

The Macarthur cabin up north materialized around us as my body temperature slowly began its climb back to normal. The moment the room solidified around us, I yanked my hands free and took several giant steps backwards. Trace's lips twisted into a smile as he watched me scurry away from him like a petrified mouse. Honestly, it seemed to amuse him.

"Alone, at last."

For all intents and purposes, it was Trace. He looked just like Trace. Not a hair on his head or muscle in his body was amiss. He even sounded just like him. But it wasn't him. I could feel it. Or rather, I couldn't feel it—the very distinct body buzz I usually got from being close to Trace.

In my shock of seeing him at All Saints, I hadn't noticed the feeling was missing.

But I noticed it now.

"You're not Trace." Surprisingly, my voice didn't shake when I spoke.

"No," he answered plainly. "Not in essence."

Lucifer. His name rolled through my mind like an incantation of evil.

The devil ignited Trace's dimples, and my heart seized at the sight of them. "It's a pleasure to finally meet you, Daughter of Hades," he said with a hint of admiration in his tone. "I wanted to thank you in person for releasing me."

I cringed at his words. "I didn't release you—I didn't. I mean, I did but not by choice! It was a mistake." The worst mistake I'd ever made in my entire miserable life, but one I intended on rectifying. I needed him to know where I stood, that I wasn't one of his followers or devotees.

I wasn't his anything.

"A mistake?" He chuckled as though I'd said something cute. "A day of reckoning that has been prophesized since the beginning of time? Where I come from, we call that destiny."

"Where you come from? You mean Hell." It pained me to even look at him. To watch this monster…this thing, use my boyfriend's body as though it were his own. As though he had any right to occupy my place of worship.

"Hades, Hell, The Underworld. My Realm has many names, though none truly do it justice." His head cocked to the side as he waited for another question.

And believe me, I had hundreds, mainly the exact steps required to nuke his ass back to his hell-tomb. But I was pretty sure he wasn't going to give me that information willingly, so I had to think of something else. Something to keep him talking, to keep him giving me inside information, and yet when I opened my mouth, there was only one question that mattered to me.

"Is he—?" Tears sprang up beneath my lids, blurring out my vision. "Is he still in there…with you?"

"Yes," he said, dragging the word out almost serpent-like. "I'm well aware that my vessel's soul is the only thing stopping you from trying to kill me right now. My consorts took every precaution."

Yes, the Roderick sisters certainly thought of everything, and I fully intended on paying them back for that.

Threefold.

"Can I talk to him?" I asked, my voice small and pleading.

"I'm afraid it doesn't work that way."

"Why not?" I asked, though it came out more like a whine than a question.

"Because, Daughter," he said and paused for effect, "I am the only one that operates this vessel now."

"He's not a vessel!" I shouted without thinking the whole thing through. "This isn't your body! This isn't your life. It belongs to someone else—a good person who deserves to see it through to the end!"

His eyes crinkled as he smiled back at me. "You say that as though it's of any importance to me."

Of course, it wasn't of any importance to him. He was Lucifer—Satan, the Devil incarnate.

Realizing I wasn't getting anywhere with him, I tried a different approach. "If you won't let me talk to him, how do I know you're telling me the truth? How do I know he isn't already *dead*?" I asked and nearly choked on the word.

"You'll just have to take my word for it."

"Take the Devil's word for it?" I made a face and waited for the punchline.

He smiled again. "I'm not all bad, you know. If you'd give me a chance, I could show you why they once called me the Light Bringer."

I was shaking my head before he even finished the proposition. The only thing I wanted him to show me was how to get his twisted ass out of Trace's body.

"After all, it is I who gave your realm knowledge—gave them *free will*." His eyes were trained on me like an unsuspecting target. "And I could give you so much more than that, Daughter. If you let me."

"That's never going to happen," I said, panic-stricken. "You're...you're crazy. You're completely crazy and out of your mind!" And apparently, *I* was uber-eloquent.

He narrowed his eyes with curiosity. "You really have no idea, do you?"

I felt my throat tighten at his ominous words. "No idea about what?"

"About how much bigger your world could be. How much better your life could be."

"My life is just fine," I lied. My life was a freakin' disaster, but I wasn't about to tell him that. "At least, it was until you showed up."

"You cannot deceive a deceiver, princess. You weren't meant for this world. You were meant for something much more than all this. And with my blood in your veins, you could have it. You can take your rightful place in the kingdom and rule as you were intended to."

"Rule? Rule what?" I had no idea what the hell he was talking about, and the rising bile at the back of my throat was telling me I really didn't want to know.

"The Underworld, of course."

My mouth dropped open as a new surge of panic rose to the top. This was not the conversation I intended to have with him. Not that I had ever planned on having any conversations with the devil, but this? This was insanity.

"I'm not...I don't...NO!" Just no. My feet were moving by their own accord, backing me up towards the door.

"I've frightened you," he said as though I hadn't been one cough away from peeing myself since the moment he ported us here. "You don't need to be afraid. Not of me. Not of the darkness. It's innate in you, Daughter, as it is in me," he said and spread his arms wide. "All you have to do is accept it. Let it in…"

At his words, I could feel a dark energy reaching out to me, slithering over my skin as it searched for a way inside. It was him, I realized. He was doing it. I wasn't sure how I knew it, but I did. He was beckoning me, calling to something inside of me that knew who he was and wanted to respond.

I slapped my skin as though I could smack the energy away. "Stop it! Stop whatever you're doing! Get it off me," I cried hysterically as I continued to scrub the invisible dark energy from my skin.

He dropped his arms, and the feeling immediately retracted as though he had called it back. I'd seen more than enough. I kicked off the ground and made a run for the door, but he was already in front of it by the time I got there.

"Where are you going?" he asked calmly as I jumped back, startled. "Back to the *Revenant*?" There was an audible hint of disgust as he said the word. "It displeases me to see my kin consorting with a lesser demon."

I honestly didn't give a flying *frock* what displeased him, but with him standing this close to me and blocking the only exit I had access to, I wasn't about to tell him that. That was the kind of thing that got people's tongues clipped.

"It displeases *him* too," he continued as an evil glint flickered through Trace's pristine blue eyes. "In fact, it daggers his heart to see you two together."

Guilt immediately sank my heart. "That's not what I'm doing. He's my friend. Trace knows that."

"Does he?" He tilted his head to the side again and gazed into the distance as though sifting through a memory bank he had no right to invade. Trace's memory bank. "That's not what he believes in his heart. In fact, just the sight of you two together sickens him to no ends."

"You don't know what you're talking about! You don't

speak for him!" I shouted, anger taking the wheel again.

"Oh, but I do. I'm the voice that speaks his truth now." His features dimmed as he craned his head towards me. "Even the truths he was too much of a coward to utter."

My throat filled with grief at the notion that Trace was keeping his true feelings hidden from me.

"What do you think it did to him to watch his *soulmate* bond herself in blood to another man—to a Revenant?" he asked, his words cutting through me like a blade. "He *hated* you for it."

The blade twisted deeper inside of me, slashing away at the protective walls I'd built around myself to keep me safe from exactly these words. My legs wanted to give out, to bring me to my knees and beg for his forgiveness.

"I never meant to hurt him," I said as tears trickled down my face.

I felt the dark energy return, licking over my skin as it swallowed up my agony like nourishment. And this time, I let it, my defenses temporarily weakened by my own grief.

"And yet you did hurt him. Over and over again." His hand came up and cupped my cheek, and I nuzzled against it, desperate for atonement. "Why do you think that is?" he asked softly as he closed his eyes. He was reading my thoughts then. Reading my entire life story, all with the touch of his hand.

With Trace's hand.

Because I'm a horrible person, I thought to myself.

"If only it were so simple," he said as he continued pushing through the layers of secrets I kept hidden inside of me. "There are boundless facets to each of us, Daughter. Every sinner was born of innocence, were they not?"

I sunk deeper into his probing darkness, unable to speak.

"Show me your truth, Daughter."

More tears fell from my eyes as he dug deeper through the

layers of my life. And I let him, too caught up in my own guilt to pull away. Seconds turned to minutes, and the minutes felt like an eternity before he spoke again.

"Well, well, well," he whispered, his breath close to my neck. "What do we have here?"

Startled, my eyes popped open.

His own eyes were still sealed shut. Still probing and reading me. "A secret cove hidden in plain sight."

"A secret cove?" I wasn't sure what he referring to, but he appeared to be deep in the trenches of it. "What secret cove? What are you talking about?" I asked, half-afraid he'd just found a tumor in my head, because well, that's the way my life usually went.

He opened his eyes tentatively and met my terrified gaze. "It seems you have a bank of memories that even *I* can't access," he added, as though that cleared up anything.

I pushed his hand away from my face. "What does that mean? Speak English."

"It means you have an infiltrator of the mind, my princess."

"An infiltrator?" With my body and mind in full panic mode, I couldn't make sense of what he was saying to save my life. Then again, maybe there was no sense to be made of it. Maybe he was just trying to confuse me, to play with my mind again and twist me into a ring of confusion.

Shit!

Terror overtook me as I realized I'd let the devil get too close to me. I let him bring down my defenses and warp my mind with his crazy-talk. This was wrong on so many levels.

"Just…just stay the hell away from me!" I warned, fear and anger melding together inside of me. I could feel it charging me from the inside out as it searched for an outlet, for a way out.

The lights flickered around us violently, and I jumped again.

"Stop doing that! Stop everything!"

He laughed heartily. "I'm not doing anything." He lifted his hand and pointed to the light show. "That is all you, Daughter."

Daughter.

Daughter of Hades.

Princess of Darkness.

"Beautiful, isn't it?" His eyes circled the room in awe. "I could show you how to harness your power. I could teach you how to use it in the most spectacular of ways. All you have to do is say the word," he said, dropping his chin.

A new level of panic slammed against me, and suddenly, I couldn't seem to catch my breath. There wasn't enough air in the room anymore. There wasn't enough air in the entire world now that the devil was walking it.

The lights continued to flicker even faster now, and my breathing shallowed until I wasn't even sure I was still breathing.

Was I dying?

Was *he* doing this to me? His darkness…

Unable to stand another second of it, I reached around him and grabbed the door knob. Yanking it open, I hurled myself past him and rushed towards the open air.

And surprisingly, he let me go.

"I'll be seeing you again very soon, Daughter. You can run from what you are, but you can never hide from me," I heard him call over my shoulder as his laughter cut into the night, echoing all around me as I ran like an angel out of Hell.

7. RUNNING SCARED

My feet pounded against the earth as I ran through the forest, each step taking me farther and farther away from the devil that had invaded my entire world. The woods were dark and foreign, but somehow, with fear and guilt pummeling me forward, I found my way through the shadows to a main road. It was only when I was absolutely certain that I wasn't being followed that I allowed myself to slow down and catch my breath.

Miles away from Hollow Hills, I pulled out my cell phone and checked to see if I had any service. I let out a lungful of relief as one lone service bar appeared at the corner of my screen.

Opening my contacts, I immediately pulled up Dominic's number, but something stopped me from calling it. Lucifer's words were replaying in my head, despite every effort to block him out.

It daggers his heart to see you two together.

I hit the back button and pulled up Taylor's number instead. Thirty minutes later, Taylor's white Beetle pulled onto the shoulder of the barren road I'd given her the coordinates to, with her music on full blast. After making sure she wasn't followed, I pushed through the brushwood I was hiding behind and ran up to the car.

"I seriously owe you for this," I said as reached over and trapped her in a hug. "Now please get me the hell out of here!"

She put her foot on the pedal and floored it. "What are best friends for if not for picking up the other one on random roads in the middle of nowhere?" she said with a playful wink. I could always count on her to be there for me without question. One of the many reasons why I loved the girl.

I glanced over my shoulder again to make sure no one was following us. After a few minutes of shallow breathing and compulsive rearview mirror checking, I finally relaxed in my seat.

"Sooo...are you going to tell me what's going on, or should I just keep gunning it Thelma and Louise style?"

"I don't even know where to start." I shook my head as though that might shake the right words loose from my mouth. This wasn't the kind of thing you just spit out. This was...insanity. It was the kind of thing they locked people up for.

"Alright then," she said with nod. "Thelma and Louise, it is."

"I'm serious, Tay. Everything's a mess. He's gone or trapped or...I don't even know. And it's all my fault."

"Okay, you're officially wigging me out." She looked over at me, inspecting me as she raced down the winding road.

"I'm wigging myself out."

"Namaste, babe." She picked up my hand and squeezed it. "Take a deep breath and start talking."

Digging deep for any semblance of clarity or composure, I went on to tell her about everything that happened from Angel's Peak right up until my stint with Lucifer at Trace's cabin. And surprisingly, she didn't completely lose her shit. I'd hoped that the more I talked, the better I would feel, but unfortunately, it had the opposite effect. Saying it all out loud just made me feel emptier and more alone, because I knew this was all my fault, and worse, I had no idea how to fix it.

I shook my head and glanced out the window at the blurring mess of trees. "I should have listened to Nikki and stayed the hell away from him."

"No one should ever listen to Nikki. Are you even listening to yourself?"

"Well, she was right, wasn't she? All I did was hurt him and now look where he is. Look at what I did to him. It's no wonder he hates me." Recalling Lucifer's gutting words put the blade right back in my stomach.

"That isn't your fault, babe, and I'm sure Trace knows that," she said as she reached over and took my hand. "You didn't do this to him. Those three bitches did! And he doesn't hate you," she continued, squeezing my hand again. "He could never hate you. He loves you, and you know that."

My eyes were welling up faster than I could blink the tears away. "All I've ever done is hurt him."

"That's not true," she said, but the truth was, she didn't know what she was talking about. She was just being a good friend and trying to say the right things to me. But I knew what I was, and I knew where I was going because of it: straight to hell with the devil.

And apparently, it was exactly where I belonged.

"Come on, Tay. I'm bonded to Dominic—to a vampire! Even Lucifer was disgusted with me. God knows what he saw— what he showed Trace when he was riffling through my brain." I dropped my face into my hands as I tried to wipe the images clean from my brain.

"I don't know, babe. If it was me, I'd be more concerned with what he *didn't* see," she said cautiously as though wary of adding any more weight to my already full load.

I lifted my head and looked at her. "Meaning?"

"You know...what he said to you about memories being hidden..." She trailed off like she was too nervous to finish the sentence. "Aren't you worried that Dominic's messing with your mind?" she finally said. "I mean, it's not like he hasn't taken memories away before," she said and dramatically pointed to herself as evidence.

"He wouldn't do that to me." Wait. What the hell was I talking about? This was Dominic. He totally would, and the worst part is he wouldn't even be remotely sorry for it. "Oh, my God. Oh, my God."

"Exactly."

The world felt as though it were crashing down on me again.

"I'm going to kill him. I'm going to end his freakin' existence!"

A breath of silence passed between us as we both sat with the weight of everything and let the implications sink in.

"This is so messed up," she said, her face ashen as she shook her head, causing her long blond locks to gently bounce back and forth.

"Welcome to my life," I said bitterly as I pulled out my cell and dialed Tessa's number again. "It's like one big shit-bomb after another." And I had no idea what to do about any of it, and now, I wasn't even sure I had a place to stay. If Dominic was somehow messing with my mind, I couldn't trust myself to be near him. Even if he was one of the only people I had left right now. "I think I need to get out of town. At least until I figure out what's going on and who to trust."

Voicemail.

Again.

"Goddamn her! Why does she even bother having a cell phone?!" I tried not to break out in sobs, but I could feel the

55

pressure building at the back of my throat again.

"Come on, babe, don't do that," said Taylor, wiping a straggling tear from my cheek. "It's going to be all right."

I gave her a have-you-not-been-listening-to-a-word-of-this look, and she promptly shrank in her seat.

"Okay, so it's pretty bad," she said, deciding to just come out with it. "But you still have me, and I'm not going anywhere. I'm your sidekick, remember? You don't have to go through this alone."

"Yes, I do." More tears fell as I looked up at her and caught the sincerity in her eyes. "I'm not putting you in any more danger, Tay. Not after what happened—"

Taylor slammed on the breaks as a sleek black car cut in front of us, forcing us to come to a dead stop behind it.

"Who the hell stops in the middle of the road like that?" she said and then started pounding her hand against the car horn. "Nice driving skills! Get out of the way, asshole!"

The driver's side door popped open and I watched in a stupor as Dominic stepped out of the car and strode over to us, his black trench coat catching air at the ends as he moved.

My heart hopped up into my throat and pretty much stayed there.

"Shit! What do I do? What do I do?" cried Taylor, realizing it was him and not some random inept driver.

I lowered my head, defeated. There was nothing to do at this point. I couldn't very well have her take us on a high-speed car chase and risk something bad happening to her. I knew Dominic, and he would not give up that easily. He'd chase me to the ends of the earth if he had to, and worse, he'd enjoy every minute of the hunt.

He walked over to the passenger side and yanked open the door, narrowing his eyes on me. "Kindly remove yourself from the vehicle. *Now*," he said in that godforsaken will-stealing voice.

I swung my legs out and then stepped out of the car. "Son of a—"

"Don't make me cut out your tongue, angel. I'm rather fond of it," he said, inspecting my face. It looked like he was searching for signs of injury, but I couldn't really be sure.

"Did you just hypnotize her again? You sick freak! I'm calling the cops," cried Taylor as she pulled out her phone.

Dominic leaned in the car and yanked the phone from her hands. "You were never here. None of this happened. You drove around for a short time and now you're going home. Goodbye." He tossed the phone into her cupholder and slammed the door shut.

And just like that, Taylor put the car in drive and took off into the night…without me or her memories.

Well, there goes my ride out of town.

My stomach dropped as I realized I was alone with the man who may very well have been lying to me this entire time. I had no idea if he was stealing my memories or even conjuring up entire new realities for me. My whole time with him could have been a farce—some demented joke Dominic came up with in his twisted little mind. It's not like he wasn't capable of it. He just put the whammy on Taylor right in front of me.

"Get in the car, angel. Don't make me tell you twice." His usual babyface features were all shadows and edges now.

"Fine. Relax. Don't have a cow." I took a few steps towards the car and then spun on my heel to make a run for it. Before I could even taste freedom, he snatched my elbow and pulled me backwards.

My back slammed hard into his chest.

"Running from me, angel? Really?" he asked close to my ear as he secured his arms around my torso. "You know you can't outrun a Revenant."

"Probably not, but I could kick the shit out of one." Ramming my elbow into his stomach, I broke out of his grip and spun before clocking him in the nose with the palm of my hand.

The sound of crunching bone was a strange kind of music to my ears.

He wiped his nose with the sleeve of his jacket and then smiled at me. "I let you have that one."

"How nice of you," I said as I threw another fist at his face.

This time, he caught my hand and used it to pull me into him. "The first one was free. You're going to have to work harder than this for the next one."

"Not a problem," I said and then rammed my knee all the way up into his crown jewels.

He dropped to his knees with a savage growl. I stood there for a moment, basking in the sight of my handy work. My enjoyment was quickly squashed by the sound of his fangs clicking out.

Shit.

He was pissed.

Time to run.

My feet slapped against the concrete road as I barreled for the woods. It was useless, really, I knew I couldn't outrun him, but I gave it my all anyway. I barely made it to the brushwood along the side of the road before I felt his body slam into mine from the back. I faceplanted into the grass as the air swooshed out of my lungs.

"Get off me!" I yelled as he turned me over, my body still trapped beneath him.

"I think you've had enough fun for one evening," he said, his face so close to mine that I could almost feel his lips on me when he spoke. "Now get in the car," he repeated, this time without giving me the option.

Damn it.

I had no choice but to obey his command, but I didn't have to be happy about it.

Glaring at him, I pushed him off me and then wrangled myself back to my feet. He was right there behind me as I walked myself back to his car and climbed into his black Audi—against my will. He slammed the door shut and walked around the car to the driver's seat.

My hands were still tremoring from the adrenaline rush as I yanked at the seatbelt and ran through all the different ways this thing could go bad. If he wiped Taylor's memory and sent her away, obviously he had nefarious intentions. Then again, this was Dominic Huntington. His intentions were always nefarious.

"How did you know where I was?"

"I have a tracker on your phone," he announced without shame.

"A tracker? Seriously? You know that's illegal, right? I'm not your kid, asshole!"

Dominic didn't pay me any attention as he pulled out his cell phone and made a call. "It's me. I have her." Tossing the phone onto the dashboard, he put the car in drive and fishtailed onto the moonlit road.

"Who was that? And where the hell are you taking me?" I asked as I rolled down the window and chucked my phone onto the side of the road.

That'll teach him to put a tracker on my phone.

"That was Gabriel, and I'm taking you back to the manor. Where else would I be taking you?" He looked over and inspected me. "I knew you were susceptible to mind games, angel, but this is just embarrassing."

I glowered at him. "Bite me, Dominic."

"I'd love to, angel." A smirk curled the corner of his lips. "Just tell me where and when, and how hard."

Was he seriously making lewd remarks right now? Obviously, his debauchery knew no bounds.

His eyes lingered on me for another moment. "Please tell me you didn't believe that nonsense back at All Saints?"

I refused to confirm or deny the fact that he had me going for a good minute.

"He was lying, angel. Every word of it."

"I know." I didn't meet his eyes when I said, "I realized it about two seconds *after* it was too late."

"Then why are you—?" He looked at me again, carefully appraising my features. "Did he hurt you?" he asked, his jaw muscle feathered with obvious tension.

"No." Well, not in the physical sense, anyway.

I couldn't help but notice his expression eased with something that looked a lot like relief.

"Then would you mind telling me what's going on?" he asked, clearly irritated. "What exactly did he say to you?"

"He said a lot of things, Dominic. Most of which only confirmed what I already knew about myself, like what a shitty person I am and how much Trace is disgusted with me because of our..." I couldn't finish the sentence, but Dominic already knew that I was talking about our bloodbond.

"I see." A weighty breath of silence passed between us before he finally spoke. "And seeing that you called Blondie instead of me, obviously you ate up every word of it."

"Well, it's not exactly farfetched."

"He's trying to break you down."

"And you know this because...?"

"Believe me, angel. I know a snake when I see one," he said, and I couldn't help but detect a hint of pride in his tone. "For some reason or another, he wants you weak and alone, and you're playing right into his hand."

I opened my mouth to deny it, but I couldn't seem to find

the words. If he was trying to get me to do something, say, take my place beside him in the Underworld, then isolating me from my friends would be a good way to start.

"What else did he say?" he pushed, somehow knowing there was more.

I wanted to tell him all about the horror story he told me, starring me as the Princess of Hell, but I still couldn't shake what Lucifer said about my memories, or Taylor's theory about what had happened to them. Unfortunately, the seed of doubt had been planted, and it was impossible to ignore it now.

"He said that someone's been messing with my mind." I shot him an accusatory look. "With my memories."

I waited for him to deny it, but all I got in return was earsplitting silence.

8. WHAT LIES BENEATH

Dark silhouettes of trees blurred past us as Dominic barreled down the long stretch of road. I stared at him for what felt like an eternity, and though it was probably only a few passing seconds, it was more than enough time to clear all moisture from my mouth.

"Why aren't you saying anything?" I asked him, though, deep down in that place I rarely ventured, I already knew the answer to that.

"I'm waiting for you to ask me a question." His gaze landed heavy on me. "That is what you're leading up to, isn't it?"

"Yes."

"Then ask me."

God, I was trying to, but I could barely get my tongue off the roof of my mouth. Reining in my nerves, I forced myself to meet his eyes. "Did you do something to my mind?"

"I've compelled you before. You know that."

"That's not what I mean."

"Then you're going to have to be more specific, angel."

My eyes narrowed as I took him in, watching for any signs of unease or deception. "Have you ever compelled me...to forget something?"

More radio silence.

"Dominic!"

He didn't look at me when he answered. "Yes."

Was he responding to my prompt, or was he answering the question? "Yes *what?*"

His eyes bore into me when he finally faced me. "Yes, I've compelled you to forget."

My stomach bottomed out as terror and panic seeped into my pores, into my bloodstream, shaking me to my core.

There it was.

The truth in his own words.

He'd compelled me to forget. To forget *what?* *When?* And how often? A million different possibilities pummeled through my brain, each one dragging in a worse scenario than the last one.

I had no idea what or when he did this, and as afraid as I was of learning the truth, that fear was nothing compared to the unbridled anger that bubbled up on the tail end of it.

"How could you do that to me? I trusted you!" My head was spinning so violently it was making me feel sick.

"It isn't what you think," he said calmly, his hand relaxed around the steering wheel.

"You don't know what I'm thinking." Oh, God, the things I was thinking. Too many thoughts. Too much motion. "You need to stop the car. Right now!"

Knowing how easily I tossed my cookies, he veered onto the shoulder and quickly killed the engine. Without looking back at him, I swung the door open and jumped out of the car. I needed air, and I needed space…and I needed to *not* throw up again. I'd done enough of that for one day.

Squatting down, I sucked in as much air as my lungs could take and tried to clear the hazy panic from my mind. From the corner of my eye, I saw Dominic walking around the car as he casually moved to where I was hunched over, but he knew better than to get too close to me.

He opened his mouth to say something, but I quickly shut him down.

"Do *not* say a goddamn word to me right now," I warned.

He promptly pressed his lips together, but his expression remained unchanged. Cold. Uncaring.

Ignoring him and his stupid careless faces, I went to war with my body's natural reflex as I tried to will myself not to throw up again. A few minutes later, I managed to get my stomach in check and felt strong enough to face him again. As horrifying as it was, as angry as I was, I wasn't going to run away from this.

Not this time. This time, I was going to hear the truth.

I pushed my back against the car and met his eyes in the dark. "How many times?"

"Once."

I swallowed noisily. "Did you...*do* something to me?"

He knew exactly what I meant. "I may be a monster, angel, but I'm not that kind of monster."

The pressure in my chest eased a little. "Then what is it? What was so bad that you had to erase it from my memory?"

"I wish you would leave this alone."

"Are you kidding me?! I'm not leaving here until you tell me what it is, Dominic."

"Angel—"

"Just tell me what you did!" I demanded, my voice echoing eerily into the forest around us.

"I didn't *do* anything." His stare was heavy with regret. "It was something I said to you."

"Something you *said*?" I balked, certain I'd heard that wrong. "You compelled me to forget something you said?" I repeated it for a second time, still unable to hide the doubt from my words.

That made a grand total of zero sense.

"I told you it wasn't what you thought."

"Alright. Fine." I decided to go with it for argument's sake. "So, what did you say to me?"

"It doesn't matter." His eyes hardened into impenetrable marble. "It was a mistake, which is why I erased the memory. Now, will you please get back in the car?"

"Um, that's going to be a big fat hell no." I pushed off the car and ambled towards him. "I want to know what you said to me. Right here and right now," I demanded and then thought of something even better. "Actually, I want my memories back." At this point, I really didn't trust him to give me the truth. I was going to need to see it for myself.

"I beg your pardon?"

"You heard me." I took another brazen step forward. "Whatever you erased from my mind, undo it."

"That isn't the way it works."

"Taylor remembered everything you compelled her to forget," I pointed out, unwilling to back down from this.

"Taylor's heart stopped. Are you saying you want me to stop you heart?" He looked at me as though I'd lost my mind.

Who knows? Maybe I had.

"No." I swallowed the knot in my throat. "Of course not. But, whatever you erased, it's still there, locked away in some secret part of my mind. Lucifer could see it. He just couldn't get to it."

He slid his hand through his hair as he stared out at the road.

"But you can." I closed the last vestiges of distance between us and forced myself into his personal space. I could smell the liquor on his breath, almost taste the chocolate in his cologne.

My heart speed up as he looked down at me.

"Compel me to remember."

Chaos stirred in the depths of his dark eyes. "You don't know what you're asking of me."

"Yes, I do." Okay, so I didn't, but that wasn't going to stop me from pushing for this with everything I had. "Please, Dominic. You have to do this for me—you owe it to me," I said, my voice straining. "I have to remember."

"Why does it matter to you what I said?"

"It's not *what* you said that matters." And that was the truth. Whatever it was he said, whatever vile name he called me, it didn't matter to me one bit. "It's the fact that there's a piece of my memory that's missing, and I don't know what it is." It didn't feel right inside—it made me feel incomplete, as though a part of me was missing.

And I didn't like it one bit.

He looked away again, considering it. The moonlight seemed to dance in the black velvet of his eyes, and suddenly, I wanted to be closer to him. My hand came up, curious to see if his skin was as soft as it looked, but he quickly caught my wrist before I could make contact. Brief as the contact was, it was enough to incite the bond.

"There are some things that are better left unsaid," he whispered, his eyes skirting over my features.

"Maybe, but I still think I should be the one who gets to decide."

Headlights drenched us in light as a lone car zipped by us.

"If there's any part of you that cares about me—that wants me to trust you again, you'll do this," I pleaded. Using his hold on me against him, I tugged him towards me so that he could see, *really* see that I meant business.

There was no way around this. I needed to have those pieces back.

And I needed to know I could still trust him.

His eyes slid down to my mouth, and my breathing quickened. I wasn't sure what was going on in that head of his, but he was at war with himself, and I could tell the exact moment he conceded.

"Alright," he finally agreed, though it was obvious he wasn't happy about it. He looked down at me and sighed. "But we're going to the Manor first. I'm going to need a drink to do this."

Well, then.

That made two of us.

9. TRUTH BE DAMNED

The grounds were crawling with fog when we pulled into the Huntington Manor a short time later. Gabriel's SUV was still missing from the driveway, which meant he'd either stepped out again or hadn't yet come home from searching for me. A small voice inside me was telling me to wait for Gabriel to come home—that it was safer to do this with a third party in the room, but damn it if I wanted the truth more than I feared the consequences.

My heart lurched in my chest as we entered the den. I tried not to think of anything too much as I waited by the fireplace, warming my hands above the licking flames as I watched Dominic fix himself a drink. Every second that his back was turned to me felt like sixty.

"Would you like something to drink?" he asked me without turning around.

Alcohol was probably the last thing that needed to be thrown into this mix, but it certainly never stopped me before.

"I'll have whatever you're having." My hands were already trembling with apprehension, and I desperately needed something to take the edge off.

After a few more grueling moments of waiting, he finally strolled over to me carrying a drink in each hand. I couldn't help but notice that my nerves immediately simmered down as soon as he closed the distance between us. Unfortunately, it didn't matter how angry he made me or even how afraid I was in any given moment. The bloodbond only wanted to give in to itself, and it overshadowed everything else.

Taking my drink from him, I knocked it back like a seasoned pro and then set the empty glass on the mantel. Liquid fire burned all the way down to my stomach, but it felt good.

His lips curved up at the corners. Apparently, it pleased him to see how far I'd come with my underage drinking. "Would you like another one?" he asked, a smug grin on his face.

"Nope. But I'll take my memories back, thanks."

His gaze never left mine as he took a long sip of his drink. "You do realize you won't be able to unring this bell once it's done. Are you absolutely certain this is what you want?"

He could utter every ominous warning under the sun. Knowing was still better than not knowing.

"I'm sure," I said pointedly.

His eyes searched mine for a moment, gauging them. "Alright. As you wish, angel. But don't say I didn't warn you," he added, his voice a low and menacing whisper.

I swallowed the lump that had wedged itself at the back of my throat as Dominic set his glass down beside mine and then cupped the sides of my face, forcing me to look him in the eyes.

I held his gaze as though it were the last ray of sunlight on earth.

"Think about the night you found out your mother was a Revenant," he ordered, and I did, remembering how devasting the news had been to me. How angry I was that Dominic, Gabriel and Trace had known and never told me.

A flash of something passed through his eyes as he opened the connection and felt my emotions. And then,

"*Remember.*" His voice crawled through my mind as fragments of forgotten memories pieced themselves together. It was so fast and natural, it was almost as though they'd been there all along, just waiting to be looked at. So, I did. I watched as the memory of that night settled in, vivid and earth shattering, and then my mouth fell all the way open.

"Oh. My. God."

Knowing exactly what I was remembering, he let go of my face and dropped his hands to his sides.

"You told me you're…in love with me?" I shook my head and stepped back from him. Because, no. I couldn't believe the words even as they passed from my lips.

Of all the endless possibilities that filtered through my mind from the moment I found out he had erased my memory, Dominic professing his love to me was never one of them.

Not ever.

He rolled his shoulders at my accusation, looking wholly irritated. "I knew you'd make a thing of this," he muttered.

"A thing? It is a *thing*, Dominic. It's a very big thing!"

He laughed, the sound of it condescending yet melodic. Picking up his drink again, he narrowed his eyes at me. "In case you've forgotten, angel lips, I was heavily inebriated at the time—drunk on blood and Scotch. I really wouldn't put too much weight on anything I said in that state."

I blinked at him. "So, are you saying it's not true then?"

He didn't hesitate. "That's precisely what I'm saying."

I paused to let that sink in. "Then why did you say it?" I asked, thoroughly confused. Had this just been another one of his games, and if so, what exactly was he playing for?

"You of all people should know the lengths I go to get what I want. I'm liable to say anything," he said, looking damn proud of himself.

"And what is it that you were trying to get from me that night?"

That smug look in his expression was back with a vengeance. "Your blood and servitude, of course. Though I must admit, binding your tongue from lying was one of the highlights of my week."

My face warmed as pieces of our Truth or Dare session fluttered back to me.

Oh, God. The things I said to him. The things I admitted…

He moved closer, lowering his head as his eyes roved over me, honing in on the color my cheeks had taken. "If you ever wish to be released from that cage of yours, little dove…" His finger danced across my cheek. "I am at your service."

I winced. He was *trying* to hurt me—to embarrass me—and he was doing a good job of it too.

Maybe a little too good.

Angry, I smacked his hand away. "Don't touch me."

"Why not?" He smiled coyly. "We both know you like it."

I narrowed my eyes at him, taking him in piece by piece. As confident as he stood, with his taut shoulders pulled back and that self-satisfied grin on his lips, his eyes held a spark of something very different. Something based in fear. Fear of rejection. Fear of letting someone see you as you truly are and then throwing you away because of it.

Maybe that's what he was doing. Maybe he was pushing me away because he was afraid that if he didn't do it, I would.

"I don't believe you," I said. My voice was soft, though there wasn't any hesitation in it. "You're trying to hurt me."

Irritation flickered in his eyes as he polished off the rest of his drink and walked back to the bar. "No. angel. You don't want to believe me," he said as he poured himself another drink.

"That is your *thing*, isn't it? Pushing away the truth until you can no longer see it from where you're hiding?"

Son of a—

Steeling myself, I followed him to the bar. "That *was* my thing. Past-tense. And at least I can admit it. That's more than I can say for you."

His shoulders tensed as I settled myself behind him. Something inside of me throbbed, probably the bloodbond, and suddenly, I wanted contact. I reached out and gently touched his back.

He raised his head, but he didn't turn around.

"Look at me," I demanded softly.

When he didn't, I slid my hand to his shoulder and turned him around. His arrogant smirk smacked me in the face like a no holds barred insult. It was meant to deter me, to force me to back down. But I wouldn't.

"Are you in love with me?"

His smile disappeared. "I already told you it was a mistake. I was intoxicated," he said, biting out the words.

"You're always intoxicated."

"Touché." He raised his glass to me and took a big, long sip.

"Are you in love with me?" I asked again. If it wasn't true, if it was just some drunken rambling, why did he want me to forget it? Why did he erase that entire night?

His features darkened. "I'm warning you, angel. I'm not in the mood to play tonight."

"Good, because neither am I."

His back straightened into a perfect line. "Then leave it alone and go to bed," he gritted out, his tone turning angry. "I'm not going to tell you again."

Narrowing my eyes, I shook my head at him and took another brazen step forward. "I'm not going anywhere until you answer me honestly." He could threaten and insult me all he wanted. I was going to get the truth out of him, even if I had to pester him all night for it. "Are you in love—"

He clamped a hand over my mouth and spun us around, leaning me backwards against the bar and barricaded me there with his body. "You ought to know better than to provoke me by now."

My gaze dropped to his exposed fangs, but I didn't falter. Not in the slightest. Pulling his hand away from my mouth, I said, "I'm not afraid of you."

"No?" He pushed me further down, arching my back as he curled his body over mine. "You should be."

Dangerous static charged the air between us as his eyes slid down to my neck, pausing there briefly before climbing back up to my mouth. His expression twisted as though he was at war with himself, at war with what he wanted to do more. And then he said, "Do you know how easy it would be to bleed you dry?"

This would have been a good time to run, to drop the whole thing and high-tail it out of there, but I didn't. Something inside of me held me there. It kept my fear at bay and urged me to keep trotting forward into the bleak unknown.

"Then do it," I taunted as a dark need nestled in my heart. "Bleed me dry, Dominic. Show me how much I don't matter to you." I pushed my hair away from my neck, clearing the path for him—daring him to follow through with it.

The glass he was holding in his other hand shattered as a low guttural growl escaped his throat.

He didn't make a move, though, and neither did I. We were in a standstill of epic proportions.

I licked my lips, searching for a drop of moisture in my dessert mouth. His hungry eyes immediately dropped to my mouth, though this time they lingered there.

I could see the desire in his eyes now—almost taste it on

my tongue. The wrath that had clouded his expression only a moment ago had dissipated into nothingness, replacing itself with something that was just as dangerous. He stared back at me intensely, his smoldering eyes narrowing as he studied my face. And then he pulled back from me, defeated.

"Leave it alone, angel." His voice was softer now, almost pleading.

"I can't," I said, my heart thumping hard in my chest as I righted myself. I needed to know the truth.

He looked down at his bloodied palm and shook away the tiny shards of glass that had wedged themselves into his flesh. "What would it change if I was?"

Everything inside of me clenched up. "I…I don't know."

"Then why do you want to know?"

"Because…I want to know how you feel about me." Saying the words out loud made me realize I'd been trying to figure that out since the day I met him, and possibly every day since then.

He opened his mouth to say something back, but the sound of approaching footsteps quickly cut him off. After a few beats, Gabriel appeared at the doorway wearing his black leather jacket and signature frown. His eyes shuffled between us, silently gathering intel before settling his troubled gaze on me.

"Are you okay? Is everything alright?" he asked, his tone terse as I straightened out my shirt.

"Why yes, brother. Everything is just peachy," answered Dominic, sliding his injured hand into his pocket.

I avoided making eye contact with either of them and instead picked imaginary lint off my sleeves.

"Well?" Gabriel waited, his face still jacked with unease. "Is anyone going to tell me what happened?"

"Nothing happened," I quickly defended, my cheeks warming with embarrassment. "We were just talking."

His eyes shifted between me and Dominic, and I swore I

could see a flicker of judgment brewing. "At All Saints," he clarified, his tone letting me know he had already passed said judgment.

"Right. All Saints." *Damn it*. If he wasn't suspicious before, he certainly was now.

"Dominic said Lucifer was there," he added, waiting for me to fill in the blanks.

"Yeah, he was there alright...impersonating Trace." My mood quickly nosedived as the awful memories came crashing back in. "He did a really good job of it too. Acted as if he had no idea what I was talking about when I called him out."

"He pretended to be Trace?"

I nodded. "He tried to convince me that Dominic compelled me to imagine the whole thing."

Gabriel crossed his arms. "And you believed him?"

It wasn't my shiniest moment, but what the heck else was I supposed to think? "Peter Macarthur backed him up. He said he was at work all week. How was I supposed to know he was lying?"

Gabriel looked at Dominic for clarification.

"He's been compromised," said Dominic as he sat back on the sofa, resting his ankle on his thigh.

Gabriel's eyes slammed shut, because he knew what that meant: a demon was now inhabiting the body of Peter Macarthur, with or without his permission. "Dammit." He had a hard time meeting my eyes just then, as though he'd lost all confidence in my judgment.

"They caught me off guard," I said, still defending myself. I hadn't exactly been ready to see Lucifer masquerading in my boyfriend's body at that exact moment, and I certainly didn't expect for him to pretend none of it ever happened. There was no training for that kind of thing. "It's not going to happen again."

Gabriel nodded, but the doomed look never left his face.

"Thanks for the vote of confidence," I muttered, taking the look personal.

"It's not that. I'm trying to understand his methods here." His eyes were distant, as though trying to put the pieces together in his mind. "Why bother with something so trivial?"

"What do you mean?"

"Impersonating Trace, turning Peter, holing up at All Saints. None of this makes sense."

"Isn't it obvious?" answered Dominic, nursing his drink from the sofa. "He wanted to get her alone, and in order to do that, he needed to get close enough to *touch* her."

Gabriel's eyebrows furrowed with unease. "Then he has control over Trace's abilities?"

I nodded that he did. "He ported us out of there as soon as he had a chance."

"Where did he take you?"

"Trace's family cabin up north."

"Which means he also has access to Trace's memories." Gabriel's expression pinched as he thought about the repercussions of that. "Everything he knew about the Order—hierarchy, weapons, techniques, practices, Scripture—Lucifer now knows."

"Well, this just got interesting," said Dominic as he swiveled the dark liquid around in his glass and then polished it off.

"Interesting is not the word I would use." Gabriel turned his weighty eyes to me. "And now he's set his sights on you, and he has the perfect weapon to disarm you."

"What do you mean?" I asked, my head already spinning faster than a tornado.

"Your feelings for Romeo," answered Dominic, his tone flat.

My knees weakened as the gravity of it all settled in. The floor felt as though it were shifting below me, conspiring to knock me on my ass again. I quickly shuffled over to the sofa and slid down into the spot beside Dominic. I needed him to quell my rising anxiety. Frankly, I didn't have the energy to try to fight it off on my own.

"You cannot trust anything he says to you," warned Gabriel, as though it were that simple. As though that weren't going to be a huge problem for me. "He'll find a way to use it against you."

"He told me Trace was still alive...that he was still in there with him."

"He's lying, Jemma." There was no hesitation in his voice, no pause for thought.

"You don't know that!"

"And so it begins," muttered Dominic as Gabriel ran a hand down the length of his face.

"Look, I don't care what either of you say. I believe him."

"No, angel, you *want* to believe him," corrected Dominic, and I quickly shot him a vengeful look.

"Jemma, he knows you won't go after him if you think Trace is still alive," added Gabriel, obviously agreeing with his brother. "I hate to say this, but you're walking right into his trap."

"And what exactly is the alternative, Gabriel?" As far as I was concerned, there were no alternatives. I needed to believe him, because if I didn't, that meant that Trace was gone, and I couldn't even stomach that thought.

"Why are you so sure Lucifer's worried about me coming after him anyway?" I continued, deciding I didn't want to have the other conversation anymore. "I'm not exactly his biggest threat. I mean, if I were him, I'd be more worried about the Order, or even Tessa for that matter." No doubt she'd slice first and ask questions later.

Dominic unfurled his arm along the back of the sofa and picked up a strand of my hair. "Unless he knows something we don't know," he said, twisting my hair around his finger as he looked at it, completely intrigued.

"Well, that's not hard being that we don't know anything about anything," I griped and sank in closer to him without even meaning to. In my defense, it was hardly my fault. His closeness felt like the sun to my frozen bones, and it was damn near impossible to stay away from something so soothing when everything inside of me ached with pain.

"You can say that again," said a familiar male voice from the entrance.

My eyes darted up to meet the intruder behind the voice and all the blood drained from my face.

Double shit on a stick.

We had company, and it was the worst kind.

10. THREE'S COMPANY

My chest swelled with a sharp intake of air as I took in the cold, unforgiving features of my uncle Karl. He was standing in a formal line along with William Thompson, the senior Magister, and another suit I didn't recognize, watching us with weighty disapproval in their eyes. I hadn't heard them walk in, and being that I was in a house with two Revenants who also didn't hear a thing, either they were spelled, or they'd ported themselves here.

Neither option made me comfortable.

"I wish I could say I'm surprised to find you here, fraternizing with the enemy," said my uncle, his voice clipped and riddled with accusations. "But of course, I'm not."

"That's pretty funny coming from you," I shot back humorlessly. My unease over what they may have overheard was quickly overthrown by my hatred of him for lying to me about who I was, about my mother, and God knows what else.

His charcoal eyes shifted from me to Gabriel, and he shook his head. "For shame, Gabriel. We've come to expect this sort of thing from your brother, but not from you."

Gabriel cast his eyes down, and suddenly, I wanted to kick him in the shin.

"By all means, barge into my home and berate me," said Dominic, his crooked smile shrouded in dark warnings. "That will surely end well for you."

My uncle was about to say something back to him when William raised his hand. Apparently, it was all that was needed to shut my uncle up. I needed to remember to try that out some time, though I doubted it would have the same effect on him if I did it.

"Gabriel. Dominic," greeted William with a curt nod. "I do apologize for the intrusion. Unfortunately, you didn't leave us with much choice in the matter," he said as he turned his full attention to me.

My body felt heavy under the weight of his stare.

"It's nice to see you again, Jemma. I do wish it were under better circumstances." A sad smile touched the corner of his lips, and despite my instinct to distrust anything associated with The Order, it seemed genuine.

My eyes veered to the other man with the shoulder-length salt-and-pepper hair and the small blue eyes. He looked like the silent-but-deadly type. The type you called when the shit really hit the fan.

William noted where my eyes had gone and quickly made an introduction. "This is Alford Benedict, Sacred Keeper of our Temple. I don't believe you two have met."

Alford nodded, but I didn't bother with any faux niceties. I crossed my arms and was about to ask them what the hell they were doing here when Dominic beat me to the punch.

"Well, now that we're all acquainted, would you mind telling me what you're doing in my house?" asked Dominic. His words were polite enough, but his tone was anything but. "Last I remember, we severed all ties."

"Indeed." William nodded his agreement. "We mean no disrespect, I assure you. We'll leave just as soon as we get what we came for."

"Dare I ask what that might be?"

William's face had the look of gloom when he answered, "We've come to bring Jemma home."

Dominic threw his head back and laughed, the sound of it hearty and insulting.

"And does *Jemma* get a say in this, or did you just decide it for me?" I balked, not believing their audacity.

"You need to be with family right now—with those who can protect you and guide you in—"

"He's not my family," I cut in through gritted teeth as I glowered at my uncle. "He's a liar and a traitor, and as far as I know, you aren't that much better. So, no. I'm not going anywhere with any one of you."

I may not have had any concrete proof to back up my claims, but I knew the Order was behind the attack on me in the woods the night of Taylor's party. The hooded assailant had come from inside the party, and since Revenants had been barred from entering, that only left them on my suspect list.

"Is that all?" I asked, pretty much shooing them away.

"Unfortunately, no." William's brows furrowed as he ran his hand down the front of his Cassock, smoothing out the invisible wrinkles. "I trust you're aware of what has come to pass, are you not?"

From the severity of his tone, I knew he was referring to the unearthing of Lucifer.

"Yes, I'm aware." I crossed my arms and glared at my uncle again. "You could have stopped this. You could have told me the truth about what I was instead of lying to me about everything. I was a bomb waiting to go off, and you just sent me out to war with blinders on. That's not what *family* does!" Because the truth was, they didn't want to warn me or prepare me. They wanted to eradicate me altogether, and that's the reason why they kept me in the dark from day one.

I knew that now.

My uncle opened his mouth to fire back at me, but William promptly raised his hand again and silenced him.

It really was a neat little trick.

"I am fully cognizant of our transgressions against you," said William, and my mouth dropped all the way open, because that was the closest thing to an admission of guilt I'd ever received from any of them.

"If we could turn back the hands of time and do things differently, we certainly would. But that is not an option here," he continued, sounding sincere enough. "If it's any consolation to you, everything we did, it was only to prevent this very event from unfolding—to defend what we have all been created to protect. Yourself included."

As much as it hurt to hear, I didn't bother arguing that back, because frankly, I could understand where he was coming from. I'd lost track of how many times my good intentions had led me straight to Hell. But still.

William took a few steps into the room, surveying the end table as he moved around it. "The only thing I can do now is to apologize on behalf of the Order and my fellow brethren, and of course, extend a helping hand to you."

"Is that right?" I couldn't hide the suspicion from my tone even if I wanted to. "And why do you suddenly want to help me? What's in it for you?" If I've learned anything during my time in Hollow Hills, it's that everyone had a motive.

"Well, for starters, we need to know who the vessel is."

"Of course, you do." My eyes narrowed as I tried to make sense of it. "And why do you need me for that? Why don't you just see who the vessel is for yourself?"

With all the powerful Descendants they had at their disposal, they could easily have a Reaper or Seer figure it out.

"Unfortunately, that particular moment on the Timeline has been *bound*, sealed with something much stronger than the magic we have at our disposal. Whoever did this made sure it could not be undone."

Hearing him admit that they didn't even have enough mojo to glimpse at the Timeline sent an icy chill down my back. The All Mighties weren't all that mighty after all.

"We mustn't be sidetracked by what cannot be done. Let us discuss what *can* be done."

"Which is what?"

"Restoring the balance on earth between good and evil. It is what we have always done."

"And how do you plan on doing that? You don't even have enough power to break the Timeline seal."

"Mind your manners, Jemma," scolded my uncle. "That isn't how you speak to a Senior Magister."

"That's quite alright, Karl. It's a valid question." He paused before continuing. "May I be frank?" he asked, grimacing.

"You can be the Pope for all I care, just as long as you tell me the truth."

The corner of his lip rose in amusement before dropping back in line. "There is another reason why we are here, and that is the most important reason of all."

Again, no surprise there. And yet, I still felt a mild anxiety attack stirring in my chest as I waited to hear it.

"Lucifer cannot be permitted to exist in this world. He must be returned to Hades at once. No matter the cost." His eyes were burning holes into my soul. "You do understand that, don't you?"

I nodded because I did. I had no desire to let Satan run rampant on earth. I just wanted to figure out a way to get him out of my boyfriend first.

His eyes smoothed out with sympathy. "And of course, you

understand that you have to be the one to do it?"

I nearly choked on my own tongue. "Why me?"

"You are the Daughter of Hades, Jemma, whether any of us like it or not. Lucifer was released by your hand, and as such, it is only your hand that can return him to where he belongs."

I knew it! I freakin' knew they would try to blame me and stick me with the task.

Well, little did they know, that wasn't happening. I'd already given up everything that mattered to me. My life, my human identity, my family and friends, and pretty much any and all chances I had of ever having a normal life. And I'd give up Trace too if that meant he would be safe. That he could have the life he deserved. But that's where I drew the line.

I wasn't killing Trace.

I shook my head decidedly. "That's not happening."

"Only you can yield the weapon—"

"NO!" I fired back as William exchanged a look with the others. "I don't give a crap about who can yield what. I'm not doing it."

My uncle quickly stepped forward, fire brimming in his eyes. "You *will* yield the weapon, Jemma," he said matter-of-factly. "There is no other option here."

I met his cold eyes and let his words sink in for a moment.

There is no other option.

My natural instinct was to distrust anything that came out of my uncle's mouth, but this time, his words were ringing true. If there was another option, another person who could take Lucifer out, they wouldn't be here right now wasting their time with me.

I really was their *only* option.

"Alright, let's say I believe you. Let's say I do this. What exactly happens to Lucifer's vessel once I yield this weapon?" I asked, deciding to play along for information's sake.

"What becomes of the vessel is neither here nor there," snapped my uncle, the irritation heavy in his tone. "That isn't a factor here."

"Well, it's a factor for *me*, and since I'm the one that has to yield the weapon, it's a factor for you too."

He pinched the bridge of his nose, as though I were giving him a migraine.

Good, I thought and crossed my arms.

"Jemma, the vessel is almost certainly already empty," answered William, reclaiming the reins. "And whatever remains of it, if anything, will be broken beyond repair."

"*Almost* certainly?" I verified, ignoring the part about being broken beyond repair. "So, basically, you're not sure."

His lack of a response was answer enough for me.

"Don't you think you should figure that out before you send me off to murder an innocent person?"

"For Pete's sake," shouted my uncle, his face turning purple from anger. "This isn't the time for your teenage rebellion! You will do as you are told!"

"Like hell I will," I seethed and lurched forward, my hands balled into fists, as though ready to sock him. "You don't get to tell me what to do anymore. You lost that right a long time ago."

William quickly stepped in front of me and tried to be the soft voice of reason. "I understand your concern, Jemma. I do. The loss of an innocent is always painful, but it will pale in comparison to the bloodshed that will come if we fail to act now. Thousands of lives are at stake here, if not millions."

His words sobered me, and suddenly, my load felt heavier. It wasn't just Trace's life that was at stake. It was all of our lives, and they were all resting on my shoulders.

"There has to be another way."

"There isn't." He picked up my arms and inspected my

Marks, his expression somber. "You've invoked."

His eyes trailed the silver runes up the length of my arms. They were nothing like any of theirs, which only served as a reminder that I wasn't like them. I was different—something darker.

Something markedly more dangerous.

"I must insist we begin training at once," continued William, mistaking my silence for acquiescence. "Now that you've invoked, you'll need to learn how to use and control your abilities, and of course, how to yield the weapon. There isn't much time," he said and nodded back to Alford, who began stalking towards me. "We must go now, or we risk losing—"

"Woah! Wait a minute!" I ripped my arms free from his hold. Sheer panic exploded in my veins, sending blood pumping into my ears as though my pulse had relocated there. "I already told you I'm not going anywhere with you, and I meant what I said!"

I was pretty sure I had made myself clear about that.

Apart from being the middle of the night, I still didn't trust any of them as far as I could throw them. And I certainly wasn't about to leave the security of the only two people I did trust to run off with my twisted uncle and company.

For all I knew, they were going to take me straight to the slaughterhouse and be done with me and my cursed blood once and for all.

Alford ignored my protest and continued stalking towards me. He had the look in his eyes that told me he wasn't above dragging me out of here kicking and screaming.

Shitballs.

"Stay the hell away from me!" I shouted, backing myself up. I could feel the pressure mounting, the kind of panic that usually set off my powers and had glass shattering all around me.

Dominic and Gabriel quickly stepped in front of me and

blocked his path.

"You heard the lady. Back up," warned Dominic.

Alford stopped abruptly and glared at him. "You do know I could banish you both with one snap of my finger."

Well, damn. He speaks.

"Then perhaps you should try using that finger on Lucifer, my good man."

"Please," pleaded William, arms outstretched. "We are all on the same side here. We all want the same thing."

Only, we didn't. I wanted to save Trace, and they...they looked at him as though he were expendable. Collateral damage. I shook my head, tears clouding my vision as the memory of his empty eyes flashed through my mind. If I didn't help him—if I didn't save him—who would?

"You don't know what you're asking me to do." A tear filed down my cheek as I blinked through the blurry haze.

He paused for a moment, studying me. His features softened as realization set in. "The vessel is very dear to you."

I refused to confirm or deny it.

"I see that now." The sympathy in his eyes vanished almost as quickly as it had appeared. "But that does not change anything, dearest Jemma. You cannot allow it to."

I shook my head because I was already passed that point. The fact that the vessel was Trace changed everything.

"I can't do what you're asking me to do. I'm sorry. There has to be another way, and I'm going to find it," I said, more to myself than anyone else. "I wouldn't be able to live with myself if I didn't try."

"And if he kills before you find a way? Could you live with the blood on your hands, knowing you could have done something to stop it?"

More tears spilled over my lashes, because I knew I couldn't live with that either.

My uncle leaned in and whispered something in his ear. William nodded and then again to Alford.

"I can see we aren't going to reach an agreement tonight," he said, his mouth puckering with pity. "Please take the night and sleep on it. When you're ready, come to Temple, where we will be waiting for you." He paused and offered a sympathetic nod. "There is no other choice, Jemma. As hard as it is, I know you will come to see that."

Perhaps he was right, I thought as my tears continued to fall. Perhaps someday I would realize there was no other way. But today wasn't that day.

He rejoined my uncle and Alford at the entrance of the den and then turned to face me one last time. "There is at least one version of this that doesn't end with the apocalypse—where good trumps evil. Of course, it won't be without great sacrifice, but it is possible. And I know you will do the right thing."

And with that, the three of them were gone, blurring out of the room like the remnants of yet another bad dream.

11. AFTERSHOCK

"Well, that was eventful," said Dominic, relaxing his stance as the three of us found ourselves alone in the den again.

Gabriel's worried eyes settled on me. "Are you alright?" he asked, noticing I was still crying.

"I'm fine." I sucked in a deep breath as I wiped away my straggling tears, doing my best to pull myself together.

"You don't look fine."

I could only imagine what I looked like: the tears, the bruises from the accident, the blood loss from the stab wound coupled with my anxiety over Trace and the gnawing bloodbond that was trying to rip a hole in my soul.

"I'm fine," I reiterated. "I don't have the luxury not to be. I have to find a way to get Lucifer out of Trace's body." And I needed to do it before they figured out a way to kill him...with or without me.

"Angel, did you not hear what they said?"

I stared at him, blank faced. "Yeah...I heard them say they weren't sure about anything."

"Here we go again," muttered Dominic as he turned for the bar.

Apparently, he had heard something else.

"Look, no one is forcing you to be a part of this," I said, talking to his back. "You can leave town like you wanted to, and I'll find someplace else to crash. I can do this on my own."

"And miss all this fun?" he said, spreading his arms wide. "That's not my style, love."

"Then stop making this harder on me and help me!" I was damn-near begging him for it.

"Alright, angel. I'll help you if that's what you want, but riddle me this," he said as he ambled back over to where I stood. "How exactly do you plan on saving him when everyone and everything is telling you it isn't possible?"

Both their gazes fell heavy on me as they waited for me to answer the million dollar question.

The sad truth was, I wasn't sure how I was going to save him. I just knew that I *had* to. It wasn't logical or practical or even something I could put into words. I had to believe there was a way to stop this—to bring him home to me safe and sound, because the alternative was that there wasn't, and he was gone, and that was too much pain for one person to bear.

Life wouldn't be this cruel. Not after everything I'd already given up.

"If Lucifer was able to find a way inside of him, then there has to be a way to get him out."

It was as simple as that.

"But you heard what William said," answered Gabriel. "He's the Senior Magister, Jemma. He knows the Scripture inside out. If there was a way, he would know it."

"Well, maybe we're reading the wrong books then," I blurted out, grasping at straws now.

"The wrong books?" Gabriel crossed his arms as he needled me with a stare. "I'm not following."

"If the Order doesn't know anything about the vessel,

maybe The Dark Legion does." The more I thought about it, the more I felt as though I were on to something. "They knew about the Ritual. They knew how to get Lucifer into Trace's body, so who says they can't—"

"Jemma, please. Do you have any idea what you're suggesting right now?" asked Gabriel, aghast. "If the Order caught wind of this, they would—"

"They would what?" I quickly cut in, not worried in the slightest. "What would they do, Gabriel? What *can* they do? They can't kill me. They can't do anything to me...and now they need me." I could feel the darkness, the desperation trilling under my skin, but I didn't care. I would let it consume me from the inside out if it meant moving me closer to bringing Trace home.

He shook his head, his jaw clenched rigidly. "I can't be a part of this. This isn't the way it's supposed to be."

"Says who?" I asked, anger broiling just below the surface. "The Order? The Magister? *God?*"

He didn't answer.

"What if it was someone *you* loved, huh? Would you give up so easily if it was your family? If it was Tessa?"

He seemed taken aback by my question—by my assumption. "I would do everything in my power."

"Then why do you expect anything less from me?"

"I'm not suggesting you give up, Jemma. But I can't support you turning to the Dark Legion for help." His forehead creased with worry. "That's a door that should never be opened."

"Right. The big, bad Dark Legion. Because the Order is so righteous and holy, right?" I said tartly, making sure he didn't miss my sarcasm. I'd seen enough from both sides to know that neither one was free of guilt.

He furrowed his brows and shook his head, apparently not

appreciating my sentiment as much as I had.

"After everything I've been through because of them…because of what they did to me, how can you still trust them?" My question wasn't harsh or judgmental. More than anything, I was curious.

"Because, Jemma. I have to." His chin rose ever so slightly, as though arming himself with his self-appointed badge of honor. "I may not always agree with their methods, but I know I'm on the right side. I'm on the side of good."

"How can you be so sure of that?"

"At the end of the day, more good than evil is done. More lives are saved than lost."

"And that's enough for you?"

His Adams apple bobbed. "Yes."

"And the evil that's done?" I asked, looking him dead in the eye. "Destroying lives and families? My family. Trace's family. Is that all just collateral damage?"

"I suppose it has to be."

I shook my head at him, disappointed. It shouldn't be that easy for him.

"You have to focus on the bigger picture, Jemma. The greater good of all."

"I wish I had your kind of blind faith," I said, saddened by the turn this conversation had taken. "But I don't see things as black and white as you do."

"Maybe not, but you will," he said with a tinge of sorrow in his words. "In time, we all do."

I wondered if that was true. If one day, I would fall in line with the Order and carry out their brand of justice without as much as a second thought to anyone around me. I hoped to God that would never be me.

"As always, duty above all else," said Dominic from over my shoulder. "Don't say I didn't warn you, angel."

That he did. He was full of warnings.

I studied Gabriel for long moment, unable to tear my eyes away from him. I could only imagine the disappointment that was smeared all over my face. "You're going to tell them about Trace, aren't you?" I realized.

He didn't answer.

"You can at least give me a heads up, Gabriel. You owe me that much."

"I've sworn allegiance to the Order," he said, working hard to keep his chin up. "I have no other choice, Jemma."

That was a copout if I ever did hear one.

I looked away, having never felt more distant from him than I did in that moment. We hadn't always agreed on everything, and that was okay, but this was the first time we've ever been on opposite sides of the line. "Then I guess we don't have anything else to say to each other."

"It doesn't have to be that way," he said, striding closer. "I can still help."

"How?" I asked, doubtful. "By reporting every step I take to the Order?"

The last thing I needed was a mole in the ranks.

"Of course not," he said, though his tone lacked conviction. "I want to save him just as much as you do. You have to know that. But I can't sacrifice all of us to do that. The Order has to be informed and prepared. We all do. Too many lives are at risk here."

I nodded, because I understood where he was coming from. I also understood that we were never going to see eye to eye on this nor was I going to change his mind. Not on matters that were black and white to him and gray to me.

"Please consider their offer," he continued, his eyes pleading with me to listen, to graze the line in the sand with the tips of my toes. "Ready yourself in the event that we don't find what you're looking for."

"I'll find it, Gabriel. I'm not letting him die."

"And what if the thing you're looking for doesn't exist?" he challenged, his dark brows pulled together. "What then?"

I let his words sink in for a moment. I knew it was coming from a good place—a place of duty and preparation and even of love—but it was hard to hear just the same. Accepting it meant I was accepting that this might not end good for me and Trace, and I wasn't able to stomach that thought. There was no other option as far as I was concerned.

"I guess I'll have to cross that bridge if I get there."

Now it was his turn to shake his head in disappointment. "I hope to God you change your mind in time," he said, his voice low and foreboding as he turned to leave the room. "For your sake, and everyone else's."

12. FIGHTING TEMPTATION

The rain tapped its fingernails endlessly against the glass windows as I watched Gabriel leave the room, leaving me and Dominic and our bloodbond to our own devices. There were still so many unanswered questions between us, so many words that had yet to be spoken, but I couldn't summon the courage to speak them now. I could barely summon the courage to look at him. It was too distracting, and I couldn't afford any distractions. Not when the clock was ticking so furiously for all of us.

"Drink with me," he said from somewhere over my shoulder.

I shook my head, still not willing to face him—to allow myself to be distracted by him. One look and I knew I'd be done for. "I think I've had enough for the night."

I started to walk away, following the same path Gabriel had taken, but he quickly snagged my hand.

"One drink."

My hand tingled from the contact. I looked down at our clasped hands and then back up at him.

"Humor me," he said, smiling coyly. While his tone was all

sweet and innocent, the look in his eyes told me another story entirely. He was hungry—for blood, for me...for God knows what else.

I noticed the awful crawling feeling on my skin had eased now that he was touching me. As much as I wanted the feeling to stay away, I wasn't willing to pay my pound of flesh for it.

"I...can't."

"Why not?" He tilted his head to the side and studied me.

"Because I have work to do." Well, research to be exact. I needed to dig up everything I could find on the Dark Legion and the Ritual they performed the night of Lucifer's unearthing, and I couldn't do that if I was busy getting high off Dominic's blood. "I have to stay focused."

"We both know you're not going to be able to focus on anything but this," he said, using our clasped hands to draw me in closer to him. To lure me in.

I hadn't even realized we were still holding hands. Horrified, I pulled my hand away, and the scratchy feeling under my skin immediately returned.

Irritation flickered in his eyes as he straightened to his full height. "How long are we going to do this?" he asked as he walked around me, frowning down at me as he circled me like his prey.

I shadowed his move and turned right along with him. "Do what?"

"Anger the bloodbond."

I didn't answer, because I knew exactly what he meant. The trembling hands, the vivid dreams, the incessant anxiety clawing just beneath my skin. It was the bloodbond calling for its offering, over and over again, and the more I tried to stay away from Dominic, the louder the calls became. My body was a mess, and my mind was in even worse shape, and even though Dominic could easily make me feel better again, I couldn't help but fear the cost of it.

"Why do you insist on making me suffer so?" he asked, his voice soft now—almost pained.

I looked up at him and saw that the edges to his eyes had been replaced with a sort of softness that made me want to move closer to him. Like a moth, I always seemed to want to get closer to that flame.

I dug my heels into the ground and forced myself to stay put.

"That's not what I'm trying to do."

"Isn't it?" he challenged, his eyes dropping briefly to my mouth.

My pulse spiked, and then I was retreating from him, using every ounce of strength I had to back away from the flame, but he was right there with me, following me until my back hit the wall.

"Then stop fighting me, angel." Wiping out the remaining space between us, he pressed his body against mine and casually tucked a loose piece of my hair behind my ear.

My skin prickled with heat as he brought his face to my cheek and took in the scent of my hair.

"Let me *have* you," he lilted, his voice a seductive whisper against my ear.

My cheek instinctively turned towards his face and nuzzled itself against the soft curve of his jaw. It wasn't what I had intended to do, but my body seemed to have a mind of its own. Pushing the rest of my hair over my shoulder, he cleared the way to my neck. His hands slid down my arms, caressing my skin as his eyes filled with enticement—with want. A shudder rippled through my body as I allowed myself to breath in his scent.

Big mistake.

I swayed towards him recklessly and without abandon, my body desperate for him to give me some way to survive the night—to survive the smothering darkness that was my life. I knew what giving into him would yield, what the bloodbond wanted, and the longer I stayed this close, the harder it was to resist it.

He lowered his face to my neck, and I whimpered as his lips grazed against my skin. My body felt as though it had caught fire from the inside out, reacting to his touch in every way possible, even despite what my heart wanted it to do. But it wasn't all pleasure. No. Guilt and self-loathing were there too, and they slashed a hole right through my fantasy.

If Trace could see me now...

I shook my head and pushed him away.

"We shouldn't be doing this," I said, my eyes flicking down to where my hands rested on his firm chest. I couldn't bring myself to pull them away. "This isn't right."

He captured my wrists and brought them down, securing them behind my back with his hand while the other hand came back up to my face, his thumb gently gliding over my lips as he said, "Then why does it feel right?"

"It doesn't. It's not," I sputtered, trying not to get lost in the dark pools of his smoldering eyes.

"You're lying, angel." His gaze locked onto mine as he sifted through my layers of truth. "I know you want this, even if you won't say it out loud. I can *feel* it." He pressed himself between my legs, and my breath caught in my throat. "I can feel your body responding to me, even when you try to push me away. Your heart races, your pulse quickens, and your skin"—he nuzzled his cheek against mine –"the heat is hotter than hell, love."

I wanted to say something back, to deny it, but all I could do was lick my lips and try to quell the thirst that was raging on the inside.

"You can refute it with that pretty mouth of yours all you

want, but your body will always give you away. It's been doing that since the day I met you."

My thighs clenched as I fought the urge to lift my legs up and trap his body between them.

Oh, my God, this was wrong. All wrong. So wrong.

His lips spread into a knowing grin, as though he could feel me battling against the pull.

"I don't want this," I said and tried to will it to be true. "I don't want you!" I pulled my hands free and shoved him back again.

His features darkened as he squared his shoulders.

"Just leave me the hell alone!" I yelled, though I wasn't sure who I was angrier with—him for doing this to me or my body for responding to it.

"Are you sure that's what you want, angel?"

"More than the air I'm breathing."

His back stiffened as he let my words sink in.

"Alright. I'll leave you alone, but hear this," he said as he picked up my hand and used it to yank me against him. Craning his head down, he whispered by my ear. "The next time you need relief—the next time your hips are writhing in pain and you can't see straight, I'm not going to lay a single finger on you. Even when you beg me to," he warned and then pressed his finger against my lips before I could protest. "And believe me, angel. You *will* beg."

"Are you threatening me, Dominic?" A slither of fear burrowed under my skin as I gazed into his menacing eyes.

"No." He angled his face to mine, his mouth so close it was almost touching my own. "Just a fair warning to be careful what you wish for," he said with a cold smile as he let go of my hand. Without glancing back, he grabbed his coat from the sofa and then walked out of the room, leaving me breathless and alone.

A few beats later, I heard the front door slam shut.

My anxiety immediately returned, and I knew he had left the house. The farther he got from me, the worse I felt, and I hated him for it. But most of all, I hated myself, because the moment he was gone, I instantly missed him.

There was something seriously wrong with me, and I wasn't sure it could ever be fixed.

13. NIGHT VISITORS

Ignoring the ever-mounting discomfort inside me, I made my way to the study as planned and was surprised to find Gabriel already there. He was sitting behind a dark oak desk with a colorful spread of books fanned out in front of him. His brows were creased with worry, and his hair was slightly disheveled from passing his hand through it one too many times.

"Doing some late-night reading?" I asked him, still hovering by the entrance with my arms folded across my chest.

"Sort of. I'm going through some of my father's journals," he said and then set the book down on the desk to give me a once-over. "What are you still doing up? You should get some rest, Jemma."

Typical Gabriel, always worrying about my well-being, even we were technically still in a fight.

"I'll rest when this is over." I tilted my head to the side and studied him. Despite the fact that he was a powerful immortal being, he looked as though he had the weight of the world on his back. Everything sagged from his shoulders to the slight downturn of his mouth.

"So, have you found any interesting family secrets?" I asked, curious about what he was trying to dig up in those books.

"No, no, nothing like that. My father was one of the High Guardians of the Order and recorded most of their happenings in these journals right here. I was hoping to find something about the Ritual."

My heart warmed upon realizing he meant what he said when he told me he wanted to find a way to save Trace.

"Any luck?" I asked, taking a small step into the room.

"Nothing yet," he said, his eyebrows still furrowed in frustration. "But there's a lot more books to cover." He tipped his chin to the mounds of books and journals piled on the floor beside the desk.

It looked like a good place to start. "Mind if I join you?"

"Of course not. Help yourself." He smiled, though barely, and then motioned to the overwhelming pile of books.

I pulled out a chair from against the wall and dragged it over to the desk. Plopping down across from him, I picked up a book from the top of the pile and cracked it open.

Flipping through the pages, I scanned the entries for any passages about the Dark Legion or their possible use of a vessel. While there were plenty of entries about demonic possession and corresponding passages outlining the various rituals of exorcism to cure them, there was nothing about Lucifer.

"Has the Order ever gone up against anything like this?" I asked, wanting to know exactly what our chances were. It was worth trying it their way, giving this a chance, though the more I heard, the more I realized I was going to need to go at this from a different angle.

"The Roderick sisters are certainly not the first to try opening the Hellgates, though they did get the furthest."

"Thanks to me," I muttered bitterly.

"This isn't your fault," he said, lowering his book again, his eyes fixed on me in a meaningful way. "You didn't know, Jemma. None of us did."

"Yeah, but it still doesn't change the fact that it was *my* blood that opened the seals."

He relaxed back in his chair and appraised me. "If you had spilled your blood with the intention of opening that Gate, we would be having a different conversation. Intention is everything, Jemma."

I nodded because I appreciated the sentiment, though I couldn't allow myself to unload my burden. It belonged on my back until I found a way to atone for my mistakes.

"How have you been holding up?" he asked gently, shifting the conversation.

I looked up and noticed he was staring at my hands. My trembling hands.

"I'm keeping it together." I shrugged, bringing them down to my lap. "More or less."

"And my brother? Is everything—?"

"Gabriel, please," I quickly cut him off, though I wasn't even sure what he was going to ask me. "Don't."

An awkward silence wedged its way between us. I couldn't bring myself to keep having these conversations with Gabriel about Dominic or the bloodbond. I wasn't sure what he thought of me, knowing that I was bonded to his brother and that I'd willingly sacrificed myself to him on more than one occasion. I imagined it wasn't anything good, and I already had enough of that as it was.

His eyes searched mine for a short moment, and then he nodded. "Understood."

I picked up the journal on my lap and resumed reading, hoping he would take that as his cue to drop this conversation.

And of course, he did. Gabriel was always good like that.

We spent the next hour combing through dozens of

journals and poorly translated Old Latin texts and found ourselves nowhere closer to the salvation I desperately sought. The more of nothing we dug up, the more my gut was telling me we were looking in the wrong place altogether. But of course, I wouldn't bring that up to Gabriel again.

I already knew where he stood on the whole let's-crack-open-the-Satanic-Bible thing.

"You should try to get some sleep, Jemma. You won't be any good to him in this state," said Gabriel, taking pity on me as I rubbed the sleep from my tired eyes.

I knew he was right, and while I certainly wasn't planning on getting a good night's rest, I was going to need at least three or four hours to keep my body functional.

I was about to call it a night when I heard two very distinct voices carrying in through the downstairs hall. One very male voice that sounded a lot like Dominic, and another high-pitched female voice that I couldn't place. Something dark and wretched coiled inside of me as realization smacked me upside the head.

Did he seriously just bring a girl home?!

My eyes snapped up to Gabriel for confirmation, but all he could do was run a hand down his face as the sound of distant giggles rebounded into the study.

My cheeks flamed as a strange, uncomfortable sensation sunk to the pit of my stomach like a piece of spoiled meat. Tossing the journal on the desk, I pushed the chair back and stood up.

"Jemma, please don't engage—"

I held a trembling hand up to silence him. *Engage my butt!*

"He's only trying to provoke a response out of you," he said, his words urging me to ignore him. To rise above it.

But of course, I wouldn't. I would sink myself all the way in it, because if a response was what he wanted, a response was what he was going to get.

14. WICKED GAMES

My feet smacked against the marble floor as I barreled down the hallway, letting the sound of their happy voices guide me to the scene of the crime. My vision blurred with rage as I turned the corner and blasted into the den to find Dominic relaxing back on the couch with a busty little blonde thing sitting on his lap. My stomach tightened as a slash of jealousy tore its way through my insides, its presence surprising and confusing me at the same time.

"Dom!" purred the woman as she smacked him in the chest and giggled like a school girl with a crush. She obviously didn't notice me standing there. But Dominic sure did.

His eyes met mine as a lazy grin pulled into his cheeks. "Good evening, angel."

Good evening? GOOD EVENING?

The guy had some nerve!

I narrowed my eyes at him and damn-near growled, "What the hell are you doing?"

The blonde spun around on his lap and gawked at me. A mixture of surprise and annoyance flashed across her pretty face as her dark green eyes took me in.

"I'm having a nightcap with my friend Sally here."

"Sandy," she corrected and then whispered to him, "I thought we were alone."

He ignored her, his eyes still fixed on mine as though he couldn't stand to look away. "What does it look like I'm doing?"

I took a step into the den, my hands balled up into tight fists at my sides. "It looks like you're trying to piss me off."

His smile widened at the corners. "Really? How so, angel?"

Ah, hell no. I wasn't about to take the bait.

"Get rid of her, Dominic. Now."

"Excuse me?" shrieked his date.

"You're excused, Sally!"

"Sandy," she corrected again.

"Does it look like anyone cares?!" I snapped. Crap. I didn't mean to. I mean, poor girl. It obviously wasn't her fault, but that didn't mean I wasn't going to take it out on her. At least a little bit.

"Now, now, angel. Is that any way to speak to my guest?" He brought his arm up from along the back of the sofa and lifted Sally—Sandy—off his lap, placing her on the sofa beside him. And judging by the toddler-sized frown on her face, she was disappointed by it.

"I know what you're trying to do, Dominic, and it's not going to work."

"And what is it that I'm trying to do?" he asked as he rose from the couch and straightened out his shirt.

"Your trying to make me jealous," I seethed.

"Is that right?" His eyes moved down the length of my body before fliting away with a chuckle.

Was he laughing at me?

I clenched my fists harder, my nails digging into the palm of my hands and drawing blood.

"And why would I do a thing like that?" he asked, walking towards me as though he were coming to talk to me, though he never bothered stopping. "You made your feelings, or lack thereof, perfectly clear to me," he said, turning his head slightly in my direction. "The only thing I'm trying to do is enjoy my friend's company."

"Bullshit."

He tsk'ed me as he sauntered to the bar and poured himself a drink. "A man has needs, angel. You may be in the business of repressing yours, but I am not."

"Oh really? And is Sandy here aware of your needs?" I asked, giving her a once-over. She still looked confused and kind of irritated, but other than that, nothing was out of sorts. "Does she know what you are?"

He turned to me with his glass in hand and leaned back against the bar. "Why don't you ask her for yourself?"

I wasn't even sure how to word that question.

Instead, I turned to the girl and decided I needed to talk some sense into her. You know, save her life and all that other birthright crap I was supposed to do.

"Listen, Sandy, you really shouldn't be here. I know you came here for a good time, and hey, good on you—who am I to judge, you know? But he isn't who you think he is," I started, but her laughter quickly halted my pep talk.

"So, then he *isn't* a vampire?" she asked, quirking her perfectly shaped brow at Dominic. "Say it isn't so."

The fact that she was in the know, and completely relaxed about the whole thing, told me all I needed to know. At least I thought it did. "You're compelling her, aren't you?!" I charged.

He clicked his tongue at me. "That hurts, angel."

"That's not an answer."

"I'm more than capable of finding myself a willing participant." His eyes ran down my body like an accusation, and my face immediately flushed with heat. "But you already know that, don't you, angel?"

"Screw you, Dominic." Frankly, the fact that I was even standing here having this conversation with him was a testament to how off the rails my life had gone.

Regardless, I wasn't about to sit here and let him feed off some innocent girl right in front of me. "You need to leave," I said as I stalked over to her, ready to physically remove her from the premises if need be.

You know, for her own safety.

"I'm not going anywhere. Dominic invited me here, and I'm not leaving until I get what I came for."

That stopped me in my holier-than-thou tracks. "And what exactly did you come here for?"

"Not that it's any of your business, but let's just say this isn't my first time." Sandy pulled her legs beside her on the couch and needled me with a glare.

"You're a blood-whore," I realized, not bothering to hide the repulsion from my tone.

She grimaced. "I prefer to call myself a happy donor."

Dominic raised his glass to her and winked.

My stomach twisted with unpleasant feelings. She could call herself a damn happy meal for all I cared. It didn't change the fact that she was indeed a blood-whore—a woman or man who sought out the company of vampires to willingly offer themselves up to them. Though, up until this very moment, I'd never actually had the displeasure of meeting one in person.

I wasn't sure what disturbed me more, the fact that she was here to give herself up to him, or the fact that I was jealous about it. The latter only confirmed that there was something severely wrong with me, though I wholly blamed the bloodbond for it.

"See, love?" said Dominic as he came to stand behind me,

his fingers grazing a trail along the top of my shoulder. "All is well here."

Only, it wasn't.

I wasn't well.

I spun around and faced him. I had every intention of telling him to enjoy his night, but that wasn't what came out of my mouth. "Make her leave, Dominic." My voice was lower now, more desperate. I honestly wasn't sure what was driving me anymore—my disdain of the entire situation or my desire to keep her away from him.

"Why? Did you want to take her place?" he asked lowly—daringly.

I resisted the urge to smack him. "No."

"Then why would I send her away?"

Because it's bothering me. Because it's making me jealous. Because I don't want you touching other women.

"Because her voice is getting on my nerves!"

Really, Jemma? Really? That's what I went with?

He laughed at my outlandish response, and I didn't blame him. The more I spoke, the more ridiculous I sounded.

He took a sip of his drink and shifted closer to me. "Try again, angel."

"Because I don't want her here."

"And why is that?" he asked, tucking my hair behind my ear and sending a parade of shivers down my arms.

"I just...don't! Okay?"

He shook his head. "Not good enough."

Damn him!

I knew what he was trying to do. He was trying to get me to admit something—to admit I had some kind of feelings for him. But that wasn't going to happen because I did NOT have feelings for Dominic Huntington.

Anything I felt for him was directly related to the

bloodbond. It had to be. So why the hell did I care what he did with his free time? Why did it bother me that he had another woman here? The answer scratched just below the surface, desperate to claw its way through, but I staunchly jammed it back down into the pit of darkness where it belonged.

I seriously needed to get a hold on myself, and damn it, I was about to do just that.

"I shouldn't be here," I said, shaking my head as I took a slow step away from him. I'd somehow allowed my jealousy to nearly drive me off the deep end. "This right here," —I flicked my fingers between the two of them— "this is none of my business." There were two consenting adults here, and I wasn't anything more than a spoke in their wheel.

"Well, that's unfortunate," he said, disappointment set heavy in his eyes. "You were so close."

"So close? Close to what?" A split second passed before I pushed that away too. "Forget it. I don't even care." I turned to leave, but he reached out and took my hand.

"Angel, wait."

"Wait for what?" For more humiliation, more confusion. I already had enough of that. "I'm going to bed."

"Ask me again," he said quietly, intimately, as though we were alone in the room.

I met his eyes and faltered. There was no bravado there, no cockiness to be found, though I still wasn't exactly sure what he wanted me to ask him: For his date to leave? Whether or not he was in love with me? I'd asked him so many questions in the last twenty-four hours that I wouldn't even know where to begin.

And the truth was, I was too beaten down to even try.

"I don't have anything to ask you." I unclasped his hand from mine and watched as he shuttered his eyes. "Goodnight," I said and then left the room, leaving the two of them free to enjoy each other's company.

15. PAY IT IN BLOOD

Back in the safety of the guestroom, I locked the door behind myself and pressed my back against it as I released the breath I'd been holding since I walked away from Dominic. From the window, I could see the moon hanging low in the distance. A soft glow of red still encased it like an ethereal prison, and as awful as the meaning of its presence was, I couldn't help but find beauty in its carnage.

I pushed off the door and walked to the bed, hoping that sleep would take me quickly. The anxiety had returned with a vengeance and was slowly chipping away at my insides again. I wasn't sure how I'd be able to get any sleep like this, and while my cure lay within a few dozen feet of me, I wasn't willing to venture down that road again.

There was too much darkness and uncertainty there.

Too much confusion.

Minutes ticked by as the noxious turmoil inside of me slowly melted into the darkness of the room, bringing me at one with it again. Footsteps sounded on the other side of the room, drawing my attention to the wall that separated me from

Dominic. My stomach lurched as I realized he was probably in there with Sandy, doing things I really didn't want to think about. I squeezed my eyes shut and tried to think of other things—anything—but instead, my mind immediately segued to the newly acquired memory of Dominic confessing his feelings for me.

I am ruinously in love with you…

His words reverberated in my head like the haunting echoes of a long-forgotten tale. I tried to make sense of it, to understand his words, but there was no sense to be made. Not after what he did tonight. I supposed that deep down, I'd wanted his words to be true, to believe that the devil did in fact care, but it had become painfully obvious that he hadn't meant a word of it. It was nothing more than a new game to occupy his time with.

But then why did he take the memory away?

And why did I even care?

The more I played back the memory of that night, the more of it I uncovered—like the things I had confessed to him when he compelled me to only speak the truth. I'd been burying my truth for so long that I'd somehow managed to keep it hidden even from myself. What did it all mean? And why was I so afraid to look at it?

Okay, so, I craved our exchanges. Big deal. It didn't mean anything. It was just the bloodbond. It *had* to be.

But what if it wasn't…?

A knock sounded at my door, bringing my attention back to the here and now.

Climbing out of bed, I padded across the dark room and felt my tension ease the closer I got to the door. Knowing full well what that meant, I turned the lock and opened the door for him.

Dominic stood on the other side of the threshold, his

forearm rested against the doorframe as he gazed down at me. Neither of us said anything as we stared back at each other through the shroud of night.

"Are you going to invite me in?" he asked, breaking the silence first.

Unable to find my voice, I shook my head.

"Why not?"

"Because I'm sleeping, and I need to get back to sleeping." Apparently, I was as eloquent as I was good at lying.

"We both know you weren't sleeping, angel. I can feel your anxiety through the walls," he said bitterly.

"Aw, you poor baby." Was he looking for pity? Because he wasn't going to find any here. "I guess you should've done your homework on me before hitching your wagon to mine, huh?"

"Oh, I've done my homework, love. I'm a very astute student." His gaze dusted over every inch of my body, and my cheeks flamed in response.

"Don't you have a date with Cindy to get back to?" I asked, pretending to look over his shoulder for her.

"I sent her home," he said, not bothering to correct her name.

Relief nestled itself into my stomach, but it only served to further confuse me. Why did I care what he did (or didn't do) with other women? It's not like he was mine. It's not like I wanted to be the one he did things with.

...Did I?

No! I shuck away the thought like a cold, wet raincoat.

"Well, that was fast," I said instead, putting on my best version of a poker face. "Are you sure you got your fill?"

An easy smile curled his lips. "Are you worried about me going hungry?"

"You could starve for all I care." I started to close the door, but he kicked his foot out and stopped it.

"Angel…" He slanted his head to the side and appraised me. The intensity in his gaze made me feel naked; exposed, like he was sifting through the layers I wore, trying to force his way down to the truth.

"What?!" I barked, fidgeting uncomfortably under his heavy stare.

"Ask me again."

My heart skipped at his words.

I knew what question he wanted me to ask him. Only this time, I was too much of a coward to ask it. I didn't have the courage or the luxury to venture down that rabbit hole with him. Not with the Order breathing down my neck and Trace's life hanging in the balance.

"I can't."

His eyes drank me in as though I were spilling secrets out of every pore on my body. He opened his mouth to say something then closed it as a grimace gradually passed over his features. Whatever he was going to say, it wasn't going to see the light of day in this lifetime. Instead, he pulled his foot back from the door and then brought his wrist to his mouth.

"What are you doing?" I asked as his fangs clicked out.

His sharp teeth pierced through the skin, drawing out two droplets of blood. "It'll help you sleep," he said as he extended his wrist to me like a peace offering. I started to shake my head when he added, "No strings attached."

My eyes locked on the drops of crimson, and I unconsciously licked my lips, water pooling readily in my mouth. I knew all about the full body restoration that a small taste of his blood would bring, and while I'd managed to restrain myself before, seeing it in front of me…I wasn't sure I had the willpower to turn that kind of elixir away.

Was it really so wrong to indulge in his blood if it meant that I'd be sharper, calmer, and more myself? I wasn't hurting anybody. In fact, I was bringing the odds in my favor, because at the end of the day, what use would I be to anyone if I was nothing but a shaky bag of nerves? Right? Right.

Somehow, I'd managed to convince myself that this was the right thing for all involved. Wrapping my fingers around his forearm, I pulled him inside the room and shut the door behind him, not wanting anyone to witness my tumble from the wagon. My eyes flicked up to his, gauging him for any signs of judgment or trickery, but there was none to be found.

He was trying to help me—to make it easier on me in his own twisted way. I could see that now, and the realization wiped away any remaining apprehension I may have had.

He watched with silent interest as I brought his wrist to my mouth and covered the two puncture wounds with my lips. The dark pull inside me took over, and before I could think twice about it, I sucked down hard, drawing out a mouthful of his enchanted blood. He winced, but he didn't pull away as I ravenously drank from him.

"I could watch you like this forever," he murmured, though his words barely registered.

I was too busy drinking him in like a lone glass of water in the middle of the desert.

There was no euphoric high, of course, as that only came from his bite, but I felt stronger, invigorated and more powerful with every mouthful of his blood I swallowed. My body was being restored, and the pain was slowly ebbing away.

He slouched back against the door with a thud, resting his weight as he watched me feed my darkness without interruption. I wasn't sure what any of this said about me, what it meant, and frankly, in the moment, I didn't much care.

"Angel, that's enough," he said lowly as he tried to unhook his wrist from my mouth.

But I wouldn't let him go. I clasped his forearm with my

other hand and pushed myself into him, barricading him against the door with my body. I could feel myself getting stronger, and him weaker, but I still couldn't stop myself from drinking.

I wanted more of him.

I wanted to devour every last drop of him.

I bite down on his skin with my own teeth as I manically tried to make the wounds bigger, but he quickly ripped his wrist away from my mouth. I stumbled back, panting and shocked by what I'd done.

Turning his wrist over, he appraised the damage, looking even more stunned than I was.

"I'm…I'm sorry," I said and covered my mouth with my hands. "I didn't mean to."

Not only had I not meant to do it, but I had no actual idea what the hell had gotten into me.

"It's fine, angel. No harm done." He smiled at me, but it was weak and feeble. "I just need a minute," he said as he propped his head back against the door.

My face blanched as I realized I'd taken way too much—so much so that he needed a freakin' minute to get himself back together. I was thoroughly and wholly mortified with myself.

"What can I do? Tell me how to fix this," I pleaded, deep in the throes of guilt. My shaky hands hovered awkwardly between us as I tried to figure out what to do with them. "Oh, my God. I'm so sorry!"

His eyes met mine in the dark, though not much else of him moved. "You never have to apologize to me, angel. I already told you that."

But I did. I so did. He came here to help me, to offer me some of his restorative mojo, and I damn near ate him alive. I was a monster! A freak! What the hell was wrong with me? I didn't even like the taste of blood! Okay, granted, his blood didn't taste like actual blood, but still!

"Here," I said, jamming my wrist in front of his eyes. "Take some of my blood!"

It seemed like a fair trade, being that I nearly sucked him dry of his.

"I don't want your blood," he said as he gently pushed my wrist down.

Um…what now?!

I blinked repeatedly as I tried to process his words. Nope. Couldn't process.

"What do you mean you don't want my blood?" I asked, trying not to sound offended, which I sort of was. I hadn't expected to hear those words come out his mouth. Like ever. Perhaps he was making good on the promise he made earlier. Something about making me beg for it…?

"But there is something I want from you." Reaching out to me, he wiped his blood from the corner of my lips. It was a simple gesture, but it made my stomach feel like butterflies were dancing through it.

"What do you want? My soul?" I asked playfully as I tried to lighten the mood, though it didn't really work.

"Nothing like that, angel." The corner of his lip pulled up into his cheek. "We both know you aren't ready for that."

I wasn't even sure if he was joking or not.

"Then what do you want?" My throat felt like sandpaper as I swallowed thickly.

He met my eyes and smiled. "I want you to kiss me."

16. THE TRUTH OF THE MATTER

Seconds ticked by, and all I could hear was the pounding drum of my own racing heart. Of all the things he could've asked me for, this was the one thing that threatened to break everything inside of me. At this point, it probably would have been easier to just hand over my soul to him. And it wasn't like I hadn't kissed Dominic before. I had; months ago when I first moved to Hollow Hills. It had been my first real kiss, and it had damn near stopped the world from spinning.

But that was a lifetime ago.

And I wasn't that girl anymore.

"You know I can't do that." My voice was soft and to the point, yet it sang with regret for reasons I couldn't explain.

"Can't or won't?" he asked, his eyes glittering as the moonlight slithered in from the window to reflect in them.

"Both."

His frown deepened. "Because of him?"

"Yes," I admitted freely. "I love him, Dominic. You know that."

The bloodbond may have been messing with my mind and

body, making it far too easy for me to do things I wouldn't normally do. But it hadn't replaced my love for Trace. He still had the starring role in my heart.

He bowed his head gracefully, accepting my claim. When his eyes met mine again, there was something vulnerable and fragile in them. Something that tugged at that secret part of me.

"And what of me, angel?" he asked as he pushed off the door and met me where I stood. He lowered his head again, his eyes landing on mine in the most intimate of ways. "Could you ever love me that way?"

My breathing ceased, as though all the air had been sucked out of the room.

Could I ever love Dominic?

I let the question simmer in my mind as my eyes roamed over him, considering it.

It was no secret that Dominic Huntington was gorgeous in that can't-think-straight, sell-your-soul-for-a-kiss, knee-buckling sort of way, and I had been attracted to him since the moment I first laid eyes on him at All Saints. That part had been easy. Effortless. But then there was the other part of him. The important part. The parts which I loathed and desired all at once. From his cocky one-liners to the way I'd catch him watching me with adoration every once in a while.

He was an enigma who left me with just enough clues to keep me coming back for more. A man who challenged me, and infuriated me, and never once tried to fix me, because to him I wasn't broken.

I was perfectly whole just the way I was.

"Yes, I could love you," I said, my tenor barely above a whisper.

The hard part was forcing myself *not* to feel anything for him. That was a battle that was getting harder and harder to win with every passing day. No matter how much I pushed him back, he somehow continued to gain ground on me.

"It would be easy to love you," I admitted and immediately lowered my eyes as my confession sounded back to me.

He picked up my chin and forced me to look at him. His face was draped in shadows and moonlight, and it was the perfect representation of the dark angel he was.

"Say that again," he demanded.

But my lips refused to part. Admitting that out loud once had been one too many.

Gripping my waist, he gently turned me around and then walked me backwards until my back hit the door with a soft thump. We were no longer two people standing in a room together. We were the only two people in the universe, and nothing existed between us but the insufficient fabric of our clothes.

"Say it again, angel. I beg of you."

There wasn't enough willpower in the world to deny him. Not when he was looking at me the way he was, so vulnerable and eager, and dangerously close to me. "I said it would be easy…to love you."

Dominic's eyes glittered something beautiful and otherworldly, and my heart rate picked up feverishly as I fought the unrelenting urge to sink in closer to him.

Grazing the back of his knuckles against my cheek, he looked down at my chest, as though he could hear the change in tempo, and then met my eyes again. I covered my heart, afraid it was going to smash a hole right through my chest.

"Don't do that." He pulled my hand down to my side and held it there. "I live for that sound, angel."

The room suddenly went all topsy-turvy on me as an unbearable pull urged me to get even closer to him, to sink all the way into him and never right myself up again.

This had gone entirely too far, but I didn't know how to

pull us out of it anymore.

"I told you to stop saying things like that to me."

"It seems to be beyond my control, angel."

"You're doing it again."

The corner of his lip pulled up into a lopsided grin, a delicious one, and my heart went all crazy again.

This was so wrong, so very very wrong.

"Please, Dominic...you have to stop. *This* has to stop." My voice was so small and forlorn, it barely sounded like mine.

"Why?" he asked and then frowned. "We haven't done anything, angel."

Maybe not technically, but we were definitely teetering around the edge of something I wouldn't be able to come back from. "You don't know what this is doing to me," I confessed, my words coming out with broken undertones. "I feel like I'm being pulled in two separate directions and it's only a matter of time before I snap."

His eyebrows creased, probably because he knew where I was going with this. Or maybe, just maybe, it was because it pained him to know that I was hurting this way.

"We can't keep going like this. *I* can't keep doing this," I said, gesturing to our touching bodies. "The guilt is eating me alive. I can't sleep, I can't think straight. I can't do anything right, and if I fuck this up—if Trace dies because I was too wrapped up in the bloodbond to think straight, I will never *ever* forgive myself for that. Or you."

He let the words sink in for a moment and then pinched his eyes shut.

"Let me go, Dominic. Please."

"I don't know how to do that, angel."

God help me, because I wasn't sure how to do it either.

The cold hard truth was, I had feelings for Dominic. Feelings that had become impossible to ignore, and while I wasn't sure exactly what that meant for me, I also wasn't in the position to explore it. Either way, I couldn't keep allowing myself to succumb to Dominic every time the going got too hard for me.

That wasn't fair to Trace, and it wasn't fair to Dominic either.

Armed with my undeniable truths, I pulled my hands free and forced him to back away from me. And while it took everything in me to pull it off, my heart knew it was the right thing to do.

I waited for him to say something cruel, or flirtatious, or even look at me in that way he does, but he did none of those things. Instead, he picked up my hand and held it in his, his thumb tracing small circles on the back of it.

"I think you already know how I feel about you, angel, and I suspect I know how you feel about me—whether you want to admit it or not. You have every reason in the world to push me away right now, and I will do my best to accept those reasons, no matter how difficult or painful it may be."

I dropped my head, feeling guilty for making him feel this way, but he quickly picked up my chin and held my gaze.

"But there will come a time when you run out of excuses, and when that day comes, I will be waiting."

I blinked, taken back by his words. Had she just vowed to…wait for me?

"Dominic, I would never ask that of you."

"I know, angel. You didn't," he said simply. "But I'll be waiting anyway."

The pressure was building in my chest again. "And what if that day never comes? What then?"

He smiled. "Then I suppose I'll wait forever."

My heart sank to the bottom of my stomach as he looked at me for a long, harrowing moment. I wasn't sure what was worse:

him pursuing and distracting me relentlessly or him waiting quietly on the side-lines.

Neither one felt right.

"Don't look so sad, angel," he said, drawing my attention back to him. Always back to him. "I'm an Immortal, remember? I have nothing if not time," he said with a wink and then kissed the top of my hand. "Besides, angel. You're worth waiting for."

And with that, he was gone.

…Gone, but ever present in my heart.

17. SAY IT AIN'T SO

The school bell wailed around me as I walked down the empty corridor of Weston Academy. There was no sign of life but for the sound of my sneakers smacking against the vinyl floors. With my books cradled against my chest, I turned the corner and followed the neat row of darkened classrooms, each one with their doors sealed shut, stopping only when the art room came into view at the end of the hall—the only room with the lights turned on.

Instinctively, I knew it was where I had to go...where I was supposed to be. Pushing back my shoulders, I continued walking, my stride and pulse gaining speed the closer I got to it.

Reaching the door, I turned the knob abruptly and then stepped into the empty room. Wet paint brushes and unfinished canvases propped on easels were scattered throughout the space, abandoned as though their owners had picked up and disappeared.

"Where is everyone?" I wondered, looking down at my watch. It was the rose-gold watch my dad had given me for my thirteenth birthday. The one I lost the night my father was murdered.

I shouldn't have this, I thought to myself, knowing it wasn't supposed to be there, and yet there it was.

"No one's coming," said a voice from behind me. "It's just us."

I spun around hastily, recognizing Trace's voice even before I saw him. His face was pale, and his eyes were a shade darker than usual, but it was him in all his resplendence.

"Hi, Jemma," he said softly and then smiled. Something about the way his smile hung at the corners made it look weighed down and sad.

"I'm dreamwalking again," I realized, my eyes growing wide.

He nodded, and I ran for him, jumping off my feet and into his waiting arms. He staggered back a step, but he never loosened his grip on me.

I buried my face into his neck and breathed in his spicy woodlands scent. "I don't want to wake up, Trace. I just want to stay here with you."

He didn't say anything back. He just held me tightly against his body, and I instantly felt the beautiful hum I always felt when I was close to him. When he finally let me go, he placed me back onto my feet and then kissed the tip of my nose. He was trying to put on a brave face, trying to be strong for me, but I could feel his despair beneath the mask. It was stealing the air out of my lungs and making it hard to breath.

"It's bad, isn't it?" I asked, touching his cheek with the tips of my fingers.

"He's getting stronger every day, Jemma. You have to stop him."

"How? How do I do that? How do I save you?" I asked, waiting on bated breath for the answer I sought so desperately.

"You have to let me go." He looked down at me pointedly.

"When you do, you'll know what to do."

I shook my head. "That doesn't make any sense."

The ceiling lights flickered above my head. Trace's eyes rounded out in horror as he glanced over his shoulder.

"He's coming," he said and then grabbed my shoulders. "You have to go. He knows I'm here."

"Who does? Lucifer? What do you mean he's coming? I don't—?"

"You have to wake up, Jemma. Right now! WAKE UP!"

My lids popped open as I shot up in my bed. My heart was racing a million miles a minute, and my skin was slick with sweat. It took me a few minutes to calm myself down, to bring myself back to reality. These dreams were becoming more and more real to me and that much harder to snap out of, and I honestly wasn't sure what that meant.

Dropping my feet over the bed, I climbed out onto shaky legs and treaded my way to the bathroom. After a quick shower and a fresh change of clothes, I left the room feeling slightly better than how I'd started the day, but I was a long way from being okay. In fact, I couldn't really remember the last time I truly felt okay, and a small part of me feared that was just the way things would be from now on.

The thought depressed me.

In the distance, I could hear the low hum of voices coming from the downstairs den. Three of them. My breathing altogether ceased as I rounded the corner and recognized the feminine one.

Tessa!

I peeked my head in the room and found her sitting on the couch, casually talking to Gabriel and Dominic as though she hadn't been MIA for God knows how long. I wasn't sure if I wanted to hug her or throat-punch her.

Her gaze met mine, and her lips pulled up into a smile, though it didn't quite reach her eyes.

Then again, it rarely ever did.

"Hey, Jemma."

My emotions took over, and my vision immediately blurred.

"Where the hell have you been?" I asked as the first tear sneaked its way down my cheek.

"Killing Revs, hunting demons. The usual." She shrugged playfully.

"No. *Where have you been?*" I repeated, another tear escaping. "I needed you, Tess."

"I know." She stood up, straightening her black skinny jeans. "I should've been there for you, but I'm here now," she said as she walked over to me and wrapped her lean arms around me.

I responded with a full-on sob fest in her hair.

"I'm so sorry about Trace," she said as she tightened her hold on me, letting me know Gabriel had already started sharing the good news.

I immediately pulled back from her. "It's not over yet," I told her, shaking my head at her words—at her condolences. "I'm going to save him, Tessa. I swear to God I will."

"Jemma—" She started to shake her head, but I wasn't having any part of it.

"Don't say it. Just don't." I didn't need another naysayer, another person telling me I couldn't do it and that this was an unwinnable task. I didn't want to hear it. "I'm not giving up on him, and I really don't care what any of you have to say about it either!"

"Okay, okay." She put her hands up to calm me, letting me know that she was leaving the Trace matter alone…for now. Her gaze shifted over her shoulder to Gabriel.

They were doing that silent-conversation-with-their-eyes thing again.

"Have you given any more thought to sitting down with the Council?" she asked, her eyes boomeranging back to me.

I crossed my arms and glared at her. Could she and Gabriel be any more meant for each other?

"Don't look at me like that, Jemma. The Order is your best bet right now."

"My best bet at what? Execution?"

She looked back at me confused.

"I guess you didn't get the memo about how they tried to kill me or how they knew Mom was in the Sacred Necropolis RIGHT UNDER OUR FEET!" I was shouting at her, and I hadn't even meant to.

"They didn't try to kill you," she answered humorously, as though I were overreacting to being served the wrong breakfast at a restaurant and not my attempted murder. "Besides, you have the Amulet. You can't be killed, Jemma."

"*I* know that. But *they* didn't. They had someone attack me in the woods, Tessa! They sliced my freaking throat wide open. If it wasn't for the stupid Amulet, I'd be standing here dead!"

She made a face at the probability of that.

"You know what I mean!" God, she was no better than Gabriel. And why the heck wasn't she shocked and appalled about our mother? "Did you hear what I said about Mom? She didn't abandon us, Tess. They had her all this time in that disgusting underground cemetery. How can you trust anything they say?"

"Because I already knew that. Uncle Karl told me about Mom a while ago." Her tone was cold and detached, and it sent a shiver right up my spine.

"You knew she was there?" My eyes widened as a tsunami of emotions rushed through me. "You knew she was Revenant?!"

"Of course, I did."

I gaped at her. "For how long?"

"Does that really matter?" she asked.

"Are you kidding me right now?" I tried to control the anger broiling inside of me.

"I don't know the specific date, Jemma. A few months I guess."

"A few MONTHS?!" I shouted, my voice pitching higher with every syllable. I couldn't believe what I was hearing. "And it never occurred to you to tell me? It never occurred to you that I'd want to know what happened to her too?"

"Yeah, it did, but frankly, I thought it was better if you didn't know."

"Oh really?! And what the hell gave you the right to decide that for me?" I was crying again, but it wasn't tears of sadness. It was anger and betrayal from the one person that was supposed to do right by me.

"I was trying to protect you."

"From what? In what kind of backwoods world of logic were you protecting me?"

"I was protecting you from yourself," she said bitingly. "From running off and doing something stupid! And lo and behold, that's exactly what you did."

My eyes narrowed into two vengeful slits of rage. "Getting her out of there wasn't stupid! She didn't belong there! Look at her! She's the splitting image of you," I said and turned to the spot we'd left my incapacitated mother, only she wasn't there. I spun around and then spun back the other way, frantically searching the room for her missing body.

"Where the hell is she?" I roared back at Tessa, knowing full well that she was behind this.

"I brought her back to Temple. It's where she belongs, Je—
"

"YOU DID WHAT?!"

Tessa flinched at my volume and then quickly recovered. "Jemma, calm down."

"How. Fucking. Dare. You." I seethed, my hands balled into fists at my sides now, poised to strike.

Like I didn't have enough adversaries, enough mountains to climb. I had to add my own sister to the list. Tears burned under my lids like broiling lava. I was seriously going to explode. How much more could I take?

Something was going to seriously snap, and I feared it would be me.

"Bring her back, Tessa, or I swear to God—"

"You know I can't do that," she answered calmly.

But she could. She absolutely could. She was simply choosing not to.

More rage. More raw emotion I couldn't handle. The lights sputtered chaotically as I glared at her, my hands shaking with anger—with energy. I could barely contain myself enough to think straight.

"Jemma, you need to calm yourself down before you—"

Too late.

Every light bulb in the room shattered into a trillion little pieces, raining down around us like some demonic light show nobody signed up for. Dominic and Gabriel barely reacted to it, probably because they were already used to my little power surge mishaps, but Tessa quickly covered her head in surprise.

Her eyes darted around the room frantically before making their way back to me. Unfazed by it, I didn't bother covering up, and she noticed it. Her features twisted with confusion as she stared back, her eyes probing and questioning.

"Did you...do that?"

"You need to fucking leave. Like right now." Frankly, I was worried she was going to be the next thing I exploded if she didn't. "I seriously can't even look at you right now."

"Jemma—"

"GET. OUT!"

She flinched as a strange combination of surprise and fear passed through her eyes. She quickly steeled herself and said, "I'm not going anywhere, Jemma. This isn't your house."

"Oh, really?!" I fired back and then paused.

Okay. Alright. So, she had a point. This wasn't my house, and I couldn't kick her out of it. But that didn't mean I had to stay here. I wouldn't. Not with Brutus sleeping under the same roof of me.

"You know what, Tessa? You're right. This isn't my house, and you—" I jammed my finger into the center of her chest "—you aren't my family because family doesn't do that to each other. So, enjoy your bed! Drown in it for all I care, but don't ever don't forget that you're the one who made it," I warned and then left the room in a huff.

Taking two stairs at a time, I bolted back up to the guest room and slammed the door so forcefully that it bounced back open and nearly hit me in the face. Anger trilled in my veins as I tried to quell the overwhelming urge to bust every single window in the house. To topple the whole damn structure to the ground.

I knew then there was absolutely no way I could stay here now. Not with her here. For my own sanity—for my own safety—I had to get out of this house as fast as humanly possible.

Grabbing my schoolbag from the back of the chair, I tossed it onto the bed. Tears continued spilling as I riffled through the drawers, looking for my things only to realize I didn't have any things.

I owned nothing, and I had no one.

The realization had my tears raining down harder and my

legs threatening to drop me to the ground.

Zipping up the bag, I tossed it onto my shoulder and pivoted for the door only to come face to face with another brick wall. My heart jumped up into my throat as I looked up and met Dominic's eyes.

He was standing in the doorway with an amused grin on his face. "Going somewhere, angel?

18. THE BIG PLAN

The rain picked up outside, raking its nails against the windows as I stood in the bedroom and stared up at Dominic. Bloodbond or not, he was the only one I could still stand to look at in this house of fallen souls, but that wasn't nearly enough to keep me here.

"I'm leaving," I said as I readjusted the strap of my schoolbag. The almost-empty bag hung awkwardly on my shoulder, and I felt silly for even bothering to bring it with me. "I can't stay here anymore. Not with her here."

"That's easily remedied, love. I'll gladly throw her and my brother out," smirked Dominic. He looked like he was chomping at the bit for the opportunity to do just that.

But I wasn't about to start a fight between him and Gabriel.

"Don't bother," I said, shaking my head. "It's not just them, Dominic. The Order knows I'm here—I have to leave."

I wasn't safe here anymore. Not with Council members dropping in and out as they pleased, and Gabriel and Tessa breathing down my neck. Knowing where they stood only made my decision that much easier to make.

"And where do you plan on going?" he asked, crossing his arms as he leaned into the doorway. "I'm guessing you don't have a secret lake house up north?"

"Nope." I lifted my chin a little. "I don't need anything or anyone. I have a plan and a few bucks for a motel and that's all I need right now." I started to walk towards him to leave the room, but he didn't clear the way.

"A motel?" His smirk morphed into a grimace. "You think I'm going to allow you to run off to some fleabag motel?"

I narrowed my eyes. "I don't remember asking for your permission."

His shoulder pushed off the wall, though he didn't step out of the doorway. "And that's precisely the problem with you, love. You don't ask my permission nearly as much as you should."

Mother—

I opened my mouth to fire something back at him, and then realized what he was trying to do. He was trying to get a rise out of me—to slow me down—and I didn't have time for this.

"Just move," I said as I tried to squeeze by him, but he stepped to the right, putting himself directly in my way again.

"Dominic!"

"Yes, angel?"

"Are you going to let me leave?"

"Alone? With Lucifer running wild?" He laughed as though I were an amusing little child, but it died off just as quickly as it started. "Not likely."

I stepped back and glared at him. "So, what then? You're just going to keep me prisoner here?"

"The thought has crossed my mind." He smiled darkly.

My sadness over Tessa's betrayal quickly morphed into a

blind rage that was consequently directed right at him. "Get out of my way!" I screamed, ramming my open hands into his chest.

He stumbled back, but barely. "Have as much of a tantrum as you want. I have yet to sit by and allow you to get yourself killed, and I'm certainly not going to start today."

"You can't keep me here," I shouted, still trying to move him. "I'll run the second you turn your back on me."

He exhaled. "I'm sure you will, angel, but that isn't what I'm trying to do."

"Then get out of my way!" I tried pushing again, and when that didn't work, my pushes turned into slaps, and next thing I knew, I was wailing on him with closed fists. And still, he didn't move.

"God damn you!" Out of gas and defeated, I shoved him one last time and threw my bag back on the bed as tears rolled down my cheeks. I wanted to scream, break something, hit him, but none of it seemed to be worth the effort.

Every time one door shut in my face, there was always somebody standing in the doorway of the next one.

"I'm only trying to help you, love."

I scoffed at him as I slapped away my angry tears.

"Angel, come on now," I heard him say quietly. "You know I hate it when you cry."

"Yeah, well, get used to it," I said, still feeling sorry for myself. "I have." And I had a feeling I was going to spend a good number of my remaining days crying my eyes out. My life just sort of sucked that way.

After a few beats of silence, I felt Dominic move up behind me. His hand came up, but he hesitated and then lowered it back to his side again. I furrowed my eyebrows, wondering what he was doing back there.

"I meant what I said yesterday. I'm here for you, angel, in whatever capacity you need me to be."

"What the hell does that mean?"

He leaned in closer to my ear. "It means get your bag. We're leaving."

My back straightened, certain I'd heard that wrong. "*We're leaving?*" I asked and then slowly turned around to face him.

"Yes. As in you and me. Do you have a problem with that, kitten lips?"

I seriously couldn't help but smile at him. Shaking my head, I said, "Not a one."

Less than an hour later, we pulled into the valet of a luxury hotel overlooking the rocky coastal waters. If it was up to me, which it wasn't, we'd be staying at some low-key motel off the freeway, but Dominic refused to entertain the idea. Vampire or not, he was born with a silver spoon in his mouth, and that wasn't about to change anytime soon. Instead, he checked us into their finest suite using a combination of his glamour, fake names, and his fat inheritance.

We took the private elevator up to the top floor, which opened up to the penthouse suite. Floor to ceiling windows greeted us, stretching all around the room as they gifted us with a picture-perfect view of the ocean.

My jaw just about hit the floor as I stood there frozen and awestruck.

"Make yourself at home," he said as he picked up a tiny remote control and aimed it at what looked like a gargantuan flat screen TV built directly into the wall. But it wasn't a TV.

Flames immediately strung up from behind the black glass, dancing rhythmically over hundreds of glittering rocks that looked just like diamonds. It was a fireplace, though I'd never seen one quite like that before.

My eyes veered back to the balcony, and then my feet were moving, slowly making my way towards it, stopping only when my feet hit the beginning edge of the terrace.

It was a hell of a long way down.

"It won't bite you," chided Dominic, encouraging me to step outside.

Ignoring him and my pattering heart, I took a small step forward and then another one, and before I knew it, I was on the balcony, drinking in the incredible view.

"It's just...breathtaking."

"I couldn't agree more," he said from somewhere over my shoulder.

I felt as though his eyes were trained on me, but I couldn't bring myself to turn away from the view. I needed to soak in every morsel of its beauty, take in all the colors of the coast and the haunting sounds of the water crashing onto the shore and then sear it into my memory.

With how my life was going, who knew if I'd ever get the chance to see something like this again?

I'd never admit it to him, but I was glad he insisted that we come here instead of the rat-hole I wanted to go to.

After getting my fill of the view, I headed back inside and took in the rest of the room. And by room, I mean massive condo. There were two spacious bedrooms on opposite ends of the suite, and at the center of them, a luxurious living room, equipped with a Grand piano, all-white seating area, and a fully-stocked wet bar.

And then there was the bathroom. Heated floors, a massive hot tub and a glass shower the size of my old bedroom in Florida. I seriously wanted to live in that bathroom.

"Which room is mine?" I asked, figuring I should let him have first pick after the big fuss I made about having two separate rooms. If it was up to Dominic, we would've been shacked up in the honeymoon suite.

"Whichever one you want, love. I've already seen the view

hundreds of times."

"Are you sure?" I tried not to sound too excited at being able to take the bigger room with the insanely beautiful ocean-front view. "Because I'm going to choose the better one."

He laughed. "Be my guest."

He didn't have to tell me twice. I strutted back to the master suite and tossed my schoolbag on the plush chaise. Flopping back on the bed, I spread my arms and closed my eyes for just the tiniest of moments. In that small span of time, nothing and no one existed. It was just me and my fancy room.

"Perfection," I muttered to myself.

"It's about as close as I've ever come to it."

I opened my eyes and met his gaze. He was leaning against the doorway with his arms folded over his chest and a strange look in his eyes as he watched me from the entrance. There was something about the way he was looking at me. It was intense yet soft. Adoring, yet frustrated. It was hard to wrap my mind around it, especially since he'd begun looking at me like that a lot more lately.

And he was still doing it.

"What? Why are you staring at me like that?"

"Like what, angel?"

"You know, all…" I was going to say goo-goo eyed, but my mouth wouldn't finish the sentence. Instead, I bit down on my lip and muttered, "Never mind."

A smolder of heat darkened his eyes as he stared down at my mouth. I promptly released my bottom lip and pretended not to notice the obvious effect I had on him. I couldn't let myself be distracted by that, or him, or anything. I wasn't here to give in to my traitorous skin that craved his touch or the bloodbond that sought to bring us together. We'd already established the line, and I needed to stay on my side of it.

Sitting up, I scooched over to the end table and pulled the

phonebook from the dresser drawer. Dominic watched me with interest as I flipped through the pages until I found what I was looking for. Grabbing the pen from the notepad, I circled the batch of telephone numbers I needed and then set the book down beside me.

Curiosity getting the better of him, he pushed off the doorway and came to stand in front of me. Craning his neck, he looked down and peeked at the numbers I'd circled.

"Owens?"

"I'm not sure which number is his," I said as I picked up the phone and dialed the first phone number listed under Owens. I really should have thought twice about smashing my phone to smithereens on the side of the highway.

"*His?*" Dominic hung up the line. "Now would be a good time to fill me in."

"Caleb Owens—he's a Caster."

"Yes. And what of him, love?"

"Do you remember what I told Gabriel last night? That maybe we were reading the wrong books?"

"Vaguely."

I paused before answering. I needed to get my thoughts together in order to present my idea as efficiently as possible, because if I didn't, Dominic wouldn't go for it. And if he wasn't for it, he was against it, which meant he would be a thorn in my ass, and I so did *not* need a thorny ass right now. "Well, that got me thinking—"

"Heaven help us."

"—Maybe we really are wasting our time digging through the Order's endless supply of books and Scripture. If the Dark Legion knew how to create a vessel for Lucifer, they must have a fail-safe if something goes wrong, right? And if anyone knows the ins and outs of a vessel, it's the Dark Legion."

He frowned, knowing where I was going with this.

"And who better than the ones who opened the Hellgate in the first place?"

"The Roderick Sisters."

I nodded. "Exactly."

"Okay," he said, dragging the word out. "And you think they're just going to hand over this information to you?"

"Not even if Hell froze over," I said, knowing full well what lies ahead of me. Unfortunately, the Roderick bitches and I left off on bad terms, so chances were, they weren't going to help me with a damn thing. Not that they'd help me even if we were on good terms. Hell was the team they played for, and that alone made us enemies.

"I need to find another way to get close to them," I began cautiously. "The only thing I can think of is to isolate one of them from the pack and then force her to give me the information I need." And by force, I mean torture until she begs to tell me everything I want to know.

"That's assuming you can get anywhere near them, which we both know isn't a possibility."

Apart from being prominent Dark Casters, they had the gift of Sight, meaning they could hear and see me coming from a mile away.

"Right." I tweaked my eyebrows. "And that's why I need Caleb."

"And what is it that you think he's going to do?"

I smiled darkly. "He's going to bind their magic."

19. BLAST FROM THE PAST

After several awkward conversations with people who were obviously not Caleb Owens, I finally called the right house and managed to get Caleb's mother to give me his cell phone number. After that, it wasn't hard convincing him to meet up with me, especially after I told him I needed his particular brand of services again.

Caleb Owens was always up for a chance to show off his talents.

Dominic and I pulled into the parking lot of Starry Beach, the lakeside park that had hosted Spring Carnival several weeks back. It seemed like such a lifetime ago that I was walking through the park with Gabriel, still learning the truth about who I was and the hidden world around me. It was hard for me to think about the past now. The more I looked back, the further I felt from it...from who I used to be.

Caleb was already there waiting for us, sitting on the hood of his yellow Camaro and fiddling with his phone when Dominic and I walked up to him. A toothy grin coiled his mouth as his eyes flicked up and found us.

"Damn, Blackburn. Long time no see," he said as he ran his hand through his chestnut hair and then nodded over to Dominic, who faintly returned the gesture. "Where've you been hiding?"

"You don't want to know," I said and gave him a quick hug. "How have you been?"

"Could be better." He lifted a casted hand as evidence. "Probably going to miss the rest of the season."

"Ouch."

"Yeah, it was worth it though. You should see the other guy's face."

"Seriously, Cale?" I shook my head at his stupidity. "I hope it wasn't over a girl again."

He laughed but didn't confirm or deny it. "So, you ever planning on coming back to class?"

"Maybe," I said, and I hoped to God I would. Even though I didn't exactly like school and I wasn't the best student, attending class again meant that the dust had settled—that I was out of imminent danger and everything was normal again. I wanted that so very much.

"Such a rebel," he smirked, brushing off my shoulder as though rebellion had anything to do with it.

Dominic crossed his arms, apparently not liking all the small talk and physical contact.

"So, anyway," I said, changing the topic. "Like I was saying on the phone, I need a favor."

"Alright. Shoot."

"I need to know if there's a way to disable another Caster's magic."

He looked at me with suspicion. "What's this about again?"

"I'll explain everything in a minute, but first I need to know if it can actually be done."

"Yeah," he said with a shrug. "The Order binds people all

the time. They really don't like us stepping out of line, you know," he added, winking at me, as though that last part was meant for me.

"But is it something *you* can do?"

"Depends."

"On what?"

"On who's being bound and how strong their magic is."

Well, that was probably my cue to come out with it. "I need to bind one of the Roderick Sisters. They're—"

"Dark Casters? Seriously, Blackburn?" He gave his head a shake. "What the fuck did you get yourself mixed up with?"

"It's not what you think. They…they have information I need."

"What kind of information?" he asked, his golden eyes darkening with curiosity.

I hesitated to give him too much information, afraid of what he might do with it. "Look, I can't really talk about that. Not until I know you can do this—that you're all in."

He scratched his head and then slicked his chestnut hair back as he thought about it. "Even if I agreed to do this for you, it wouldn't work with just me."

"What do you mean? You're not strong enough to do it?"

He didn't like that conclusion. "It's not that. A spell like this is big business. And the Roderick Sisters? They're even bigger business."

"Could Carly help you?" She was his twin, after all. I figured she had to be at least as powerful as he was.

"I'd need at least two other people to do this—a Trinity— and even then, there's no guarantees. They'll have to be some seriously powerful Casters, and you're not going to like it, but there's only one person around here that fits the bill."

Dang it. I really didn't want to bring that bitch into this.

"Nikki," I guessed.

"The one and only." He shrugged her name off like it was no big deal. "I mean, unless you know another Caster."

I didn't.

Great. How on earth was I going to convince Nikki to do me a solid? And worse, how was I going to stop myself from rearranging her facial features long enough to ask her?

The only thing worse than having to ask Nikki for a favor was having to go to Temple to do it. Apparently, Hollow Hills' number one Caster was dutifully attending an emergency meeting called by the Council. One in which all Anakim near and far were required to attend. Being that I destroyed my cell phone, I wasn't sure if my invite got lost in the mail or if I was purposely left off the guest list. Either way, I wasn't about to let that stop me from going.

The rain was a light drizzle by the time Dominic and I made it to Temple. The parking lot and surrounding streets were filled with expensive cars, which only served to deepen my apprehension. The place was packed with powerful Descendants that could easily take me out with their little pinky nail. It wasn't the kind of place you wanted to hang out at when you happened to be *the* Daughter of Hades.

Halfway up the walkway, I considered waiting for the meeting to finish and catching Nikki outside. It wasn't because I was afraid of the crowd—not with my trusty Amulet, anyway. It was who was in the crowd that was worrying me. Tessa. Gabriel. Nikki. Morgan. Julian. My uncle. William...And God knows how many other people I'd rather not see. There were far too many people who could get in my way, and even more ways this thing could go wrong.

Then again, I didn't exactly have the luxury of time.

Conceding, I sucked in a deep breath and opened the door.

After a series of thumb scans and passcodes, Dominic and I

were finally inside the cryptic building. From the entrance, I could already hear a strong, commanding voice booming through the atrium, letting us know the Council meeting had already started. We followed the sound all the way down the elaborate corridor until we got to the meeting hall. Taking in another breath, I cracked open one of the double doors and then slipped into the packed room with Dominic right behind me.

We quickly blended into the shadows and listened to the speech from the back of the room.

"With the threat of the end of days fast approaching, it is imperative that all the factions band together as one," said William at the front of the room. He was planked by my Uncle Karl, Alford, and another man I didn't recognize. "We cannot allow the Dark Legion to undo centuries of service our kind has contributed to the mortal world. Now, more than ever, we must fight the evil that threatens all of us."

"With all due respect, Magister. How are we supposed to do that?" asked a middle-aged woman I'd never seen before. "The Hellgate has already been opened."

Another man stood across the room. "And we still have no idea if Lucifer is earthbound or not!"

"We need answers!"

"How do we protect ourselves? Our children?"

A roar of agreement rippled through the crowd.

"Please." William rose his hands to quiet the mounting upheaval. "There's no need to panic. We have already assembled our top Rigs, who are out gathering information as we speak. This battle is far from over." There was a quiet confidence about him, almost as though he knew exactly how this whole thing was going to play out.

I thought that was strange, being that he didn't even know who the vessel was.

"So, what do the rest of us do in the meantime?" asked a

younger man from the audience. He looked about twenty.

"The best thing any of us can do right now is to continue to live our lives—honor your duties and your studies, and for God's sake, check in with your superiors and Handlers. Demon activity has been on the rise throughout the entire west coast, so please be prepared and stay vigilant."

"Interesting tactic," whispered Dominic in my ear. "He's giving them the bare minimum of information."

I'd noticed that too.

"Why do you think that is?" I wondered, my eyes narrowing with suspicion.

"Why do you think, love?" he said, and I could hear a smile behind his words. "It's easier to control people when you keep them in the dark."

I suppose Dominic would know that better than most. He wasn't exactly a spring of information.

"Do you see her anywhere?" I asked, having heard enough of this angel meeting.

He shook his head. "Negative."

"Maybe she decided to ditch." I wouldn't put it past her. She was probably out in the woods sacrificing animals. That, or stalking Devil-Trace somewhere.

When I turned my focus back to the front of the room, my uncle had taken the podium. "Those of you interested in training with the High Casters, please see me at the end of the meeting. Again, Elite Casters only..."

Then again, if Nikki was running late, maybe I still had a chance to catch her outside—alone.

I ticked my chin to the exit and then followed as Dominic led us back into the corridor. I was about to tell him about my plan to wait the witch out, when I saw her come around the corner like a cursed gift from the heavens.

I narrowed my eyes and watched as she flipped her hair to

the side and then continued banging away on her phone, strutting down the hallway as though it were her own personal runway.

Something broke loose inside of me—anger, revenge, hatred—and it rattled through me like tremors from an earthquake. All I could think about was the way she left me to die. The look on her face as I begged for my life.

Suddenly, I couldn't remember the reason I was here in the first place.

I couldn't remember anything but her betrayal. I ran towards her, my feet hitting the marble floors like gunshots firing through the building as the sweet nectar of revenge settled on my tongue.

Nikki Parker was going to get her just desserts, and I was going to be the one to serve them.

20. WILD CARD

Nikki's eyes flicked up and met mine a fraction of a second too late. I was already gunning for her at full speed when I whipped out my arm and clotheslined her neck, knocking her ass straight to the ground. She hit the floor fast and hard, the air rushing out of her lungs with an audible swoosh.

"You stupid bitch! *Recedite!*" snarled Nikki as she threw her palm out at me. The incantation sent an invisible force of energy barreling into my stomach and knocking me back several feet away from her.

And to my dismay, it kept me there.

My anger quickly morphed into something more primal as I envisioned myself ramming that magic energy all the way down her throat. I slashed my arm through the invisible force, fighting it as though I could somehow push it away, and surprisingly, it worked.

With a small taste of freedom, I charged at her again just as she threw another wave of her mojo at me, though this time, it barely slowed me down.

"*Recedite!*" she screamed again, panic staining her tone as I continued to push my way through the force. The image of my fingers wrapped around her throat, driving me forward with the sweet promise of repayment.

Her eyes doubled in size as she frantically shuffled backwards, desperate to put space between us now that her magic wasn't working. I closed the last bit of distance and threw myself down on her, my knee pressing into her gut as I grabbed her by her neck and squeezed.

Terror and lack of oxygen painted her eyes red, but even that didn't stop me from pressing down harder against her windpipe.

I may as well have been standing outside my body, because I sure as hell wasn't in control of it anymore. All I could think about was making her pay—making her suffer the way I suffered at the hands of Engel for all those weeks.

And I squeezed harder.

"As much as I'm enjoying this little show, I think you've made your point, angel," said Dominic as he wrapped an arm around my waist and attempted to peel me off her.

But I refused to budge, even for him.

"You're going to kill her," he warned, and while I could somewhat understand the words he was telling me, they barely perforated my awareness enough to make the slightest difference.

"Angel!" he shouted, this time firmer. "Get a hold of yourself! You *need* her!"

"My ass I need her!" I snapped back and then inwardly cringed as Trace's beautiful face floated through my mind.

Dammit. I *did* need her—I needed her to help me save him!

Putting his salvation above my own need for revenge, I released my death-grip on her throat and sat back on my knees as the rest of me slowly regained lucidity. Nikki immediately began coughing and gasping for air as she frantically tried to refill her lungs.

If you asked me, she was trying to sell it way too hard.

"You crazy bitch," she croaked hoarsely as she crawled backwards on her elbows. "You almost killed me!"

I probably should have felt some sort of remorse for that, but I didn't.

"Don't act as if you didn't have it coming."

"I hardly think the crime fits the punishment," she said, still clutching her neck. "You seriously need help."

"You watched me get my throat sliced and then handed me over to Engel so he could finish the job, and you think I'm the one that needs help? I should hang you by your feet and bleed you out, you stupid—"

I hadn't realized I'd lunged at her again until I felt Dominic's arm yanking me back out of thin air.

"Oh please," she said as she clumsily pulled herself back to her feet. "Don't pretend this is about that when we both know it's about me and Trace."

"You and Trace? Are you deranged?" I practically laughed in her face.

She dusted off her jeans and then gave her head a little shake. "I told you he would come back to me."

My back stiffened at her words. "What the hell are you talking about?"

"Like you don't know. Like it's some big coincidence that you decided you wanted payback exactly one day after me and Trace hook up. Give me a break. You're not that good of an actress, Jemma."

The room no longer had enough oxygen.

"You hooked up with Trace?" I couldn't get the foul words out of my mouth fast enough. "Last night?"

An evil grin twisted her lips. "Twice."

"Oh, my God." I threw my hands over my eyes as images of her with devil-Trace pummeled through my consciousness, threatening to knock the ground out from under me.

"You little hellion," laughed Dominic as I nearly threw up in my mouth.

Nikki's eyes thinned as she took in my reaction. "Wait...you really didn't know?"

I was still trying not to throw up when I said, "I'm so disgusted, I can't even look at you right now."

A pleased smile brushed across her face as she realized this was brand-new information to me and she had just gotten herself a front row seat to my reaction. "Look, no hard feelings, kay? It's not like I didn't warn you he'd come back to me."

"He didn't come back to you, you dumbass. That wasn't Trace!" I gnashed my teeth together to keep from lunging at her again.

"Oh, okay, then who was it?" She half scoffed, half laughed and didn't bother waiting for me to respond. "Believe me, it was all Trace. I would know."

"Obviously not." My fingers were itching to smack that whorish grin off her face. "Trace is Lucifer's vessel."

"Lucifer? Lucifer *who*? The devil?" She burst out laughing as though anyone in their right mind would ever joke about something like this. "You really are a freak, Jemma. Only you would come out with something as ridiculous and desperate as this." She tried to walk passed me, but I stepped in front of her, blocking her exit.

"If you would've bothered to get to Temple on time you would know the Hellgate's been opened. Lucifer is earthbound, and Trace is his vessel."

"Riiiight," she said and rolled her eyes at me, as though I'd make something like this up.

"I watched it happen with my own eyes."

"Yes, I'm sure you did," she said and patted my head before trying to walk off again.

Obviously, I wasn't getting through to her at all. The delusion was strong with this one.

"Dammit, Nikki. He wouldn't choose you over me," I said, stepping with her so that she couldn't walk away from me—from this. "And deep down you already know that."

She paused, squaring her shoulders in an attempt to hide the impact of my words. "Well, apparently he would, because he did," she said, scowling at me now. The deathly look in her eyes let me know she was out for blood. "Trace is over you, Jemma. Maybe you should try getting over yourself too," she spat and then pushed her way passed me.

Dominic, my last line of defense, stepped out in front of her. "When you decide to remove your head from your ass, you can find us here," he said and slipped a piece of paper into the palm of her hand.

She quickly turned the paper over and read it. "Wow. Shacking up in a hotel, huh? That's low, Jemma. Even for you," she said and then threw the piece of paper back at him before storming off.

"Well, that went super well," I said bitterly as I watched her disappear around the corner.

Leave it to me to try to kill the one hope we had of saving Trace. Literally.

Not that it mattered now. She didn't believe us anyway.

"She'll call," he said with absolute confidence, though I had no idea where he was getting it from.

"And if she doesn't? What the hell are we going to do?" I said as we made our way out the building. The dewy air pressed around me like a soggy blanket. "We need another Caster or we'll never be able to bind the sisters."

Dominic unlocked the passenger door and opened it for

me, his gaze shifting away from me briefly. When his gaze returned, his eyes looked harder—troubled even. "I may know of someone," he finally said.

My eyes widened with surprise. "Who?"

"Just someone I used to know."

Well that wasn't cryptic at all.

"Why am I only hearing about this now?" I asked, unimpressed with his blatant withholding of information.

It felt like forever before he spoke again.

"Because, angel, she's my sire," he said, his eyes as dark as a star-lit sky. "And believe me when I say, she's a last resort."

21. PERSON OF INTEREST

Dominic and I didn't say much to each other on the drive back to the hotel. As much as I was dying to know anything and everything about this secret sire of his, I could see he was bothered by the mere mention of her. And Dominic was never bothered by anything, which had to mean that she was either *that* bad, or they had history.

Honestly, I couldn't decide which one was worse.

As soon as we were back in the room, Dominic didn't waste any time marching straight to the wet bar and making himself a drink. He quickly downed the first glass and then started to make a second one when his phone buzzed in his pocket. He took a quick peek at the screen and then held it up so that I could see the caller I.D.

Tessa.

Again…

"Perhaps you should speak to her," he suggested.

He was probably right. But not because I owed it to her. I'd just had enough of her incessant phone calls. Snatching the phone from him, I hit the accept button and put it to my ear as

I walked out onto the wrap-around balcony.

"Where the hell is my sister?" I heard her shouting on the other side of the line. "I swear to God, if you did something to her—"

"He didn't do anything to me. I'm perfectly fine," I said, irritated by her mock-concern.

She paused for a second and then barked out, "Where are you? I'm coming to get you."

"If I wanted you to know where I was, I would've left you a note." I leaned over the railing and looked down at the rocky coastline. "Do you see a note anywhere?"

There was a stint of silence on the other end, and if I knew my sister, she was using it to compose herself. "This isn't cute anymore, Jemma. You need to get back here *right now*—we have a meeting with the Council first thing in the morning."

"No, *you* have a meeting," I corrected. "I haven't agreed to anything."

More earsplitting silence. "Look, I don't know what kind of a point you're trying to prove, but this is getting really old. You don't just sneak out of the house in the middle of the day and—"

"Oh, kind of like you did with our mother's body?" I quickly shot back.

"JEMMA!"

"Go to Hell, Tessa."

I ended the call and tossed the phone back to Dominic. He was sitting on the couch with his arm draped along the backrest, watching me with those dark eyes of his.

"That was fast," he remarked.

Truthfully, I'd intended to have a longer conversation with her, to even hear her out. All she had to do was shut her big mouth for once—maybe even take responsibility for something and apologize for it. But no, not Tessa. She was going to run her mouth until the end of days. Literally.

"I'm done with her." Turning my back to him, I leaned over the balcony again and stared out at the storm clouds as they leisurely rolled themselves in front of the sunset. And it wasn't just her I was done with. I was done with all of them. They could keep their lies and half-truths and unwillingness to help me save Trace and shove it up their asses. I didn't need them anyway. I was going to find a way to do this on my own.

"I'm sure you don't mean that," said Dominic as he came to stand beside me. "She's your sister, love."

"And? When has she ever acted like it? When has she ever been there for me?" I didn't give him a chance to answer. "Never. That's when." Angry tears began sliding down my cheeks, and this time, I let them. It was becoming a full-time job trying to suppress my emotions, and I just didn't have the energy to keep doing it.

"Angel." I could feel his eyes on me, but I couldn't bear to face him.

"Whatever. I'm fine," I said, though it was clear to both of us that I wasn't. "I don't need her anyway. I don't need anyone. You can't miss what you never had, right? I mean, that *is* what they say, isn't it?"

"I really wouldn't know."

I met his eyes for a moment, and suddenly, my heart hurt for him. Here I was complaining about my family problems, yet again, while he just stood there listening—without any family to speak of. Not only did his mother pass away during childbirth, but his father blamed him for her death, and then later disowned him when he Turned. All he had was Gabriel, and they couldn't be more at odds if they were trying to do it on purpose.

"I'm sorry. I shouldn't be going on about all this to you. You already have your own problems to deal with."

"I only have one problem to speak of, and it's really more of a waiting game than a problem," he said calmly, watching the sun creep its way down the horizon.

"Is that right?" I quirked a brow at him. "And what non-problem would that be?"

"Do you really want to know the answer to that?" he asked, side-eyeing me. Something about his daring tone made me think he was referring to me—to this thing between us.

"Hm…probably not," I decided.

He chuckled to himself, though he didn't say anything else on the matter, probably because he knew better than to poke me when I was already teetering around the edge of losing it. Instead, he just remained next to me, not saying anything, and somehow that was enough.

"I wish it could always be like this," I said, taking in the view and the momentary stint of peace I had. "So calm and beautiful."

"Yes, but you wouldn't appreciate it if it was," he answered softly, without meeting my eyes.

"Why not?"

"Because, love, you have to know the storms to be able to appreciate the calm." His eyes never veered from the horizon, as though he couldn't bring himself to look away, and suddenly, something occurred to me.

"When was the last time you watched the sunset?" I asked, turning myself to face him.

Up until that moment, I hadn't even considered how special this may have been for him. Revenants, like in most vampire lore, could not withstand the sun, but after the walls of Sanguinarium were torn to shreds, it somehow gave Revenants the ability to walk with the sun.

"It's been a very long time," he admitted without taking his eyes away from the picturesque sky before us.

"I can't remember the last time I watched it either." Though I had no excuses or magical barriers preventing me from seeing it. I just never took the time, and I wasn't sure which one of our stories was sadder.

A long stretch of silence passed between us, though there was nothing awkward or uncomfortable about it. In fact, it was the exact opposite. For the first time in a long time, I felt calm and present in the moment I was in.

Of course, the silence didn't last for long, as we had important matters to discuss.

"So, are you going to tell me about this sire of yours?" I finally asked, having dug up enough courage to bring it up again. "What did you say her name was again?"

"I didn't."

"Funny," I deadpanned.

"Her name is Priscilla."

"And...?" I motioned for him to continue.

He paused briefly, still gazing out at the sun as it slowly slipped away from the world. "There isn't much to say, love. She was a Caster before she Turned, and if need be, she's powerful enough to bind the sisters."

"A Dark Caster?"

He shook his head. "The only allegiance she has is to herself."

"Oh. Well, that's good, right? She might be willing to help us if she hasn't pledged herself to the Dark Legion."

"She'll help. But it'll come with a cost."

"Awesome." I huffed out an aggravated breath, causing a loose piece of hair to flutter in front of my face. "I have about eighty bucks to my name."

"It's not that kind of payment, love. She prefers to be paid in favors and flesh."

A chill crept down my back. Already, I didn't like the

sound of her. "What do you mean by flesh, exactly?"

"Never you mind that, angel." He met my gaze again, and for the first time ever, I could see color in the depths of his dark eyes. With the sun hitting them just the way it was, they looked almost amber. "If we have to cross that bridge, I'll be the one to take care of it."

I wasn't sure I liked the sound of him dealing with Priscilla and her payment of flesh.

Especially if it involved *his* flesh.

"Were you two ever together?" I blurted out, and then swallowed down the nasty aftertaste the words left in my mouth.

The corner of his lip pulled up ever so slightly. "Curious, are we?"

"No—I mean, I just think I should know if you two had some kind of history," I said, doing my best to sound casual about it. "You know, in case it interferes with our plans."

"Of course." He turned back to the sun, which had almost completely disappeared into the horizon. "There's always history with a sire. The bond is deep and rather complex, but I assure you, angel, it will not interfere with anything."

Deep and complex? I wasn't sure why, but hearing him speak about his bond with her rubbed me the wrong way.

"Were you in love with her?" I asked him before I could think the question all the way through.

He met my eyes again and searched my face as though his answer were hidden somewhere among my features. The intensity in his gaze made my heart speed up. It felt like a lifetime before he spoke again.

"No, angel. I wasn't in love with her."

I released a breath of air that felt a lot like relief. When I looked back up at him, he appeared to be studying me.

"Does that please you?" he asked, his voice low with curiosity.

Shrugging, I glanced down at my hands and remarked how badly my nails needed a manicure. I stared at them for a long time, hoping he'd forget he asked me a question.

But of course, he didn't.

"Angel—?"

"Yes, it pleases me." I felt my face warm at my admission.

Another stretch of silence wafted between us, but I wasn't brave enough to meet his eyes again, even though I knew that he was staring at me as though I held the key to all of life's mysteries.

He leaned into me, his shoulder brushing up against my own. "Why do you think that is?" he asked tentatively.

The truth was, there were a lot of reasons why that made me happy. Because I had feelings for him. Because I didn't like the idea of him with other women. All of which would further complicate my life at a time when I needed the least amount of complications.

"Because it's one less distraction for me to worry about," I said, deciding to go with the least problematic answer. "You know, if we end up having to work with her."

"I see." He shifted his attention back to the evaporating horizon and ran a hand through his pale hair. "Then you needn't worry about that, angel. For what it's worth, you have my full attention," he said and looked back at me.

I bit my lip, working hard not to let his words sink into my heart.

His gaze immediately dropped to my mouth as a heated look passed through his eyes. "You have for a very long time." He reached out and touched the palm of his hand to my cheek, his thumb brushing softly against my bottom lip.

"I think Cindy would disagree," I said and burrowed my cheek deeper into his hand.

His lip twitched as though trying to suppress a smile.

"You're incredibly cute when you're jealous."

"I'm not jealous," I said and yanked his arm down. That snapped me right out of my daze. "I'm making fun of you—there's a difference."

His smirk morphed into a full-blown grin. "Oh, is that what you were doing?"

"Dominic, get over yourself!"

And now he was laughing. At me. I moved to shove him away from me, but he quickly caught my elbow and used it to pull me in front of him. Locking me against his chest, he wrapped one arm around my shoulder and the other one around my torso, making it so that I couldn't move even if I wanted to. And with the way he was nuzzling his cheek against mine and holding me as though I belonged to him, I wasn't entirely sure I wanted to.

"Dominic…"

"I know, angel," he whispered against my hair, breathing me in. "Just give me this minute and I promise I'll let you go."

The minute came and went quickly, and he was still clutching me to his body. And I was still allowing it to happen. And as much as I didn't want to enjoy it, it felt nice to be held by someone.

Probably a little too nice.

A brisk knock at the front door interrupted our moment, saving me from having to drum up the strength to pull away from him.

"Time's up," I said, my voice cracking at the end.

Dominic grunted and then slowly peeled his arms from me. I straightened out my shirt and watched as he sauntered over to the door, his countenance unreadable. With one hand flattened against the door, he leaned in and peered through the peep hole. He tossed a grin in my direction and then opened the door.

Apparently, he liked what he saw.

"Fancy seeing you here."

"Where is she?" I heard Nikki ask him.

He pulled the door all the way open and ticked his chin in my direction.

Nikki rushed past him and then stopped in her tracks upon seeing me standing by the balcony door.

"I really hope you have a plan," she spit out as she crossed her arms over her chest. "I want that hellspawn out of Trace's body!"

"So do I." My eyes briefly met Dominic's before settling back on Nikki.

"Then start talking, because I need this shit-show over and done with, like yesterday," she said gesturing around us as though we were standing in the midst of said shit-show. "How do we kill him?"

"We don't."

"Excuse you?" Her eyebrows puckered together. "I know I didn't hear that right."

I walked around the back of the couch and then sat down on the arm rest, motioning for her to join me. There weren't any words that could describe how wrong it felt sitting in the hotel room with Nikki by my side as though she were some kind of ally and not the backstabbing bitch who tried to have me offed.

"Alright. Explain," she demanded, as though it were that easy.

How the heck was I going to explain that Trace was Lucifer's vessel for better or worse?

"The thing is…we can't just…like…" Apparently, I couldn't finish sentences anymore.

"Jesus. Just spit it out!"

"I'm not sure we can kill one without killing the other," I said and blew out a frustrated breath.

"They're tethered?" Her eyes flashed with fear and then with something else...with hopelessness.

"Apparently."

"But you *do* have a plan, right?"

"Well, the way I see it, if the Roderick sisters found a way to get Lucifer into Trace's body, then there has to be a way to get him out. And who better to tell us than one of the sisters?"

"And you think they're going to willingly do that for you? They're not one of your little boy-toys, Jemma."

"I'm aware of that, Nikki," I spat back in the same biting tone. "And no, I don't think they're going to tell me anything *willingly*. But they will tell me what I want to know."

She arched her perfectly manicured brow at me. "And how are you planning on pulling that off?"

"By whatever means necessary."

A flicker of amusement flashed through her eyes. "So, you're going to like, what? Waterboard them?"

"If I have to." I shrugged, even though I had no idea what the heck that even was.

Whatever. I could *Google* it.

"And you actually think you're going to get within ten meters of them without their magic blowing you into next Tuesday?"

"No, but that's where you come in."

"Ohhh, I get it. You want them to blow *me* into next Tuesday?" She stood up abruptly. "I'm not interested in going on one of your little suicide missions."

"It's not a suicide mission. Sit down and relax," I said, rolling my eyes at her. "You're not going to be anywhere near them for any of this...I will."

"You?" Her eyebrows shot up with disbelief. "And which army?"

I refused to let that sting. "Look, I'll worry about me and

my army. I just need you and Caleb to disable their magic long enough so that I can get close to them. Together they're unstoppable, but if I can separate one from the pack, they'll be just as vulnerable as the rest of us." And I planned on taking full advantage of that. "You think you can handle that?"

"So, basically, you want me and Caleb to disable their magic so you can snatch one of them up and then beat the information out of her?"

"Yeah. More or less." I really didn't like her patronizing tone. "Unless you have a better idea," I challenged.

Her failure to offer up an alternative solution let me know she didn't have one.

"And what if it doesn't work?" she asked, her tone markedly softer now.

"It will," I said and swallowed thickly.

It had to, because as it stood, I really didn't have a plan B.

22. A SHOT IN THE DARK

Dominic and I spent the next hour ironing out the details of our plan with Nikki. Everything was set and ready to go except one very important factor: We had no actual idea where the sisters were holed up.

"Can you do a locator spell?" I asked, remembering the Roderick sisters doing one for Trace, though in hindsight, the whole thing was probably just a farce. They knew exactly where Trace and my mother were the entire time, being that they were the ones who brought them to Angel's Peak.

Nikki shook her head. "I'd need their blood or hair to do the spell."

"Damn it." We sure as shit didn't have either of those. "How the hell are we going to find them?" I bounced a look between the two of them, hoping one of them had another idea. "They could be anywhere!"

Literally anywhere on this planet and beyond.

"We start with the most obvious places and narrow it down from there," offered Dominic.

"That could take weeks, maybe even months. We don't

have time for trial and error."

"Then what do you suggest, angel?"

"I don't know, but there has to be a better way. Maybe a Seer could help us. Or maybe there's another spell we're not thinking about." I turned to Nikki for confirmation. She appeared to be lost in her own world—probably fantasizing about her romp in the sack with devil-Trace. "Nikki?"

"I think I might know where they are," she said suddenly, her aquamarine eyes glimmering like two precious stones that had the power to compel and destroy all in one look.

"Where?" Dominic and I asked at the same time.

"Trace's house."

"That's a little basic, don't you think?" chided Dominic.

"Trust me, they're there. I'm sure of it."

"What makes you say that?" I asked, curious how she'd gotten to that conclusion.

"He made a really big deal about not going there. I didn't think anything about it at the time, but I'm guessing that was the reason why," she said as she waggled her eyebrows.

Well, it was a bit of a stretch, but at this point, it was the only lead we had.

"I'll ask Ben to track the house tomorrow night," I said, ready to get this plan off the ground. I wasn't exactly thrilled about involving any more people in this, but this was Trace we were talking about, and Ben was his best friend. Helping us is exactly what he'd want to be doing. "How long after he confirms their location can you do the spell?"

"I just need to get a couple of things," she said as she stood up from the couch. "But I'll be ready by tomorrow."

"Get whatever you need now," I said, making sure not to mince words. "This is our one and only chance. If we mess this up, they'll know we're coming and we won't get another opportunity to get close again." Of that I was sure.

"I'm already on it," she said as she smoothed out her dark jeans before starting towards the door. "You just worry about you and make sure you have that army of yours ready," she said over her shoulder.

Little did she know, my little army of one had been ready and waiting to end those bitches the moment they shoved that mega-demon into Trace's body.

"I'll call you on loverboy's phone when I have everything," she added and then left the room, slamming the door shut behind herself.

I rolled my eyes at the door.

As irritated as I was of having to work with Nikki, I was glad she came through for us. And by *us*, I meant Trace. I knew the only reason she was doing this was for him, but that was one hundred percent good enough for me.

My gaze slid across the room to Dominic. He was leaning against the balcony railing, both hands buried in his pocket as he watched me with an undecipherable look in his eyes. He was probably wondering how I'd managed to drag him all the way into the middle of a war that had nothing to do with him and was conspiring to come up with a way to get out of it.

I'd save him the trouble.

"There's still time for you to get out of this," I said as I made my way over to him. He needed to know I didn't expect him to do anything for me. Especially not to help me save my boyfriend from Lucifer—the freaking devil himself. No one in their right mind would expect that of someone. "I wouldn't blame you if you did."

"I know you wouldn't." He tilted his head to the side and studied my features, all the while his own expression remaining a blank mask that gave nothing away.

I folded my arms across my chest, though I wasn't sure if it was because of the light rain peppering my skin or because of the intense way he was staring at me. "Is that a no?"

"A firm one." He smiled lazily.

It was beyond me how he managed to remain so composed at a time when so much was at stake. Obviously, he wasn't getting the gravity of the situation. He wasn't understanding that this was life or death for all of us, including him.

"You do realize that this could go really bad tomorrow, don't you?" I asked and then bit the inside of my cheek.

"Yes, I'm aware of that, angel."

"Are you sure?" I said and took a step closer. "Because you seem really calm, being that tomorrow could be the last day of your entire existence."

"I've had a good life." He smirked, flashing me that lopsided grin that was all his. "I suppose tomorrow's as good a day as any."

"That's not funny."

His smile slipped away. "I can take care of myself, angel. You needn't worry about me."

"Yeah, well, I can't help it," I muttered.

His eyebrows drew together as my admission dangled in the air between us like a piece of dirty laundry. I couldn't figure out for the life of me why I couldn't stop confessing every little feeling or thought I had about him to him. It was as though there were no other place for my foot to go except all the way into my mouth.

"You worry about me?" he asked, his honeyed voice low but penetrating.

How could he ask me that? "You know that I do." I shifted on my foot and quickly tried to change the subject. "We should go back inside. It's starting to rain."

Dominic made no attempt to move. Instead, he continued watching me, his eyebrows drawn together closely.

The air suddenly felt heavy around us, like a magical force

working to push us together—to bring us to that borderless place I dared not venture. I had to put the brakes on.

"Look, it's not a big deal. I just don't want anything bad to happen to you is all."

"Nor I you."

"Then it's settled. You want me safe and I want you safe, and that's all there is to it. Two friends wanting to keep each other safe." It tasted like a lie even as I spoke the words, but I spit them out anyway. Deep down I knew there was so much more to it, but I wasn't even *almost* ready to fess up to any of it. "Agreed?"

"If you say so, angel." He reached out and tucked a strand of my hair behind my ear.

The brief contact made me shiver, but I refused to let it sidetrack me. "I do say so."

And that wasn't all I was saying. The closer we got to facing off against the sisters, the more nervous I became about all the ways it could go wrong.

"No matter what happens tomorrow, I'll be okay as long as this stays around my neck," I said as I wrapped my fingers around the Amulet, grateful for once that I had this magical safety net to catch me when I would inevitably fall. "But if you're seriously planning on coming tomorrow, you're going to need my help whether you want to admit it or not."

"Is that right?" Typical Dominic taking everything I say as some kind of challenge.

My eyes never left his as I carefully rolled back the sleeve of my shirt and exposed my skin to him. His gaze dropped from my eyes to my wrist before making their way up again.

"What's this?" he asked, raising an eyebrow at me.

"You know what it is."

His eyes darkened as he took me in. "Are you offering yourself to me, angel?" There was no mistaking the daring turn his voice had taken.

"Yes." I swallowed hard, my throat already bone dry. "For your protection."

We both knew that the more of my blood he had in his system, the more protected he would be if something were to go wrong. On the surface, that was all that this was about, though if I dared to go just a little deeper, I knew that there were so many more reasons I wanted this, reasons that were tormenting me just below the surface.

We both knew it, and yet he still hadn't made the slightest move to take the bait. All he did was stand there and stare at me, burrowing himself into my soul with those penetrating eyes.

"Why are you just standing there?" I shifted my feet, still holding my arm out.

"I'm enjoying the view," he said with a lazy smile.

"I mean, why are you not—?" I bit my bottom lip as I tried to figure out a less vulgar way to ask him why he wasn't feeding off me. "Are you not…hungry?"

"For you?" he asked as his pupils dilated. "Always."

A strange sensation fluttered through my stomach. It felt a lot like butterflies.

"Then why aren't you taking my blood?"

He cocked his head to the side, as though considering my question, debating it.

Slow burning seconds came and went until it seemed as though I were standing there for an eternity. The rain continued to fall on us, harder than before, though I could no longer feel the chill over my heated skin.

I dropped my arm and frowned. "Is this about what you said to me yesterday? About not laying a finger on me? Because I'm not doing this for me," I quickly clarified, though it came out far too speedy and defensive to sound truthful. "I'm just trying to help you."

"Is that what you're doing?"

I clenched my jaw shut and glared at him. The corner of his lip twitched as though he were fighting back a smirk.

Apparently, this was amusing to him.

"You know what? Forget it. If you don't want my blood, then I'm not going to force it on you," I said and spun on my heel to leave, but he quickly reached out and grabbed a hold of my wrist, pulling me back to him.

Torturous electricity prickled my body as he pressed me all the way up against his chest, our bodies separated only by a hairbreadth. My lips parted to protest, but he quickly pressed his finger against my mouth and silenced me.

"One of these days, you're going to have to face your truth, angel. And for my sake and yours, I hope that day comes soon."

"What's that supposed to mean?" I asked, my heart steadily hammering a hole through my chest.

"I think you know precisely what that means." His eyes flicked down to my mouth.

"Are you saying I want this?"

"You tell me."

Chills fluttered over my skin at the sound of his fangs releasing, and I immediately bristled, knowing he'd done that on purpose. He knew full well that I'd react to it. He was a total prick that way.

"That's not fair, Dominic. I never asked for any of this," I said, struggling to keep the tremble out of my voice. It was taking every ounce of strength I had just to stop myself from sinking into him—into the bloodbond.

"No, you didn't," he agreed and then captured my jaw, angling my face up. "But you want it now, don't you, angel?" he asked and then slowly lowered his head to my neck, gently grazing his lips and teeth against my skin.

It took every bit of willpower I had not to climb up his

body like a feral animal. After all, that was exactly what he wanted: me losing control over myself...throwing myself at him...begging him.

I'd be damned if I gave him the satisfaction.

He lifted his head when I didn't answer, his eyes settling on my mouth. "It's a simple question, love."

"No, it's not." It was loaded and complicated, and the consequences impossible to carry.

My heart galloped furiously in my chest for too many reasons to name, but mostly because he was still staring at my lips as though he wanted to kiss them—to consume them—and I wasn't entirely sure I had the strength to stop him if he tried. Something was seriously wrong with me, and the sickness was growing stronger by the day.

"Please stop looking at me like that," I pleaded, my voice almost as weak as my knees were.

"Like what, angel?" His gaze lifted for a brief second.

"Like you're going to kiss me," I said breathlessly.

"Do you want me to kiss you?" he asked and then met my eyes again.

It took me a long moment to choke out an answer. "No."

Grinning, he leaned in beside my ear and whispered, "Does your body know that?"

I didn't have to look down at myself to know that my fingernails were digging into his lower back and my traitorous skin was practically glowing from the heat.

Instead, I glared at him. "I know what you're trying to do, and it's not going to work."

We'd already had this conversation back at the Manor. Regardless of what secret signals my stupid body was sending him through the bond, I'd made my position clear.

At least, I thought I had.

He smirked though it melted away just as soon as it

appeared. "You can relax, angel. I have no intention of kissing you or doing anything else to you for that matter," he said and released me from his grip.

My arms flopped to my sides as I looked back at him disbelievingly.

"That is what you wanted, isn't it?"

"Yes." I bit my lip to keep my shoulders from slumping. "But what about tomorrow? What if something happens to you—?"

"It won't," he said, as though his saying so was even remotely enough to calm my unease.

I needed a guarantee. One written in blood.

"You can't just stop cold turkey. What about the bloodbond? The repercussions?" We both knew that the longer we refused to exchange blood, the more brutal the withdrawals would become. And since I was already hyperventilating like a junkie who hadn't had her fix in days, I wasn't particularly interested in finding out how much worse it could get.

He stroked the back of my cheek again, and my stomach tightened.

"Relax, angel. We'll be fine," he said as he slipped his hand into his pockets and produced two small vials. One of them was empty, but the other one looked like it had been filled with thick, red blood.

"For the withdrawals—as per my brother's recommendation."

"You can't be serious." I gaped at him. When it became clear he was in fact serious, I reached forward and snatched the vials from his hand to get a better look at them. I quickly turned the full one around with my fingers, confirming that it was indeed blood. "Since when do you listen to Gabriel?"

"Since it became what's best for you."

My gaze snapped to his. "So, all of this is for my benefit?"

"Entirely." His jaw muscles feathered as he smoldered me with his eyes. "I wish to be many things to you, angel, but a regret is not one of them."

"Well, I guess it's all settled then. Problem solved, right?"

Ducking his chin, he slipped his hands into his pocket and stood there stoically—completely in control. But something about the way his eyes flared told me he was working hard to stay on his best behavior.

I took a small step back, my eyes never departing from his as an uncomfortable feeling of disappointment settled deep in my belly. I didn't understand why the disappointment was there at all, but I didn't stick around to question it.

"I'll have this ready for you by morning," I said and then forced my feet to turn around. I could feel his eyes on my back as I walked away from him, but I never did muster up the courage to look back at him.

23. A DREAMWALK TO REMEMBER

Back in the privacy of my hotel room, I sat down on the edge of the bed and looked down at the vial of blood in my shaky hands. I still had so much to do tonight, so much to mentally prepare myself for, and I wasn't particularly looking forward to any of it. Especially the part where I had to call Ben and tell him what had happened to his best friend.

As much as it pained me to admit it, I was going to need a little push to get me through the night.

Flipping the cap off, I brought the vial to my lips and then tossed it down. The minute the enchanted elixir was in my system, I immediately felt my anxiety ebbing away until nothing remained but me and blood's magic.

I sighed and then sucked in a deep, cleansing breath.

Honestly, if pharmaceutical companies ever got a hold of Rev blood, they'd be hitting the jackpot. There wasn't anything like it, and although I didn't feel great about needing it, the benefits usually outweighed my disdain for it.

Finally feeling like myself again, I hopped off the bed and sauntered over to the phone to call Ben.

After a very long and tiring conversation with him, explaining everything from what happened at Angel's Peak up until the plan we had in place for tomorrow, I changed into a long t-shirt and dragged myself to bed. Even though I had intended on training a little tonight, by the end of the call, I was entirely too drained.

Somehow, the simple task of having to explain all of this to Ben in plain English had been so much harder than actually living through it. Probably because a part of me was still in denial, living through it like some dream—some nightmare I could skirt in and out of as needed. But the more people I involved in this, the realer everything became for me and the harder it became to bounce out of it.

The truth was, I was scared out of my wits. Scared of what tomorrow would bring. Scared of screwing this up. Scared of losing Trace forever.

I had to think of everything, to cover all my bases, because if one little thing went wrong, the entire plan would fall to pieces and it would be all my fault. That was a kind of pressure I'd never felt in my life. It was the kind of pressure that could buckle your knees just by thinking about it too long.

So, I wouldn't.

For now, all I could do was pray to everything above that the sisters would be at Trace's and that Nikki's spell would work. I knew that if I could just get one of them alone, I could make her tell me everything I needed to know to bring Trace home and send Lucifer back to where he belonged.

But what if there was no way to get him out?

What if Trace was really gone?

I shook away the petrifying thought.

There *would* be a way.

There had to be.

This life wouldn't be that punishing—not after everything

I'd already lost. I had to believe there was a happy ending waiting for me at the end of all this grief. I had to believe this would all work out.

Turning on my side, I tried to find a comfortable position to fall asleep in. I needed to talk to Trace. I needed to clue him in to the plan for tomorrow, and there was only one way I knew how to do that.

Dreamwalking.

I'd managed to do a little digging since the last time he visited, and it turned out that *dreamwalking* really was a thing. A *Reaper* thing. From what I understood, he had the ability to astral project himself into my dreams, secretively meeting me in my subconscious. I didn't fully understand the mechanics, nor did I really care to—just as long as it worked.

And it would work, because while I couldn't enter his subconscious, I could force him to enter mine.

Dreaming about Dominic was always effortless. Those dreams came to me even when I didn't want them to. Even back when I wanted nothing more than to force him out of my existence. So, of course, when I'd fallen asleep thinking about him, the subsequent dream that followed was no surprise. It never was, and yet, this dream was different.

It felt too real to be just a dream, yet too hazy and disjointed to be anything but.

For one, there was no sign of the red sky. Just the same old tired rain battering down against the windows as Dominic and I stood in his bedroom at Huntington Manor. There was a deep and penetrating agony that touched every part of my body. A pain so unforgiving that it made it hard for me to take in air. Even in this dream state, I knew something had gone terribly wrong and there was nothing I could do to fix it.

He cupped the sides of my face, forcing me out of the

thralls of pain and back to the present moment. I leaned my body into him, pushing myself all the way against him in a way I'd never done before. It was brazened and suggestive, and suddenly, he was kissing me, walking me backwards until my legs hit the foot of his bed.

He pulled his mouth from mine and said something to me, though the words were drowned out by the thunderous sound of my pounding heart. His mouth stopped moving, his eyes probing me as he waited for a response. For some kind of sign that I'd gotten his message.

I kissed him hard on the mouth.

Gripping my waist, he spun us around and then sat down on the bed, pulling me onto his lap. My soaking hair hung in ropes along my face, and my clothing clung to my body like a second skin. Transparent and exposing. But I didn't care. I wanted him to see me. To see *all* of me.

His eyes drank me in, flirting over my body like butterflies as he pushed my hair over my shoulders.

His mouth found mine again as his hands drifted down to the edge of my shirt. I sucked in a breath as he lifted it up over my head and tossed it onto the floor behind us. There was a very real and conscious part of me that knew where this was going, that knew I'd come here for exactly this reason, so when he slid us backwards on the bed and pulled me down on top of him, I went easily.

I wasn't the Slayer who brought on the apocalypse, and he wasn't the Revenant I was bloodbonded to. We were just two people riding our attraction for each other in the only place it was allowed to happen.

He touched his lips to mine tenderly as I slid my hands between our bodies and unbuttoned his shirt. I wanted to feel his bare skin against mine, to know if he felt as good as he looked.

His Adam's apple bobbed as he gazed up at me and mouthed something. I still couldn't hear what he was saying, but I knew that he was telling me that he loved me. I could see it on his face, feel it in my heart.

And in that moment, right there and then, I loved him too.

The sound of someone clearing their throat snapped me out of my lust-filled haze. With my palms still flattened against dream-Dominic's bare chest, I looked over my shoulder and found Trace standing at the foot of the bed, watching us.

Guilt sucker-punched me in the stomach as I took in the pained look in his eyes.

Mortified, I quickly tried to climb off Dominic, though my stupid foot caught under the sheet and tangled me up. In my clumsy rush to dismount him, I stumbled off the bed and landed butt first on the hard, wooden floor.

This dream was quickly becoming a nightmare.

"I know what this looks like," I said to Trace as I scrambled back to my feet. I tried not to look back at Dominic, who was still lying half-naked on the bed where I'd left him. He hadn't moved nor made a sound. Probably because this was my dream and I didn't want him to.

Trace flexed the muscles in his jaw, his eyes fixed on Dominic.

"I needed to talk to you, and this was the only way I knew to get you here." A clap of thunder exploded outside the windows as I closed the distance between us. "I'm sorry you had to see that. It didn't mean anything."

The painful look in his eyes intensified at my words, though I wasn't sure why.

He slowly peeled his eyes away from Dominic and finally met my gaze. "What did you need to talk to me about?" he asked, his voice low and hollow.

I hated that I'd just done this to him, that I'd just caused him all this pain.

It's for a good reason, I reminded myself and then remembered that I had to talk to him.

"We have a plan. Is it safe to talk here?" I asked and looked over my shoulder, half expecting Lucifer to drop into my nightmare and really make this the world's absolute worst dream.

"For now." He nodded. "I don't have much time, though."

"We're going after the Roderick sisters tomorrow. If anyone knows how to get Lucifer out of your body, it's them."

He squeezed his eyes shut. "Jemma—"

"I just need you to hold on a little longer, okay?" I said and slipped my arms around his waist, wanting to feel his warmth again. "I wish this never happened to you, Trace, but I swear to God, I'm going to make it right. We're going to bring you home. I promise."

"Jemma, I'm not coming home," he said and gently pushed my arms down.

My bottom lip sagged, though words never made it passed my lips. I couldn't fathom why he would say that, and the truth was, it stunned me silent. Had he already given up? Did he not *want* to come home?

"I don't understand," I said as hurt and confusion soaked into my voice.

His eyes veered back to Dominic, though he wasn't looking at him as much as he was looking through him as though lost in some distant memory only he could see. An icy chill scratched its way down my back as he turned back to me.

"I need you to listen to me," he said as he picked up my chin. His eyes were a storm of pain and loss and regret, and the more I looked into them, the more I wanted to cry.

"I want you to move on with your life and forget about me. If that means being with Dominic, then so be it," he said speedily without looking away from me. "I know he loves you, and I know he'd protect you with his life if you needed it. Right now, that's the only thing that giving me any kind of relief—"

"What?! Stop it!" I said and shoved his hand down. "Why are you saying this to me?"

He lowered his head as moisture filled his eyes. "I need to know you'll be taken care of and that you'll be happy—"

"I *will* be happy—with you! Just like we promised each other."

He started to shake his head.

"Why are you doing this? Why are you giving up already? Is it because you think I can't do this? Because I can. I swear to God, Trace, I won't stop until I find a way."

"Dammit, Jemma. Don't you get it? There *isn't* a way!"

His words slapped the air out of my lungs as the walls around us shook, flickering in and out of existence.

"You don't know that."

"Yes, I do." He pushed his hands through his hair as his body momentarily faded out like a lambent light trying to hold on. "I'm as much a part of Lucifer as he is me. I know his thoughts. I know what he has planned, and I know there isn't a way to separate him from this vessel. Not without killing both of us, and I've already accepted that."

Tears were dripping down my cheeks faster than I could wipe them away.

"The Order knows how to kill him. You have to listen to them, Jemma. It's the only way to stop him."

"No," I said, shaking my head, because I knew exactly what that meant. It meant killing him.

Something I already knew I could never, ever do.

"You can't ask that of me, Trace. You can't."

He reached out pulled me into his arms. "I love you, Jemma. I'll always love you, but you have to let me go."

"How am I supposed to do that?"

"By putting them before us," he said, his voice echoing ominously in my head. "Let me go, Jemma. Find a way to do it, or everyone dies." His voice grew weaker—more distant.

I shook my head and sobbed into his shirt, but he just kept going—kept spearing me with his words.

"The blood will be on your hands, and you won't be able to live with that. I know you'll do the right thing. I know you'll make me proud." He squeezed me harder then, and I knew he was telling me goodbye.

But I wasn't ready for goodbye.

We still had our whole lives to live. "Don't you dare leave me, Trace. I can't lose you!"

"You won't," he said and kissed the top of my head. "I'll always be with you, Jemma. Always."

"Dammit, Trace! Don't leave me!" A guttural cry ripped out of my body as I tried to hold onto him, to keep him with me forever, but it was no use. He faded away until nothing but air remained in my arms.

I fell to the floor in a heap and sobbed until I woke myself up.

24. WAKE AND BAKE

My cheeks were wet with tears as I sprang up in the dimly lit room and looked over at the clock. I was back in my hotel bed, and though my body never physically left the bed, my mind and heart had, and I wasn't sure I was going to be able to recover from what had just happened.

Trace had given up.

He'd already resigned himself to his death, to his own slaughter by my hands. How could he expect me to do that to him? To kill him. To give up on him. After everything we went through. After everything we promised each other.

Something wasn't sitting well with me.

It wasn't like him to give up so easily. Trace was a fighter. A leader. Was he throwing in the towel because he really believed there was no way to save him, or was it something else?

The more I thought about it, the more the pieces fell together. Hadn't this been exactly what Morgan had seen in her vision all those months ago? Me killing Trace. His blood on my hands. Maybe he knew this day was coming all along. Maybe he believed this was his destiny. He sure as hell didn't believe there was a way to bring him back.

But I did.

I refused to give up on him, to surrender to these faulty destinies that were drawn up by someone else's hands. I would find my own way out of this mess, even if it killed me, and I was dragging Trace's Reaper ass right along with me, whether he wanted it or not.

Deciding to ignore everything Trace had said, I got out of bed and stalked to the shower. The sooner I got this day started, the closer I'd be to bringing him home again.

I stood under the cascading water for several minutes, letting the warmth pour over my skin. Most of the bruises had long since disappeared, and the stitches were almost completely healed. I wasn't sure if it was because of my own Angel bloodline or if it was because of the vampire blood I'd been drinking. Either way, I was relieved to be back at full strength, because now more than ever, I was going to need it.

Stepping out of the shower, I grabbed a towel from the shelf and dried myself. After twisting my hair into a messy top bun, I brushed my teeth and got myself dressed. I didn't have a change of clothes with me because I was bright like that, so I had to get back into my outfit from yesterday. There was something epically wrong about getting into dirty clothes after a nice clean shower.

Whatever. I'd been covered in much worse.

Twisting the doorknob, I yanked open the door and nearly had a heart attack at the sight of Dominic standing in the doorway. The smug grin on his face told me he'd been standing there for a while.

"Breakfast?"

"I'm good, thanks," I said and tried to step forward, but he didn't bother getting out of my way.

"You have to eat something," he insisted.

"I'm not hungry." After all, I scoffed back a vial of his blood last night, which would surely hold me over better than any eggs and bacon could.

Mmm bacon.

"I'm sure you're not, angel, but you're still eating something." He picked up my hand and towed me out of the bathroom and through the bedroom.

Begrudgingly, I followed him, knowing that he wasn't going to let up until I shoved a few bites into my mouth. He walked us into the living room to a small table with two chairs by the window. The table was outfitted with a crisp white tablecloth and several covered dishes that I couldn't see the contents of but could definitely smell.

"Sit," he ordered, and I did. But not before rolling my eyes at him.

He pulled the lid off the first dish, revealing a fully loaded omelet with a side serving of fresh fruit. My eyes slipped shut as I breathed in the delicious scent. I could have sworn I wasn't hungry, and yet my stomach moaned with hunger pangs upon seeing the food.

"I guess I'm a little hungry after all," I said as he poured me a glass of orange juice and then sat down on the chair across from me.

He didn't have a plate in front of him, but he did have a glass of something thick and red with a celery stick sticking out of it.

"I hope that's a Bloody Mary," I said, eyeing it suspiciously.

"Emphasis on the Bloody." He winked.

I paused, gauging if he was joking or not. He wasn't.

"Where did you get the—?" I shot up from my chair. "Did you attack someone?" I screeched, looking around the room, half expecting to see a dead body slumped in the corner.

He leaned back in his chair and clicked his tongue. "Honestly, angel. Do you take me for some kind of animal?"

I wasn't sure how to answer that, being that he was half vampire half wolf.

Giving his head a shake, he said, "I called for delivery, and I assure you, angel, no one was hurt in the processing of my meal." With that, he rose the glass to me and took a long, hearty sip.

He had to be telling the truth. He wouldn't be stupid enough to attack someone with me here. Besides, after witnessing his date with Cindy or whatever her name was, he was clearly capable of finding willing participants.

"Now can we please enjoy our meal together?" he asked, his pale blond hair looking almost white in the light of day.

Rolling my neck, I sat back down in my chair and picked up my fork. I intended to only take a few bites just to get him off my back, but once I started eating, I couldn't seem stop myself. A few short minutes later, I'd already wiped my plate clean and even had to stop myself from eating the decorative garnishing.

When I looked back up at him, I found him smirking at me.

"What? Haven't you ever seen a girl eat before?" Probably not, I thought, remember how rail thin Cindy was.

"I was just remarking how beautiful you look when you're *satisfied*." His grin widened at the corners as something sinful flickered across his eyes. "I'd like to see more of it."

A blush swept across my cheeks. "Well, you'll see it good and long when I jam Lucifer's ass back in his tomb."

"I'm looking forward to it," he said and took another swig of his drink—meal. Whatever.

I reached in my back pocket and pulled out the now-empty vial of blood from my jeans. "Thank you for this," I said and handed it back to him.

"My pleasure, angel."

I reached into my other pocket and pulled out the other vial—the one that was meant for my blood. "I didn't fill it," I admitted and then tossed it back to him.

He caught it without taking his eyes off me. "May I ask why not?"

"Because you're going to drink my blood the good old-fashioned way."

He relaxed back in his chair and stared back at me. "Is that right?"

"Yes. At least for today you are." I stood up from the table and began rolling back the sleeve of my shirt. "I need you alive, and since we've only ever tested my blood directly from the source, that's how you're getting it."

Chances were, my blood would work just as good if he drank it from a teacup than if he drank it from my vein, but we'd never actually tested that out, and I wasn't about to start taking chances. Especially not today.

Dominic parted his lips to say something, but a hard knock at the door interrupted him.

"I'll get it," I said since I was already standing. I didn't even get a chance to start walking before Dominic was already at the door, looking through the peephole.

"It's the witch," he said and then opened the door.

My stomach bottomed out as Nikki barged into the room, her expression twisted with apprehension.

"What is it? What happened?"

"The hellspawn happened."

I looked back at her, annoyed. "What about the hellspawn, Nikki?"

"Oh, nothing. Just that he's currently meandering around Weston." Her eyes darted back and forth between me and

Dominic as she waited for us to say something. "At *our* school."

"What?" My head recoiled. "Why would he be at school?"

"Exactly," she said, planting her hands on her slim hips. "Something's up. I can smell it."

My gaze quickly careened back to Dominic.

"I'll get my coat," he said and then took off for his room.

"Did he say anything to you?" I asked, trying to get as much information from her as possible.

"He didn't get a chance to. I high-tailed it out of there and came straight here as soon as I spotted him."

"What the hell does he want with Weston Academy?" I asked, mostly to myself.

"After you," said Dominic as he rejoined us by the door.

One by one, we filed out of the room and made our way to the elevators.

"Was he talking to anyone?" I asked as I pushed the button for the lobby.

"Not that I noticed."

"It doesn't make any sense," I said as the elevator slowly came to a stop on the floor below us.

An old couple with an adorable white Poodle walked onto the elevator. I smiled politely and then rode in silence the rest of the way down.

"We'll take my car," said Dominic as we walked through the front doors of the hotel.

One minute he was walking beside me and then next he was groaning in agony as a very distinct sizzling noise stopped him in his tracks.

"Oh, my God!" I yelled, realizing he was being charred by the sun. Without thinking, I ripped off my jean jacket and threw it over his head as I hauled him back into the safety of the building.

"What the hell was that?" asked Nikki as I grabbed Dominic's face and inspected it.

"Shit! It's really bad," I cried as I looked over his features. There were visible sores all over his once-pristine face that looked a lot like third degree burns.

"It's fine, angel."

"You're completely burnt, Dominic! It's not fine!" I lifted my hand to touch him, to somehow magically rebuild him, but he quickly flinched away from my touch.

"It'll heal, angel. Just give it a minute." He gently brought my hands down and glanced over my shoulder, glaring at the sunlight that had nearly cooked him to the bone. "I wasn't out there long enough to cause any real damage."

But the fact that there was any damage at all made one thing clear:

"The Order must have sealed the rift." And by rift, I meant the big giant hole in Sanguinarium that was allowing Revenants to daywalk.

"I'd say so." His features darkened as he let that settle in.

I looked him over again and released a breath upon noticing his wounds had already begun disappearing.

Thank God for accelerating healing.

"So, now what?" asked Nikki with her hands plastered back on her hips. "How are we supposed to get to Weston with Sir-Bakes-A-Lot?"

Dominic scowled at her.

"Nothing's changed. We'll just take your car," I said to her and then turned back to Dominic. "Don't leave the hotel. I'll meet you back here in an hour."

I started to turn on my heel, but he promptly grabbed my elbow and hauled me back.

"You don't actually think you're going there without me, do you?"

I pulled my wrist free and glared at him. "I'm perfectly capable of getting myself there without you."

"It's not the navigational part I'm worried about," he said and leaned closer. "You're walking into a trap, angel, and I'll be damned if I let you do that alone."

"I'm aware of how much of a bad idea this is, Dominic, but what choice do I have? There's hundreds of innocent people there. My *friends* included. I'm not just going to hide out in a hotel and leave them all to his mercy."

"Why not?" he asked, completely serious.

"Because I—look, this isn't up for debate. I'm going!" I took half a step before he grabbed my hand again and held it, though this time, he didn't say anything.

My gaze lifted from where he was holding me to his eyes, and I faltered.

There was so much worry swirling in them, so much fear. I'd never seen that kind of emotion from him before and certainly never so blatantly aimed at *me*.

Realizing what this was really about, I closed the gap between us and then lifted on my toes so that I could whisper in his ear. "I promise I'm coming back. I have the Amulet. Just trust me." I tried to pull back to read his eyes, to see if the fear had left them, but he quickly slinked his arm around my waist and held me there against him in a sweet embrace.

"Don't make me walk out into the sun to come find you, angel," he warned, his voice a quiet whisper against my ear. "Because I will," he said and then released me from his hold. Hearing his message loud and clear, I smiled at him once more and then walked out of the hotel lobby with Nikki freaking Parker by my side.

25. DEVIL IN THE DETAILS

A cold chill crept down my spine as Nikki and I walked through the front doors of Weston Academy. The hallways were brimming with students, laughing and chattering without a care in the world, completely clueless to the fact that they were currently occupying the same building as the Devil himself. This could very well be the last day of their lives for all they knew, and not a single one of them could be bothered to look up from whatever it was they were doing.

I had no idea what Lucifer was doing here in my school, but I imagined it was nothing good. An intense feeling of foreboding slipped under my skin as I turned the corner. The building was filled with innocent, unsuspecting kids, and Lucifer knew that. This really was the perfect place to cause a whole lot of devastation.

"We need to figure out a way to get all these people out of here," I said to Nikki as we stalked the hallways.

"Well, don't look at me. I need time to prepare for a spell like that," she said sounding a tad bit defensive.

"Cover me," I said and then cut in front of her. Plastering

my back against the wall, I motioned for her to come and stand in front of me. "Just pretend you're talking to me."

"And what exactly would you like me to say?" she said and crossed her arms over the chest. "Maybe I should start with how ridiculous we look standing here pretending to talk when we're supposed to be finding Lucifer."

"Yeah, sure. Totally," I said, and scanned the area around us. When I was sure no one was looking at us, I took a sideways step and then yanked down the red lever that sounded the fire alarm.

The blaring bell blasted throughout the school, causing the students and teachers to rush frantically towards the exits.

"Nice one." Nikki nodded her approval, looking as though she were actually impressed. "Now what?"

"Now you go outside with everyone else and I find Lucifer."

"By yourself?" She arched an eyebrow at me.

"It's what he wants," I said, and while I had no actual proof that that was the case, I felt it in the pit of my stomach.

"Fine by me. Just make sure you come back in one piece," she said and took a step back. "You know, for Trace's sake."

I nodded and watched as she pivoted on her heel and then disappeared around the corner we'd been standing near.

Nervous adrenaline swarmed through my body as I ambled down the corridor by myself, carefully checking each classroom as I passed them by.

I knew he was in here somewhere. It was just a matter of finding him, and I would, no matter how long I had to walk these halls to do it. By the time I made it to the back of the building, the entire school was barren and eerily quiet.

This was it, the end of the line. And then just like that, I knew I wasn't alone anymore.

"Nice to see you again," said a familiar voice from over my shoulder. Everything in me clenched up as the sound of his voice registered as Trace's.

I turned slowly and faced Lucifer.

"Judging by your lack of a bodyguard, I take it the Revenant received my gift this morning?" he asked and then smiled, setting off Trace's dimples at the same time.

I narrowed my eyes at him. "That was you? You closed the rift?"

"Of course," he said and bowed his head. "I told you before, Daughter. I'm not all bad. I can do good too."

"Right," I scoffed, because I already knew from Engel that Lucifer and his Dark Legion despised Revenants. Simply put, they viewed them as dispensable lesser beings. Not to mention my constant bodyguard happened to be one. "I already know you hate Revenants, so stop pretending you stopped them from daywalking for anyone but yourself."

He grinned darkly. "You've been doing your homework."

He had no idea. "Why are we here?" I asked, cutting right to the point.

He took a small step towards me. My muscles tensed as I fought back the urge to cower away from him even though we still had a good five feet of distance separating us.

"How else was I supposed to get you to come out and play?" he asked sweetly.

Icy pinpricks covered my skin as my throat twisted into a knot. "Well, here I am. What game are we playing?"

"I like the way you cut right to the chase. No foreplay, no skirting around the topic."

"Kind of like what you're trying to do right now?"

Trace's dimples made another appearance, and my heart sank. I was starting to get the feeling that he brought me here just to torture me.

"What do you want from me, Lucifer?"

"The same as I've always wanted."

"Which is what?"

A dark glimmer passed through Trace's eyes. "To spend time with you, Daughter. To gain your friendship, your trust, and maybe even your allegiance someday."

I could hear sirens blaring in the distance, but I kept my eyes fixed on the devil. "I already told you I'm not interested."

"That you did," he said and pursed his lips as he took another careful step in my direction. "And I was willing to let that go. To give you time and space to come around on your own. Because you *will* come around. It's really only a matter of time." His smile slipped away, revealing something much darker and deadlier in its place. "But then a little birdie told me you were at Temple yesterday, and that made me very unhappy. I don't like being unhappy, Daughter."

My heart stuttered in my chest, as though it couldn't figure out what speed to beat at.

"I suppose I should thank you for that," he continued thoughtfully.

"For what?"

"For giving me another reason to despise them even more than I already do."

"The Council?" I asked, not sure I was following any of this.

"The Order," he corrected, his tone growing rougher and more agitated by the second. "Misguided abominations that should have been eradicated a long time ago. The entire lot of them!"

I swallowed the brick-sized knot in my throat and took a small step back. He was getting amped up, and I really didn't want to be around for that.

"Did you know they were the ones that locked me away in that hell tomb?" he asked, but he didn't bother waiting for my answer. "Thought I'd be in there for all of eternity too. That is, until you came along." He dipped his chin as if to salute me.

"There was nothing they could do to stop the one destined to bring me back. No, sir. Not with that Amulet," he said, eyeing it with desire.

My hand instinctively moved up to my neck and clutched the Amulet.

"But I digress," he said as he lifted his hand and waved the conversation off. "None of that matters. Not now. Vengeance is upon us. I've been given a second chance, and I intend to make good on it, starting with that no-good Temple of yours."

The hairs on the back of my head shot up.

"I just needed to make sure you were safe first." His dimples blinked back at me as his lips pulled into a crooked grin. "Don't say I never did anything for you, Daughter," he added with a wink.

"What the hell did you do?!" I bellowed, panic exploding under my skin as I realized this was all just a diversion.

Temple had been his target all along.

"See, that's the funny thing about Hellfire," he said, his eyes pooling with wickedness as I backed away. "There isn't a single thing on earth that could put it out."

I kicked off the ground and ran for my life.

26. HELLFIRE

A large crowd had already gathered across the street, watching morbidly as the firemen rushed in and out of the burning building. Even the earth-shattering thunderstorm that had started on the way over to Temple couldn't stop the flames from slashing unrelentingly into the overcast sky.

I stood on shaky legs, taking the chaos around me. Smoke consumed the neighborhood for several blocks in each direction, making it hard to pull in a satisfying breath. My eyes drifted frantically over the slew of people lying scattered on the sidewalks, paramedics giving them oxygen and tending to their wounds as the firemen continued bringing out victim after victim after victim.

I knew then there was no way they would be able to get everyone out. The building was too big and the fire too unstoppable. How many lives would be lost?

How many people will be dead because I refused to do the impossible—because I refused to kill Trace?

"Get back," yelled one of the firemen, directing the crowd to move further back onto the other side of the street. But I couldn't do that. My feet were frozen in place as I stared up at the bluish tinged flames, petrified to my core that my sister and Gabriel were in that building.

Bile shot up into the back of my throat as I barreled up the front steps, my feet pounding against the concrete as I ran for the door. The truth was, I had no idea what I was going to do once I burst through the flaming doors, and I never had the chance to figure that out. I barely made it halfway up the walkway before a fireman threw his arm around my waist and snatched me up from the ground, hauling me back to the safety of the street.

"My sister might be in there!" I shouted, bucking against his strong hold as he dragged me further away and then plopped me down to the ground. "Please! I have to find her!"

"You're not going anywhere near that building!" he shouted back, his hands firmly planted on my shoulders. I could see droplets of sweat trickling down his temple from under his helmet. "If she's in there, we'll get her out. You need to stay out of the way and let us do our job! You hear me?"

"You don't understand...I can help, I can *go* in there!" I wanted to explain that I could do more than just watch helplessly from the sidewalk as the building went up in flames, with or without my sister in it. But I couldn't, because how was I going to explain that while I looked like a normal (albeit currently hysterical) teenager, I was actually wearing a necklace that pretty much made me Immortal.

"If you go anywhere near that building again, I'm putting you in restraints. Do you understand me?" he said, his words popping off in my head like firecrackers.

Feeling utterly trapped and powerless, I nodded my head and then watched as he rushed back to the burning building without me.

"You really do have a death wish, don't you?" said Nikki as

she settled beside me, her arms folded tightly across her chest and her eyes fixed on the catastrophe unfolding before us.

I ignored her and asked, "Do you have your phone on you?"

"Does the sun set in the west?" She reached into her back pocket and pulled out her cell.

Taking it from her, I quickly dialed my sister's number and waited, never taking a single breath until she finally answered.

"Hello?" she answered, though I barely gave her a chance to get the whole word out.

"Thank God! You're okay!" I clutched my heart and then crouched onto the ground to avoid passing out from hyperventilating. "Please tell me Gabriel's with you?!"

"Yeah, he's right here. Why? What's going on?" she asked, sounding worried.

"Temple's on fire, Tessa. People are still inside!" And it's all my fault...

She let out a colorful string of curse words and then said, "Uncle Karl had a meeting there this morning."

I swallowed the ball in my throat.

"Do you see him anywhere?" she asked.

My eyes scanned the scene, looking for signs of my uncle amid the crowd of injured and onlookers.

"No, I don't see him," I said on the verge of hysterics. I mean, I obviously hated my uncle, but I didn't wish him dead, and certainly not like this. Burning alive was a fate I didn't wish on anyone. Except maybe the Roderick sisters. "Are you sure he's still here?" Maybe the meeting ended early. Maybe he stopped for a latte on the way.

She didn't answer except to say, "I'm on my way."

Tessa arrived less than fifteen minutes later, accompanied by a tall, dark-haired guy I'd never seen before. I wasn't sure if he was her friend, Keeper, or boyfriend, but I knew he was definitely Anakim judging by the Marks on his arms, which were mostly hidden by extensive tattoos. They immediately parted ways, with Tattoo Guy going towards the building and Tessa running up to me and Nikki.

"Did you find him?" she asked, panting as she tried to catch her breath.

I shook my head. "They've stopped going in to save people," I said without meeting her eyes. The flames had engulfed the building and rendered it too dangerous to enter.

"The building's spelled," she said, standing shoulder to shoulder with me as we watched the firemen fruitlessly douse the bluish tinged flames with water. "They'll be okay."

"It's hellfire, Tessa." I wrapped my arms around myself as tears trickled down my cheeks in bold, anguish-filled streaks.

"Hellfire?" she whispered, her voice almost completely lost in the noise. "How do you know that?"

I could feel her heavy eyes on me, scrutinizing me, but I didn't turn to meet them. "Lucifer told me. It was his punishment to me for going to Temple."

She swore under her breath, knowing exactly what that meant. The fire would not stop until nothing but ash remained. And there would be casualties—so very many of them.

"This is all my fault." I could feel a heaviness pressing over my heart, pulling me down deeper into the darkness—into that place that was void of all hope and salvation. "People are dead because of me."

I wasn't sure how I was ever going to be able to live with that—to be okay with it. There was no coming back from something like this. That burden of guilt would remain with me for the rest of my days.

"Look, I'm not going to stand here and tell you I told you so," said Tessa, her voice cold and flat. "But this is only the beginning unless you do something to stop it."

My eyes squeezed shut as I struggled to take a breath.

This must be what drowning feels like.

"How many more people are you going to let die, Jemma?" She grabbed my shoulders and forced me to face her. "How many people are going to perish because you were too afraid to do the right thing? The hard thing? You can't let this continue. Not when you have the power to stop it."

More tears fell, because while I did have the power to stop this, to stop Lucifer, I would have to kill Trace in the process, and that wasn't just a hard thing for me to do. It was the impossible thing—the thing that would inevitably slaughter my heart from the inside out.

I stared at the dark circles that had taken up residency under her eyes. She looked so tired and worn out, so small in the face of all we were going up against. I wondered where she got all her courage from? I wondered if she even still felt fear, or had she stopped feeling altogether?

I shook away the disturbing thought and crossed my arms over my chest. "Even if I wanted to, half of the Council is dead, Tessa, and the weapon is probably nothing more than dust by now."

Or at least it would be once the Hellfire finished with it.

Even as we stood there talking, the fire continued ripping away at the building, piece by piece, room by room. The sacred Temple they'd spent decades building and protecting would soon be a pile of ash.

"The weapon is safe," she said quietly so only the two of us could hear.

"What do you mean?" I searched her face for clues.

"Carter and I are its Keepers." Her voice dropped as she held my gaze. So, Tattoo Guy had a name. "I can train you. I can teach you what you need to know to do this."

A thick lump wedged itself at the back of my throat.

"You can still do the right thing, Jemma. It's not too late."

Her words, so similar to what Trace had said to me, echoed in my mind as I realized I was being squeezed out of any other choices. The body count was steadily rising, and Lucifer had no plans on stopping. I had to do something…to at least be ready if my plan for the Roderick sisters went straight to hell.

I couldn't be stupid or selfish about this. Not when so many lives were at stake.

"Okay." I nodded, my cheeks soaked with fresh tears. "Show me what I need to know.

27. THE SWORD OF ANGELUS

The rain fell in sheets as Tessa and I pulled up to Huntington Manor. Dominic's Audi was already in the driveway, which probably meant that he'd already heard the news about Temple from Gabriel. As much as I wasn't giving up hope that our plan to entrap one of the Roderick sisters would work, I knew that I had to be prepared in the event that it didn't.

I still wasn't sure how I would ever be able to follow through with something as inconceivable as killing Trace, so I decided not to think about it until I absolutely had to.

"We're back," shouted Tessa as we walked into the house, our clothing dripping wet from the rain.

Gabriel came to meet us in the hallway, his eyebrows pulled together in concern. "How many?"

"At least eleven," answered Tessa, referring to the confirmed causalities. "There's still twenty-two people unaccounted for, my uncle included."

"I'm sorry."

"Don't be," she said and walked passed him. "He's not dead until I see the body."

With my head hung low, I didn't say anything as I followed her into the den.

Dominic was sitting on the couch in his usual position with his arm stretched along the back of the sofa and a drink in hand. His face had all but healed, and while he was staring at me as though he wanted to say something, or do something, he didn't, and that was fine by me. I really wasn't in the mood to talk anyway.

Quietly, I walked to the sofa and sat down in the spot beside him.

The scratching unease under my skin immediately eased as I settled in closer to him. I could feel his eyes on me, appraising my body for damage, probing me for answers to his questions, but he didn't trouble me with voicing them.

Instead, he turned to Tessa and Gabriel and asked, "What now?"

"Now I train her," said Tessa as she peeled off her soaking wet leather jacket and tossed it onto the coffee table. She was wearing a black tank top and a pair of black skinny jeans, which were both equally wet, though it didn't seem to bother her. "Can we use the basement?"

"Of course," said Gabriel as he started to lead the way.

"Just me and Jemma," she said to his back.

He turned and nodded curtly, and my mouth went bone-dry.

The Huntington basement was wall-to-wall concrete and weaponry. There were no safety mats for practice, no benches to rest, no holes to crawl into and hide. This was clearly a space that was meant for pain and destruction, and I could only imagine the infinite number of hours Gabriel had spent down here in his youth, training to be a killer.

Hugging my arms for warmth, I followed Tessa to the center

of the room. My jean jacket was soaked and clinging to my skin like wet sandpaper, making me shiver under its cold embrace.

"How in control of yourself would you say you are?" she asked and then turned around to face me.

"What do you mean?"

"Your abilities—can you control them?"

"Not really," I admitted indifferently. "I mostly just short-circuit and blow shit up."

She nodded, probably remembering the light show from earlier. "You know you can control that, don't you?"

"That's what everyone keeps saying." I looked at her expectantly, because up until now, no one's bothered to explain how I might go about doing that.

"You control them by controlling your emotions."

I huffed out a humorless laugh. "In case you haven't noticed, Tess, I'm not very good at suppressing my emotions."

"Not suppressing them," she said as she gathered her hair back it into her hand. "Harnessing them."

"What's the difference?" I asked, watching as she tied a black elastic band around the ponytail.

"Suppressing your emotions pushes them into places they're not meant to be. The minute you get worked up, bam! Everything comes out backwards. But harnessing them is understanding your emotions, its filing them away in exactly the right place so you can pull them out at exactly the right time." Her eyebrows waggled with excitement. "The rage, the sadness, the fear… they fuel you, and that's a good thing. You just need to figure out how to drive them. Visualize the act, own the emotion, and your body will do the rest."

My mind flashed to my fight with Nikki at Temple. I'd been so furious with her that I was somehow able to push through Nikki's magic even though it was forcing me back.

"The sword works pretty much the same way," she said as she

knelt to the ground and pulled her pant leg up. She was wearing what looked like a gun holder around her calf, but I knew it wasn't a gun. No, this weapon was so much deadlier that a gun could ever hope to be.

"The Sword of Angelus was forged from the bone of a Gargoyle and the essence of an Archangel," she said as she released the weapon from its sheath. It was much smaller than I had anticipated, closer to the size of a dagger than a sword, but something about its silver gleam let me know its size had no bearing on its power.

"There's nothing on earth that can destroy it," she said and met my eyes briefly. "It's existed almost as long as we have and will be there long after our people are gone." She maneuvered it through the air with ease, twisting it around and then transferring it to her other hand in the same fluid motion.

I was mesmerized, not only by the sword but by the graceful way she handled it.

"This sword right here is the only thing we know of that can vanquish Lucifer, and there's only one bloodline that can ignite its power—the Morningstar bloodline." She flipped it over once more and then extended it out to me, hilt first. "Your bloodline."

My hand shook as I inched my fingers toward the handle, both afraid and curious of what would happen once I picked it up. Obviously, I knew that my blood would ignite its power— Tessa had just said as much—but I had no actual idea what that meant.

Ignoring the erratic pounding in my chest, I wrapped my fingers around the grip and then gasped as the sword lit up in my hand. I couldn't tell if the strange blue glow was coming from the inside of it or just emanating all around it. The only thing I knew for sure was that it didn't look remotely natural. Frightened, I dropped the sword and gawked as the unearthly light disappeared the moment the weapon left my hand and hit the ground.

"What the hell was that?" I asked and gaped at her.

She quickly bent down and picked the devil-sword back up. She seriously couldn't stand to see the thing on the floor. "There's nothing to be afraid of. It just means you were the one meant to do this."

Easy for her to say. She wasn't the one that had to do it.

Flipping it over in her hand again, she pushed it back out towards me, urging me to take it again.

"You knew that was going to happen, didn't you?" I accused, crossing my arms.

"Not exactly. I mean, I've heard stories, but I've never actually seen it light up like that," she said and shrugged her shoulders as though it were no big deal. As though my blood didn't just light up a freaking devil-killing-sword.

"How about a head's up next time?"

"Right. Sorry," she said, her eyes looking a lot more excited than remorseful. "This is new for me too."

I eyed the sword curiously, but I never moved to take it from her. "Why did it do that?" I asked instead. Maybe if I could understand the mechanics behind it, it wouldn't be so frightening to me.

"Its power is based in the purpose it was created with. Your blood, the very existence of it, awakens that power and calls it to action."

I blew out a heavy breath. That didn't help in the slightest.

"Just trust the sword, Jemma. It would never hurt you," she said, nodding into it.

I didn't particularly like the way she kept referring to it as though it were some living, breathing entity. It was weird and just plain wrong.

And yet as creepy and unsettling as it was, I knew there was no way out of this. I had to take the sword, knowing that there was no going back from this. I would learn to yield the weapon, and if all hope vanished, I would have no choice but to use it. If I didn't, Lucifer would destroy us all, one by one, city by city.

Relaxing my tense muscles, I took the sword in my hand and slowly brought it in towards my chest. Once again, the sword lit up, though this time, it didn't scare me.

Okay, maybe this isn't the worst thing ever, I thought as I carefully turned it around and admired the blue glow as it radiated in my hand.

"Do you feel it?" she asked, speaking softly now.

I turned it again, tossing it gently in the air and then catching it—testing its feel against my skin. It felt right holding it, almost as though it had been crafted to fit perfectly in the palm of my hand.

"It's a part of you as much as you're a part of it. Allow yourself to accept its power, to be at one with it," said Tessa as she watched me maneuver it through the air, each time catching it by the hilt.

It was as effortless and natural as breathing. The grip wanted to be in my hand. There was no other option but for me to catch it—to connect with it.

"That's it. Nice and easy," she said softly as she began to circle around me. I wasn't sure what she was doing, and even though I wanted to follow her movements, my eyes couldn't turn away from the blade.

One moment she was walking behind me, and the next she was on my back, whipping her arm around me in an attempt to grab the sword from my hand. Without hesitation, I clutched her wrist and yanked her over my shoulder, slamming her down hard against the concrete floor, all without loosening my grip on the sword.

I stared down at her, confused. Confused about why she'd

just done that, but even more confused about how I was able to move so quickly to defend myself without even so much as loosening a finger around the hilt. I mean, I'd come a long way since moving to Hollow Hills, but that was beyond anything I'd learned in training. It was almost as though I'd seen the attack coming long before she even made a move.

Her lips pulled into a knowing grin as she looked back up at me. "Did you see that? That was amazing."

"See what? What the hell just happened?"

"It's exactly what the prophesy's been saying all along," she said and jumped back up to her feet in one fluid motion. I wasn't even sure how that was possible with the skin-tight jeans she was wearing. "As long as that sword is in your hand, you will always protect it. Whether you want to or not."

Whether I want to or not? I recoiled at her words, not liking the way they felt as they made their way into my reality.

I didn't need another thing controlling me.

Another thing taking away my free will.

Shaking my head, I threw the sword down and stepped back from it. "I don't like this."

"Jemma, there's nothing to be afraid of," she said as her shoulders slumped. "The sword is doing exactly what it's supposed to do."

And that was precisely my problem.

"I don't know how I feel about being controlled by a weapon that no one on earth can destroy." Just saying the words out loud had me trembling. There was too much power in that sword for any one person. Especially when that person was a teenage girl who hadn't even finished high school yet.

"You can't think of it like that, Jemma."

"Easy for you to say. You're not the one that's being controlled by it," I fired back, unable to keep the cynicism out of my voice.

"Neither you nor the sword are in absolute control. You're just a Slayer, and the sword is just a blade, but collectively, you're a force that will not and cannot be stopped."

I wasn't sure if that was supposed to make me feel better or worse.

"You're the girl that is destined to save the world, Jemma," she said with a gleam in her eyes, "and this sword is going to help you do it."

"I really wish you'd stop glorifying this like it's some prize I won."

"It is a prize," she answered sharply. "Do you have any idea how many Slayers out there would give anything to have this fight? This honor? This is the ultimate battle, Jemma."

"You think I'm going to feel *honor* using that thing on Trace?" I said as I tipped my chin to the blade. "You have no idea about the burden I'm carrying right now or the Hell I'm going to carry for the rest of my life if I do this."

"Look, I know it's hard for you, but—"

"No," I quickly cut in before she could finish the sentiment. "You don't know, and you know what, Tessa? I hope to God you never have to find out."

Using this sword on Trace was the worst thing I could ever conceive of, and there wasn't anything she could say or do that would ever make me feel better about it.

She folded her arms across her chest and met my determined eyes. "Duty will always come before love, Jemma. It has to. You have to think about the bigger picture here."

"I'm so sick of everyone saying that to me! It's easy for you to say. It's not your life that's on the line."

"It wouldn't change anything if it was," she countered, looking like she really meant it.

"Really? So, you'd feel the same way if you had to use that sword on me?" I challenged.

"Yes."

Alrighty then.

I wasn't sure what hurt more. The fact that she'd answered yes or the fact that she didn't even remotely hesitate.

"You could've at least pretended to think about it," I said, shaking my head at her.

"It doesn't mean I don't love you, Jemma. It doesn't mean I wouldn't do everything I knew of to try to save you first. But if I came down to you or the rest of the world, you would lose. You would have to—as would I. That's just the way it is. One person, no matter how much we love them, cannot overshadow everyone else."

Tears were stinging the corners of my eyes, because while I hated what she was saying, I also knew she was right.

"I think we should break for the rest of the day," she said, glancing away from me. "It's a lot for you to take in." For the briefest of seconds, I thought I saw some emotion in her eyes, though it could have just been a piece of dust.

"Thanks," I said, grateful for her reprieve. I was going to need a hell of a lot more time to process this.

"Yeah, well, what are sisters for, right?" she said as she stalked to the sword and unceremoniously picked it up.

The minute she took the sword back, something inside of me broiled to life, and suddenly, without even meaning to, I'd reached out and snatched the sword back from her, once again igniting its power in my hand.

Woah... Why the hell did I just do that?

"That's really cute," said Tessa, though nothing about her face was saying she was amused. "Now hand it over," she said, holding her hand out to me, palm up.

I shook my head, clutching the sword by my side.

"Stop playing around," she snapped. "Give it back."

"I'm sorry, Tess, but I don't think I can do that."

Narrowing her eyes, she moved to take it from me, but I quickly stepped back.

I could hear her grinding her teeth, and even though I knew that was a bad sign, I refused to give it to her. The truth was, there wasn't a single person in the entire universe I trusted to carry this thing, and that included my sister.

"You're going to give me that damn sword," she said and then tried to snatch it out of my hands again, but I seemed to be one step ahead of her each time.

"That's not happening, Tessa."

"I swear to God—"

"The only way you're getting this sword from me is if you pry it out of my hands," I interrupted her calmly, knowing full well that she didn't have a chance in hell of taking it from me.

She paused, assessing me as though seeing me for the first time. She was probably deciding whether or not she could take me. Hell, she probably could, one on one, but not when I had this kind of magical advantage over her.

Realizing she wasn't going to win this one, she shook her head at me and dropped her hands. "You realize you're putting a target on your back by carrying that around with you?"

I had no doubt of it.

"It's not the first one I've had, and I doubt it'll be the last."

I waited for an answer, another argument, and when none came, I released the breath I'd been holding. Bending down, I pulled my pant leg up and revealed my own holster—the one Dominic had given me—and then carefully slid it into the sheath where it belonged.

"I really hope you know what you're doing."

"So do I," I said and straightened myself out. There was no point in denying it. I was in way over my head and didn't have the slightest idea what I was going to do. The only thing I knew for sure was that there wasn't a damned person on this entire planet who was going to take this sword out of my hands. In fact, I really wanted to see them try.

28. COUNTDOWN

Tessa and I rejoined Dominic and Gabriel in the upstairs den shortly after our little standoff. Neither one of us had bothered to share what had happened in the basement, and I was relieved not to have to live through it again. I didn't particularly enjoy pissing off my sister, especially when I already had so many people against me, but there was no way in Hell I was going to let that sword out of my sights. The truth was, while I'd taken the sword and agreed to be trained by her, I wasn't letting go of hope that our plan would work—that we would find a way to save Trace and bring him home again. As far as I was concerned, using the sword was an absolute-no-other-choice last resort.

Tessa's phone rang as I rejoined Dominic on the sofa where I'd left him. He watched me closely as I sat down beside him, possibly trying to read my expressions for any clues as to how it went, but he didn't get a chance to ask.

"What's up?" said Tessa into her phone. Her brows knitted closely together as she listened to whoever was on the other side of the line. "Are you sure?" Another pause. "I'm on my way."

She ended the call and promptly directed her heavy gaze back to me.

That was never a good sign.

"What is it?"

"They think they've found uncle Karl's body."

"His *body*?" The words hissed from my mouth like a gust of wind, and I instantly felt the blood rush away from my head. "Are you sure it's him?"

"No, but I'm going there now to find out."

"I'll get my keys," said Gabriel.

Tessa's eyes never left mine, though I couldn't for the life of me figure out what they were saying.

"Should I—I mean, do I need to come...?" I couldn't even bring myself to ask the question. There was no way I could stomach going with her to identify the body. I hated my uncle, but he was still my uncle, and he looked far too much like my father for me to be able to see him like that.

She shook her head. "Not unless you want to."

My face twisted as I gawked back at her.

"I didn't think so. Just stay here with Dominic until I get back," she instructed as she grabbed her jacket from the coffee table and then glared over at Dominic. "You think you can manage to keep your hands off my sister while I'm gone?"

"I can certainly try," he said as he unfurled his arm along the back of the sofa. "But I'm not making any promises."

"Funny," she deadpanned and then turned back to me. "I mean it, Jemma. Don't leave this house."

Less than half an hour later, Dominic and I were in his Audi, speeding over to the hotel to meet up with Nikki and the others. We'd gotten *the* call minutes after Tessa and Gabriel left. Ben had confirmed the sisters' location after spending the better part of the day in wolf form doing recon work. He'd observed at least two of the sisters coming and going from the MacArthur house several times that afternoon.

They were definitely staying there, and worse, they weren't even trying to hide it.

Obviously, they weren't afraid of being found out or even remotely worried that we might be coming for them. I suppose I wouldn't be either if I had the kind of magical mojo the sisters had. Then again, too much of anything was never a good thing. Over confidence can easily make a person drop their guards.

I'd learned the hard way that it was best to keep your feet firmly planted on the ground, especially when so many people were gunning for you.

"Thank you for doing this," I said to Ben as I climbed out of Dominic's car, dragging my schoolbag out with me.

"Don't mention it, Jem. You know I'd do anything for that pretty boy idiot." He was smiling playfully through the words, but I could tell it was a façade. The worry had all but etched itself into his expression.

"Was he there?" I asked, and we both knew who I was talking about.

He shook his head as he ran his hand over the crown of his shaved head. "No, and I'm kind of glad he wasn't. I don't know what I would've done if I'd seen him like that. You know?"

I nodded that I did, glad that he didn't have to experience the horror of witnessing Trace's body being worn by some demented fallen angel from hell.

"I just hope he stays gone while we're there," I muttered, not particularly wanting him to show up in the middle of operation-snatch-a-witch.

"Where do you think he is?"

"Your guess is as good as mine. He's been hanging out at All Saints a lot," I said with a shrug, though he could have just as easily gone back to Temple to watch it burn to the ground.

I heard psychopaths loved returning to the scene of their

crimes.

"Are the others here yet?" I asked as we walked towards the front entrance of the hotel.

"Yeah, they're waiting inside. Carly, a.k.a. the delicate mortal, was too cold," he said with annoyance.

He was always entirely too hard on that girl. I guess he just didn't understand what it felt like to not want the life you had, to wish for something more—for something different.

Inside, we walked through the atrium and found the three of them hovering by the elevators. Nikki was talking quietly with Carly while Caleb lingered around the edges, puttying around on his phone.

You could literally feel the tension between them, and while I didn't particularly care about their relationship issues, I hoped it wouldn't interfere with anything.

"It's about time," snapped Nikki as her gaze flicked up from Carly and found us. "Not like it's the end of the world or anything."

"I had some business to take care," I said, deciding to leave out the details about the sword. I really didn't want to go there until I had absolutely no choice left.

The elevator doors opened, and the six of us filled in with me and Dominic on the tail end.

"Everything's ready, right?" I asked Nikki as she ran her fingers through her long, silky hair.

"Do I look like the kind of girl who comes unprepared?" she asked and now it was my turn to roll my eyes.

Once we were back inside the room, Nikki wasted no time getting herself set up in the living room. Dominic had already fixed himself a drink, but not before drawing all the blinds closed. The last thing we needed was to be seen by somebody. Granted, we were like fifty floors up, but we weren't about to take any chances.

"Where should I sit?" asked Carly as she hovered awkwardly beside Nikki, who was already sitting on the carpet, legs crossed, setting out candles at the center of the space.

She didn't look up when she answered, "I need one of you on each side."

"Which side?" asked Carly, her caramel eyes bouncing between Nikki and her brother.

"I don't give a shit which side you sit on, Car. Just make sure you remember the incantation and do what you're supposed to do when I tell you to do it."

"Right," she said sheepishly and then lowered herself to the floor from the spot she'd been standing in.

"Um, are you sure you're all, you know…equipped to do this?" I asked as politely as I could. Honestly, seeing Carly so unsure of herself made me a hundred times more hesitant than I was coming into this.

"If you're asking if I can pull this off, the answer is: with my eyes closed," said Nikki. She obviously didn't like being questioned, and definitely not about her abilities. Apparently, that was a hot button issue for her.

I filed that away for a rainy day.

"Don't worry about us, Blackburn," added Caleb as he joined his sister and Nikki on the carpet. "We wouldn't be here if we didn't think we could do this. You can trust us," he said, nodding into it.

Exhaling sharply, I turned my attention to Dominic who was quietly watching the exchange. My eyes searched his for confirmation, for reassurance that we weren't completely in over our heads. He dipped his chin as to answer my silent plea and I instantly felt myself relax at his gesture, grounded once again.

"How long will it take to do the spell?" I asked, dragging my gaze from Dominic.

"I don't know," Caleb answered and then looked at Nikki for

confirmation. "I'd say ten to fifteen minutes?"

She nodded without looking at me.

"Can you guys narrow it down a little more?"

"No, we can't," blurted Nikki as she lit each of the candles in front of her. "This is magic, Jemma, not a casserole."

"Thanks, smart ass. So how exactly are we supposed to know when to go in?" I needed to make sure we were on point tonight and didn't burst through the doors three minutes before the spell was finished.

"I can text you," offered Carly with a shrug. I could tell she was trying to be useful.

"That works," I said and then grabbed her phone to program Dominic's number.

Handing it back to her, I straightened out and took in a shaky breath. The closer we got to this, the more erratic my heart was beating. Deciding to distract myself with preparation, I threw my schoolbag onto the couch behind me and unzipped it. I didn't have enough time to pack everything I wanted, but I'd still managed to fill my schoolbag all the way to the top.

I pulled out the shoulder holster first, the one Gabriel gave me the night Trace was taken, and I quickly put it on. As soon as the buckles were fastened, I immediately started equipping it with everything I brought, from throwing knives to brass knuckles.

"That's a lot of weapons," noted Carly, her gaze filled with worry as she watched me arm myself with weapon after weapon.

"I'm not taking any chances," I said as I slid in the last baton and then zipped my schoolbag shut. "We're already outnumbered, and if they're as strong as they're magic is, it's not going to be an easy fight."

Carly swallowed noisily. "Is Ben going with you guys?"

"Yeah," he answered, but I quickly shut him down.

"That's not happening, Ben."

"You can't stop me, Jem. Daughter of Hades or not, he's my best friend."

"Exactly why I need you here. If something goes wrong and we don't make it out of there, you're the only one left."

"Hey! What am I, chopped liver?" snapped Caleb, obviously insulted that I'd passed right over him.

I looked at him skeptically. It was no secret that Trace and Caleb had fallen out long ago for reasons that happened to be sitting in the middle of the living room, lighting up candles and incense.

"Don't look at me like that, Blackburn. We've had our problems, but I still give a shit about the guy."

"Well, when you put it that way..." I pursed my lips.

"You know what I mean."

Seeing signs of sincerity in his eyes, I nodded. But it still didn't change anything. "Either way, I need you guys here. You're his last hope if me and Dominic fail."

"Of course, that won't be happening," said Dominic confidently. "I've gone up against far worse than the *Witches of Eastwick*. I'm hardly worried."

"The witches of who?" asked Caleb, confused.

"Dude. Rent a movie once in a while," scowled Ben.

"The first rule of war is to never underestimate your opponent, Dominic." I shot him a pointed look across the room.

"Is that right, angel?"

"They're strong, and they're *sisters*. They're not going to make this easy on us, especially if we're planning on leaving the house with one of their own." I walked over to the wet bar and poured myself a drink. My nerves were already frazzled, and I needed something to calm myself down. I threw the glass back and then winced as it burned its way down. "And that's if the spell even works, which, let's face it, we have no guarantees of."

A strange smile settled across Dominic's face, though I had no idea what it was for. As beautiful and distracting as it was, I forced my eyes to look away.

"How much longer setting up?" I asked Nikki as she wiped her hands on the top of her jeans.

"I'm just about done." Her eyes flicked up to mine. "I don't know how long the spell is going to last once we do it. You need to get in there as soon as you get the text."

I nodded that I would and then looked over at Dominic. "You ready to do this?"

That grin was still plastered on his face when he answered, "I'm at your service, angel."

29. BLOODY DRIVE

Fissures of lightning lit up the sky as the windshield wipers sloshed back and forth, desperate to keep up with the downpour beating down over Hollow Hills. The closer we got to Trace's neighborhood, the harder it became to fill my lungs with air. So much was riding on this one mission, this one moment, and if we screwed it up in any way, the sisters would not be giving us another chance to get it right. Everything had to go perfectly. Flawlessly. Because not only did we need to make it out of there alive tonight, we needed to have one of the sisters with us.

"Pull over," I ordered as soon as he turned onto the boulevard that would inevitably take us to Trace's street.

Dominic quickly veered the car onto the shoulder, probably thinking I was going to throw up all over his fine Italian leather seats.

I couldn't fault him either. I had a tendency to lose my dinner in these kinds of situations.

"I don't want this to be a fight," I said as he killed the engine. Rolling my sleeve up, I laid my arm across the arm rest and exposed my wrist to him. "You're taking some of my blood, and you're taking it right now."

His eyebrows shot up as the corner of his mouth hitched into his cheek.

"I'm not playing, Dominic," I quickly warned him. I needed to make sure that he was coming out of there alive and well. By the grace of God, I still had the Amulet, and I knew that no matter what happened to me, they couldn't kill me. But Dominic was an entirely different story. They would use him against me and would not hesitate to end him just to spite me. "Drink. Right now."

"Have I ever told you how unbelievably sexy you are when you're giving me orders?"

"You can tell me all about it when we get back to the hotel in one piece," I said and eyed my wrist expectantly, signaling for him to do as he was told.

Wetting his lips, he picked up my hand and slowly brought it up to his mouth. My heart pummeled itself against my rib cage as he kissed the top of my hand and then turned it around, never once breaking eye contact from me. His lips brushed against the palm of my hand, soft as a feather, before moving further down to my wrist.

I braced myself, knowing what was coming.

Wanting what was coming.

His fangs dropped with an audible *click* and then swiftly burrowed into my skin. It only took a split second before I felt the familiar droplets of heaven trickling into my blood stream like medicine from an IV drip. Overcome by the rush, I pushed back against my seat, my heels digging into the floor of his car as he openly and freely drank from me.

Every small effort to stop it from affecting me, from completely consuming me, was futile. The pleasure coursing through me was impossible to ignore. It impressed itself upon every cell in my body and then settled over me like a warm blanket made of magic and all the stars in the sky. I never had any chance of fighting it, and every part of my body knew it, from the tips of my curled toes to the small moan that escaped my lips.

At the sound, Dominic pulled back and sucked in a sharp breath. I looked up at him and blinked, my vision still blurry and out of focus. It was better like this; easier to hide from the truth of what I had done. But alas, his features slowly sharpened before completely coming back in focus and revealing the dark angel I was constantly hiding from.

With my chest rising and falling at dangerous speeds, I watched as he licked his lips clean and gazed at me longingly. There was so much need in his eyes, so much lust that it made it hard for me to think clearly.

Every time he drank from me, the cord between us shortened, and I knew that it was only a matter of time before there was no more give left in the line.

Breaking eye contact first, I pushed my head back against the headrest and tried to re-center myself.

"It's your turn, angel," he said, drawing my attention back to him. His eyes were heavy pools of emotion—desire, longing, excitement. They were all dancing freely in the depths of his dangerous eyes.

I tore my gaze away and instead watched as he made two small puncture holes in his wrist.

Wrapping my fingers around his forearm, I quickly brought his wrist to my mouth and drank, knowing that I needed a little help from his blood to anchor myself back to this world. And surely enough, as soon as his blood settled in my system, I could feel my feet slowly touching ground again.

Every exchange between us was like a rollercoaster ride of mind-numbing highs and heart-pounding lows, and as much as I feared the loss of control, I couldn't figure out how to get off the ride.

"Alright, angel. That's enough," he said softly as he pulled his wrist back.

I didn't know how he did it, but he always managed to stay in complete control of our exchanges. If it were up to me, we'd probably be in two body bags by now, side by side and completely drained of all our blood.

Apparently, my level of self-control was in the negative.

"How are you feeling?" he asked tentatively, his eyes surveying my features.

"Better," I said and released an easy breath. "You?"

His lips twisted into a grin. "Never better, angel."

"Good," I said and pulled my seatbelt back around me. "How much time do we have left?"

He glanced at his watch. "Eleven minutes."

That was more than enough to get to Trace's house and set ourselves up. If all went well, we'd have plenty of time to spare before the text came in.

And God knows we needed it.

30. RING OF DEATH

The rain continued to beat down violently as Dominic and I made our way around the side of Trace's house on foot. The lights were on at the front, signaling *someone* was home, but we had no idea who, or how many people were actually in there. Something we should have probably confirmed before coming here.

As long as Nikki's spell went off without a hitch, I was confident we could overpower at least one of the sisters, and I had my sights set on the one I wanted, but that plan could easily go to hell if there were more people in the house than expected; particularly Lucifer or one of his demon minions.

Deciding to play it safe, we watched the house before choosing our point of entrance, spotting an unfamiliar, long-haired blond man in the kitchen, rummaging through Trace's fridge while the sisters sat together in the adjacent living room. From the windows, I could see that they were curled up on the sofa and relaxed. The TV was on, though they didn't appear to be watching it.

Just as I'd hoped; their guards were all the way down.

"Can you take him?" I whispered to Dominic as I assessed Tall, Blond and Hungry.

Do you even need to ask? He responded telepathically.

"Use the kitchen door," I instructed as I ticked my chin to the back door. "It's probably locked, but it's mostly glass." Something Dominic could easily break through. "I'll take the sisters and go through there," I continued, gesturing in the opposite direction towards the patio door.

Are we catching and releasing or shooting to kill? he asked.

"Shoot to kill," I said icily and then looked down at the phone as it vibrated in my hand.

Four little word stared back at me on the screen:

It's done. Good luck.

My heart lurched, hammering so savagely against my rib cage that I could hear the reverberations of its pounding in my ears. There was no going back now, no time outs, and no do overs. This was our one and only chance to get this right.

"This is it," I said hoarsely and then reached over to grab him by the lapels of his coat, bringing his face within inches of mine. "You make damn sure you come back to me, you hear me?"

A hint of a smile touched his lips. "I'll see what I can do, angel."

Nodding to him, I released my hold on him and watched as he shifted into his wolf form, his eyes glowing like two amber stones caught in the moonlight.

I'll see you on the other side, he said as we parted ways, each of us heading in separate directions at the back of the sprawling estate. Within a few seconds, I heard a loud crashing noise—the distinct sound of wood and glass smashing out of existence—and knew that he had made his way inside.

My turn.

Grabbing the banister, I pulled myself onto the back porch and then barreled straight for the glass doors. Using every emotion I owned—fear, anger, desperation, loss—I channeled them into something that felt so much bigger than me or this moment, and then aimed it at the patio doors, shattering the glass before I even touched it.

The sisters' heads snapped in my direction. They had already been standing up, gawking in the direction of the kitchen as they tried to figure out what the commotion was. And judging by the looks of shock on their faces, I could tell I was the absolute last person on earth they expected to see here.

"Well, well. Look what the cat dragged in," said Annabelle. The look of surprise had quickly morphed into one of amusement. "You're even stupider than I thought," she said and then threw her head back and laughed.

My hand flexed at my side as I took each of them in, quickly assessing whether they had any weapons and how many points of escape they had access to. The odds were in my favor.

My eyes zeroed in on Arianna—stupid, traitorous Arianna—and then my feet were moving, walking themselves towards her as though they had all the time in the world to get there.

"*Recedite*," shouted one of the sisters, though I didn't bother turning around to see who. "*Recedite*!" she bellowed again when it clearly wasn't working.

The spell had worked.

Their magic was disabled, and that was all I needed to know to pounce.

Like a starving shark with a small taste of blood, my feet kicked off the ground as I dove into Arianna, my body slamming into hers like a head-on collision and then tumbling to the ground with her body trapped beneath mine. Before she could even *think* about recovering, I was already pummeling my fist into her face.

"Get her off of me!" cried Arianna as she fruitlessly tried to block my blows.

"I'm trying!" shouted Annabelle, panic streaking her voice. "My magic's not working!"

I was able to land four more hits before a pair of hands found their way into my hair, fisting through my long waves and then using them to yank me backwards off Arianna. I landed on my back and looked up at Anita as she dropped her body on top of mine, using her weight to hold me down.

"Get your shit together, Annabelle!" she scolded her sister.

"I'm trying to! *Aqua suffocent*," screamed Annabelle, her fist clenching and unclenching so frantically that she was drawing blood from her palms. "Something's wrong," she said, dropping her hand and turning to her sister. "She did something to my magic," she said and then turned her accusatory finger at me. "What did you do, you little bitch?!"

"Who, me?" I asked innocently, though the smile on my face let them both know I was proudly claiming responsibility. "Oh, that's right. I evened the playing field," I said and then reached up and grabbed Anita by her throat, yanking her off my chest and flipping her onto the ground. I threw my leg over her body and straddled her chest, locking her arms against her body. Her eyes widened as I tightened my grip around her throat and squeezed as hard as I could.

Her legs flailed aimlessly as choking noises sounded from her throat, but it only made me squeeze harder.

The darkness that I had worked so hard to suppress was coming up faster than I could control now. It was angry, and it wanted revenge, and for the first time in my life, I was letting it take the wheel.

"Stop it! You're killing her!" screamed Annabelle as she grabbed a lamp from the table and threw it at my head.

I wasn't sure if it was the adrenaline or my dark desire to choke the shit out of Anita, but the pain of the lamp smacking me upside the head barely registered.

"Dammit, Ari! Get up and help me!" shouted Annabelle, useless now that her magic was no more.

My gaze snapped to Arianna, who was struggling to get back on her feet. Her face was already swollen and the cut above her eye was bleeding profusely, dripping red ooze down her face and making it impossible for her to see even two feet in front of her face. She lost her footing and dropped back to the ground.

Satisfied that she wasn't going anywhere any time soon, I turned my full attention back to Anita just in time to watch her eyes lids flutter for the last time before her eyes rolled back into her head.

A small smile twisted my lips as the darkness continued to ride me.

My intention had only been to choke her out—to put her to sleep—and at the moment, I wasn't sure if I'd gone too far, but the truth was, I didn't give an actual shit if I had.

I released her throat from my grip and climbed off her limp body.

Annabelle was screaming in tongues I couldn't understand, probably trying to summon her magic as I marched towards her. She quickly jumped back over the sofa, as though that would stop me. I hopped up on the coffee table and watched as she cowered behind the furniture while throwing inanimate objects at me.

I paused for a moment, allowing myself to bask in the sight of it. Annabelle Roderick, hiding—from *me*.

"What's the matter, Annabelle? You scared?" I asked, easily dodging her throws.

"Fuck you!" she spat and threw another book at me.

A freaking book.

I clinked my tongue at the pathetic-ness of it all.

"You didn't actually think I was going to let you get away with what you did to him…did you?"

Her lips pursed together, but I could see them quivering even from where I was standing.

My deadly stare shifted over my shoulder as Dominic's wolf came racing into the living room. "Took you long enough," I quipped, quickly running my eyes over him to make sure he wasn't hurt.

Sorry, angel. My date brought friends, he answered silently as he prowled over to Arianna. With his lip curled back over his teeth, he planted his paw on her chest and ruffled her, checking for signs of life.

She's still breathing, he said.

"Good."

What do you plan on doing with that one? he asked, referring to Annabelle.

"I'm still deciding if I want to kill her, or just make her wish I had."

Then by all means, as you were, he said, watching intently as he guarded Arianna.

He knew more than anyone how long I'd waited for this day.

I faced Annabelle again. She was hiding behind an end table, chanting in hushed tones in a last-ditch effort to summon her magic. Her lips pressed together upon catching my stare.

"You don't have to do this. We can work something out," she pleaded as she held out her open palms to me.

I refused to dignify that with an answer. After what she did to Trace, she needed to pay.

They all did.

Ignoring her plea, I jumped from the edge of the coffee table to the sofa and then leapt over the back of it, closing the gap between us. As soon as my hit feet the wooden floor, she took off running in the opposite direction, barreling for the nearest exit. My heart filled with delight upon realizing how drastically the tables had turned.

Sprinting forward, I caught her by her long blond hair and yanked her backwards, sending her sailing several feet behind me. Realizing she wasn't going to outrun me in this lifetime, she jumped up to her feet and took a fighting stance.

I snorted, because by the looks of her sloppy posture and limp right arm, she was in way over her head. At least she had enough self-respect to put up a fight. However futile that would be.

"I don't wa-want to d-do this," she said, her voice shaking almost as much as her closed fist was. "You've m-made you're point, okay?"

But I hadn't made my point. In fact, I hadn't even gotten started.

Darkness coiled in my stomach as I took two giant steps towards her and then dropped to the ground, kicking my leg out and using it to swipe her feet out from under her.

She hit the floor with a loud thump, the air rushing out of her lungs with a grumble.

"You won't get away with this," she bellowed, staring up at me with unabridged terror in her eyes, arms outstretched and trembling between us. "*He's* going to make you pay for this!"

Her words only served to further enrage me. Visions of Trace's vacant eyes assaulted my mind, blurring out the edges of my vision until all I could see was red. I dropped down on top of her and pulled my trembling fist back as I held her jaw with my other hand.

I had reached my boiling point, and like a rubber band with no more slack to give, I snapped.

31. DRIVEN TO KILL

The rain was still pattering down against Dominic's windshield as we sped away from Trace's house. The last thing I remembered was sitting down on Annabelle's chest with my hand balled into a fist, ready to make her pay for what she had done to Trace. Everything had gone black after that point, and I realized I had lost complete control over myself. I wasn't sure how many times I had hit her or how long the beating lasted. The only memory I had was that of Dominic's arms around my chest, dragging me off her bloody body as she lay motionless in a pool of her own blood.

I looked down at my fists and swallowed hard. I couldn't recognize them as my own. They were swollen and cut and covered in blood that I was sure didn't belong to me.

Turning my head slightly, I glanced back at Arianna's motionless body slumped over in the back seat. Dominic had thrown her over his shoulder and carried her out to the car while I followed in my post-murderous haze behind him.

"How many times did I...?" I asked without meeting his eyes. He knew what I wanted to know. He knew I'd lost track of time and needed to put the missing pieces back together.

"As many times as she deserved," he said evenly and then stroked my cheek with the back of his knuckles. He was trying to comfort me, to lessen my burden.

"Was she dead?" I asked him, my voice hoarse and distant.

"She was still breathing when we left. *Barely*," he added almost too softly for me to hear.

"I lost control," I said, dropping my gaze when he met my eyes. "I'm not sure what happened. Everything just went…black."

"The only thing you need to remember is what *they* did to *you*." He leaned over and took my hand in his. "They came into your life, angel, not the other way around," he reminded.

I knew he was right—they had caused this, asked for it even, but something still felt off inside of me. I was numb. Hollow. The faint ray of light that once lived within me seemed to have disappeared.

All I felt now was the darkness.

Less than forty-five minutes later, we pulled up to the abandoned mine on the outskirts of town. With no houses or businesses for miles in each direction, we knew that we'd be completely alone here, and that no one would be able to hear the screams that were inevitably going to come.

With Arianna draped over Dominic's shoulder, bound and gagged, I followed him into the cavernous mine. Long tunnels stretched out into the rocky mountain, some going up while others took us further down into the ground. We walked for what felt like an eternity, blindly following the railed tracks until we came upon a cave-like opening.

He dropped Arianna face-first onto the ground and then rolled the kinks out of his shoulders. When she didn't immediately wake up and spring into action, I walked over to her and poked her with the tip of my foot.

She was out cold.

"What now?" I snapped, staring down at her, irritated. It was going to be pretty hard to beat the information out of her while she was already unconscious.

"We wake sleeping beauty," he said and then crouched down over her.

"Any idea how to do that?" I asked as I tried not to be bothered by the fact that he called her beauty.

"I'm a Revenant, angel. Who do you think?" he said and then brought his wrist to his mouth. He pierced two small holes in his flesh and then brought the bloom of blood to her lips. Rubbing a small drop of his blood on her lips, he pulled his wrist back and then straightened to his full height.

I crossed my arms and watched as her eyelids began to flutter to life. It took about a minute for her to fully regain consciousness, and when she finally did, her eyes doubled in size as she realized she was hog-tied and shit out of luck.

I knelt down before her and pulled the bandana from her mouth.

"Where am I? Where are my sisters?" Her eyes were wide with alarm and brimming with terror.

"They're dead," I lied, needing her to feel nice and scared and hopeless.

Her expression quickly morphed from one of fear to one of panicked disbelief. "That's impossible...you're lying," she said as a strangled sob escaped her throat.

"Are you sure about that?" I asked and then scratched my nose so that she could see the blood on my hands. "They looked pretty dead when I left them."

Her eyes widened into saucers, tears quickly filling them.

"And not to be cliché or anything," I said and leaned down over her. "But you're about to join them unless you start talking." I grabbed her by the collar of her shirt and yanked her up so that she was sitting on her knees, her hands still tied behind her back and anchored to her feet, making her body arch backwards unnaturally.

It looked painful, to be honest, but I didn't give the tiniest of fucks.

With my fist still tangled in her shirt, I jerked her forward to me, close enough that I could smell her soured breath. With my free hand, I reached into my holster and pulled out a knife. Her eyes flared with fear as they met the blade.

"I'm giving you one chance to answer this question," I started, my voice eerily calm, "and then I start cutting."

She swallowed thickly but didn't move other than that.

"How do I get Lucifer out of Trace's body?"

Arianna's mouth opened and then closed, as though struggling to find the right answer. That, or she was just trying to come up with a good enough lie.

A second late, she exhaled roughly and said, "You can't."

"Wrong answer." I brought the knife up to her shoulder, pressed it down against her flesh and then dragged it halfway down her arm.

An earsplitting scream tore from her lungs as thick red liquid blossomed from the wound and slowly oozed down her arm. Her scream turned into sobs as I brought the knife up to her neck, pressing the edge down against a spot just below her ear.

"What do you think, Dominic? Should I give her another chance?" I asked him without taking my eyes off her.

He chuckled and said, "Nah."

"That means no," I told her and then leaned in a little closer to whisper in her ear. "Between you and me, I probably would've given you another chance."

"I'm telling you the truth!" she said, her voice warped with fear and frustration.

"You better hope you're not," I said and twisted the blade clockwise, just a bit, nicking her skin and drawing a droplet of blood from her neck. "You hungry, Dominic?" I asked over my shoulder.

"Only for you, love," he answered, his voice a slice of fresh honey comb in my ears.

Her narrowed eyes turned to ice as she glowered at me. "You can cut me up all you want, feed me to your little vampire for all I care, it's still not going to save your boyfriend," she said proudly and then hawked a big glob of spit at my face. "We made sure of that."

Gnashing my teeth, I wiped the spit from my cheek with the back of my arm and then slammed my elbow into the bridge of her nose. The crunching sound of bone breaking echoed in the cavern as another scream ripped out of her.

"Unbelievable," I said, still feeling her nasty spit on my face. "You see what I get for being nice?"

"How many times do I have to tell you, angel? Nice guys always finish last."

I leaned in closer to Arianna, my eyes narrowed like a heat-seeking missile. "Do that again and I'll cut your lips off your face," I warned. And I meant it too.

Her strangled cries of pain and suffering turned into a maniacal laugh that made the hairs on the back of my neck stand up. "I'm going to enjoy watching Him eradicate your kind, you Hollier-than-thou do-gooders. You think you're so much better than us. Well, you're not!" she said, turning her head to the side to spit the blood from her mouth. "You shed just as much blood as we do, yet you think you're free of sin. Your hypocrisy makes me sick!"

"Tell it to someone who cares," I said and jerked her forward again. "That's not my war. The only thing I give a damn about is getting your demon-Master out of my boyfriend's body!"

"Like I said before," she said, spitting on the ground again. "You can't. His soul is tied to Lucifer and his vessel. Taking one out automatically kills the other one."

My throat tightened until it felt as though I were being strangled. "You're lying," I said, even though, deep down I already knew that she wasn't.

"Do you honestly think we would've made it *that* easy for you to undo everything we worked so hard to do?" She laughed again, and this time it felt like a knife to my chest. "He's a goner, baby. You might as well kiss his ass goodbye."

Everything inside of me hardened into stone as I listened to the words I had been secretly fearing since the moment they put that monster into Trace's body. Tears scorched the corners of my eyes as every remaining fragment of hope vanished from my heart, leaving nothing in its wake but the unbearable agony of loss.

He really was gone, and there was nothing I could do to get him back.

I'd failed him...

And it was all *her* fault.

A dark need for vengeance bore into my heart as I dropped the knife and grabbed the sides of her face. I had every intention of making her suffer, of beating her to a bloody pulp and then leaving her here to wither away and die, but in the moment, all I could think about was my need to see the life drain away from her eyes.

"Angel!" warned Dominic, but it was too late.

My hands were already moving, twisting her head around until I heard her neck snap. She fell to the ground in a lifeless heap, and all I could do was cry.

32. THE BODYCOUNT

The drive back to Huntington Manor was a haze of suffocating darkness and tears that seemed to have no end. Every breath I took scorched my lungs as though I were breathing under water, as though I were slowly drowning to death, except that my end never came. There was no break from the storm, no place to hide for sanctuary. The grief was all-encompassing and unwavering as it wrapped itself around every organ in my body, strangling me from the inside out.

"It isn't over yet, angel. We'll find another way." Dominic's words only briefly cut through my agony, but they were too fleeting and baseless to hold onto. So, I didn't.

I shut him out right along with the hope I'd held onto for so long.

I could no longer allow myself to believe that this was going to end well, because the truth was, it wouldn't, and I couldn't suffer through that realization all over again.

There was no way to get Trace back.

The sisters had made sure of it.

There was only one thing left to do, and I couldn't even

stomach the thought, let alone picture myself doing it.

We pulled into the driveway behind several cars and an SUV. I immediately noticed Nikki's red Jeep and Caleb's Camaro. They were waiting for the good news. Bile turned in my stomach as I realized I was going to have to relive the whole thing and tell them the truth: that there was no hope of getting Trace back.

He's a goner, baby. You might as well kiss his ass goodbye.

Dominic killed the engine and turned to me, but I didn't even have the strength to face him. All I could do was stare forward, blank-faced and broken.

"Let me help you, angel," he pleaded. His voice was solemn and soft and something else...pained.

I shook my head, knowing there wasn't anything anyone could do to help me now. This was my living nightmare, and I was never going to wake up from it.

"I can't bear seeing you like this," he said and then captured my hand in his.

I stared down at our interlaced fingers through a blur of tears.

"Let me take the pain away," he whispered quietly, though I never had a chance to answer his plea.

The front door of his house swung open, stealing my attention. I immediately recognized Ben and Caleb as they bolted down the steps towards us, their expressions sullen and twisted with apprehension, and I instantly knew they weren't just coming here to collect the fruits of our labor. They were coming to deliver bad news.

I sucked in a breath as Ben yanked the passenger door open and crouched down beside the car.

"What happened?" I said, my voice a strangled whisper.

"It's bad, Jem." His expression pinched. "Hannah's dead."

Hannah's...dead?

I blinked through my tears as I tried to understand the words he was telling me. Hannah was dead? How could Hannah be dead? When? Why? "What are you talking about?" I asked, panic infiltrating my voice.

"Some demon just delivered her body to the front door like a pizza," explained Caleb as he leaned in over Ben. "They left a note, Blackburn…" His voice trailed off as he shook his head.

There was no way to brace myself for what came next.

"Jem, he has Taylor," said Ben, his voice cracking on her name as he ran a hand down his face to wipe the rain from his eyes. "Lucifer has Taylor."

I pushed them out of my way and sprang from the car, running up the driveway and then bolting up the front steps, taking two at a time. Panic rode me as I hurled the front door open and immediately found Nikki and Carly. They were huddled together, sitting side by side in the entrance.

Carly was still crying hysterically, while Nikki had her arm around her, trying to comfort her. And judging by Nikki's bloodshot eyes, I could tell she had been crying too.

"Where is she?" I asked, bouncing my eyes between the two of them.

"The den," answered Nikki hoarsely, pointing as Carly continued to sob on her shoulder.

Leaving them, I ran for the den, bursting in and then stopping short as the awful smell of brimstone hit my face the moment I entered the room. I knew exactly what that meant: demon.

Ignoring the stench, my eyes landed on Tessa and Gabriel. They were standing together near the entranceway, talking quietly amongst themselves. I shifted my gaze over their shoulders to the sofa—to the golden locks of hair cascading over the edge of the sofa. I followed their trail up to the head it was attached to, and my heart immediately dropped to my feet.

Hannah's lifeless body lay motionless on the sofa as the orange light from the fire danced over her form.

"Nooo," I cried out, my head shaking back and forth. "This isn't happening!"

She was an innocent *human* girl who had nothing to do with any of this. She didn't deserve to die, not like this.

"I told you not to leave the fucking house," growled Tessa, picking the absolute worst possible time for a lecture. "What the hell did you do? Why does he think you have his consort?"

All I could do was stare at Hannah in a guilt-ridden stupor.

"Answer me!" she snapped. "He sent a demon here! What do you think would've happened to your friends if we weren't here to vanquish it?" she said, pointing with her thumb to the dark corner of the room.

My eyes darted over to the stinky body huddled over in the shadows. Undoubtedly, the demon and the reason for the putrid smell. "I really don't need this right now, Tessa."

"Like hell you don't!"

"Where's the note?" I demanded, my gaze whipping back to her as I tried to piece together what had happened here.

"I have it," she said without producing it.

"Give it to me."

"I think you need to—"

"Give me the goddamn note, Tessa!" I cut in, taking an aggressive step towards her.

She bounced a glance at Gabriel and then exhaled. "Fine," she said as she reached into her back pocket and pulled out a folded sheet of paper. "I really need you not to do anything stupid, Jemma. For once in your life, be smart about this," she warned before handing over the note.

Snatching it from her, I unfolded the paper and read the words:

Dearest Daughter,

Bring my consort or Taylor is next.

All Saints.

Come alone.

Yours eternally.

I crumbled the paper in my hands and then swung around on my heel to leave, but Tessa quickly grabbed my elbow and hauled me back.

"Where do you think you're going?"

"To get my best friend back. Where the hell else would I be going?"

"You can't just waltz in there alone, Jemma. We need to think this through."

"What's there to think about?" I asked as I pulled my arm free from her grip. "He wants me at All Saints, so that's where I'm going."

"First of all, you're not going there alone. Second of all, I need to get these bodies to the Council. Once that's done, we can talk about this and figure out our next move. You don't know what he has planned. Besides, the minute you give his Caster back, they're going to use their magic to bury you in *his* hell-tomb!"

"I wasn't planning on giving her back." I crossed my arms and looked away from her. "I couldn't even if I wanted to. She's already dead."

Tessa immediately started cursing profusely as Gabriel stepped up beside her, his worried eyes fixing me under the weight of their stare.

"What happened?" he asked softly.

"What do you think happened, Gabriel?" I bit out and then dropped his gaze. "I killed her."

"What do you mean you killed her?" asked a pissed-off voice from somewhere behind me. I didn't have to turn around to know it was Nikki. "What about Trace?!"

I lowered my head as his name assaulted my soul.

With my back still turned to her, I sucked in a breath and shook my head. "There's no way to save him." The air in the room thinned as I recalled Arianna's world-shattering words. It took every bit of strength I had not to crumble to the floor in pieces. "The Order was right. You were right," I said, bouncing my glance between Gabriel and my sister. "Their souls are tethered together. If I kill one, the other one dies. The sisters made sure of it."

"And how exactly do you know they weren't lying?!" snapped Nikki as she grabbed my shoulder and spun me around to face her. "You just killed our only hope of saving him!"

"If there was a way, she certainly wasn't going to tell us," interrupted Dominic as he ambled into the den. "The witch chose death, which either means she was telling the truth and there is no way to save him, or she was willing to go to her death to keep the secret. Either way, Jemma did the right thing."

"Of course *you* would say that!" barked Nikki. "You've had a hard-on for her since the day she moved here. Nothing she does is ever wrong to you," she accused bitterly.

Everyone in the room fell silent as Dominic causally leaned back against the bar and locked his eyes on Nikki. An easy smile curled his lips when he said, "That may very well be true, but that doesn't change the fact that she's right."

My cheeks flushed red as I realized what he'd just openly admitted in front of everyone.

"Thank you for proving my point, asshole," she said and then glared back at me. "Morgan's vision was right all along. Even if you didn't kill him by your hands, you're still the reason he's gone," she said and slammed her palms into my chest.

I stumbled backwards and hit the wall, though I didn't bother raising my hands to defend myself, because I knew she was right. I *was* the reason he was gone.

"That's enough," warned Tessa. "Touch her again and I'll rip your insides out from your mouth."

Vengeful tears pooled in Nikki's eyes as she looked back at me with disgust. "I should've buried you when I had the chance. Maybe then Trace would still be alive," she seethed and then slowly backed out of the room.

A few seconds later, I heard the front door slam shut, and I dropped my head, too ashamed to look at anyone.

"She's just upset," offered Caleb, though I wasn't sure if he was trying to comfort me or defend Nikki.

Maybe it was a bit of both.

"She's also right." Lifting my chin, I faced my judge and jury.

Caleb and Ben were hovering near by the doorway with a mixture of sympathy and pity on their faces while my sister hung back looking wholly ticked off, probably at Nikki. And, of course, Gabriel wore his usual troubled expression, his eyebrows knitted together with never-ending worry.

I couldn't even look at Dominic.

"Come on, Jem. We all know you didn't do this to him," said Ben, his voice straining to remain even. "The only people responsible here are devil-worshipping bitches that cast the spell in the first place."

I didn't answer, because honestly, it didn't really matter what any of them said. None of it would change the fact that Nikki *was* right. This *was* my fault. Sure, I wasn't the one to put Lucifer in Trace's body, but I'd cursed his life the moment I'd walked into it. Long before the Roderick sisters ever strolled into town. Morgan had seen it all those months ago and stupidly, I refused to believe it.

Because I didn't want to believe it.

And now he was gone because of it.

With my back still pressed against the wall, I lowered myself to the ground, crouching down as I tried to contain the hurricane rioting inside of me. The lights flickered in the den, a visible sign of my spiraling emotions, and while Ben and Caleb probably chalked it off to the end-of-spring thunderstorms, my sister and the brothers knew better than that.

"Look at me, Jemma," said my sister as she knelt down in front of me and picked up my chin. "You need to calm down and get your shit together."

But I wasn't sure that was physically possible anymore. Losing Trace that night was bad enough, but now I had to be the one to take his life, to put that final nail in his coffin and bury him.

How on earth was I ever going to be able to do that?

I couldn't.

I'd sooner die than watch the light vanish from his eyes—eyes that had brought me so much love and solace when all I had left in my world was darkness. But then…what about Lucifer? Was I just supposed to just let him continue killing innocent people? Hope that he would stop and decide to change his ways? That was never going to happen. He wasn't ever going to stop until someone made him, and no one had the power to do that but me.

My gaze veered over her shoulder to Dominic. His features were strained, as though it were painful to look at me. Not even he could help me now, I realized. I was unredeemable. A lost cause. My stomach lurched as the agony and guilt coiled itself around my stomach, squeezing the contents until I could taste bile at the back of my throat.

The fire roared to life, exploding from the fireplace as every bottle of liquor exploded on the bar.

"Dominic!" shouted Tessa as the lights continued to sputter uncontrollably. "A little help here?!"

He was beside me within a split second, swooping me up into his arms, and then carrying me out of the den—away from the darkness that chased me incessantly.

We could run all we want, I thought to myself dryly, but there was nowhere for me to hide.

Lucifer had said as much, and now, I finally believed it.

33. DARKNESS RISING

A clap of thunder reverberated against the glass window as Dominic carried me into his bedroom. The room was dark, save for a slither of light coming in from the hallway, but even that disappeared as Dominic kicked the door closed and walked me to his bed. Pressing me down against the soft down comforter, he remained close, hovering above me as his eyes roamed over my features, searching my face for any signs of life.

"I think I'm going to be sick," I warned, giving him ample time to put some space between us.

He remained perfectly still. "You're fine, angel. Just take a few deep breaths," he said, his voice soothing me as he whispered to me through the darkness.

Focusing only on the words he was telling me and nothing else, I pulled in a slow, shaky breath and then another.

His closeness to me helped soothe the storm of emotions that were rocketing through my body, but it did nothing to fix the hollowness that was left in their wake.

Everything inside of me had busted wide open, leaving remnants of the life I once had splattered all around me. Trace was gone. Hannah was dead, and now Taylor had been taken. It didn't matter which way I tried to spin it, they were all in this mess because of their connection to me.

"I really fucked it all up this time, didn't I?" I covered my eyes with the inside of my arm. I didn't want him to see the tears that were preparing to fall. He'd seen enough of those to last him a lifetime.

"Hardly," he said, gently pulling my arm back to my side. His brows were pulled down over his dark eyes, and his smooth jaw was set in a hard line. "When are you going to stop blaming yourself for things you cannot control?"

"I don't know, maybe when I stop getting everyone around me killed?"

"You're doing it again," he chided.

I sucked in another jagged breath as I struggled to pull my unraveling self back together.

Okay, so maybe I couldn't control everything and everyone around me. I'd give him that. No one could do that. But I could've controlled myself and stayed the hell away from them. Instead, I'd selfishly tried to hold onto my human life despite what everyone had told me. They'd warned me that it wasn't possible. That it wasn't safe to do so. But I did it anyway. I was desperate for any semblance of normalcy, and I'd somehow deluded myself into believing that I could have a happily ever after at the end of all this horror. That I could have a best friend, a boyfriend, and maybe even a husband and family someday. But none of that was real.

It was all just a lie I'd told myself; some fairy tale life meant for somebody else.

Someone *normal*.

The sad truth was, I wasn't normal, and I never would be, no matter how much I wanted it. I was a Slayer, and my only purpose in this world was to hunt monsters on the fringe of society, in the shadows—where I belonged. Every one of my friends were better off without me, and the sooner I accepted that, the safer everyone around me would be.

Realizing that was the easy part. Figuring out how to rectify everything was a whole different story. I had to find a way to bring Taylor home, and I had to send Lucifer back to where he belonged.

The Order had said it.

Tessa said it.

Hell, even Trace had said it.

They were all just waiting for me to hear it.

Unfortunately, I still couldn't fathom using the sword on Trace...but maybe there was another way? Maybe I could make a deal with him—with Lucifer. One that would save Taylor and put Lucifer back in the place he belonged.

Put me where I belonged...

"I have to go to All Saints," I said as I tried to lift myself off his bed, but he quickly pushed me back down.

"We will." He brushed a piece of hair from my forehead. "After you've calmed down."

"I'm calm," I lied, ignoring the *we* part. This was my fight, and I was fighting it alone.

He arched his eyebrow at me, knowing I was lying through my teeth.

"What? I'm calm, okay?!" I said as I pushed up on my elbows, bringing my face dangerously close to his. "See? Calm as a snail. Can I please go now?"

"No, you cannot," he said with finality. "I can feel your emotions, angel, and they're all over the place. The last thing you need is a storm in that pretty head of yours, particularly when you're planning on facing off with the king of Hell."

My body stiffened at his words.

When he put it that way, I probably could use a few minutes

to simmer down.

"Fine." Begrudgingly, I lay myself back down and pushed out an antsy breath of air as I tried to come up with some sort of plan to ditch him. There was no way I was letting Dominic anywhere close to that building. He would try to interfere, and that was if he even made it through the door alive.

"Now, while we're waiting, would you mind telling me what you think you're going to accomplish by going there?" he asked, pulling back for a better view as he sat beside me. "We both know you have no consort to speak of."

"I haven't really gotten that far in my plan yet."

He quirked a doubtful eyebrow at me.

"Okay, so I don't have a plan," I admitted. Well, none that involved anything other than barging into All Saints and begging him for his mercy. "It's not like I have an infinite number of options here, Dominic. He wants Arianna back for Taylor, and Arianna is dead. So…" I broke away from his gaze. "I'm going to give him the next best thing."

"Why am I getting the feeling I'm not going to like this?"

His jaw muscle feathered as I quickly pushed myself up from the bed and crossed my legs so that I was sitting face to face with him.

"Lucifer told me something the day he took me to Trace's cabin. He said I wasn't meant for this world, that I was meant to be beside him…in the underworld." Just saying the words out loud sent an icy chill skittering down my back.

"Care to explain why I'm only hearing about this conversation now?" he asked, his tone clipped.

"Because…it didn't matter then. I wasn't planning on going *then*," I said as though it were so obvious. "But he was right, and I see that now. If I agree to go with him, he might be willing to spare Taylor, and that would be good enough for me. Everyone around here is better off without me anyway—"

"Angel—"

"And maybe this way, I could keep him contained, you know? Keep him away from everyone else—"

"ANGEL! ENOUGH."

My plea died at the back of my throat. I had never heard Dominic shout before, and frankly, it stunned me silent.

A meld of fiery emotions flickered through his eyes as he clamped down on his jaw and pushed forward into my personal space. "You. Are. Not. Going. Anywhere. With. Him."

Fighting the urge to cower away with him, I held my ground, though my voice lacked any real punch when I muttered, "I don't think that's your call to make."

His eyes tapered as a devious smile impressed itself upon his lips. "If you think I'm going to stand by and allow you sacrifice your life to Lucifer, for a useless human no less, you have gravelly misunderstood who I am or what I am willing to do to get what I want. And make no mistake about it, angel. *You* are what I want."

I chose to ignore the last part of his statement, even though it made my stomach feel as though I'd just taken a swan-dive off a cliff.

"If you think that Taylor is a useless human, you have gravelly misunderstood who *I* am," I quickly fired back instead.

"Perhaps not in your eyes, angel, but in the grand scheme of things, she most certainly is."

"If I don't give him something he wants, she's going to die!" Of that, I was certain. He would not hesitate to kill her just the way he did Hannah and the people at Temple. None of us meant anything to him.

"Then she dies," he said flatly, his tone and expression void of any emotion.

Just hearing him utter the words sent a torrent of rage through my body. "I'm not going to let him kill my best friend!

That's not even an option!" Pissed off, I hopped off the bed and tried to put some much-needed distance between us, but he was already in front of me, blocking my path by the time my feet hit the ground.

"I will follow you wherever you wish to go, angel, fight as many of these doomed wars as you wish to fight," he said, craning his head so that we were at eye-level. "I'll even help you save these unserviceable humans you call friends, but I will not, under any circumstances, allow *you* or anyone else to extinguish your light."

"You can't stop me," I challenged, though I regretted it as soon as the words sounded back to me.

"I most certainly can," he laughed icily, his dark eyes glimmering with something sinister and foreboding.

Shit. He *could* stop me. Pretty easily too. I needed to back us up, to bring us back to neutral grounds before he went ahead and did something stupid, like compelling me to run off to Paris with him.

"Look, I can save her, Dominic," I said, my voice softer now as I quickly tried to explain myself. "I know I can, and maybe just maybe, I can save everyone else too. If I can get him to agree to take me instead and trick him into coming back to Hades with me, we can figure out a way to close the Gates and trap him there."

"And what of you?"

I shrugged, because it didn't matter. "I don't belong in this world, Dominic. Everything I touch turns to shit."

"I wholeheartedly beg to differ."

"Yeah? Name one good thing that's happened since I came here," I challenged.

He straightened his back and lifted his chin, making me feel as though he were towering over me. Heat pooled in my stomach when he gazed down at me and said, "You're looking at it."

I wasn't sure what to say to that.

"I like to think that you've made me a better man, angel," he said and then cracked a mischievous smile. "Well, much better than I was when you found me."

As sweet as his words were, I shook my head at him and said, "That doesn't count."

"Why not?" He appeared to be offended by that.

"Because we're bloodbonded," I answered gingerly.

"What does that have to do with anything?"

"I don't know. It just seems like something that should disqualify you." I looked away and then muttered, "Either way, it isn't good enough."

Not when I got my boyfriend trapped, Hannah killed, and my best friend kidnapped—twice. Not to mention the countless others that have been hurt or killed indirectly because of me. The list wasn't even almost even.

"I have to do something, Dominic, and this is the only thing I know of that doesn't involve plunging a sword into Trace's heart."

"Has it ever occurred to you that perhaps you should be considering that alternative?"

My nostrils flared as my eyes locked onto his. "I'm not killing Trace. I can't do that to him."

"You *won't* do that," he corrected. "And let's be honest, angel. You're not fighting against this because of him. You're doing it for yourself."

My head flinched back as though he'd just sucker-punched me. "The hell I am."

"Every second that you hesitate, innocent people die—"

"Dammit, I know that!" I quickly cut him off.

He paused and let out a sharp breath before continuing slowly, softly. "What you have failed to consider is that Romeo is being forced to bear witness to those slayings by his own hands."

Everything inside of me froze.

"Every day that you refuse to do what you know in your heart to be the right thing, you are forcing him to live another day trapped in a vessel that he no longer controls, and while I do not particularly care what becomes of him, I know that you do. I know you would not want this for him."

My hands shot up to my face, hiding myself away from the pain of his words.

In my mad race to find a way to save Trace, to finding an alternative to vanquishing Lucifer, I'd failed to fully grasp the fact that Trace was still in there. That he'd been an imprisoned spectator while Lucifer killed Hannah and all those people at Temple. He'd watched his own hands light the flame that caused so many innocent deaths.

A strangled sob escaped my throat as I realized he had been forced to watch his father take on a demon. My knees buckled beneath me, and I crumbled to the floor in shock.

He'd begged me to let him go—to stop Lucifer, and I didn't.

Dominic lowered himself to ground, placing himself directly in front of me. "The last thing I ever want to do is cause you pain, angel, but you would have come to see it on your own, and by then, the damage may have been irreversible." He brushed back the strands of hair that had fallen across my face. "Please do not hate me for this."

My shoulders shook as tears rained down my cheeks like waterfalls.

"As intolerable as it may seem, you have the ability to put an end to this tonight."

"How am I ever going to be able t-to do that if I can't even stomach th-thinking about it?" I sputtered through sobs and then met his troubled eyes. "I might as w-well put the sword in my own heart, because I won't be able to l-live with myself. I just won't."

Dominic lowered his head. He knew I was right. I wasn't strong enough or cold enough to live with something like that. The moment would haunt me for the rest of my life, eating away at my soul until it eviscerated everything that I was.

"I can take the memory away for you afterwards," he whispered softly through the darkness. "As much or as little as you need."

My chin quivered as I sucked in a tear-filled breath.

"You could leave Hollow Hills and find a place far away from here where you could mourn your loss." There was something so real and vulnerable in his eyes when he added, "I could come with you if you needed me too."

I broke away from his gaze, knowing that none of that would ever happen. I didn't deserve the easy way out. I'd done this to Trace, and I earned my right to suffer for it for the rest of my life. The gaping hole in my chest was only a prelude of what was to come, and I would take my penance for it.

The bedroom door swung open as Ben stepped into the darkened room.

"Jem?" he called as his eyes dusted over the room before landing on me. "We need to talk."

34. THE RECKONING

Wiping my cheeks with the back of my hand, I struggled up to my feet, my heart pattering erratically as I crossed the room to where Ben stood solemnly. Even in the darkness, I could see his eyes were wet with moisture, and I instantly knew this "talk" was going to be a bad one.

My lips parted to say something to him, but my dread quickly shoved the words back down my throat.

"Tessa and Gabriel left with the bodies," he said, rubbing the side of his face as his eyes slid briefly to Dominic and then back to mine. "I figure that gives us at least a couple of hours."

"To do what?" asked Dominic.

Ben didn't answer right away, which only made my heart race faster when I asked, "To do what, Ben?"

"To get Taylor back," he finally answered. "I'm going to All Saints, Jem, with or without you. But I'm kind of hoping you're planning on coming too."

My stomach dropped at his words. "You can't go there, Ben. The note said I have to go alone."

"Come on, Jem," he answered with a slow shake of his head.

"You know me well enough to know that's not going to happen." He ticked his chin to Dominic. "And I'm pretty sure he's not letting you go alone either."

Dominic nodded his head in agreement.

"Besides," he continued before I could say anything else on the matter, "if we plan this out properly, we can take him out before he even sees any of us coming."

"Take him out?" I repeated, certain I'd heard that wrong. If it was anyone else, I would have believed it, but not Ben. He was Trace's best friend since as far back as either of them could remember.

He dropped his head and shoulders. "You heard what they said. There's no way to separate them."

Shaking my head, I rubbed the horrified expression from my face. It appeared that everyone had already reached this insufferable conclusion long before I was even ready to look at it.

"We can't just let him keep killing people, Jem. Trace wouldn't want this. You know it, and I know it."

I tried to blink back my tears, but it was useless. They were spilling down onto my cheeks, picking up exactly where they'd left off not even two minutes ago.

Dammit. Would I ever be able to stop crying?

"Look, I know you can stop this. I know you have the sword," he said, glancing away when I looked back at him surprised. "I overheard your sister taking about it with Gabriel."

Fucking shit.

"We can't just stay here and wait for him to kill her," he said, his tone sharper and more urging.

"Don't you think I know that?" I fired back, panic strangling me.

I knew it, and yet my feet still refused to move.

No matter how many times I'd heard the saying, "between a

rock and a hard place," I'd never truly understood its meaning until that very moment. I was between two rocks right in the middle of hell.

It didn't matter which way I looked at it. Someone I loved was going to die tonight, and the blood was going to be on my hands, and mine alone. Everyone else would be able to leave it in the past and move on with their lives, but I was going to have to live with this ghost for the rest of my life. Maybe that's why it was so much harder for me to see the bigger picture. I was the only one that was going to be irreversibly changed by it—haunted by it.

The bigger picture wasn't so big when you were looking at it through my eyes.

"You can either come with me and help me save your best friend or you can sit here and let him kill more innocent people. What's it gonna be?" he asked, his dirty blond eyebrows arched high, challenging me.

"I'll go," I said, my voice barely above a whisper. Of course, I would go. I had to. I was the only one who could stop Lucifer. "But on one condition."

"Don't ask me to stay here, Jem. I'll give you anything you want, except for that."

"I won't be able to concentrate on what I have to do if I have to be worried about watching your back."

"You don't need to watch my back," he fired back, audibly offended. "If anything, we'll be watching your back," he said, wagging his finger between himself and Dominic. "Besides, Lucifer ain't coming alone, and you know that. We're just making the fight fair."

"Dominic, can you please back me up here?" I asked, turning to him for help.

"Unfortunately, angel, I happen to agree with him."

Of course he did. "Thanks a lot," I ground out in a tone that was anything but thankful.

"So?" prompted Ben with determination in his eyes. "Are we taking his car, or Caleb's?"

I shook my head, drawing the damn line. "Caleb is *not* coming with us. Two of you is already bad enough."

"Bringing a Caster is just good business. He's powerful, Jem, and besides, there's strength in numbers."

"Not when Lucifer said to come alone," I reminded him.

"You won't be saying that *when* things pop off, and trust me, Jem, they *will* pop off, especially when he finds out you already killed his witch."

I swallowed the thick lump in my throat.

This was bad. Like stupid bad. The worst part was, I knew I wasn't going to be able to convince any of them to stay out of it. Ben was determined to save Taylor and refused to listen to reason. And Dominic…well, Dominic was going to fight by my side, no matter what. Sitting out on the sidelines was never his style. And even if I could convince Caleb to sit this one out, he wouldn't let himself look like a coward.

Not when Ben and Dominic had already signed themselves up to go.

"We'll take Caleb's car," I finally said and then hung my head in defeat.

Like I said, stupid bad.

35. KISS ME DEADLY

We had less than twenty minutes to come up with a stellar plan that wasn't going to get the whole lot of us killed, or worse, set off the damn apocalypse. Dominic and Ben did most of the talking while I sipped on black coffee and periodically stepped in to try to convince them to stay behind and let me handle this by myself. Of course, none of them would hear any of it, though I did at least manage to get them to agree to remain hidden until I gave the signal. And really, that was all I needed, because little did they know, that signal was never going to come.

I had absolutely no intention of involving them in this fight. None.

This was my battle, my devil-sized cross to bear, and I intended to carry it alone. I was the one who brought Lucifer into this world, however indirectly it may have been, and I would be the one to take him out of it. I only hoped I'd stay alive long enough to make my plea, because not only was I showing up to All Saints sans consort, I was also bringing two Shifters and a Caster along for the ride.

Lucifer was going to be very, very unhappy, and that was

never a good thing.

Climbing into the back of Caleb's Camaro, I pulled my seat belt around my body and clicked it into place. My gaze veered out the window as I watched the rain streak against the glass.

Regardless of what Dominic had said, I had every intention of making a deal with the devil. I would agree to go anywhere with him, to do anything, with one very minor stipulation: that he release Taylor *and* Trace as his vessel.

At this point, it was the one and only card I had left to play.

And yes, I was well aware of the fact that I was pretty much dooming my own life to an eternity of misery and insufferable agony, but even an eternity in Hell with Lucifer was better than a life on this earth without Trace.

I wasn't sure I could survive that, and I wasn't interested in trying either.

A penny for your thoughts? asked Dominic to my mind.

He was sitting beside me with his legs pushed open as the shadows from the outside flickered across his face while Caleb and Ben rode up front, arguing over the best way to get into the ceiling vents at All Saints.

I shook my head and offered him nothing, though I couldn't bring myself to fully meet his eyes.

We were bloodbonded, after all, and I feared he would sense something was off if I allowed him to look at me—to see me the way only he could.

I turned my gaze back to the window as I watched the outline of trees cast their shadows into the night. My mind switched to auto-pilot, refusing to think about Trace or what it would do to him if he knew what I had planned. He would try to stop me. He would try to sacrifice his own life in exchange for mine, and it would be easy for him. Almost as easy as it was going to be for me to do the same thing for him.

"We're almost there," said Ben, turning his head slightly in my direction. "Remember, Jem, you need to keep him talking long enough for us to find Taylor and get her out of there. Dominic will cover you until we come back."

I nodded, playing my part as I pretended to go along with our plan. And then something occurred to me. "What if she isn't there?" I met his eyes through the shrouded darkness. "What if he's keeping her someplace else?"

"Then you back out. Tell him it's no deal until you see she's okay."

I nodded again, hoping that she was there, and that he would agree to let her go...in exchange for me. I didn't want to prolong this thing for even a second longer than it needed to be. The sooner we made the deal, the sooner Taylor and Trace would be free to go back to their lives. The lives they had before I strolled into town and ruined everything.

Dominic placed his hand over mine, stealing my attention back to him. "You're shaking, love," he remarked, his eyebrows gathered into a concerned knot.

I looked down at my trembling hand and swallowed thickly. "It's just my adrenaline," I said without meeting his eyes.

Of course, that wasn't the only reason I was shaking like a leaf, but it was all he was getting.

"Angel...are you sure you're ready to do this?" he asked, his tenor barely more than a whisper.

Was he doubting that I could?

Strange. It wasn't like Dominic to doubt me.

I pushed the uncomfortable thought away and nodded. "As ready as I'll ever be."

And it was as close to the truth as I would get tonight.

It wasn't like this were the kind of thing you could ready yourself to do. You sort of just had to do it—to jump feet first into the symbolical lion's pit and hope to God you didn't get torn to shreds before your feet even touched the ground.

A short stretch of silence passed between us, and I relaxed back in my seat, thinking he had let it go. And then I felt his arm slide along the back of my headrest as the side of his body pressed up against mine. He had completely invaded my personal space, and while my brain was telling me to shove him back to his corner, my body was having no part of it.

"Angel." His mouth was so close to my ear that it made my body shudder.

My eyes slipped shut.

"Will you please look at me?"

My pulse quickened as I pulled in a breath and prepared myself to meet those knowing eyes. Only, I never turned. I couldn't bring myself to face him—to say goodbye to him.

I inwardly cursed at myself for being such a coward.

"Why won't you look at me?" he asked, suspicion creeping into his honeyed voice. If he didn't suspect anything before, he definitely did now.

Turn, dammit. Turn or he'll know something's up!

Shuttering myself, I slowly turned my head and met his eyes. My heart immediately sank to the bottom of my stomach, but I held his gaze nonetheless. "Happy?"

"No." His pupils dilated as he narrowed his eyes at me. "I felt that."

"Felt what?"

"*You.*" Lines creased his otherwise perfectly smooth skin as tension swept across his forehead. "Something's off. I can feel it, and I don't like it."

"You're being paranoid, Dominic," I said as evenly as I could manage. "I'm just mentally preparing myself to do this. Everything's fine," I lied and then started to turn my focus back to the window, but he quickly captured my chin and forced my attention back to him.

In that moment, we were so close, our breath was practically making out.

"I don't believe you." His eyes roamed over my face, taking in my features as though trying to decipher a ten-thousand-piece puzzle. "You're hiding something."

"I'm not." The words left my mouth in a breathy whisper. It was taking every morsel of strength I had not to succumb to him, not to sink all the way into his arms and make myself a home there.

"*Then look at me,*" he demanded, this time without giving me the option.

Having no other choice but to do as he said, I surrendered to the compulsion and allowed myself one final parting good look at him.

His expression softened as I took in the forgiving edges to his face, the fullness of his lips, the boundless depths to his sinfully dark eyes. Eyes that I could easily get lost in. Curls that begged for me to run my fingertips through...

Shit.

I was in some big-ass trouble.

"Dominic," I growled.

"Yes, angel."

"How long are you going to make me do this for?" I meant for it to sound angry, but it came out weak and suppliant.

He cracked a smile, enjoying his temporary hold over me. "For as long as you *want* to."

At his words, I felt the heaviness of my free-will return, but oddly, my gaze never broke away from his. I'd fought so hard to avoid looking at him, *feeling* for him, that now I couldn't seem to do anything but that.

The man was as beautiful as they came, a masterpiece in his own right.

Seconds ticked by, and I was still staring up at him, frantically trying to memorize each one of features—his expression, his inscrutable countenance—wanting so badly to remember every inch of his face. To remember all the ways he looked at me and how alive it made me feel inside.

I would tuck those memories away in my heart—someplace so deep and hidden that not even the devil himself could find them—and I'd hold onto them for as long as my heart was permitted to beat.

My gaze was still locked on his when he smiled down at me, the faintest hint of a knowing smirk. He knew he was affecting me. He knew I was completely wrapped up in him, soaking up every edge and line of his beautiful face and eating him up in droves. He knew it, and I didn't even care that he knew it.

I needed to remember it. To remember all of him.

My belly clenched as I silently vowed to never forget a second of my time with him, or all the ways he had come to my rescue when I was drowning in a sea of never-ending despair. He had stuck by my side, no matter how bad it got, or how much danger he put himself in, and he had made me fall so incredibly hard for him because of it.

Tears prickled the corners of my eyes as I realized I would never get a chance to thank him, to let him know just how much he really meant to me.

And I'd never get a chance to have that kiss.

"Dammit, angel, what is going on in that pretty head of yours?" he whispered as his finger came up and wiped away a fallen tear. His eyes were peeled on me as though trying to get a proper read on my spiraling emotions.

Good luck with that.

I shook my head and sighed heavily. "You don't want to know."

"I beg to differ." His eyes darkened as though I'd challenged him.

I knew that look. "Dominic, don't you dare—"

"*Tell me what you're thinking*," he commanded softly before I could finish getting my warning out.

My eyes dropped to his mouth as his lips twisted into a delicious, self-satisfied grin. He wasn't even remotely sorry for his blatant misuse of his power.

I glared at him and then admitted, "I was thinking about kissing." And it wasn't a lie. I *was* thinking about it. It just wasn't the only thing I was thinking about.

"Kissing?" He eyes were hooded with interest. "*Elaborate.*"

"I was thinking about kissing you," I clarified as a deep blush swept across my cheeks. "That I want to."

He pulled back a little and examined me like he hadn't trusted his ears.

Jeez. Was it so hard for him to believe that I'd want to kiss him? Hadn't I asked him to kiss me all those weeks ago in Engel's castle? Then again, I'd also turned him down just as many times.

Talk about mixed signals.

Looking back on it now, I supposed I just assumed I'd have more time. That the dust would have eventually settled, and I'd have all the time in the world to do all the things I'd always dreamed of, to visit all the places I'd only ever read about in books. To have as many kisses with him as I wanted.

I thought I'd have more time, but my time had abruptly run out on me.

Shaking my head at the unfairness of it all, I unclicked my seatbelt and did the unthinkable: I climbed onto his lap and seized his face in my hands. His eyes immediately flared with surprise and confusion, and then with something else.

With want. With pure unfiltered desire.

If I'm going to Hell, I might as well earn myself a ticket.

His questioning eyebrows drew together as he watched me lower my head, stopping only when my face was less than a hairbreadth away from his. I could smell the liquor on his lips, taste the sweet aroma of decadent chocolate on his skin, and my stomach tightened. It was a beautiful smell, and I was going to miss it.

"Angel..." He whispered my name like a plea for salvation, and my unsated eyes snapped to his mouth. The world screeched to a halt as though collectively holding its breath for me—for us. For this moment.

I watched as he slowly wet his bottom lip, and at the sight of it, I unraveled. Erasing all remnants of the space between us, I greedily pressed my mouth against his and kissed him with everything I had and all that I never would.

It only took a split second for his shock to dissipate, and then he was kissing me back just as hard. His hands immediately found my hips and clutched onto them, holding me possessively as I moved my body over his and deepened the kiss.

All I could think about was the soft feel of his lips against mine, the way his breath tasted like whiskey and mint, and my need took over, giving way to something far more primal than anything I had ever felt before. All semblance of guilt and self-control disappeared, leaving nothing but the bare-boned truth in its wake.

A deep groan rumbled at the back of his throat as I parted his lips and tasted his tongue, reveling in it as though he were mine for the taking. I rolled my hips in response and he groaned again, a savage growl at the back of his throat.

"Woah," said Ben from the front seat upon spotting me straddling Dominic.

But even the realization that I had an audience couldn't stop me from taking the thing I had denied myself of for so long. The fire between us had become all-encompassing, feral, and I wanted nothing more than to burn in it.

And judging by the way he was kissing me back, he felt the

same exact way.

My fingers weaved into his hair, reveling in the silkiness of his soft curls as his own hands slid up the back of my shirt, sending a geyser of heat through my veins that kissed the most scared parts of my body. And then his hands were on my butt, squeezing and kneading as he pushed me down harder against him. My thighs clenched as a soft moan rustled to life inside my chest, but it was quickly swallowed up by the fierce devotion of his mouth against mine.

What had started out as a goodbye kiss, a small token of my appreciation, had quickly turned into something so much more than a kiss. It was primal, and it was dangerous, and it needed to stop, or I'd never be able to muster the strength needed to walk away from him. And I really didn't need another thing to anchor me down to this life. Not when I was about to condemn myself to an eternity in Hell.

Breathless, I pulled back from him, my hands shaking as I tried to regain some semblance of self-control. Dominic's lips chased mine through the darkness, but I held him back, letting him know that our moment had come and went.

"I beg you not to stop," he pleaded, his voice low and raw.

If only that were an option…

"I have to."

He pressed his forehead against mine, his hands still planted on my butt, and I swore I could feel his heart thundering in his chest. "You cannot allow me to taste heaven like that and then take it away from me," he said, his breathing coming out in rapid bursts, letting me know he was still winded from our kiss.

I smiled, realizing I had done that to him. Even if for only the faintest of moments, I was alive again.

"I'm sorry," I said through my smile, though truth be told, I really wasn't. As much as I didn't mean to start something I couldn't finish, there wasn't a single cell in my body that regretted it.

His lids lifted, revealing eyes that burned with carnal sin. "You truly are going to be the end of me, you know that?"

The leather seat protested as he shifted his hips below me. I could still feel his hardness pressed against me, but I pretended not to notice, even though it was making my thighs clench.

"Death by way of an interrupted kiss? Not likely," I teased, trying to break some of the sexual tension.

He smiled, though the intensity in his gaze never let up as his eyes dusted listlessly across my features, moving from my swollen lips, to my rosy cheeks, and finally settling on my eyes.

"Did you like it?" he asked painfully soft, sending my heartrate into another tantrum.

"Did I like *what?*" I couldn't hide my smile.

"Did you like kissing me?" There was no challenge in his question, no ulterior motive to get me to admit my feelings for him. He wanted to know where I stood—where we stood.

Even though my heart was telling me he already knew the answer to that, I still couldn't find the courage to say it out loud. To admit that there weren't strong enough words to describe just how much I had *liked* kissing him, or what it had done to my body. I supposed we all had secrets we couldn't share, stories we'd never tell…

Maybe this was one of those things for me.

When he realized I wasn't going to offer up anything, he pulled back a little and studied me—his hungry eyes searching mine once again. Always searching, always mining for the truth.

Nervous that he would see through my poorly-constructed façade, I offered a small smile and then tried to climb off his lap, but he quickly gripped my thighs and held me down against him. He wasn't ready to let me go, though something was telling me he'd never be ready to do that.

"Ask me again," he demanded as shadows from the passing

lights continued to dance across his face.

My heart sputtered chaotically, slamming into my chest every which way because I knew exactly what he wanted me to ask him, and this time, I needed to hear it—to memorize the sound of it as it imprinted itself on my soul.

"Are you in love with me, Dominic Huntington?"

"With every fiber of my being, angel."

I tried not let his words affect me, to completely embed themselves inside of me, but they had already burrowed into my heart by the time he finished speaking them. I knew they would make walking away from him, from this life, that much harder, but damn was it ever worth it.

"Thank you," I whispered.

He crooked an eyebrow at me. "For being in love with you?"

"For saving me." I padded my finger across his decadent lips. "You made the unbearable bearable."

He cupped the back of my neck and drew me forward, our breath once again mixing together like a forbidden tonic I couldn't help but breathe in. "I could do a lot more than that, love. If you'd let me."

He was a fraction of an inch from touching his lips to mine when Ben interrupted us from the front passenger seat.

"You two about done back there? We're less than three minutes away, and we kind of need your heads in the game here."

His words were a like a needle scraping against the thin rubbery surface of the balloon I was floating in. And just like that, the balloon popped.

"We're done," I answered without bothering to meet his eyes. My gaze was still locked on Dominic, drinking him up, from the steadfast resolve in his eyes to the lust-filled heat he was sending my way.

Even after everything that happened, and everything that was coming at us, I couldn't seem to get my fill.

See now, that's where you're wrong, angel, said Dominic to my mind, the fire in his eyes still burning wildly as it threatened to burn us all to the ground. *We aren't done. We haven't even started.*

He was right about that.

This thing between us had barely lifted off the ground, and unfortunately, grounded was where it would have to remain. Along with the rest of my life and any other stupid dreams I may have had for myself. He certainly wasn't the only thing I was going to have to leave behind, but it felt like he would be the hardest.

Sorrow clamped down around my throat again as I climbed off his lap and unceremoniously returned to my seat. The bubble had burst, sending me back head-first into my reality. Pulling the seatbelt across my body, I drew in a breath and tried to re-center myself to the moment that was coming at me full speed ahead.

Mindlessly, my finger drifted up to my lips as my eyes veered back outside the window.

I could still taste him in my mouth...

And then I memorized that too.

36. NO TURNING BACK

Angry storm clouds gathered in the distance as we pulled into an abandoned steel factory about two blocks from All Saints. Apart from the fact that Caleb still needed to Cloak himself and the others, Ben wanted us to go over the plan one more time, as though repeating the idiotic suicide mission would make it any less idiotic.

I opened my door and stepped outside into the cool night air, stretching my legs as I tried to calm my ever-present anxiety while Ben and Caleb hauled ass to the front of the car to look over the blueprints for All Saints. I let them do their thing without interruption, even though I knew it was pointless. We wouldn't be executing that particular plan no matter how many times they memorized the ins and outs of the building.

My eyes drifted to Dominic. He appeared to be lost in thought as he leaned back against the trunk of the car with both hands buried in his pockets. I calmly walked around the Camaro and joined him at the back.

"A penny for your thoughts?" I asked, rubbing away the droplets of rain that had begun to pepper my arms.

"That's my line," he answered matter-of-factly.

"Well, I happen to like it, so it's mine now."

The corner of his mouth lifted. "Do you always just take what you like, angel?"

"Don't you?" I countered, though it came out more like an accusation.

His voice sounded bitter when he answered, "I certainly did before."

His expression turned contemplative again as an uncomfortable chill spread over my body.

I wasn't used to seeing him like this...so bothered and distressed. That was generally Gabriel's schtick, and it just didn't look right on Dominic. He was supposed to be aloof and carefree and untouchable.

"And what about now?" I asked, watching as his jaw hardened.

"And now it's taking every morsel of control I have not to compel you to leave with me."

My stomach tightened. "You wouldn't do that."

He laughed, the sound of it dark and biting. "I most certainly would," he said, still facing forward.

There was nothing in front of us but a deserted road with broken streetlights and overgrown grass, but it somehow held his interest. Behind us, the old factory stood guard, bruised and battered and no longer of use to anyone.

"You *won't* do that," I corrected myself, eying him pointedly.

He didn't respond except for a small tick of his jaw muscle.

But I knew Dominic, and I knew he'd let me have my fight. As long as I was fighting it. But what would he do once he realized I wasn't there to fight at all?

He would get in my way. He would do everything in his power to stop me, and let's face it. He had a whole lotta power over me.

I had to find a way to ease his worries, to calm him enough to drop his guard and stay back.

"Look, you really don't have to worry about me," I said, keeping my voice as light as possible. "I'll always be okay as long as I keep this little trinket around my neck. You know that."

He met my eyes and held them. "Do I?"

"It's not the first time I've had to face-off against—"

"This is different," he interjected, his tone and expression equally smooth. "You are different."

I could practically feel the tension seeping out of his pores.

"Why? Because I kissed you?" I asked, and then chewed my bottom lip as the memory of his mouth against mine rushed back in.

"Yes, because you kissed me. *You* kissed me," he gritted out, suddenly looking upset by it. "The mere fact that it happened at all is not sitting very well with me."

What in the freak was that supposed to mean?

"Are you trying to say you didn't want it to happen?" I asked, trying to remain calm, because, what the freak?

His lusty eyes immediately dropped to my mouth. "Of course I did."

Phew. "Then what's the problem?" I asked, still thoroughly and completely confused.

"The problem, angel, is that you've been pushing me away for so long that it actually feels natural to me, yet tonight of all nights, you accosted me in the car—"

"*Accosted* you?" I pushed off the car and faced him. He didn't seriously just say that.

"Yes, angel, accosted me. Try to keep up."

My cheeks flamed with anger as I rammed both hands into his chest—hard. "You know what, Dominic? Screw you," I said and then tried to storm away, but he promptly snatched my elbow and propelled me back to the spot I'd been standing in, only this time, he was in front of me, boxing me in as he towered over my five-foot-seven frame.

"Get out of my way before I *accost* you with my fist," I warned him, and I wasn't even kidding.

He flattened both hands against the trunk and leaned in, searching my eyes like a fiend scouring the street for his drugs. "There it is." A mischievous smile curled his lips.

"There *what* is?" I snapped, trying to break myself out of his crazy-town prison.

"That fire and fight of yours that I like so much." He was looking directly into my eyes, mining me once again. "They've been missing all night." Narrowing his eyes, he leaned in closer. "I'd like to know why that is, being that you're heading into the biggest fight of your life tonight?"

Shit. He was on to me. The freaking jig was up!

"I don't know what you're talking about," I said dismissively, lying my ass off almost as easily as I breathed in air.

"I think you do." He practically sang the words, but the dark undertones made it sound like anything but a song. "It's as though you've already given up. As though you have no intention of winning whatsoever. Honestly, angel, if I didn't know any better, I'd think you were—" His voice dropped off a cliff as an icy film of realization settled over his eyes.

Everything halted. Me, him, time, my heart…

"You aren't going there to kill him at all, are you?" he charged, his tone sharp and accusing. "You're going there to sacrifice yourself."

I gnashed my teeth together, refusing to answer as my hand covertly drifted to the back of my jeans.

"*Answer me truthfully!*" he ordered in his stupid, pain-in-my-ass, will-stealing voice. "*Are you going there to kill Lucifer or not?*"

"Not," I answered honestly, because well, I had no other choice in the matter.

"I knew it," he said, his teeth clamped down so tightly that I'd barely seen his lips move.

"This is the only way I know of to save them both, Dominic. You know it's true, and you can't stop me."

"Watch me." He grabbed my jaw roughly, primed to compel my decision away from me, but it was far too little and far too late.

I had already pulled my stake from behind my back and plowed it into his heart before he had a chance to get the first word out.

His eyes widened with shock before turning cold as the life slowly disappeared from his face. He crumbled to the street in my arms, his once luminous skin now a sickly shade of ash.

It's only temporary, I told myself as my heart seized in my chest at the sight of his lifeless body. As soon as this nightmare was over, the stake would be removed, and he too could return to the life he had before I came here.

All of them would.

"What are you guys doing back…?" Ben's question died at the back of his throat upon spotting me on the ground with Dominic in my arms, and a stake protruding from his chest. "Jesus, Jem. What the fuck did you do?!"

"What is it?" asked Caleb, the sound of his sneakers smacking against the pavement as he rounded the corner. "Holy shit, Blackburn." His mouth hung open, gaping at me like I was the starring freak of the carnival sideshow.

"I think she lost it, man," said Ben, his panicked tone hushed, but still loud enough for me to hear.

"I didn't lose it." I glared up at them as a lone fat tear slipped down my cheek. "I did what I had to do."

This wasn't the way I wanted to end things with Dominic. It wasn't the way I wanted my last memory of him to play out, but I had no choice.

276

"Help me get him back in the car," I choked out, working hard to keep more tears from spilling out.

Neither Caleb nor Ben made a single move. At this point, they weren't even blinking.

I snapped my head up and fixed each of them a look. "Help me, dammit!"

Ben was the first to break out of his stupor. He knelt down on the ground before me, his nervous eyes examining my face, as though looking for signs of full-blown mania. He thought I was crazy.

I wasn't crazy.

"He was going to compel me from going." I needed him to understand me. To know that I wasn't some deranged lunatic for doing this to Dominic ten minutes after I *accosted* him in the back seat.

"Why would he do that, Jem?" he asked delicately, speaking to me in the same tone you'd use if you were speaking to a frightened child. Or a crazy person. "He was here to help us."

"Because I'm not going to All Saints to kill Lucifer, Ben. I'm going there to make a deal with him."

"What deal?" asked Caleb. Even though he was still keeping his distance from me, I could tell his eyes had gone all small and squinty like I was speaking some foreign language.

"What are you talking about, Jem? What deal?" echoed Ben.

"Me in exchange for Taylor and Trace."

"*What?*" Caleb practically hissed the word out.

"Woah wait a minute," said Ben, shaking his head. "You're planning on sacrificing yourself...to the devil?" Ben flinched back at his own words. "You can't be serious."

"Does this sound like something I would joke about?"

He blinked, struggling to wrap his mind around what I'd just said. And then, "What makes you so sure he'd take you in exchange for them?" he asked, a hint of curiosity stirring his voice.

"I'm *not* sure," I answered truthfully, because I wasn't sure. "But I have to at least try."

"This is crazy," said Caleb, pushing his hands through his hair. "I didn't sign up for *this*."

"Dude, calm down," said Ben, though Caleb didn't seem to get the message.

He was pacing back and forth like a caged animal. "Do you even realize what you're saying, Blackburn? This isn't just crazy. It's suicide. No—it's worse than suicide."

"And what's the alternative, Cale? Do you actually think there's any part of me that can go there tonight and ram a sword into Trace's heart?! Do you? Because, spoiler alert: I can't do it."

His judge-y eyes flicked down to Dominic, and I understood the look perfectly.

"This is different. I didn't kill him! He's incapacitated, not dead," I quickly defended.

"Yeah, that's debatable," answered Ben, though he appeared to be lost in his own world as he stared down at Dominic.

"You know what I mean." I shook my head as more tears slipped from my eyes. "I can't kill Trace. I just can't. Not when there's a chance that I can save them both."

Ben appeared to be mulling it over, and I knew I was slowly inching him over to my side.

"If this works, if he accepts my offer, you can have both of them back tonight, and everything around here will go back to normal. Don't you want that, Ben? Don't you want them both home again?"

He nodded, though it was so faint and barely-there that I wasn't sure he realized he'd done it.

"And what about you, Blackburn? What happens to you?"

"It doesn't matter what happens to me," I said, suppressing a wave of nausea that slashed through the pit of my stomach.

"The only thing that matters is that everyone will be safe and that no one will ever be able to use me to do something like this ever again."

Caleb frowned, but I could see that I was getting through to him too. Without the distorting veil of loving somebody, it was easy to see what needed to be done. Dominic couldn't see it because he loved me, but Ben and Caleb could.

"Now, will you please help me get him back in the car so we can end this thing once and for all?"

And with that, the two of them finally scrambled forward and helped me carry Dominic's body back to the car.

37. A DATE WITH THE DEVIL

Fissures of lightning spiderwebbed across the sky as I slowly made my way to the front entrance of All Saints. The air seemed inexplicably thinner here, less abundant, and strangely...impure. I couldn't tell if it was my mind playing tricks on me, or if it was Lucifer's mere presence contaminating the air around us.

All Saints was always dark and eerie during closed hours, but somehow the shadows felt thicker tonight, almost as though they were alive and working with Lucifer to conspire against the light. I wondered if the boys were getting the same vibe at the back of the building, or if it was just me being uber-paranoid because I was going at this alone.

Even though they'd agreed let me do this my way—to offer myself up in exchange for Trace and Taylor—we decided it was still a good idea for them to keep watch in case something went wrong. And if it didn't, and everything went according to plan, they would be here to clean up the mess after I was gone.

I rubbed my sweaty palms against the back of my jeans, sucked in an unfulfilling breath of air, and then pulled open the door. My skin immediately prickled with unease as I stepped inside the building that was once my place of refuge. The main hall, usually swarming with people and loud music, was empty and as quiet as a grave.

The tremble in my hand was back, and it was snaking its way down to my legs now.

Ignoring the mounting alarm, I drew in another breath and scanned the room, searching for any signs of life. I noticed the air was just as sparse and fruitless inside the building as it was on the outside. Or maybe I was just hyperventilating to death.

It was definitely a possibility.

Something moved in my peripheral, and my gaze snapped to the bar. I narrowed my eyes as I took in the tanned man standing behind the wooden counter, wiping down shot glasses with a bar towel in his hand.

Zane... All Saints' number one bartender.

In that brief instant, it didn't occur to me to wonder what the heck he was doing here. Instead, I ran straight for him, half-petrified and half-relieved to finally find *somebody* inside the otherwise lifeless building.

"Zane! What the hell are you doing here?" I whisper-yelled from across the countertop. I quickly threw a glance over my shoulder to make sure we were still alone. "You have to leave! You can't be here!"

I mean, seriously, hadn't he noticed something was off about his two bosses? Or did they just continue to run the bar as though it were business as usual?

Before I could put the obvious pieces together in my mind, Zane cocked his head so far to the side that it no longer looked human. Unease zipped down my back as I gave him a second, more thorough look. His eyes were as black as the night and were fixed on me in the most peculiar way. It made my entire body feel as though a million scurrying insects were crawling underneath my skin.

"Zane isn't available at the moment," he said. "But if you leave him a message, I'll be sure to pass it along for you." A cruel smile crept across Zane's face as I realized it wasn't Zane at all.

It was some demon imposter squatting in his body.

My stomach twisted as I shuffled back from the bar counter. And then I smelt it. The faint smell of brimstone in the air. The calling card of all demons. God only knew how many more of them were in here...

In this town.

How many people had Lucifer possessed? And would I be able to save any of them?

Probably not...

"Where is he?" I scowled, my hands unconsciously clenching and unclenching at my side. I could feel the anger rocking my body, feel the adrenaline rushing away from my extremities as it hollowed out my limbs and turned my legs to jelly.

"Where are any of us, really?" answered demon-Zane, making no sense whatsoever. "That is the real question, isn't it?"

I blinked a few times, waiting for the punchline, because this was obviously some kind of underworld joke.

Silence was followed by more silence.

Okay, it wasn't a joke.

"Riiight." I dragged the word out nice and slow for the weirdo. "So, he's not here then?" I verified, secretly hoping that he wasn't. Not because I hadn't already resigned myself to doing this, because I had—I would give my life a thousand times over to save Trace's. But being here in the moment, so close to my end, I couldn't help but want for one more day to do the things I never had a chance to do. To watch one more sunset before I had to say goodbye to it all.

I wasn't sure if that made me selfish or not.

"He's wherever you want him to be," he drawled, spreading his arms out wide, with a glass in one hand and the rag in the other, gesturing around us as though Lucifer were some invisible summer breeze.

More like an air-born plague.

I'd had enough of this idiot.

"Look, pal, the only place I want Lucifer to be is in Hell," I barked back, growing exceedingly annoyed by his complete lack of sense. "And last I checked, he wasn't there, so either point me in the right direction or go find a dark corner to exorcise yourself in."

The sound of a tongue clicking reverberated in my head like a gunshot.

"Well, that's not very nice now, is it, Daughter?"

My face blanched at the sound of Trace's deep baritone voice. Still frozen and facing forward, I watched Zane's lip hike itself all the way up into his golden cheek as he continued wiping water spots from the glassware.

Thanks for the heads up, mother fudger.

"Leave us, Malphas," said Lucifer from behind my shoulder.

I still hadn't summoned enough courage to turn. I was too busy trying to get my damn legs to stop shaking.

"Of course, my liege." Demon-Zane, a.k.a. Malphas, bowed his head and then disappeared in a murky cloud of smoke. A cloud of smoke that reeked of sulfur and burnt flesh.

I resisted the urge to fan the fumes away with my hands.

"Alone again," said Lucifer, hissing out the words like a promise of vengeance, and my heart responded by stopping cold in my chest.

Everything inside of me was screaming at me to run. To run so damn fast and far away that no one in this world or beyond would ever be able to find me. My legs were damn-near quaking for it, and I couldn't even blame them for it. This wasn't some run-of-the-mill demon or Revenant that I was up against. This was Lucifer, the first and most powerful fallen angel, the one and only reigning King of Hell.

And I was a high school kid.

"I believe we have some business to discuss," he continued expectantly.

Correction: A high school kid that killed his consort.

Seriously, eff my life.

But even with all that, with my body begging me to flee, I would not run. Not from this. I was here for a reason—for two very important reasons—and I wasn't going anywhere until I got what I came here for.

"Yes, we do," I finally managed to answer. Ignoring my body's plea for flight, I turned around and faced my judge, jury and would-be executioner, ready to plead my case.

He was standing in the middle of the empty room, wearing Trace's perfect dimpled smile and matching Adonis body, as though he had any right to occupy the same space as him. His broad shoulders were proudly squared, and his jet-black hair was slicked all the way back, just the way Trace used to wear it.

My already balled fists tightened as I tried to shake the overbearing urge to rip him out of Trace's body and send him back to Hell in pieces.

"I have to say, you're much braver than I gave you credit for." The words by themselves were a compliment, but that's not the way he was delivering them. "Coming here…*alone*. After what you did to my consorts." His eyes thinned with condemnation. The dark look in his eyes made me think he was contemplating my punishment.

A shiver raced down my back, and I quickly folded my arms across my chest to keep myself from trembling at his feet. "It's not like you gave me much choice."

"We always have a choice, Daughter," he said, his eyes holding me captive. "You could've chosen *not* to disfigure my consorts. You could've chosen to leave us alone. Those are all choices, are they not? You may not like the choice, but it is a choice nonetheless. You just happened to make the wrong one."

"Maybe," I shrugged, swallowing down the burgeoning fear. "But I'd make it again if I had to."

Even though hand-delivering the Roderick sisters' karma had been the best decision I'd made all month, I had no idea why I'd gone ahead and admitted that to him.

I supposed a small part of me wanted the victory, wanted him to know that he couldn't scare me into inaction. I may have been throwing in the towel, giving myself up for the greater good of all, but at least I'd have that.

"So, you liked it, did you?" He took a slow, calculated step towards me, and my body recoiled.

There was something entirely wrong about staring across the room into the eyes of the boy you loved, hearing *his* voice, *his* vocabulary, seeing *his* face, yet knowing there wasn't a single part of him there with you. It was cruel and unnatural, just like the creature inhabiting his body.

"Liked *what*?" I asked, my eyes never leaving his person as I closely monitored every inch he moved in my direction.

"The bloodshed. Giving in to the darkness." He cocked his head to the side and scrutinized me, using Trace's stormy eyes to wash over me like a rogue wave. "I bet you loved every second of it."

I lifted my chin, refusing to let his words—his voice, his eyes—affect me. "They deserved what they got."

"Even at the expense of your dear friend Hannah." It wasn't a question. It was a hard-hitting in-your-face accusation. "I told you, you weren't meant for this world, Daughter. But did you listen to me?" He slapped me with a slow shake of his head. "And now look how many people are dead because of you. And your response is *what*? That you'd do it again."

I tried not to flinch. "That's not what I said. That isn't what

I meant!" I protested, but he was already grinning victoriously, like he'd accomplished exactly what he set out to do.

My thoughts scattered into a million different directions as I realized he had egged me on, used my own words against me and backed me into a shame-filled corner. He wanted me weak and vulnerable. He wanted me broken. It was easier to manipulate your victim that way.

But I was no victim.

I refused to cower away. I refused to let his carefully woven words of deceit confuse and disarm me until I wasn't even sure what I was doing here anymore. I knew exactly what I was doing, and not even the devil himself could distract me from that.

I pulled my thoughts back together and narrowed my eyes at him. "Look, I didn't come here to chit-chat with you about my feelings," I said, unfolding my arms as Trace's lips spread into a beautiful, dimpled grin. "I'm here to save my friends."

His eyebrows shot up. "Your *friends*?" Obviously, he didn't miss the pluralization of my mission.

"Yes. My *friends*," I reiterated, and then, against every natural instinct I had, I closed the remaining distance between us. "I'm here to make a deal with you, Lucifer," I said, stopping just short of where he stood. I looked up at the beautiful raven-haired Reaper from my dreams, and I faltered.

In a matter of mere seconds, an entire would-be lifetime with him flashed before my eyes. Him standing at the altar, waiting for me to make my way down the aisle to him. The two of us leaning over a bassinet, his arm around me as we stared lovingly at our first-born child. Endless nights in his arms. Laughter that seemed to have no end. Rocking chairs on a porch, side by side, still holding hands and loving each other as much as we did the first day we kissed.

My throat thickened with grief, and I quickly choked down

my tears, right along with the fantasy.

He'll still be able to have that, I reminded myself. It just won't be with me.

"Well?" he asked expectantly when I didn't do anything but stand there with glassy eyes and my lips slightly parted. "Are you going to tell me what it is or not? The suspense is *killing* me."

I could feel beads of sweat breaking out against my lower back.

Am I really going to do this?

Trepidation scraped its way into the pit of my stomach, turning everything around on its head before looking for a way out. Suddenly, I could taste the vomit rising at the back of my throat, but I quickly swallowed that down too.

I *was* doing this. No take-backs. No do-overs.

It was now or never.

"You were right," I mumbled, hating that I sounded so frail and insecure. "I don't belong here."

"I'm sorry, Daughter. Can you say that again? I didn't quite hear that."

Gloating bastard.

I cleared my throat and tried again, this time with my chin and shoulders slightly raised. "The thing is, I've had some time to think about what you said the other day, about your offer—"

"This just got a hell of a lot more interesting."

"—And I've decided I want to take it." My mouth was so dry, I wasn't even sure how I was managing to speak at all. "I will come with you to Hades, and I'll take my place beside you. No questions asked."

His eyes flared at my offer before quickly narrowing again. "In exchange for what?"

"In exchange for Taylor and Trace as your vessel."

"Ah," he said, nodding as though he knew that were coming.

"That is what you wanted, isn't it?" In that moment, I wasn't entirely sure why he wanted that—me—in the first place, and while a shudder assaulted my body at all the possibilities, I refused to allow myself to think about it.

"Yes, Daughter. That is what I want." He stepped forward and cupped my jaw, angling my face to his. "It's the only thing I want."

My eyes flew wide as I realized he had come here for me.

But why? What use did he have for me? What exactly did he plan to do with me? I wanted so bad to ask those questions, but I wasn't sure I could bear to hear the answers.

It was easier to face the dying light when you were already standing in the dark.

"Then we have a deal?" I asked instead.

He pursed his lips. "If this is some sort of scheme, Daughter—"

"It's not," I quickly interjected, my voice poignant. Honest. "You can see for yourself."

He was still holding my face in his hands and knew what I meant.

Trace's brilliant blue orbs disappeared as thick sooty lashes came down over his cheeks, and suddenly, I wasn't alone in my mind anymore. I could feel somebody there with me, riffling through my secrets, my plans, ripping the veil out from over my life. And I gave the devil carte-blanche to do just that.

Satisfied with what he saw, or rather with what he didn't see, he slowly reopened his eyes and released my jaw. Every cell of my being was numb, disconnected to the world around me, but somehow, it was better this way.

"You will pledge yourself to me in blood," he said, and again, it wasn't a question. It was a requirement—part of my end-of-life plan.

"Fine."

"A Blood Oath is not something to be taken lightly,

Daughter," he reproached, sounding upset by it. "You enter into it willingly, wholly, knowing that it can *never* be broken."

"Fine," I repeated, this time firmer.

His eyes bore into me, and I swore I saw of flicker of excitement pass through them. "Not just for entirety of your life. For *eternity*."

His words echoed in my head like the harsh finality of a gavel slamming down. Was he trying to scare me out of the deal, or did he just want to see how far I'd be willing to go?

"I said I'll do it. I don't care what it takes or what I have to do."

A pleased smile coiled his lips at my admission, and then his eyes darkened to the color of the open sea. "And you will give me the Sword of Angelus."

My breath caught in my throat. Um, hell no. "That wasn't part of the deal—"

"It is now." He looked at me with all the darkness of a looming storm. "I know you have it, Daughter. I can feel it's power radiating on you."

"I'm not going to use it on you," I whispered, trying to back away from the darkness, from the impending storm, but it seemed to be moving with me.

"I know you won't," he said plainly, almost humorously. "You don't have it in you."

My back stiffened at the affront, and he chuckled spiritedly.

"Don't look so offended, Daughter. There's a reason my consorts choose your soulmate as my vessel."

My soulmate...Trace *was* my soulmate.

My mind flashed back to the night we danced together at Caleb's party. He'd asked me if I believed in soulmates. Had he known I was his all along? I shook away the thought, refusing to allow it to hold me back, and the memory scattered away like a cockroach running from the light.

"I'm not giving you the sword," I said, crossing my arms.

"Then we have no deal."

"It isn't mine to give," I said, grasping at any straw I could grab a hold of.

"It's always been yours, Daughter." He smiled kindly, and for the faintest of moments, I'd almost forgotten who I was talking to. "You are the only living soul in all the realms that can yield the weapon, but my bloodline is eternal and far-reaching, and there will always be another you to serve its power."

Good, I thought, but I kept that thought to myself.

"I'd be a fool to allow that to happen," he said pointedly.

And I'd be a fool to not. There was no way I could hand over the only thing in this entire universe that could put an end to his reign of terror. He may have been agreeing to leave this world with me, and return to Hades, but would that last forever? What if he changed his mind? What if he decided to return and make happen the one thing that could end us all?

I may have been desperate, but I wasn't an idiot.

"The sword stays with the Order," I said, refusing to back down even an inch. "You'll have my Blood Oath, and I'll have my own reassurance that you'll keep your word and stay in Hades."

His eyes glimmered as he looked me up and down. "You drive a hard bargain, Daughter. I like that."

And then the trepidation was back, pushing bile up the back of my throat. The way he was looking at me...it wasn't the way you'd look at relative or *Daughter*, as he called me. It was the way you looked at someone you planned on doing very bad things to. It made my stomach dip and roll as though something necrotic was eating its way through it.

"Then we have a deal?" I asked again, having no other choice but to ignore my body's scream to empty itself.

"We have a—" His words broke off as a loud crash blasted at

the back of the building.

Both of our heads snapped in the direction of the employees-only area at the same time.

The sound of furniture breaking followed by a piercing wolf howl blew through my ears, raising the hairs on the back of my neck. For a moment, I panicked, thinking Dominic had somehow magically come back to life before his time and was back there tearing everyone to shreds, and then I remembered he wasn't the only wolf Shifter that had come along.

Ben was here too!

I immediately tried to run towards the noise—towards Ben. I needed to see for myself what the hell he was doing here, and then knock a thousand pounds of sense into him by way of my fist, but Lucifer had already snatched me by the waist and yanked me back into his chest, stopping me from going even a foot further.

"Do not move another muscle," he warned me, his breath ruffling my hair as he spoke by my ear. "I warned you not to cross me, Daughter."

"I didn't!" I said, my back still pressed against his broad chest. "I swear to God I didn't—"

He spun me around and grabbed my arms, his fingers clamping down so hard around my arms that I thought I'd heard my bone snap. "NEVER speak of Him in my presence, or it will be the last thing you ever do!" he growled murderously, shooting tiny specks of spit onto my face as he bellowed the warning.

"I'm s-sorry," I stuttered, my voice failing me as it scurried away to hide.

But he was still squeezing me, still glaring at me as though he were going to rip my body in two. And then, as if God himself had stepped in and intervened, his eyes began to flutter, blinking and rolling back, his body shaking violently as though he were having a seizure. It was the perfect time to break out of his hold and run, but my feet were like two blocks of concrete, cemented into the ground.

I was confounded, my eyes unable to look away for even a second.

As quickly as it started, the seizure halted, giving way to a humming electrical current that made my entire body hum.

"Do it now, Jemma! Do it before it's too late!"

The voice. The eyes. The hum. It couldn't be...

"Trace?" Every nerve ending in my body woke up as though I'd been sleeping through this life without him. "Trace! Oh, my God, it's really you. Please stay with me. Please. Please. Please! Just hold on. Don't leave me again!"

"AARRGH!" A scream tore out of his lungs, penetrating and sharp, as though he were being ripped away from his own body, and the convulsions quickly restarted, harder and faster this time.

I stood frozen with panic, terror infusing every inch of my being as I watched his body shake with a ferocity that was violent enough to make his body split in two.

And then, just as quickly as it had started, everything stopped.

My heart sank to the pits of Hell as the soft humming of my soulmate vanished, leaving only the presence of the cruel fallen angel that had stolen his life.

Lucifer exhaled sharply, almost painfully as he rolled his shoulder and locked his eyes back on mine. I couldn't tell if he was angry or...amused? "Annoying little thing, isn't he?" he said and then cracked his neck.

The realization that Trace had just come through, that it actually happened, slammed me upside the head. He'd somehow managed to overpower Lucifer and regain control of his body. But how?

And could he do it again?

"I wouldn't count on it," answered Lucifer. He was still holding me by my arms and could hear every thought that was running frantically through my mind. "That won't be happening again. This time, I made sure of it."

He made *sure* of it?

"What did you do to him?! What did you do?!" I wailed, tears aching to break free as I struggled to break out of his impossible grip.

My cries never had a chance to be answered.

The sound of doors crashing open pulled his attention over my shoulder.

"Well, what do we have here?" he said as he released my arms and swung me around so that I could see.

I stumbled back into his chest, my legs turning to jelly as I watched six of Lucifer's demons walk into the main hall, one of them carrying a bound and gagged blonde with denim-blue eyes that were silently screaming with terror.

"Taylor!" I pushed off Lucifer and tried to run to her, but he promptly grabbed my neck and hauled me back, holding me in place as though I were nothing but a useless bag of feathers.

The last demon filed into the room, forcefully dragging a collared wolf behind him. I blinked several times as I catalogued the glowing leash around Ben's neck. It seemed to be on fire, only it wasn't burning him.

"The little beast dropped right out of the ceiling like an Angel," said Malphas, laughing as he stood beside the dark-skinned meatsuit of muscle that was holding the other end of the leash.

Lucifer didn't appear to find it amusing. "Reveal yourself," he ordered, but the wolf just continued to buck and whimper against the chain. "Reveal yourself or Talon snaps her pretty little neck."

He nodded to Talon, the orange-haired buffoon, who promptly wrapped his hand around Taylor's neck and lifted her off the ground, dangling her in front of the wolf's eye so he could see they meant business.

That was all that was needed. The wolf immediately blurred into a miasma of darkness, shifting and reshaping itself before reappearing in human form.

Ben's human form.

"You got me, aright?" snapped Ben, his tone more angry than afraid. "Now let her go!"

Talon glanced back at Lucifer who responded with a curt dip of his head. With that, Taylor's feet were back on solid ground, but she was far from being out of the clear.

"You're a fool for coming here," said Lucifer, shaking his head at his idiocy.

Ben's eyes met mine and for the first time ever, I saw fear in them. "I'm sorry," he mouthed.

But that wasn't even *almost* good enough.

"What the hell were you thinking?" I scolded him through strangled sobs. "You promised me!"

"I'm sorry, Jem," he said again, rattling his head from side to side, the collar still fastened around his neck and restricting his movements. "I heard him say he wanted the sword…I knew you wouldn't give it to him…I had to do something," he explained, his voice as wild and desperate as his eyes were.

"And now you'll pay for it…with *her* life," said Lucifer, calmer than a sleeping baby.

"Wait!" I yelled, my arms flailing out frantically. "We had a deal! We had a deal!" My legs tried to give out, but Lucifer held me up, keeping my head facing forward to make sure I got a front-row view of the massacre.

"Kill the girl."

At Lucifer's words, the orange-headed demon holding Taylor

by her neck grabbed the sides of her face and twisted her head around until it snapped, the sound of it echoing through the building like a single gunshot to the head.

Her lifeless body crumpled to the ground as an ear-splitting scream tore out of my body, flaying the inside of my throat as it bludgeoned its way out of me. "NOOOO!"

"I'll kill you!" screamed Ben as he tried to pounce on Talon, but Muscles promptly yanked the leash towards himself, repelling him backwards so that he couldn't reach Taylor's lifeless body. "Kill him, Jemma! Kill him!"

My feet were already pounding against the floor as Ben's screams rippled through every bone in my body. I wasn't sure if I'd escaped Lucifer's grasp, or if he let me just to see what I would do, but I didn't stop to question it.

Within seconds of reaching Talon, I was on top of him, savagely ripping a hole through his chest with my bare hands, gouging the cavity, as though taking his own heart might somehow make Taylor's beat again.

My body went numb as I wrapped my fingers around the beating organ and squeezed until Talon's eyes rolled back into his head. Before I could fully absorb the satisfaction, an arm snaked around the front of my neck, hauling me backwards as I clutched the still-beating heart in my hands.

"Now look what you did," said Lucifer as he pressed his forearm against my windpipe and locked me to his chest. "How many more are going to have to die tonight? Hmm?" His hot breath blew against my ear as I bucked and kicked against his hold.

Realizing I was still holding the dead heart in my hands, I tossed it on the ground and then grabbed his forearm with both hands as I tried to rip, and claw, his arm away from my neck, but my hands were covered in warm, slippery blood, making it impossible to get a decent hold on him.

"Tell me, Daughter. Do you have any more surprises waiting for me in the ceilings?" asked Lucifer as he pulled me off my feet by the rim of my neck, cutting off my oxygen. "Or should we just go ahead and kill the boy now?"

Unable to speak or suck in a single drop of air, I punched and scratched at his arm, silently screaming at him to let me go. *I can't breathe! You're choking me!*

"Yes, Daughter," he whispered by my ear. "That's the point."

The lights flickered all around us as terror trilled through my bones. He was going to kill me—to strangle me to death right where I stood, or worse, just keep me lucid enough to watch another one of my friends die.

The lights flickered harder, flashing in and out of existence as my head grew heavy with fog. In and out. In and out. Blackness then light. Blackness then light. And then, I realized it was me, slipping in and out of consciousness.

I had to do something—but what? My hands were too slick with blood and sweat to do anything but slide right of his arm. And then it hit me. Panicked, I pulled my bloody hands from his arm and moved them to my neck, frantically coating myself in the blood in last-ditch effort to wiggle my way out of his iron-clad hold.

And it freaking worked!

One moment I was standing pinned against his chest, slowly suffocating to death, and the next, I was spinning on him, grabbing his arm and twisting it around so violently that his shoulder popped right out of its socket. He screamed out in pain as terrifying pools of red lava began swirling in his eyes.

My stomach knotted at the petrifying monster standing before me.

Red eyes.

Satan's eyes.

"You will regret that, Daughter," he said as he grabbed his

arm and snapped his shoulder back in place.

I could hear chaos breaking out behind me, and I instinctively knew that Caleb had joined the fight. A part of me wanted to help him, to drag him and Ben out of this building and bring them someplace safe, but I couldn't turn my back on Lucifer. I couldn't give him the chance to get away. He had to pay for what he did.

To Hannah.

To Taylor.

To Trace...

My brain clicked off to everything around me, but him, and I attacked.

The force of my chest slamming into his knocked him off his feet and sent us both tumbling to the ground in a messy heap of good and evil. My fingers clutched his throat as I climbed on top and locked his body between my legs.

He wasn't going to kill any more of my friends.

He wasn't going to kill another living soul, because I wouldn't let him.

"Mmm," he moaned lewdly. "We're finally getting somewhere good," he said, pushing his hips up towards me, and I responded by socking him in the nose. Twice.

"Ah, you like it rough then?" he went on, his bloody lip curling into a twisted snarl as he bucked his hips again. "That's my kind of girl."

"Shut up! Just shut the hell up!" I screamed as I rained down three more blows to his mouth, hoping to break it enough to stop him from speaking. To stop him from using Trace's voice, ever again!

"But this is Trace's voice," he said, catching my fist before I could land the fourth hit. He squeezed his palm around my fist, crunching the bone and then using it to toss me off of him.

Within seconds, he was on top of me, straddling my body

under his weight. "If you could only see the things he wanted to do to you, Daughter." His grin turned into a sneer as he leaned down and whispered, "*Dirty* things."

I rammed my elbow into the side of his head, knocking him back a notch, but not enough to get him off me.

"Why don't you be a good little girl and throw the guy a bone, hmm?"

I threw a left hook instead, clipping him in the nose as he ducked back.

"You're really riling him up now! Can you feel that?" He was moving his hips again, rolling them over me as though he were riding a bull.

"You're sick! You're fucking sick!" I said and then slammed the palm of my hand all the way up into his nose.

His hands shot up to his face at the sound of crunching bone, giving me a chance to buck him off and reclaim the upper hand. With my knee pressed against his torso, I reached back to my other leg and pulled out the Sword of Angelus.

That shut him up real quick.

The moment the sword touched my hand, its power ignited, turning it blue in my hands, and mesmerizing me with its grippingly beautiful deathly glow. Even Lucifer couldn't help but drop his hands from his face and stare up at it, almost as though transfixed by the power. I flipped the blade in my hand, taking it by the hilt and angling it down to his chest.

And then I hesitated.

The red flames in his eyes had extinguished themselves, leaving only the magnificent blue eyes of the boy I loved. I knew he had done it on purpose to distract me, to make me falter, and it had worked.

His lips curled into a smug grin as he pushed up onto his elbows. "I told you you couldn't do it, Daughter. You can't kill me no matter how much you want to. Not when that means taking your soulmate down with me."

The Roderick sisters had thought long and hard about choosing the perfect vessel for Lucifer. They had me pegged from the start, knowing I was weak and inexperienced, and that I would let my heart rule my mind.

"And they were right, weren't they, Daughter?" he asked, listening in to my private struggle.

I nodded, tears dripping off my jaw and dotting his shirt below me. I knew now, without a doubt, that killing Lucifer would kill Trace too, and I'd sooner choose death by my own hands than be the reason that he was no longer living.

And they'd known that all along.

My chest heaved as I sobbed uncontrollably. "I'm sorry."

"An apology isn't going to save you," he sneered back up at me, his eyes glowering with vengeance.

But so were mine when I said, "I wasn't talking to you."

His brows furrowed with confusion as he tried to put the pieces together, but he would never get the chance.

"I love you, Trace, and I'm so fucking sorry," I said and then drove the sword into his heart.

38. THE LIVING DEAD

Even as the billowing rush of black smoke swirled in the air around me, I could do nothing more than stare into the lifeless blue eyes of the boy I loved. A chasm of grief opened inside my heart, so deep and wide that I knew it would never again be filled. Everything inside of me withered up and died a thousand times, the pain so excruciating that I contemplated taking the sword out of his heart and plunging it into my own.

You don't deserve the easy way out, I told myself as tears rained down my cheeks like gushing waterfalls. I did this to him—I killed Trace—and I was going to take my lifelong punishment for it. Even as the black smoke disappeared and the numbness inside me began to creep its way in, I pushed it away, refusing to allow myself even one moment of reprieve from the agony I felt inside.

I may have been alive and breathing, but inside, I was dead.

"Blackburn!" shouted Caleb from somewhere over my shoulder. "Get the doors! They're getting away!"

But I couldn't move.

I couldn't look away from what I had done. What I was

forced to do. I had to sear it into my memory, scar it into the deepest part of my heart so that I never forgot the pain of it. I would carry it wherever I went. Carry it all the way to my dying breath. Because that was what I deserved. And only when I took my final breath would I let the pain of it go.

"Blackburn! Get the fuck up and help me!" he shouted again, and this time, the bone-rattling panic in his voice roused me from my slumberous nightmare.

I couldn't let another one of my friends die.

Not today, and not on my watch.

Squeezing my eyes shut, I pulled the sword from Trace's chest and spun around, my body still low to the floor and vibrating with vengeance.

There were only two demons left; Malphas and Muscles, who was still holding Ben by the leash. The other demons had already been eviscerated. That, or they'd run off when Lucifer got his comeuppance.

But they weren't all gone, and someone was going to pay for this.

Kicking off from the ground, I bolted forward like a feral animal, running straight for Muscles and his godforsaken leash. If he hadn't been holding Ben back, he could've gotten to Taylor in time. He could've saved her.

Rage prickled my skin as I snatched up every morsel of pain and anger I had, and I funneled it into a crosshair that was consequently aimed right at him.

A flash of fear flickered in his eyes a moment before my foot slammed into his stomach, the impact folding his body in half. A painful gust of air pushed out of his lungs as he stumbled backwards and dropped the leash. I didn't give him a chance to recover. I kicked my foot out again, and then again, slicing at his chest with my blade before ducking to the ground and spinning, knocking him off his feet and forcing him to crash to the ground like a slaughtered tree.

I jumped on top of him, ready to finish the job, ready to make him pay with blood, but a pair of hands had slinked themselves into my hair, grabbing a fistful of it and then using it to haul my ass backwards. My scalp screamed in protest as I kicked my legs out, frantically looking for something to brace myself against.

I looked up and met Malphas' black eyes just as Caleb appeared out of nowhere, body checking him as he sent him flying several feet to the left of me. I scrambled back on my feet and moved for Muscles again.

Flipping the blade in my hand, I closed in on him as he smiled back at me—welcoming the fight. I slashed the blade through the air, but he quickly jumped back and then threw his arm out in an effort to knock the blade from my hand.

Good luck with that, I thought. My fingers were wrapped so tightly around the handle that he would've needed the Jaws of Life to pry it away from them. Pulling the blade back, I swung my other arm out, slamming the back of my elbow into his throat and stunning him just long enough for me to pounce on him again.

He went down easily, and I took every advantage of that, propping myself over him like a watchful gargoyle. With the blade poised in my hand, I glared down at him and whispered sweetly. "Tell your maker I said hi." And then I rammed the sword into his chest as easy as slicing through warm butter.

I didn't bother to stick around for the smoke show either.

One down. One to go.

Climbing off his unresponsive body, I turned around and gauged the room. My nearly broken fist was throbbing, but my adrenaline was pumping too hard to fully grasp the pain. My eyes zeroed in on Malphas, who was busy making mashed potatoes out of Caleb's face.

The moment our eyes locked, he jumped off Caleb and slowly backed away, palms out, as though he had any chance of making it out of this building alive.

The demon, that is. Not Zane.

"Can you do Ritual?" I asked Caleb as we stalked Malphas' retreat side by side. Enough people had died tonight. If there was a way to get the demon out of Zane's body without killing him, I was all for it.

"I think so," he answered.

"You think so?" I threw him a sidelong glance.

"I mean, I've studied them, but I've never actually done an exorcism before," he admitted, never taking his eyes off Malphas as we closed in on him.

Whatever. That was good enough for me.

"No time like the present time," I said and swung at Malphas, landing a sharp right hook in the center of his jaw. Spit ricocheted from his mouth as he spun around like a ballerina and slammed face-first onto the ground.

"Damn, *Tyson*. Where'd you learn how to hit like that?"

"Practice," I grumbled as I ambled to Malphas.

Grabbing his shoulder, I flipped him over and appraised the damage. I doubted he would be out long, so I climbed up on his chest and perched myself there, hoping my weight would at least slow him down when he came to.

I glanced up at Caleb, who was just standing there, taking it all in, as though we had all the time in the world.

"Any day now, Cale."

"Right. Sorry," he said and rushed around to my side.

As if on cue, Malphas twitched below me and then quickly regained consciousness. I braced myself, knowing it would only take a few seconds to shake away the fog before he would be frantically throwing fists at my head, and just as predicted, that was exactly what he did. While I'd managed to dodge most of them, he did land a good one right in the center of my mouth, evidenced by the warm, metallic taste seeping out of my bottom lip.

"You're not going to be able to hold him down like this for the whole ritual," said Caleb, watching as I struggled to contain him under my weight. His eyes darted across the room to Ben. "Dude, come on. Get up and help us!"

But Caleb's plea was futile. Ben wasn't going to move even an inch away from Taylor's side. He was hunched over her body now, crying like a broken child.

"Forget him," I said, punching Malphas in the throat again. "Just help me hold him down so I can knock him out!"

At my words, Caleb dropped down in front of us and grabbed a hold of Malphas' shoulders, pushing them flat to the ground as I rained down blow after blow over. I needed to hit him hard enough to knock him unconscious again without permanently disfiguring Zane's face, or worse, killing him.

It was a fine line to walk, and I was barely teetering on the edge.

"Alright, that's enough, Blackburn! He's out. He's out," he said when I finally landed the perfect shot. He quickly rolled up his sleeves to his elbows and readied himself to do the ritual.

Reining myself back in, I sucked in a breath as my eyes skirted around the room. I tried not to look at all the bodies scattered everywhere, but it was like trying not to look at a giant pink elephant standing in the middle of the room.

It was impossible not to look, to see the death all around me.

Tears immediately brimmed beneath my lids, blurring out my vision.

"Hey. Stay with me, Blackburn. I need you. I can't do this by myself," he pleaded, noticing I was two seconds away from a complete nuclear meltdown. "It's just me and you and this guy right here. Alright? Focus."

I nodded, sucking in a lungful of air as I tried to bring my focus back to what we were doing.

"Atta girl," he said, squeezing my chin. Feeling confident that I wasn't going to completely lose my shit, he focused his attention back on Zane, softly nudging him to made sure he was still out cold.

"Alright," he said, pushing out a breath of air. "Here goes nothing."

And with that, he began the Old Latin incantation that would inevitably—hopefully—cast the demon out of Zane's unsuspecting body and send him back to Hell with Lucifer.

Even though it was the first time I'd ever witnessed the ritual being performed, I could barely concentrate enough to take in a single word of it in. In the stillness of my inactivity, my mind kept racing back to Trace, to what I had done to him, and with the thought, my gaze would quickly follow.

Grief strangled my throat as I took in his motionless body lying unceremoniously on the ground, a prelude of what was to come, of the unwavering agony I was going to suffer for this. It wasn't going to matter which way *they* would try to spin it, or how they'd choose to justify it. His blood was on my hands both literally and figuratively, and I would never be able to wash it away.

"Jemma..."

I hadn't noticed that tears were running my cheeks again until Caleb reached forward and wiped the side of my face with his hand. He was done, the ritual was over, and I hadn't heard a word of it.

"You did what you had to do, Blackburn," he said, his voice cracking as though he hadn't used it in days. He had seen where my eyes had gone, and he knew where my mind was. "You get that, right?"

Here we go.

I lifted myself off a still-unconscious Zane and shook my head at him. "Please, Caleb. Don't."

It was all I could say to him, but it was enough. He understood. He understood that I didn't want to hear his words of commiseration. Not today. Not after what I did. There was nothing he could say to me that would ever lessen my burden, and I didn't want him to try.

My eyes scanned the room as I took in the carnage around me. Trace and Taylor were dead. Countless demons had gotten away, and Zane was barely hanging on by a thread.

It wasn't supposed to happen like this.

They weren't supposed to die...

Angry and heartbroken, I looked over at Ben, who had gathered Taylor's body in his arms. I couldn't even bring myself to look at him—to go anywhere near them.

"I didn't mean for this to happen," he said, as though he could sense I was staring at him. "I was trying to save her." His shoulders were slumped forward and trembling as he cried over the girl he loved and lost.

A part of me wanted to say something, to take away some of his hurt, but I was too damn angry at him to even try.

If it hadn't been for his selfish rush to deviate from the plan, Taylor and Trace would be alive right now, and I'd be somewhere in Hell with Lucifer. Instead, I was covered in Trace's blood, staring down the barrel of a lifetime of sorrow-filled misery and insufferable guilt. And I hated him for that.

My stomach lurched, and suddenly, I was vomiting all over my shoes.

"Shit," muttered Caleb as he rushed over and placed a supportive hand on my back.

I tried to swat him away from me, but he refused to bugger off.

"You okay? Should I get you something?" he asked as I wiped

my mouth with my back of my hand.

I shook my head and pushed him back a step. I needed space. I needed air. There wasn't enough air in the room—there wasn't enough air in the entire planet now that Trace was no longer living in it.

"I can't be here anymore," I said, barely keeping it together enough to get the words out. My chest was heaving erratically. I couldn't seem to fill my lungs. "I need to leave. Now."

And I wasn't just talking about this moment or this building. I couldn't be in this town anymore. I needed to go. No—I needed to run. Too much sorrow. Too much pain. Not enough damn air.

"Call the Council," I told him, knowing they would be able to cover up what needed to be covered up and make the rest of it go away. I wasn't sure how they did it, and at this point, I didn't care.

He nodded that he would, though the apprehension in his eyes never did leave.

"And Dominic." I was already backtracking my steps, the sorrow rushing in faster than I could stand.

"What, uh, what should I tell him?" he asked, worry etched in his eyes.

"Tell him…tell him I did what I had to do," I said breathlessly. *Cowardly.* I owed him more than that, so much more than that, but in the moment, I had absolutely nothing left to give.

Not an ounce or drop of anything.

I spun on my heel, ready to make a grab for the door, except my eyes tripped on the escape route and instead, landed heavy on Trace. My throat grew tighter and tighter the closer I got to him, until I wasn't even sure I was breathing anymore. Kneeling beside him, I gently touched my palm to the side of his face as a hazy mess of tears sprang from my eyes.

His skin had already begun to turn cold, and the realization that he was truly gone only served to push me further into the realm of the living dead.

"I'm so sorry, Trace," I said, my voice a broken whisper as I softly brushed the fallen strands of hair away from his eyes, one last time. "I tried."

39. A RAY OF LIGHT

The days that followed were a blur of funerals and suffocating darkness that seemed to have no end. The final body count had risen to the dozens, sending a black cloud of grief over Hollow Hills. Local schools and business had temporarily closed their doors, while flags were being flown at half-staff all around the city. The entire town was in mourning, but even their cumulative sadness couldn't begin to touch the anguish that had permanently taken residency inside my heart.

It had been days since I had allowed myself to see anyone— to see Dominic. I still couldn't bring myself to face him after everything that I'd done. Mostly because I knew he would forgive me. He would try to be my sanctuary from the blizzard of sorrow that had taken over my life, and I didn't deserve to have his shelter from the storm.

Not this time.

Instead, I had rented myself a room in some dingy fleabag motel two towns over, where I could be alone with my thoughts. Alone with the agonizing memory of draining the light from Trace's eyes. I replayed the moment in my mind like a ghostly reel, each time letting the pain burrow deeper into my heart.

It was what I deserved.

The pain of losing my friends—of losing him—had proven to be unsurmountable, but I took the agony wholly and willingly, refusing to allow myself even a moment of reprieve. Every minute I spent alone with the pain only deepened my suffering, encouraging me to keep drudging on, deeper and deeper into the darkness where I belonged.

A soft knock sounded at the motel door, momentarily breaking through my self-appointed sentence. My eyes darted across the room, slicing through the darkness with ease. I had become accustomed to it—to the shadows. My eyes had long since acclimated themselves to the absolute void of light.

It was just as well, really; a perfect mirrored reflection of how I felt inside.

I furrowed my brows and stared at the doorway, half expecting Lucifer to blow through the door and finish the job he started. But I knew that wouldn't happen. That would be far too easy of a punishment for what I had done.

Ignoring the knock, I pulled my legs up to my chest and dropped my chin onto my knees. The only person who knew where I was staying was my sister, and I really didn't want to see her right now. And since I already knew that if I ignored her long enough, she would go away, that was exactly what I did. Just like I did that morning. And the night before. And the morning before that.

Another knock sounded, this time harder, and I ignored that one too.

Anxious for her to get the message and leave me alone, I leaned my head back against the wall and shut my eyes, once again allowing the darkness to wither in and consume me.

But instead of the deafening screams of my personal demons, I heard the door rip open before slamming full force into the stopper on the other side of the wall. My heart jumped up into my throat as my eyes rushed across the room, angry and eager to curse my sister out for daring to intrude when all I wanted was to be alone with my misery.

Only it wasn't Tessa. It was Gabriel.

He was standing in the doorway, his feet spread apart, as the motel lights dusted his form from behind, making him look like a glowing angel that nobody sent for.

His eyes quickly scanned the dreary room before finding me huddled in the corner. My knees still tucked into my body. My cheeks eternally streaked with tears.

"Jemma." His features were shadowed from the dimness of the room, but I knew he was frowning.

"She told you where I was?" I asked, disbelief marring my voice. I don't know why I was even surprised. Tessa told Gabriel everything. Certainly more than she ever told me.

"She's worried about you." He took a small step forward, though he still hadn't entered the room. "We all are."

"I'm fine, Gabriel." I squinted up at him as the light from the outside passageway assaulted my eyes. "I just want to be alone."

"You've been alone for days," he countered, as though I wasn't aware of time anymore. "You look like you haven't eaten or slept in a week."

"I told you I'm fine. I just want to be left alone. Now, will you please shut the damn door and leave me the hell alone?"

At my request, he slammed the door shut, except he was now standing on the wrong side of it. Instead of leaving me to my demons, he flicked on the floor lamp by the window and folded his arms over his chest, grimacing down at me.

"Turn it off!" I cried, feeling like a frail street rat, running from the light.

He didn't budge an inch.

"Turn the damn lights off, Gabriel!" I was shouting at him now, but he still wasn't moving. "Dammit! Can't you people just leave me the hell alone?!"

"You need a shower, and you need to eat," he said, looking down at me with disappointment. Or maybe it was sadness? I couldn't tell anymore. "You can either do it alone, and willingly, or we can do it the other way."

"Are you threatening me?" I narrowed my swollen eyes at him.

"I'm trying to help you, Jemma."

"I never asked for your stupid help," I fired back, looking for a brand-new outlet for my pain.

"No, you didn't," he agreed, his eyes moving over me pitifully. "But I'm your Handler, so you're getting it anyway."

"*Temporary* Handler," I corrected, pouring venom into the status, as though it were a dirty word.

"Correct," he said and then stalked across the room towards the bathroom. "But that doesn't make me any less your Handler right now," he said and then flipped the bathroom light on.

My eyes were immediately bombarded with mint-green tile and wallpaper, seeping out of the bathroom as the flickering florescent light struggled to stay on. Furious, I squeezed my eyes shut and tried to telepathically shatter the lightbulb, but of course, my sorry state of being couldn't seem to pull enough mojo together to do anything but grunt and moan in the corner of the room as the radioactive glow poured its eye-gouging light into my personal space.

I scowled at Gabriel's back as he shuffled across the bathroom, grabbing a towel and then turning on the water.

He really had some nerve.

"You don't actually think you're getting me anywhere near that cesspool, do you?"

He didn't answer except for the sound of his boots

clomping against the tile as he lumbered around the bathroom. A few moments later, he reappeared at the doorway, steam fogging the glass behind his head.

"The shower's ready," he said expectantly, like he had any chance in hell of getting me in there.

I laughed at him. It was humorless and dry, but it was a laugh nonetheless.

He grimaced again. "Don't make me do this the hard way, Jemma."

"I'd really like to see you try," I said, knowing he didn't have it in him. This was one war I definitely wasn't going to lose.

His frown deepened, gathering his eyebrows together and propping them down over his eyes.

Just like I thought.

"Shut the lights on your way out," I said and flopped my head back against the wall, closing my eyes again.

"Fine. Last chance," he warned.

I cracked my eye open and snuck a peek at him. He was holding his cell phone in his hand, waving it back and forth as though it were a gun or some magic weapon that could make me do something against my will.

"What are you going to do with that? Tweet me to death?" I rolled my eyes at him.

"No," he answered, unamused. "I'm going to call Dominic with it."

My heart seized in my chest at his name. He was playing *dirty*.

"Like I said, we can do this the easy way, or we can do this the hard way."

And just like that, another war was lost.

As angry as I had been when I stomped my way to the

shower and slammed the door in Gabriel's face, the moment I stepped under the medicinal warmth of the running water, all the blood, tears and anger trickled off my body like falling rain, only to be swept away down the drain. I had intended to only be in there a few minutes—just enough time to get him off my back and put that damn cell phone away, but when I finally stepped out of the bathroom, it was almost thirty minutes later.

"You look better," said Gabriel, and I decided to take his word for it. I didn't have the courage or the desire to look at my own reflection, so I hadn't.

"What is that?" I asked, toweling my hair as I stared across the room at him. He was standing beside the grungy table by the window, holding a tinfoil plate that looked a lot like takeout.

"Chicken and potatoes," he said and then held the platter out, coaxing me closer.

My stomach rumbled loudly as the smell of food wafted across the room, and despite my want for continuous penance, my feet were already shuffling around the bed to him, desperate for some kind of sustenance to keep them alive.

I dropped the towel on the bed and took the plate from him.

"Thank you," I grumbled and sat down on the edge of the bed. I didn't waste any time ripping the cover off the plate and diving into the dish.

"When was the last time you ate?" he asked as he lowered himself into the chair by the window. He dropped his forearm on the table and studied me.

"It's been...a while," I said, not entirely sure how long it had actually been.

Between the agony of losing Trace and the withdrawals from being away from Dominic, my entire body was a wreck. So much so that I couldn't tell where one injury ended and where the next one began. The pain just seemed to run into each other, never ebbing, never wavering, just a continuous ache that disemboweled every inch of my being.

"You can't stay here forever, you know," he said, his voice a gentle warning. "You have to go home eventually."

"And where would that be?" I asked him, hoping he had an answer to that, because as it stood, I really had no idea where that was anymore. When he failed to produce an answer, I took another bite and said, "Exactly."

"You can always come back to the Manor. You know that."

"That's the last place I can be right now." I didn't bother elaborating, but I assumed he knew why. "Besides, I don't plan on staying here forever. I'm taking my finals next week and then I'm leaving for the summer with Tessa," I said and shoveled another piece of chicken into my mouth.

His head recoiled. Obviously, he wasn't aware of this plan.

"Well, I'll be damned," I said and puffed out another sour-kissed laugh. "There's actually something she didn't tell you about me? Wonders never cease."

"You're leaving?" He appeared to be taking the news a lot worse than I'd anticipated. "Jemma, you can't just leave," he said, his expression turning sullen as tension crept across his forehead.

"Well, I sure as shit can't stay here. This place is…this whole town is…." I shook my head, fully decided. "I just can't be here anymore. Enough people have died because of me."

His brows snapped together. "Because of *you*?"

I looked at him like he was daft. "Everybody that comes near me ends up dead, Gabriel. Or did you miss that part?"

"Don't be ridiculous. You can't blame yourself for—"

"Do you seriously want me to run through the death toll right now?" I snapped, refusing to allow him to finish his sentence. I couldn't stand to hear him try to justify this. He was lying to himself, and we both knew it.

"I'm cursed, Gabriel. It's as simple as that." I held up a hand when he tried to protest. "I get it now, and I accept it. This is what's best for everybody. I'm not just some regular teen with a bright future ahead of her, so I need to stop acting like one. If I leave with Tessa, I'll get the experience I need to do the thing that I'm *actually* supposed to be doing."

As painful and ugly as the truth was, *this* was the life that I'd been dealt, and I needed to stop playing pretend with it. My purpose was to hunt demons and vampires. Demons like the ones that killed my best friend and vampires like the one that killed my father. And it wasn't something you could do with one foot in and one foot out like I'd been doing. You had to be all in, all the time, because if you weren't—if you tripped or hesitated or let down your guard for even the slightest second—innocent people wound up dead.

And I finally, *finally* understood that.

He leaned back in his chair, absorbing it. He knew I was right. I could see it in his face, yet the apprehension was still there. Was he worried that I wasn't ready to go on the road yet? Or was it something else?

"Stop looking at me like," I said, chancing another look at him in between bites. "I'll be fine."

"I know you will," he said without the slightest hint of hesitation or doubt. "You're one of the strongest Slayers I know. Even if you don't believe it yet."

I felt my eyes well up at his words, for just a second, and then I jammed the emotion away. The only tears I allowed to fall were tears of pain. Not of compliments. Not of good sentiments.

"So, what's with the gloomy face then?" I asked, putting the conversation back on track.

"It's just that..." He frowned again, searching for his

words. "You and Dominic are—"

"Bloodbonded," I answered for him and shoved a forkful of potatoes into my mouth.

I had already thought about that and decided it would just be another layer to the pain I would be taking with me. I expected it. I *wanted* it. I was on a mission to atone for my mistakes, and self-inflicted pain was the only way I knew to do that. "If I can take it, so can he."

He mulled that over silently as I finished up the last of my food, grateful that he'd forced it on me.

"When are you going to tell him?" he asked after a while, and my heart seized in my chest.

"I was sort of...hoping...that..." I looked up at him under my lashes, "you would do it?"

"Jemma," he reproached.

"Don't look at me like that, Gabriel. I have a lot of loose ends to tie up before I go. I just thought it would be better if you did it." I was such a lying coward, it wasn't even legal.

"He should hear it from you."

I didn't argue that, because he *should* hear it from me. But I didn't know how to tell him goodbye, and I was too afraid to try.

His frown deepened when he said, "You know he loves you very much."

My eyes shot up to his. "He told you that?" I asked, surprised since Dominic wasn't exactly a well of information, even on a good day.

"He didn't have to," he said plainly. "I know my brother. It's written all over his face when he looks at you."

My throat constricted with grief as my gaze skirted away from him.

Dominic was going to be the hardest thing to walk away from. I already knew that and had accepted it, but that didn't mean it wouldn't hurt like hell to hear it.

"Is he okay?" I finally asked, my vision blurring as I met his eyes again.

"No. He's not," he answered grimly, and it speared a hole right through my heart.

"But he will be, right?" I wasn't sure what I was looking for from Gabriel just then. Some reassurance? An okay that I could pick up and leave Dominic after everything that happened between us?

How could I pick up and leave Dominic after everything that happened between us?

God, I was such a shitty person.

"He'll be okay," he finally agreed, though something about the way he said it made me think it would be a long time before that happened. "And so will you, Jemma. You're going to survive this, even if it doesn't feel that way right now."

The weak dam around my heart shattered, giving way to a flood of tears that nearly drowned the both of us.

"I really don't think that I will," I admitted between sobs. At least not without losing a huge piece of myself—of who I was, and who I was meant to become. If I survived it at all, I'd only be a shell of the person I was supposed to be. No longer whole. No longer living. Simply just…existing.

"You did what you had to do, Jemma, and any one of us would've done the same thing."

I guessed that was supposed to make me feel better, but it didn't. "You say that, but you don't really know, do you? Because I'm the one that had to do it. I killed Trace—I watched the life drain from his eyes. Not you, Gabriel. Not them. Me. And I'll never be okay with that. Not ever." Tears were streaming down my cheeks faster than I could keep up with.

"You're right. It was you," he admitted. "And I couldn't begin to imagine what you're feeling right now. But let me ask you something…" He looked at me for a harrowing minute. "What would you do if it had been the other way around?"

I met his eyes and sniffled, wiping my cheeks with the back of my hand. "What do you mean?"

He pushed forward, his forehead creasing as he propped his elbows on his knees. "What if Lucifer had taken you as his vessel and Trace was the one who had to yield the weapon?"

"That's different," I answered easily. "I know he would've done everything imaginable to try and save me."

"Like you did?" he asked.

"I mean…I guess so," I shrugged, feeling like I didn't do enough. If I'd done enough, he would be alive right now.

"And if he couldn't find a way? If he had tried everything he knew of and was left with no other choice but to do exactly what you had to do…would you forgive him?"

I didn't even have to think about it. "Of course, I would forgive him."

He nodded like he'd already known the answer. "Then don't you think he would want the same for you?"

My mouth opened to say something back to him, to protest his absolution, but all I could think about then was Trace's words urging me to move on with my life…to let him go…to do the *right* thing.

He knew it was coming. He knew we were going to end up in exactly that place at exactly that moment. And he'd given me permission to do it. Had I done the right thing after all? And if so, why the hell did it feel so wrong?

40. JUDGEMENT DAY

My visit with Gabriel had been short and bittersweet. He'd come by one more time after that night, and we'd said our goodbyes to each other. Though he'd made it clear to me that he didn't like that I was leaving, he also said he understood why I needed to do it, and it felt good to finally be on the same page again. And, after a little coaxing and pleading on my part, he also agreed not to tell Dominic where I was until I was ready to say goodbye to him—in person. I owed him at least that, though I had no idea how I was ever going to be able to say those words to him.

I figured I'd have to do it quickly and painlessly, like ripping off a bandage.

Or a limb.

Even though the days that followed Gabriel's visit were much of the same tears and isolation from the previous week, it somehow felt different. Maybe even a little better. Of course, I was still crying for Trace, grieving my loss of him and the life we had planned together, but I didn't hate myself quite as much as I had the days before, and I think I had Gabriel to thank for that.

Even still, the hollow days came and went tirelessly, broken up only by the few hours that I forced myself out of the motel to bus it back to Hollow Hills. I wasn't sure how or why I was being allowed to take my final exams two weeks earlier than everyone else, but I had the sneaking suspicion that Tessa and the Council were somehow behind it.

I didn't spare it much thought, though, and just took the small blessing as it came.

The night before me and Tessa were set to leave on our Slayer-sister-road-trip, I'd finally worked up enough courage to head back to town and face Dominic. Strangely, the closer I got to the Manor, the worse my anxiety became. It was odd being that my proximity to him was usually the only thing that could calm me.

My heart sank into my shoes when I finally reached the house on foot. The lights were off, and Dominic's black Audi wasn't in the driveway either. I realized then that I probably should've called before coming. If only I could've drummed up enough nerve to do it.

Having no other option, I plopped down on his front stoop and waited.

Even when the rain started pouring down on me like a sideways curtain of water, I waited.

And then, nearly an hour later, when I was just about to give up and bus it back to the motel, a pair of headlights rounded the corner. My heart leapt up into my throat as I watched the lights turn into the driveway and then make their way up to the house. The car idled for a moment, the headlights beaming over my huddled, soaking wet form like a spotlight, and then the engine cut, along with my heart, the latter only restarting when Dominic opened the door and stepped out of his car. His eyes were trained on me through a mask of emotions I couldn't read to save my life.

He stood there for what felt like an eternity, the rain hammering down on him as though God himself were throwing buckets of water down from the heavens, and then he was walking towards me, slowly and carefully, as though I were a wounded animal that he might frighten away. I stood up slowly to greet him at the top of the steps, my clothing sticking to my body and revealing more of myself than I wanted to.

He stopped when he reached the bottom of the stairs and lifted his eyes, his gaze roaming slowly up my body from my feet to my chest and then finally settling on my eyes.

"I'm sorry," I said, water dripping off my face as though I'd just broken through a rogue wave in the middle of the ocean.

His eyes cut away from mine as he started up the steps, passing me quietly and then making his way to the door. I heard his keys jingle followed by the sound of a door unlocking, and I dropped my head in defeat.

At that point, I was fairly certain he had no intention of ever speaking to me again, and honestly, I couldn't even blame him. I lowered my foot onto the step below me, ready to take myself out like yesterday's trash, when I heard his voice slice through the pattering of the rain.

"Get inside," he ordered, and while his tone sounded harsh and kind of pissed off, it didn't scare me.

I welcomed it, because at least he was talking to me now.

Pushing the wet hair away from my forehead, I turned around and faced him. He was holding the door open expectantly, still staring at me in the same intense, unreadable way as before.

I held his gaze and walked back up the steps, letting it go only when I reached the doorway and passed under his arm. He shut the door behind me, but he didn't move after that.

Nervous, I snuck a peek at him from under my eyelashes.

Unfortunately, he was standing so close to me that I could only see his neck from the angle that my head was in. Digging deeper for courage, I lifted my chin and let my gaze climb up higher until I finally met his eyes.

Icy, angry eyes.

"I'm sorry," I muttered again.

"You're sorry." It wasn't a question. It was more of a reiteration of something so stupid and incredulous that you had to repeat it out loud just to believe it. He took a step forward, forcing my back against the door. "You stake me, leave me for dead in Jockstrap's car, and then disappear for days, and you're *sorry?*"

Jesus, when he put it that way…

"I—"

"Spare me, angel lips." His tone was so clipped that it made me flinch. "You've already made your lack of regard for me painfully obvious."

"Dominic, will you please let me explain?" I asked, but that only seemed to further incite him.

"What exactly would you like to explain?" he rumbled lowly, boxing me in with his body as he craned his head down to mine. I could feel his chest rising and falling against my own, and I knew he was working hard to contain himself.

"Do you have any idea how worried I was about you?" he asked, his eyes darkening with every syllable. "How many times I drove around and—" He clamped his mouth shut and then punched the door beside me.

I started, not because I thought he was going to hit me though, because I knew he wouldn't do that, but because the door shook so violently from his hit that it nearly bounced off its hinges.

And because he was out there…looking for me.

My guilt smothered me. "What do you want me to say,

Dominic? That I'm a shitty person?" I said, tears welling up under my lids. "Fine. I'm a shitty person. I can admit that."

"No, you don't get to do that," his gritted out, his eyes glimmering like two onyx stones. "You don't get to deprecate all over yourself to avoid this." His pained eyes lingered on mine, and suddenly, I wanted to crawl away and hide. "You didn't even have the courtesy to take the stake out yourself," he said, his words excruciatingly low and wounded as he pushed off the door and walked away from me.

He'd only made it a few steps before I was right there behind him, chasing him down in the hallway like a junkie looking for her fix.

"Dominic, stop! Don't walk away from me," I said and grabbed his shoulder.

He spun on me, laughing. *Laughing!* "Why not? You did."

I narrowed my eyes at him. "You were going to compel me to—"

"To stop you from killing yourself," he cut in, his face a hairsbreadth away from mine.

"Right," I said, my breathing coming out ragged from his impossible closeness. "But that wasn't your choice to make."

"If that's what you think, angel…if you think I had any other choice but to do anything and everything in my power to stop you, then you don't know—" His words cut away as his Adam's apple bobbed in his throat, seemingly swallowing down whatever he was going to say.

I waited for him to finish, for his words to come back up, but they never did come out again.

"I'm just trying to apologize to you," I said, though this time, I didn't actually say the word. I'd said it so many times tonight, it didn't even sound like a word anymore.

"That's all you're looking for, isn't it? A means to clear your conscious." His mouth upturned at the corners, as if to smile at me knowingly, but there was so much hurt in it, it looked more like a frown. "Well, then, princess," he said with an exaggerated bow. "Your wish is my command. You are forgiven. Now kindly get the hell out of my house."

I recoiled from his words, angry tears spilling onto my cheeks in droves. Was that what he really thought of me? That I was only here to satisfy my own selfish need for clemency?

Was that the reason I was here?

Did I just want to clear my conscious before I severed all ties and disappeared from his life again?

No! God, no.

"That's not fair, Dominic. That isn't why I'm here, and you know it."

"No? Then why are you here?" he asked, his voice gruff as he closed in on me, walking me backwards until my back hit the wall. My heartrate spiked as he clicked his fangs out and then lowered his head to mine.

"Is it for this?" he asked, licking his lips as his fingers moved up to my throat. "Did you want to slum it with me one more time before you pick up and leave tomorrow?"

I looked up and met his gaze, and suddenly, I could see the pain circling in his eyes, feel it through our connection. And it hurt like hell. And I couldn't stand it. "You know I'm leaving?"

"I have exceptionally good hearing," he said flatly. "Unfortunately, my taste in women leaves much to be desired, but I reckon I'll get a chance to work on that while you're gone."

My body prickled with what felt like fire—with anger and embarrassment and regret. "You know what, Dominic? Fuck you! Fuck you and your stupid fucking face!" I spat incoherently, messy tears dripping down my face as I pushed him back and raced out of his house, slamming the door shut behind me on my way out.

Hopefully in his face.

41. STRIPPED DOWN

I stomped down the street in the rain, cursing under my breath and ruing the day I met him, though I made it all but thirty steps from his house before my regret caught up with me. The faster I tried to walk, the more it burrowed under my skin, distracting me and poking at me, until my feet stopped moving altogether.

I'd come here with the intention of apologizing to him, of saying goodbye to him, and instead I told him to kick rocks and stormed out of his house. Was I really going to leave things between us like this after everything we went through together? So, he was rude and arrogant and out of line. What else was knew? That wasn't all he was, though. He was also hurt and upset, and he was pushing me away because it was easier to let someone go when you were mad at them.

Because he loved me.

I muttered a string of curses under my breath as I turned around and started back up the road towards his house.

It seemed that I was going to have to put on my big girl pants and take whatever fire he decided to throw at me, because

I needed to tell him how sorry I was, and just how much he meant to me, and I needed to do that knowing and accepting the possibility that he may not forgive me.

Because that's what big girls do.

Because if I didn't make this right tonight, I'd be closing this door forever.

By the time I made it back to his house, there wasn't a dry inch on my entire body, and even though I was shivering pitifully from the hordes of wet fabric sticking to my skin, I barely noticed it enough to let it slow me down.

I had one goal, and that was to set the record straight between me and Dominic. Once and for all. And he was going to hear me out, whether he wanted to or not.

Without bothering to knock, I opened the door and walked into the house like I owned it, making my way straight to where I knew I would find him. And he was there, in the den, standing by the fire with his back turned to me, and a drink in his hand. The man really did drink too much, but that was altogether a different story.

As if sensing my presence, he lifted his head, though he didn't inconvenience himself enough to turn around. "I suppose you think I owe you an apology now?"

"No," I said, still standing in the doorway.

"Good, because I wasn't planning on giving you one."

Nothing new there.

"That's fine, because I didn't come here for that," I said and shifted onto my other foot, drumming up the courage to say all of the things that needed to be said. To lay all my cards on the table and let the chips fall where they may. "I came here because there's something I need to say to you. Well, a lot of things actually, and you're going to listen to me until I'm done, because I think you owe me as much, and you can still hate me afterwards, and choose never to forgive me, but I'm going to say what I need to say. And I really hope that you don't."

"Don't what?" he asked, still not turning.

"Hate me."

He laughed dryly as he put his drink on the mantel and finally turned around. His face was a mask of feelings and secrets I knew I'd never be able to understand, to fully digest, but I drank them up anyway.

"I don't regret what I did to you at All Saints, and that might make you angry to hear, but I won't lie about it," I said, watching as his jaw muscle feathered. "But I should've come to you after. I should've been the one to bring you back, and for that, I'm sorry. But it hurt too damn much, Dominic. What I did to Trace…" I dropped my head, my words fluttering away like butterflies caught in the wind. "I knew you would've tried to make the pain go away, because that's what you do…and I would've let you, because that's what I do."

Realization settled his hard eyes. "And you wanted to suffer for it," he said knowingly, and I may as well have been standing there naked with how exposed I felt.

"I still do," I conceded, doing my best to stay honest with him, and with myself. "But I'm learning to forgive myself," I offered with a shrug, because it was a process, and I wasn't even almost there yet.

His expression changed—softened, and it gave me the courage to keep going.

"I know you think I don't care about you, and I guess I can't really blame you for thinking that. But you're wrong."

His eyes turned curious. Expectant.

"I worked really hard to fight my feelings for you, because I didn't understand them. I didn't understand how it was possible to be in love with Trace but still be falling for you at the same time. And it scared the hell out of me."

He slipped his hands into his pockets as he stared back at me with such a visceral intensity that I almost toppled over from the head rush.

"It still scares me," I admitted, my tenor barely a whisper now.

This *really* wasn't what I thought I'd be saying to him right now, but I couldn't stop my mouth from saying it, and then I couldn't stop my legs from moving, from walking over to him like a moth eternally drawn to the burning flame.

His back straightened as I met him where he stood, almost as though he were trying not to be affected by our closeness, but I knew he felt it—the torturous electricity between us. Because I could feel it too.

I always felt it.

"When I fell in love with Trace, it was so fast and so hard that I was sure that was it for me," I said and watched as his jaw clenched at my admission. "And then you happened, and I felt it all over again, but in a different way. And it felt right, and wrong, and good and different, and I didn't know what to do with that."

His expression remained cool, but his eyes were completely captive, almost *hopeful*. "And now?" he asked.

"And now, I still don't know what to do with it, but I'm working on figuring it out." I lowered my head, because I knew that wasn't quite what he wanted to hear. But it was the truth. My truth. And it was the only truth I had to give. "I just thought you should know that before I leave."

He didn't say anything or do anything except stand there with his hands neatly tucked into his pockets and an undecipherable look on his face.

"So that's it," I said, feeling awkward and exposed. "I guess I'll…I'll leave you alone now."

I started to turn, but he reached out and took my hand in his, holding it but not pulling. A hundred different emotions stirred inside of me like a storm slowly gathering strength over the horizon. I looked up and met his eyes, my hand tingling from the contact as a strange ache nestled inside my heart.

"Stay," he said, his voice silky and alluring and completely irresistible. "Stay with me."

I wasn't sure if he was asking me to stay for the next five minutes, or for the night, or for my whole damn life, and in that moment, I didn't much care. The only thing that registered was my need for him. My irrevocable, undeniable aching need to be consumed by this man. To be wholly and completely devoured by him.

And that was a very, very bad thing.

"I don't think that's a good idea," I said softly, not trusting myself enough to be alone with him like this.

"Why not?" he asked, looking down at me with enough heat to set the ocean on fire. "Are you worried I'm going to do something to you?"

I swallowed noisily. "Define *something*."

"Hurt you?" he asked as he brought his fingers up to the lapels of my jean jacket and then tugged me forward.

I stumbled towards him and then shook my head. "I know you won't hurt me."

"Compel you?" he asked as he began to peel my jacket away from my shoulders, sliding the wet fabric down my arms and then letting it drop to the ground behind me.

"Uh-uh," I said, my voice breathy from how thin the air had suddenly become.

His eyes flicked up to mine. "Make love to you?"

My heart slammed into my chest as I tried to wrangle out an answer. My head was spinning so quickly I thought I might pass out from the sudden fever breaking out over my skin. "No...I mean, not unless I wanted you to."

His eyes coasted down the length of my body as his fingers

picked up the hem of my wet shirt and slowly began lifting it, peeling it away from my skin at an excruciatingly slow pace. "Are you worried you'd want me to?"

My breath stuttered, heading towards the panting side.

"Mm-hmm," I murmured as I lifted my arms up above my head and let him slide my shirt all the way off my body.

"And that's wrong?" he asked, his lust-filled eyes were everywhere, moving from my eyes to my mouth and then all the way down to the hills under my silky white bra, before making their way back up again.

Strangely, the urge to cover up never came. Instead, I felt empowered by the way he looked at me.

"It's not wrong, it's just that…" I'd meant to tell him that I was still a virgin, that I'd never done this before, but that wasn't what came out. "I'm leaving tomorrow."

"I know," he said hoarsely, slipping his arm around my waist as he flattened his hand on the small of my back and drew me in closer. "But stay anyway."

At his words, I felt my body shudder, but it was the delicious kind, and that only made me more nervous to stay.

"We don't have to do that, angel," he said, his honeyed voice scraping against my nerve endings. "We can do other things. Or nothing."

"Nothing?" I looked up at him with disbelief—with disappointment.

"If that's what you want." He grinned lazily and pulled his hands away from my body, folding them behind his back. "I won't touch you until you tell me to."

Even though he drew his hands away, his face was still so close to mine that it was impossible not to breathe him in. So, I did. I breathed in a lungful of his intoxicating aroma, his sweet smell of milk-chocolate and malt, and I unraveled.

"Okay," I said, my eyes transfixed by the way his lips closed around his words. I could feel my body pooling with heat, with need, begging me to taste him all over again. To feel those lips closing around me.

"Okay *what?*" he asked deliberately, his voice husky and low.

I looked up and met his eyes, my skin prickling with heat. "Okay—touch me," I murmured.

A deep rumble sounded at the back of his throat. "Where?"

"Everywhere."

He growled again. "Pick a spot, angel."

"My lips," I said speedily, needing for him to kiss me.

He inched his mouth to mine as his hand came up and cupped my jaw. My breath hitched as he gently parted my lips with his thumb, and then grazed his tongue along the opening, feather-soft and tantalizingly slow.

Holy shit balls.

"More," I panted, arching into him hungrily as he smiled against my lips and then deepened the kiss.

His fingers laced through my hair as he pushed my mouth open and swept his tongue against mine, kissing and sucking and nipping my lips until I was nothing more than putty in his hands.

"Pick another spot," he ordered as he pulled away, leaving me breathless and pooling with need.

I knew this was going to mouthwateringly bad places, but I didn't know how to stop myself from going. "My neck."

He licked his lips and lowered his head, tilting it down to my neck as he brushed his mouth against my skin, inciting a fever of heat all over my body as he painted my skin with strokes of his tongue.

"What else?" he asked, his mouth and tongue still against my neck.

"Teeth," I whimpered. "Use your teeth."

His fangs clicked out at my command, and my heart raced

off into heart-attack territory as he grazed his pointed teeth along my skin, hard enough to excite me, but not hard enough to break the skin.

"Like this?" he asked mischievously, knowing it wasn't enough.

"No."

"Then how?"

"Dominic, please."

"Say it, angel."

"Feed...I want you to feed."

His fangs burrowed into my neck as he drew out a small taste of my blood. "Like that?"

"More," I panted as he bit down harder, drawing out more of my blood.

Waves of pleasure immediately filtered into my bloodstream, kissing every cell in my body and then washing them under like a tidal wave with no end. I wasn't sure how long it had been since he last drank from me, but it felt like I'd been waiting an entire lifetime in agony. The sweet release took over, and suddenly, it felt like I was floating.

Needing more, I slipped my arms around his neck and pulled him closer. I could feel the cord between us—the bond—tightening with every ounce he drank, but I had lost the desire to fight it altogether now.

He pulled away, as if knowing the exact moment to stop—to keep me lucid enough to keep asking him for what I wanted. "What else?" he asked looking far too in control of himself as he licked my blood from the corner of his mouth.

I, on the other hand, was not in control of myself or my volcanizing need for him. My body was damn near writhing in pain for it.

"What else, angel?" he asked again when I failed to produce words.

"My clothes," I whined, unable to stand the heat rocketing through my body.

"What about them, angel?"

"Take them off," I pleaded, needing to feel his masterful hands all over me again.

A dangerous smile curled the corner of his mouth. "Right here in the middle of the den?"

"No." I knew where this was going, and by the way he was looking at me, so did he.

"Then where?" he whispered huskily, his eyes blazing with desire.

"Upstairs...in your room."

Another dangerous growl sounded as he picked me up in his arms and hauled me out of the den.

42. NO STRINGS ATTACHED

With my legs wrapped around his waist, and both of his hands splayed beneath my ass, he walked me backwards into his bedroom, and then kicked the door shut behind us. I could feel his hardness pressing into me as he wet his lips and then released his hold, letting me slide down his body until my feet were touching the ground again.

Running his heated eyes down my body, he reached back and locked the door. Anticipation clung to my skin like a perfume as I bit my lip and watched him close the gap between us. With his eyes fixed on mine, he brought his hand up to my stomach, dusting my skin with shivers as his fingertips slowly glided around my side and then up the center of my back. With a simple twitch of his fingers, my bra clasp came undone, and then his hands were moving higher, racking against my shoulders and then dragging my bra straps down the length of my arms and dropping it on the floor between us.

The cool air brushed against my chest, tightening everything.

"Are you sure you want to keep going?" he asked, his voice a bold challenge, as though there would be no going back after this moment. Not because he wouldn't stop if I asked him to, but because he knew I wouldn't want him to if he started.

"Yes," I said, my back arching with desire.

"Then pick a spot."

"Stop torturing me," I pleaded, needing for his hands to be everywhere, and all at once.

He grinned wickedly. "Pick a spot, angel."

I glared at him and then said, "My breasts."

That seemed like a good place to start, being that he hadn't been there yet.

Another delicious growl sounded at the back of his throat as his hands glided up along my waist, around my right breast and then down the middle of my chest. "Like that?"

"I hate you."

He smiled. "Like this?" he asked as he cupped my breast with his hand, teasing the sensitive part with his thumb.

"Like that," I murmured and then pressed my eager mouth to his. Unfortunately, I got to taste his mouth for about two seconds before he broke away from the kiss.

"Patience, angel," he said as he lowered his mouth to my breast and mapped out the ridges with his tongue.

My head drifted backwards as I looked up at the ceiling and tried my best not to pass out. The way his lips and tongue were gliding and flicking over my chest made me feel as though I weren't even on solid ground anymore.

And then he was lowering himself to the ground, bending his knees as he knelt down before me, blazing a trail of kisses along my abdomen, each one dropping lower than the last and making my temperature spike with madness.

"Where else?" he asked, his fingers unbuttoning my jeans and then sliding them down to the ground.

I quickly stepped out of them, and then whimpered as he hooked his fingers into the elastic band of my underwear and paused, his eyes moving back up to mine.

"Where else, angel?"

"*There.*"

"Here?" he asked as he kissed me through the thin fabric.

I'd meant to say yes, but instead produced what could only be described as a squeak.

He smiled as he dragged down my last line of my defense, leaving every inch of my body completely naked and exposed for him to see. And boy, was he seeing. His eyes were running wildly all over my body, drinking me in as though he didn't know what part he wanted to play with first.

"You're impossibly breathtaking," he murmured, as though speaking to himself. His gaze left mine and then settled just below my waist, his mouth soon following as he scorched my core with a flick of his tongue.

Fireworks went off in my head as I gripped his shoulders and held on for dear life.

"Like that?" he asked, looking up at me under hooded eyes.

A soft moan fluttered through my lips. It was all I could do.

Another flick of his tongue and my grip on his shoulders tightened.

"Should I stop?" he asked, torturing me to the point that I was a hairbreadth away from begging him.

Apparently, he'd gotten his wish after all.

"Only if you want me to hurt you," I said, my voice shaking with frustration.

He grinned and straightened to his full height.

Before I could follow through with my threat to seriously injury him, he was walking me backwards across his room, matching every step I took with his own forward march until the back of my legs hit his bed. I fisted my hands into his dress shirt to keep myself from falling backwards.

"You'll like it more if you lie back and relax," he said, his voice coaxing my hands out of his shirt and down to my sides as I carefully lowered myself to his bed.

Apparently, it wasn't the right spot, because he quickly reached down and gripped my waist before gently tossing me further back on the bed. My heart felt as though it were going to beat a hole right out of my chest as I watched him unbutton his shirt and then peel it from body.

I pushed up on my elbows, my gaze lingering on his torso as I took in the lean, taut muscles that bulged and flexed at all the right places. And then my eyes were back on his as he climbed on the bed and dragged his body over mine, covering me like a blanket before pressing a teasing kiss against my lips. I tried to trap him in my arms, to deepen the kiss myself, but he was already lowering himself back to my happy place.

My breathing turned ragged and labored as he teased the inside of my thigh, gently kissing and nipping my skin before moving his mouth to my core. Every nerve ending in my body came alive as he flicked his tongue along my center, each movement slow and deliberate and designed to rouse a response from me. The more breathless my responses, the faster his movements became, like a game of chess that I was inevitably going to lose. Back and forth, back and forth, teasing and touching and licking until my entire body arched with anticipation before exploding into a blazing storm of fireworks.

A pleasure-filled scream ripped out from me as wave after wave of ecstasy shot through my body, making it buck and weave every which way. Dominic's tongue continued his assault, riding the waves with me as he softened his movements into barely-there touches, stopping only when my body settled with a tremble and then slowly drifted back to shore.

"Oh. My. God." My legs were still quaking as I dropped back on the bed and tried to catch my breath. I had never, ever, in my entire life felt anything quite like *that* before.

"You're welcome," he said as he licked his lips and gazed at me from between my legs.

I couldn't help but laugh. Mostly because I felt giddy, though I had no idea why. "You're entirely way too good at that," I said, not allowing myself to wonder just how much practice he'd gotten to get *that* good.

He lifted himself from between my legs and then lay himself down beside me, propping himself on his elbow as he stared down at my naked body. The need in his eyes was palpable.

"I could look at you like this forever," he said, soaking up the satisfied look on my face.

Biting my lip, I reached over and started to unbutton his pants—which were being stretched beyond their limits—but he captured my hand and held it.

"You're not obligated to repay me, angel. You can just enjoy it."

"I know, but what about you?" I asked, confused because you know, blue balls and all that.

"I'll be alright." He winked.

My gaze skirted away as I mulled that over. A moment later, my eyes boomeranged right back to his. "Don't you want to sleep with me?" I asked, trying not to sound offended.

"You *are* kidding, right?"

"Right," I said, except that I wasn't.

My face must've shown it, because he quickly took my chin in his hand and angled my face to his. "Of course, I want to sleep with you, angel." His eyes flared with heat and then with something else. Restraint. "You couldn't possibly imagine the things I want to do to your body or the ways in which I wish to possess you."

Heat rippled across my cheeks at his words. "Then...I mean, why aren't you...?" I asked, wanting to know more about these things he wanted to do to me. Obviously, I was missing something here.

"Because, angel," he said, his eyes brightening with something that looked a lot like love. "You're still grieving, and I don't want our first time together to be tainted."

"Oh." My heart swelled in my chest, wondering when the hell he had become so...sweet.

"Besides, I already told you. I have all the time in the world to wait for you," he said as he stroked my cheek with the back of his hand. "However long it takes."

The icy film around my heart melted just a little more for him.

"You may not feel it now," he said as he propped himself on his pillow and then pulled me into him so that I could rest my head on his chest. "But you will heal, and you will be whole again someday, and when that day comes, I'll be there waiting to collect my prize." He waggled his eyebrows, and I smacked him in the stomach.

Chuckling softly, he reached over and grabbed the edge of the comforter and then draped it over me, tucking me in as I pressed my ear against his chest and listened to the melodic thumping. He played with my hair, twirling it around his lean fingers as I tried especially hard not to fall asleep.

I wasn't ready for this night to end.

"Do you really think I'll be whole again someday?" I asked suddenly, looking up at him under my lashes.

His eyes were fixed on a strand of my hair as though it were some fascinating new specimen of life. "Don't you?"

"No." I picked my cuticles as I tried not to let the grief rush back and strangle me just yet. I just wanted one more moment, one more beautiful, fleeting night before I let the darkness back in to suffocate me.

"He would forgive you, angel. You know that, don't you?"

I looked up and met his unwavering gaze. "How can you say

that?" I asked, growing upset by his baseless words. "You didn't even know him, Dominic. Not the way I knew him."

He stopped playing with my hair. "I don't need to know him, angel. I know he loved you, and if he loved you and knew your heart even half as much as I do, he's *already* forgiven you."

My heart swelled with the kind of hope that moved mountains. I didn't want it to, but I couldn't help but be affected by his words, by the sureness in which he spoke them.

"You can't know that," I said, swatting the hope away like a bothersome fly, but all the while, yearning to trap it in my hands and never let it go.

"But I do, angel. I *know* he's already forgiven you, because *I* would've already forgiven you."

I looked up and met his eyes again, though I could barely see through the blur of tears trying to fight their way out.

Maybe Dominic was right. Maybe Trace had already forgiven me, and maybe now I just needed to forgive myself.

"Will you visit me during the summer?" I asked him, realizing in that moment just how hard it was going to be to not see him for six weeks. He had become such an integral part of my days, of my being, that I wasn't sure I'd make it the whole summer without him.

"Why? Are you going to miss me, angel?" he asked mischievously as his lips curled into a lopsided grin.

"You know I will."

"You can always stay here with me instead," he offered, his eyes darkening seductively.

"And do what? Exchange sexual favors all summer?" I teased.

That delicious growl at the back of his throat was back with a vengeance. "Well, now that you mention it…"

"Be serious, Dominic," I said and smacked him in the chest again.

"I *am* being serious." The intensity in his eyes picked up at he gazed back down at me. "I meant what I said to you in my car that night. I want to make you forget, angel. And I don't mean with compulsion."

The way he was looking at me just then…I almost took him up on his offer.

But alas, I knew that wasn't a possibility. Because things were different now.

I was different now.

"Forgetting what happened won't make it go away," I said softly, my voice soft and reflective. "It'll just set me up to make the same mistakes again, and I can't let that happen. I need training, and I need real-life experience, and if I go on the road with Tessa, I know I'll get that."

He exhaled gruffly as he let my words sink in. He didn't like it, I could see that, but he knew I was right.

Going on the road with Tessa would make me stronger, make my skin a little thicker, and take me one step closer to the Slayer I was meant to be. And I knew Dominic wanted that for me, no matter how much it hurt to let me go, because he loved me, and when you loved someone, you sometimes had to let them go.

"Fine," he said begrudgingly as he folded his arm under his head and stared up at the ceiling. "But I'm going to need an exponential amount of those sexual favors."

My mouth spread into a grin. "Does that mean you'll be visiting me?"

He met my gaze and held it. "Any time, any place, angel. You only have to say the word," he said and then drew me in closer to him until I was tucked all the way against his side, breathing him in like a second chance at life.

43. ONE MORE FOR THE ROAD

I left Hollow Hills the next morning under the blanket of an ever-gray sky. I wasn't sure where Tessa and I would be headed first, or what kind of adventures would find us on the road, but I knew it was where I was supposed to be, and for the first time in my life, I was ready to be there.

So much had changed since that first day I'd come to Hollow Hills all those months ago. My *life* changed. The people in it changed...even the season changed.

But most importantly, *I* had changed.

I wasn't that same naïve girl who was scared of her own shadow and petrified of all the things that go bump in the night. I'd learned how to fight since then, and I'd learned how to stand up for myself, even when my voice was trembling.

I'd learned about strength—real strength. Not the kind that comes to you freely and easily from the absence of fear, but the kind you build up slowly over time. The kind that burgeons from within when the world is closing in on you and you can't see two feet in front of your face, but you somehow manage to pull yourself off the floor, put one foot in front of the other and keep on going.

I may not have had the life that I'd dreamed of, or the happily ever after I'd always yearned for, but I was still here. I was still alive. My heart was still beating, and my lungs were still taking in air, and I was going to do something with that. I was going to do something with my life. Something meaningful, and maybe even heroic.

I owed it to Taylor, and I owed it to Trace.

Climbing into my sister's 1972 black Cadillac Deville, we pulled out of the Huntington Manor and headed for the open road, watching the town slowly disappear from my sideview mirror. The rain peppered down over us, bathing us in its melancholy beauty one last time, as if to kiss me goodbye as I sauntered into the next chapter of my life.

As hard as it was to leave Dominic, I knew this thing between us had only just begun. He'd keep a watchful eye on me while I was out there slaying my demons, and he would give me the space I needed to fly, but most importantly, he would be there waiting for me when it was finally time to land.

People always say that everything happens for a reason. That one door closes so that another one can open, and that in the end, everything will always work itself out, and if it hasn't, it simply isn't the end. I'd never really given that much thought before, one way or the other, but at this moment in my life, I liked to think it was true. I liked to think that things would somehow find a way to work themselves out, and that after all the heartache and disappointment, I might still get my happy ending after all.

I left Hollow Hills that day feeling hopeful about what the future would bring. That maybe, just maybe, I'd get to see that sprawling rainbow at the end of the storm someday.

Maybe…

Unfortunately, what I didn't know—and what would

inevitably pull the ground out from under me and wrench my happily ever after right out of my hands—was that while I'd been away, grieving the loss of the first boy I'd ever loved, Nikki had been back home, raising him from the dead.

Bonus Material

Visit the author's website for information on new releases, bonus content, and exclusive teasers from the upcoming Season Two of The Marked saga.

www.biancascardoni.com

Facebook, Twitter, and Instagram:
@biancascardoni

GLOSSARY

ANAKIM
A race of people born with the spirit of man and the blood of angels; Descendants of Nephilim

CASTER
A Descendant of Magi Angels; ability to cast magic, control elements, and manipulate energy

CINDERDUST
Magical powder created by High Casters that sends a Revenant to Sanguinarium

DARK LEGION
Descendants that have turned against the Order; pledged to the dark side/ Lucifer

DAUGHTER OF HADES
Descendant of Lucifer, prophesied to raise Lucifer and bring on the end of days

INVOCATION
An ancient ritual used by the Order to invoke Anakim abilities

LUCIFER
The first angel to be created and the first to fall; imprisoned in a tomb in Hell

REAPER
A Descendant of Transport Angels; capable of teleporting, time travel, and mind reading through touch

SANGUINARIUM
Realm of perdition for Revenants that have been vanquished

SEER
A Descendant of Messenger Angels; ability to communicate with the Spirit Realm and predict the future

SHIFTER
A Descendant of Guardian Angels; capable of shifting into animal form, and telepathy

SLAYER
A Descendant of Warrior Angels; possess super strength and ability to sense demons, siren-like blood

THE ORDER OF THE ROSE
A secret organization that oversees all Anakim affairs

ANAKIM INDEX

SLAYERS *(Warrior Angel Descendants)*
Jemma
Tessa
Gabriel+
Karl
Thomas*
Jaqueline+

REAPERS *(Transport Angel Descendants)*
Trace
Peter
Linley*

CASTERS *(Magi Angel Descendants)*
Nikki
Caleb
Carly

SHIFTERS *(Guardian Angel Descendants)*
Dominic+
Ben
Julian

SEERS *(Messenger Angel Descendants)*
Morgan

DARK CASTERS *(Pledged to the Dark Legion)*
Arianna
Annabelle
Anita

* Character is deceased
+ Character is a Revenant

ACKNOWLEDGEMENTS

Thank you to my amazing friend, Tricia Simpson, for not only proofreading this book, but for being a constant source of support in my life. You started this journey with me two years ago (when you read Inception and told me you thought it was good enough to publish) and you have continued to be that guiding light for me *four* books later. I hope you know how much I cherish our friendship, and just how grateful I am for you <3

Thank you to Alicia Rades for also proofreading my book. Your notes were extremely helpful, and your comments had me laughing out loud. It was an awesome experience working with you (and your five thousand commas).

Thank you to my amazing cover designer, Ana, for perfectly capturing my vision. I seriously cannot stop staring at this cover. It's so dang beautiful.

A special thank you to my dad, Victor, for not only reading my first three books, but for loving them (probably) just as much as I do. Your support and constant enthusiasm about this series means the world to me. Having said that, do NOT read this book, and definitely not chapters 41 and 42. That is all. Love you!

Thank you to my love, Jeffrey, a.k.a. Peanut, for making sure everything around me was perfect so that I could sit down and finish this book. I could not have dreamed up a better man for me, or a better father for my son. I hope you know how grateful I am to have you, and just how much I love you.

Thank you to my crazy toddler, Jaxon, for always keeping me busy and on my toes, and for being so damn adorable. Everything I do is for you, my love. So, remember that when I'm old and gray and blowing up your phone.

And finally, thank you to my readers. Words cannot express how grateful I am to be able to sit here and write those words. You have *literally* made my dreams come true, and I think about that every single day. Thank you for your unwavering support and continuous excitement over this book—even when it was looking like there would be no book. Your messages and comments have gotten me through some of my darkest days, and for that, I am indebted to you.

ABOUT THE AUTHOR

BIANCA SCARDONI is a paranormal fiction writer who resides on the East Coast of Canada with her family. She graduated from college with a degree in web design and went on to build an online writing community in 2004. When she isn't writing, she spends her time reading, watching vampire shows, eating junk food, and staying up too late.

For upcoming book releases, bonus material, and additional information on the author, please visit her website: www.biancascardoni.com

Made in the USA
Middletown, DE
18 January 2019